I ♥ the 80s

Megan Crane is a full-time writer and she lives in Los Angeles with her husband and various pets. Her most recent novel is *Everyone Else's Girl*.

Praise for Megan Crane

'A hugely enjoyable novel with brilliant, convincing characters and dialogue. It's romantic, funny, intelligent, believable and gripping. I couldn't put it down'
Marian Keyes

'Megan Crane rules! Cancel your evening plans: you won't want to stop reading until you've devoured every delicious word'
Meg Cabot

'Crane's style captivates and brings the story to life'
Buzz

'A fresh, upbeat read ~~~~ ~~~~res what it's like finally to have it out with ~~~~~~~~~~~~~~ ~~~~'
~~~~~~or

Deligh~~~~ ~~~~zine

ALSO BY MEGAN CRANE

English as a Second Language
Frenemies
Names My Sisters Call Me
Everyone Else's Girl

I ♥ the 80s

Megan Crane

Quercus

First published in Great Britain in 2011 by

Quercus
21 Bloomsbury Square
London
WC1A 2NS

A CIP catalogue record for this book is available
from the British Library

ISBN 978 1 84916 999 8

10 9 8 7 6 5 4 3 2 1

Typeset by Ellipsis Books Limited, Glasgow
Printed and bound in Great Britain by Clays Ltd, St Ives plc

*For everyone who grew up in the Eighties
and can still sing along*

Acknowledgements

Thanks to Julie Barer – for everything, again and always. Thanks also to Caspian Dennis in the UK. And to Charlotte Clerk and everyone at Quercus for loving this book the way I do.

Thanks to Louise Austin and Jon Reinish, for all things 80s in NYC. Any mistakes are mine.

A million thanks to Louise Austin, Josie Torielli, Kim McCreight, Liza Palmer and Kristin Harmel – for reading the first draft and being so excited about this crazy idea.

To Jeff Johnson for being such a great storyteller, time-travel nitpicker, reader, husband, and champion. Always.

And to all my favourite Eighties bands for the music. All that wonderful music.

PAST

Crystal blue and deep bone shine
My complicated Valentine
Lucky penny, lucky penny
How can I make you mine?

The Wild Boys, 'Lucky Penny'

Not enough your rough and tumble symphony,
Not enough your carelessness and apathy,
Not enough my fullness and your scarcity.
My misery loves your company.

The Wild Boys, 'Misery Loves Company'

1

'Oh, Jenna,' came the sad voice from the doorway, making Jenna Jenkins jump in her chair and nearly spill her afternoon latte all over her keyboard – right in the middle of a gripping online throw-down on the Eighties Band Fans Forever Bulletin Board regarding the endless controversy over *which* mascaraed Eighties-era keyboard player was the hottest in 1985.

She did not have to look up to know that it was her best friend and favourite co-worker Aimee who stood there in the doorway of her office. The strength of Aimee's concern could no doubt be felt all the way down the wet stretch of Times Square in the summer rain outside the windows. It made Jenna's shoulders hunch up closer to her ears.

'I'm fine,' she said automatically, moving the still-steaming venti latte to a less precarious spot on her cluttered desktop. She clicked out of the Bulletin Board and looked over at her friend. She forced herself to smile brightly, though she doubted either one of them was fooled. 'I mean, hi. How are you?'

Aimee sighed, and moved further into Jenna's office. She looked around as if she'd never seen the dark little cave before, when Jenna knew the truth was that the mess probably kept OCD Aimee up at night.

Jenna pushed back from her desk and looked around herself, trying to see whatever Aimee saw that made her frown so ferociously, with her eyes so sombre. But she could only see her normal, everyday office. It was small and not even remotely neat, with files spilling out from the cabinets and four seasons' worth of an emergency wardrobe hanging off the coat rack near the door or piled in heaps on the floor.

'Okay,' Jenna said. 'Granted, I could probably clean this place up.'

Aimee shook her head slightly, and faced Jenna as if she'd been plotting out what to say in her head. Jenna felt unease snake down her back. Because there was really only one subject Aimee ever *plotted out* how to approach, and Jenna didn't want to talk about it. Still. Eight months later, and she *still* wanted nothing at all to do with that topic. Much less the memories that went with it.

'I guess I never really paid attention to how much you've, uh, gotten back into that whole Eighties obsession of yours,' Aimee said, the compassion and worry in her voice making Jenna's stomach hurt. She waved a hand at the walls, inviting Jenna's inspection, as if Jenna hadn't decorated them herself, and didn't know exactly what hung there.

'I wouldn't call it an *obsession*,' Jenna protested. 'A keen interest? Maybe. A certain focused enjoyment? Sure.'

Aimee pressed her lips together and looked around the office, leaving Jenna no choice but to do the same. She saw what she always saw: pure Eighties perfection. The office was decorated exactly the way her bedroom in Indiana had been when she was a twelve-year-old girl, almost twenty-five years ago. She'd had it that way for years – although, in truth, over the past few months she had dug some more classic pieces out of the collection of posters she usually kept in storage.

A huge, six-foot poster of Tommy Seer from the Wild Boys dominated the wall behind her desk. She pivoted around so she could better appreciate Tommy's glowing green eyes and full, sensual mouth. She sighed happily, her automatic response and the reason the poster was *behind* her, because she would otherwise never get any work done at all. Her gaze travelled across the rest of the wall, where smaller posters of the band, and close-ups of Tommy's gorgeous face, hung anywhere else there was space. She had a whole separate wall dedicated to other Eighties loves, like Duran Duran and Wham!, but it could be argued that Jenna's professional environment was a shrine to Tommy Seer.

Much as her adolescence had been.

She failed to see why that was an issue.

'Remember that guy Mark?' Aimee asked in an offhand, casual sort of voice that Jenna knew better than to let

5

fool her. 'The one Ben and I set you up with after the Fourth of July party?'

Jenna had to fight not to roll her eyes. Aimee and her husband Ben were wonderful in every respect except this one: they believed that no one could possibly be happy single, especially Jenna, especially after The Unfortunate Event That Could Not Be Named. Hence the constant stream of blind dates and set-ups, in some misguided attempt to 'get her back on the horse', a direct quote from Ben. If Jenna said no, she had to withstand further emotionally taxing conversations like this one – so she usually gave in and simply went on the dates. She was convinced these exercises in social humiliation might, in fact, kill her one of these days, if she didn't kill herself – or Aimee – first.

'Which one was Mark?' Jenna asked, trying to exude patience and calm. 'Was he the alarmingly morose fitness instructor who wanted me to train for a half-marathon for, quote, the good of my soul? Or the pompous male nurse who lectured me on my dairy intake and made me buy a copy of *Skinny Bitch* after dinner?'

'Mark is a consultant.' Aimee shook her head as if Jenna's words wounded her. Personally. 'And he's *nice*, Jenna. He's a really nice guy.'

'Oh, right. Mark.' Jenna rolled her eyes this time, because she knew all there was to know about *nice guys*, thank you. She'd been close to marrying one once, hadn't she? Not that she was talking about that! 'The consultant – whatever that means – with such a busy, busy corporate life that he hasn't had time to read a book since the mid-Nineties, right? What a winner.'

Aimee crossed her arms over her chest and looked as if she was fighting for patience. Jenna pretended her teeth were not on edge, and her shoulders were perfectly relaxed.

'We had him over for dinner last night, and asked him why he never called you again,' Aimee said. Her voice was too kind. Much too kind. Jenna braced herself for the inevitable blow. 'And do you know what he said?'

'I can only imagine.' Jenna had blocked most of that date – and, in fact, most of every date Aimee sent her on – completely out of her mind. Better to repress than remember and weep, she always said. Or would have said, had Aimee allowed her to complain about these things without looking as if Jenna had kicked her.

Being single and in her mid-thirties in Manhattan should have been exciting, as there were so many other people in exactly the same situation. There ought to have been some camaraderie, or a sense of shared adventure. Instead, it felt a lot more like being an unpaid partici-pant in a gruelling reality show.

And the fact that her fiancé had left her for a perky aspiring yoga instructor eight months ago was, Jenna told herself, completely irrelevant.

'He said that when you mentioned that you worked here at Eighties TV, he naturally asked you what your favourite Eighties band was.' Aimee's gaze made Jenna uncomfortable, and she looked away, towards the Wild

Boys Live in Rio poster spread she'd put up near the door just last week. 'And he said that he laughed when you told him you loved the Wild Boys, which isn't unreasonable, and then you ranted at him. *Like a mental patient.* His words, Jenna.'

The worst part, Jenna thought dimly, was that Aimee's voice was still so kind. Concerned.

'He was lucky I didn't throw something at him,' she said now. 'He's the mental patient if he can't accept I take the Wild Boys very seriously.'

'I know you do,' Aimee replied. 'I'm beginning to think you need an intervention. I know you keep saying that this has nothing to do with Adam and that you're fine—'

'Since when do we speak his name?' Jenna was outraged. 'Some things are sacrosanct, Aimee!'

'Look at this office, Jenna.' Aimee's voice was low, urgent. She spread out her palms in front of her. 'Look at *you.*'

But Jenna didn't want to do either of those things. Not the way Aimee wanted her to, anyway.

'This office has a Wild Boys theme to it, yes,' she admitted, walking out from behind her desk and leaning back against the edge of it. 'I like Tommy Seer. And I can see how this might be a problem if we worked in, say, an investment bank downtown. But seeing as we work at Eighties TV, what's the issue?'

'Some of us *work* at Eighties TV,' Aimee countered gently, 'while living in the real world. The real world which is in the twenty-*first* century these days. But you're acting like it's still 1987, Jenna, and it's not healthy!'

'Again,' Jenna said, temper mixing with the other, darker things and feeling almost like a relief next to that whole mess, 'an encyclopedic knowledge of all things Eighties can only be an asset in this particular office. It's my job.'

Aimee waved her hand up and down, indicating Jenna's outfit. 'Come on,' she said. 'You're a few bangles and a side ponytail away from looking like a member of Bananarama!'

'So what?' Jenna demanded, stung. 'Leggings are totally in. I saw at least ten starlets wearing them in the pages of *US Weekly*!'

She was wearing black leggings beneath an artfully torn denim miniskirt. Complete with bright pink ankle boots and a T-shirt, she felt this comprised a normal workday outfit at Eighties TV, a subsidiary of the giant Video TV, which she and Aimee had worked for since graduating from NYU together. They ran only Eighties videos, all the time. The VJs were much worse than Jenna was in their commitment to Eighties fashion. Sabrina St Clair was known to wear her own version of Michael Jackson's famous glove on the air, and sometimes even out to dinner.

Jenna wanted to say something about Aimee's outfit, but, of course, there was nothing to say. There never was. Aimee always looked polished, even at Eighties TV where professional staff were encouraged to dress 'funky'. Even when they'd been eighteen, Aimee had effortlessly radiated cool competence from the top of her smooth blonde head to her always-pedicured toes.

Jenna, meanwhile, had wild curly brown hair only a

member of Heart circa 'All I Want to Do Is Make Love to You' could appreciate, and her fashion sense was pretty much the same as it had been when she was in high school. Which, she reminded herself, was a good thing, given her place of employment.

'I don't want to debate the merits of Bananarama,' Aimee said, shaking her head again.

'What's to debate?' Jenna replied at once. 'Frankly, I think they're underrated. "Cruel, Cruel Summer" stands the test of time – more than people think.'

'I want to point out that you've been obsessed with Tommy Seer and the Wild Boys since you were in the sixth grade,' Aimee said in that too-conciliatory tone, as if Jenna was mentally unstable. Jenna found she hated that tone. Passionately. 'And while it made sense that you would, you know, sink into all that again when Adam broke up with you—'

'Is this mention-the-unmentionable day?' Jenna interjected. 'What the hell, Aimee?'

'—it's been a really long time,' Aimee finished, ignoring Jenna's interruption. 'It's been almost a year since you guys finally broke up, and you know things were bad for a long time before that.'

Jenna rubbed at her face with her hands, surprised to see that they were shaking.

'Why are you talking about this?' she asked, her voice too low to pretend Aimee wasn't getting to her.

'It's time to let Tommy Seer go,' Aimee said gently. Pityingly. It made Jenna's eyes well up, and she hated that.

She'd finished crying about Adam and his betrayal a long time ago. She stared out her window, and fought to bring herself back under control.

'It was sort of adorable and quirky that you were so into the guy when we were in college,' Aimee continued. 'I know you saved all those B-sides and 45s, and that's cute. It is.' Her gaze was pleading. 'And I understand why obsessing about the Wild Boys is some kind of safe haven now. Adam was a shit. *Is* a shit. But we're in our mid-thirties.'

'Don't remind me, please.' Jenna had never planned to be thirty-five and single, living in a tiny one-bedroom in Hell's Kitchen all by herself. She and Adam had been together forever, and then engaged for almost two years before he'd bailed on her. This wasn't how her life was supposed to be. She was supposed to be just like Aimee. Married. Happy. Not the discarded fiancée, humiliated after all those years of waiting for Adam. Waiting for him to call her his girlfriend. To move in with her. To settle down. To propose. To set a wedding date.

This was not the plan.

'Tommy Seer has been dead for nearly twenty-five years,' Aimee said firmly. As if Jenna had missed that unpleasant fact somehow, and the news might come as some surprise. 'And you're using him as a way to hide from the world. This is your life, Jenna. Right here, right now. You have to live it.'

'I'm trying—' Jenna began.

'You are not trying,' Aimee interrupted her fiercely.

11

'You've given up.' She made a low noise. 'Adam's moved on, Jenna. The truth is that he moved on a long time ago. When are you going to do the same?'

'Aimee.' She could barely get the name out past the lump in her throat. She was momentarily blinded by the wet heat in her eyes, and was terrified she might actually weep. 'Stop,' she hissed. 'Please.'

There was a small silence. She could hear Aimee breathing, and could feel the weight of her love, her concern, floating between them like all their history. It made her hurt.

But then Aimee sighed slightly, and when Jenna glanced over at her, she was smiling. Not brightly, perhaps, but it was a smile.

'At the very least,' she said quietly, her blue eyes seeing too much, the way they always did, 'you have to quit talking about your Wild Boys thing on the first date, okay?'

Why should I give up the Wild Boys when I've been forced *to give up everything else?* Jenna wondered some hours later, still sitting in her office. Okay, maybe Aimee had a point – maybe she was a little bit obsessed – but who did it hurt? What else did she have?

It was late and almost everyone else had already gone home to their spouses and children and grown-up lives. None of which Jenna possessed. *Thanks, Adam,* she thought sarcastically. She very much doubted he and his yoga-loving girlfriend were sitting around brooding over their life choices tonight. The last time she'd seen them, in fact, they had both been equally, repulsively arrogant about the *necessity* of their love.

That was what he'd said, the back-stabbing, cheating liar. Right to her face, new girlfriend in tow, as he packed up his stuff. *My love for Marisol is a* necessity, *Jenna. You wouldn't understand.*

God, she hated him. More, she sometimes thought, than she'd ever loved him in the first place.

The halls around her office were quiet. Outside, Times Square looked like a video game, with lights streaking in every direction and crowds of people jostling together on the corners in miserable clumps as the late-summer storm poured down on top of them. Thunder rumbled ominously from the low clouds and lightning sliced open the sky. It was all very dramatic, and perfectly appropriate for her mood. She swivelled her chair around so she could prop her legs up on the windowsill, stare at the rain, and really, truly brood.

Jenna had loved the Wild Boys for as long as she could remember. Her favourite aunt Jen, for whom she was named, had encouraged this love – sending Jenna concert T-shirts and limited-edition 45 r.p.m. singles and always making herself available to discuss the band, in satisfying detail.

Jenna knew that the band's first album had come out when she was about five, so there must have been whole years without them, but she couldn't remember a *before*. It felt like she had always known every detail there was to know about the four boys from England who had taken the world by storm. Nick was the shy one who played drums and various other percussion instruments. Sebastian was the too-cool-for-school guitar player. Richie played the keyboards and was the jokester of the group. And finally there was Tommy.

Jenna couldn't help the sigh that escaped her then. She didn't have to look behind her at the wall to conjure up a perfect picture of his face, or to hear the sound of his voice. She could feel them both inside her, as if they were a part of her, and she didn't care how crazy that might sound.

From almost the very start of the Eighties, Tommy Seer had been one of the most famous men in the world. Thanks to his brilliant songwriting and model good looks, the Wild Boys had been one of the first bands to use the just-born concept of music television to catapult themselves into the heart of every pre-teen and teenaged girl in America, including and especially Jenna. Back in Indiana, she had been convinced that if only she and Tommy could meet, they would fall in love and live happily ever after. The fact that she had been all of twelve when he was at his peak, and he'd been in his thirties at the time, was irrelevant.

Jenna had loved him with every fibre of her being and every last cell in her pre-teen body. She had loved his luxuriant dark curls that he wore in the pompadour Eighties style. She had spent years weeping over his soft lips. And she had never seen anything quite as beautiful as his sparkling green eyes.

14

Almost twenty-five years ago, Tommy Seer had been driving across the Tappan Zee Bridge sometime before midnight one October night, after a fight with his fiancée, the model and occasional actress Eugenia Wentworth. He'd lost control of the car, shot over the side of the bridge into the cold waters of the Hudson river, and sunk.

His body had never been found.

And on some level, Jenna had mourned for him ever since. Other people got over their girlhood crushes, but Jenna had never quite managed to shake hers. It had ebbed and flowed over the years, to be sure, but it had never quite left her. So maybe it wasn't so surprising that when her real-life love had turned out to be fake, she'd reverted back to the fantasy love that had never done her wrong and never, ever would. Maybe that was the point.

She tipped her chair back to look at her ceiling panels instead of the depressing storm outside. After all, when idols lived, they tended to topple off their pedestals, change dramatically, or simply fade into the background. George Michael had come out of the closet years ago and broken heterosexual female hearts across the globe, David Bowie had settled down into married bliss with Iman, and Sting talked a little too much about tantric sex. Madonna had become increasingly irrelevant, while Cyndi Lauper appeared on *Gossip Girl*. Heart cut off all their hair and performed acoustically. Michael Hutchence died under questionable circumstances and INXS used Reality TV to find his replacement. John Waite and Rick Springfield had completely disappeared. If they stuck around too long, legends dried up or imploded or became fixtures on Lite FM.

But that had never happened to Tommy. He remained as perfect as the picture of him Jenna had on her wall – the one that she'd carefully saved since she was a girl.

And the fact was, he was a whole lot of perfection. Jenna drank in his poster. What *consultant* could compete with a man who could sing ballads in a voice so low and sweet it made grown women weep? What angry New York guy with male-pattern baldness was likely to hold any sort of candle to a man who looked good in sprayed-on leather pants and a glittery headband? If it hadn't been for Aimee's feelings, Jenna wasn't sure she'd even bother trying to date anyone.

No real men in Jenna's life had ever so much as approached her feelings for Tommy Seer. They might have been *real*, but they'd never made her heart thump the way Tommy could just by sending out a sidelong glance, like he did repeatedly in the video for 'Careless Lips Kill Relationships'. She'd been with Adam for years, even lived with him, and he'd never managed to inspire her in that dizzy, magical way. She'd told herself that was because real life meant *settling*, real life meant *being practical*, real life meant *compromise*.

But maybe real life wasn't all it was cracked up to be. Maybe her fantasy life was better.

It certainly hurt less.

Jenna knew it sounded crazy, which was why she knew

16

better than to mention it out loud, but more than twenty years past his death there was a part of her that still believed that she and Tommy Seer had been meant for each other. Never mind the age difference, or the enormous bridge between the small life she'd led as a girl in Indiana and the rock-star life he'd had in New York. She'd gotten over that conviction as she'd grown older, but over the past eight months she'd revisited it. On some level she couldn't let go of the idea that he'd been supposed to be with her, and fate had just messed it up somehow.

But this wasn't something she could tell Aimee. Or anyone. She pretty much only admitted that crazy little fantasy to herself, at moments exactly like this one. She knew Aimee would view it as further evidence that she'd given up on life. Jenna didn't think that was true at all. *Life* was fine; it was *her life* that she had serious issues with. Fate had a whole lot to answer for.

The only person who had ever responded positively to Jenna's notion was her aunt Jen, and even she hadn't exactly *supported* the idea. She'd only smiled enigmatically and said, *stranger things have happened, Jenna*. Which Aunt Jen should know, having managed to cash in on Microsoft *and* Apple stock years before anyone else knew about either company.

Jenna stretched in her chair, thrust her self-pity aside with great effort, and noticed the time. It was getting late, and she had to be back at work bright and early the next day. Her boss was pretty relaxed as middle-management office types went, but he nonetheless insisted the office-drone section of Eighties TV act like the office drones they were, not TV stars, and thus be behind their desks by nine o'clock sharp for invoicing and data checking, oh joy. If she left now she could still order some beef and broccoli, maybe an egg roll because she was feeling blue, and catch up on her TiVo.

Jenna got to her feet and, as if on cue, the overhead lights went out.

If there was anything creepier than standing in her office in the pitch black, Jenna did not want to know about it. Outside, the lightning seemed twice as bright, and also closer to the building. The Video TV building had a grand history of being struck by lightning – once in the late Nineties during a tribute concert to the Cure, once in the summer of 1987, and once again a couple of months later in 1987, coincidentally, on the night Tommy Seer had died. An outage at midnight, as if Video TV had mourned his passing. Funny how that bit of trivia didn't make Jenna feel any better about standing there in the dark.

Earlier that day her desk lamp had gone out, and she had been too lazy to replace the bulb. Now she regretted her laziness. Even if there was something wrong with the overhead fluorescent lights in the building, which there appeared to be as they weren't flickering back to life, her desk lamp might work with a new bulb.

Feeling enormously put upon, and not at all like the expendable chick in the opening scene of a horror movie,

Jenna headed out of her office and down the hallway towards the supply closet. As she walked, the overhead lights burst back on with a faint hum, and lit up one by one in front of her. Since she was already on a mission, Jenna kept going – who knew when the overhead lights would go out again? She pushed her way into the supply closet, and let the heavy door thump shut behind her.

Jenna wasn't a fan of the supply closet, which always seemed to be obscenely crowded and purposely disorganized. She didn't understand why Delia, the stereotypically OCD office manager, overlooked the chaos behind this door, when she was perfectly happy to send outraged memos about the overuse of the printers for personal reasons and the shocking theft of three-hole punchers.

The light bulbs were located on the highest shelf facing the door, about three feet above Jenna's head. Naturally. She groaned, and stood on her tiptoes, stretching her arms as high as they could go, but her fingertips only grazed the cardboard shell and sent the bulbs skittering back from the edge towards the wall.

Terrific.

Hiking up her miniskirt, Jenna wedged one leg on the wall and put her other foot on the first shelf. Then, tentatively, she put her weight against it. It was one of those metal industrial shelves, and it seemed sturdy enough. Emboldened, she started to climb. Not that 'climb' was the right word. It was more like she hoisted herself upward. Rock climbing without a belay. Or rocks.

A sheaf of paper fell on top of her as the shelf shifted

a little bit beneath her weight, but that was the worst of it. Jenna let out the breath she was holding. It didn't take long to manoeuvre herself up to the top shelf – some five or six feet from the ground.

She grabbed for the package of light bulbs – which by this point had slid to the far back of the deep shelf – and put them on the shelf below, which was where her foot was currently braced. The other foot was across the narrow closet, braced against the wall.

Jenna was pleased with herself and her acrobatics, having last scaled anything resembling a wall during gym class back in high school.

So, of course, the lights went out again.

'You have to be kidding me,' Jenna groaned.

Just then the shelf buckled beneath her, letting out a metallic crumpling sort of noise. Not a good sound at all.

Panicked, Jenna threw out her hand to brace herself, and slammed it up against the light bulb in the centre of the ceiling. The bulb shattered, and she ducked her head to avoid getting glass in her face.

She didn't have time to register whether or not she'd sliced open her palm, because the shelf beneath her foot made another noise, and she groped wildly above her head, her legs locking, trying to find a handhold.

It seemed as if everything around her sizzled, and then wobbled.

There was a buzzing sound, loud like bees, and she could feel it in her skin. As if the power were about to surge back on.

Jenna had the sensation of falling, as if through a long tunnel, but she knew that she wasn't actually falling because she could feel the shelf in front of her and the ceiling above.

Oh my God, I'm electrocuting myself, she thought in a panic. And then she felt nothing at all.

2

Jenna came to slowly.

She was on the floor of the supply closet. Her head throbbed and her throat felt as if she'd been out carousing in dire places, for about a week straight. It was an unpleasant reminder of a very debaucherous summer in her largely misspent early twenties.

Jenna sat up very, very carefully, and took stock. Nothing protested too strenuously. There was no blood, not even on her palm, though there was a scrape across the centre of it that hadn't been there before – yet looked old. She frowned, and continued her inventory.

No broken neck, or sprained head, as far as she could tell, and she was certain she *would* be able to tell: a broken neck wasn't something that could be overlooked. Her miniskirt, embarrassingly, was up around her waist – very attractive – and she was fervently glad she'd been wearing leggings. No crotch shots for the paparazzi, thank you. In fact, she felt more or less fine, except for her butt, which kind of ached, suggesting she'd landed on it. This struck her as completely unfair. Sure, she was lucky she hadn't landed on her head. But who was going to tell a story about a fall that culminated in a sore butt? That would be just inviting ridicule and abuse, something she had learned to avoid after surviving middle school.

Jenna climbed to her feet, feeling sorry for herself, and threw open the supply-closet door. She immediately felt even worse, because she could clearly see *daylight* down at the end of the hall. Fantastic. Did that mean she'd knocked herself out and spent the night on the floor of the supply closet? What did it say about her life that no one had cared enough to come find her? That there was no one who noticed she was missing in the first place? *Thanks again, Adam*, she thought. And what did it say about her place of employment that no one bothered to go into the supply closet, anyway?

Highly aggrieved, Jenna dragged herself down the hallway towards her office, clutching the package of light bulbs to her chest, her sore butt protesting all the way. As she walked, something niggled at her, but refused to form into a full, coherent thought. Then it came to her: the carpet looked different. Maybe she'd hit herself harder on the head than she'd originally thought, but she could have sworn the carpet was a sort of dingy grey last night. So why was it royal blue this morning?

Maybe you should lie down, she told herself. Jenna wasn't above locking her office door and having an illicit snooze from time to time. She accepted that this said things about her. That she was often tired at work, for one thing, especially when VH-1 ran the Wild Boys *Behind the Music* rockumentary at two in the morning. More importantly, it said that she was unlikely to charge up that corporate ladder while napping. But then, she was over thirty years old and still in lower-middle management, so this was not exactly news.

Her office door was closed, and, she discovered when she pushed on it, locked. That was weird, too, since she knew she'd left the door wide open when she'd gone off in search of a light bulb. But Jenna was used to the odd and capricious whims of the janitorial staff, and dug her keys out of her pocket. She inserted the key into the lock, and stood there, stupidly, when it didn't turn. She wiggled it a few times, but the door remained locked.

The hell?

Feeling disoriented, Jenna stepped back and looked around. It was the same long, narrow hallway she had walked down last night, even if the carpet looked different. She had started out in the cubicles on the floor below, and had moved up to the lower-management level and her own office about three years ago. The hallway was the same hallway. This had always been her office. This had always been the key that opened her office door. Sighing a little bit, Jenna's eyes fell to the nameplate, where she was used to seeing her name. Instead, she read a different name: PETER HALE.

Now she was really confused. How long had she been

on the supply-closet floor, anyway? Long enough to be replaced? Surely other people in her office required printer paper, binder clips, and staples? Surely they weren't all such self-obsessed New Yorkers that they'd actually reached *over* her comatose body, miniskirt at her waist, and *left* her there?

Relax, Jenna ordered herself sternly. There was no sense indulging in her ingrained Midwestern hysteria. Aimee was unlikely to just abandon her to an unknown fate – she couldn't even leave her to her own form of mourning for her lost life with Adam. There was no way *Aimee* would have allowed Jenna to simply sprawl on the supply-closet floor for days on end, while her office was handed over to someone new. There had to be another explanation.

Straightening her spine on that thought, she placed the package of light bulbs on the floor outside the office that was apparently no longer hers, turned on her heel, and headed down the hallway towards the reception area. This certainly wouldn't be the first time Video TV had done something crazy without informing its employees, and it wouldn't be the first time Jenna would have to go with the flow of that craziness, possibly even while wearing a big smile. *Office politics*, Aimee would say with a shrug.

Jenna rounded the corner, expecting to see the usual receptionist Gianna sitting behind the desk, all waifish and Kate Moss-y. Instead, there was a new girl in full-on

Eighties mode. Oversize T-shirt beneath suspenders attached to high-waisted pants, bangles up the arm, and, to complete the look, sporting that awful girl-pompadour hairdo that, in Jenna's opinion, hadn't even looked good on Princess Diana.

Wow, Jenna thought. Judgementally. Then she was gleeful. Because how could Aimee suggest that Jenna was overidentifying with Eighties icons when there was a girl walking around the office with Princess Diana hair? This chick made Jenna look like sanity central, thank you very much.

'Hi,' Jenna said, trying to sound cheerful and welcoming despite the bad hair and her own odd circumstances.

'Where have you been?' Princess Diana Hair snapped. 'Everyone's waiting for you down on set!'

That, like everything else this morning, made absolutely no sense. Jenna shook her head as if that might clear it.

'What do you mean?' she asked.

Jenna was very rarely on set, as she was neither a crew member nor one of the talent. Jenna tallied up costs and maintained customer accounts. She only snuck down to the set when they were filming exciting specials, like when they'd interviewed that awful Eugenia Wentworth last year and she'd told huge lies about her relationship with Tommy Seer. She'd called him a cheater and an alcoholic, among other slanderous falsehoods. Jenna had fumed about Eugenia's betrayal with all the rest of the members of the Wild Boys online Bulletin Board for months. Imagine being lucky enough to touch Tommy Seer and then bitching about it years after his death? To say nothing of the lies! The nerve!

'What I mean is, you need to hurry up and get down there,' Princess Diana Hair said in that same snotty tone, like Jenna was acting brain-dead on purpose, just to annoy her. 'What are you waiting for? Like, an engraved invitation?'

'Um, okay, thanks,' Jenna muttered. She wasn't sure where all the attitude was coming from, given that she and Princess Diana Hair had never laid eyes on each other before. Of course, Jenna was not a receptionist. Nor was she wearing her hair in homage to a long-dead princess. So maybe acting like a snotty bitch was par for the course with someone who was the former and was doing the latter.

Jenna went over to the elevator and pressed the down button, surprised when the doors opened immediately. That almost never happened. When she stepped inside, she could see that Princess Diana Hair was still glaring after her. Very much as if Jenna had done something to wrong her, personally.

Jenna frowned as the elevator began to move. Did she know Princess Diana Hair from somewhere? Or – and this made her stomach clench in horror – did she feel as if she'd gone on some week-long bender *because she had*? Jenna had certainly had a night or two that had disappeared into the black much sooner than they should have, but this felt entirely different. Jenna would have sworn on a stack of Bibles that she had never met that girl before, but the way she'd looked at Jenna suggested she would not say the same.

And Jenna still didn't know who Peter Hale was, or why he was in her office.

3

Down on the lower floor, Jenna made her way across the lobby and into the studio, moving at a fast clip until the general weirdness all around her started to make an impression.

Everyone was dressed oddly. Ridiculously oddly, in fact.

There was a woman in a cherry-red Eighties power suit marching down the hallway, her shoulder pads like wings. Where one could even find a power suit like that, cut to mimic long-gone divas of night-time television, Jenna could not imagine. Alexis Carrington Colby would have been proud. Then she noticed more Eighties extravagances, like the two men having a conversation in the corner, both in pastel suits with pastel T-shirts underneath, and loafers without socks. It was so Sonny Crockett, it hurt. Jenna slowed her pace without meaning to, as she found herself looking around at one far too realistic and strange outfit after another.

It was one thing to throw out a little Eighties flair on

the Eighties TV floor, Jenna thought, bewildered. A side ponytail here, a skinny tie there – that was the job. But it was something else entirely to rock vintage *Miami Vice* apparel on the Video TV studio level, where they filmed all the shows that were supposed to compete with MTV. It was like someone had announced a company-wide dress-up day, but had forgotten to tell Jenna.

But then, Jenna was getting the feeling that there was a lot someone had forgotten to tell her today.

'Jen, thank God!' a nasal voice cried.

Another person Jenna had never seen in her entire life ran up to her and grabbed her arm. He was a tiny little man, wearing an outfit that would not have looked out of place on Jon Cryer in *Pretty in Pink*. Right down to the skinny tie and high-tops. Jenna smiled automatically as confusion washed through her, as much because this person was talking to her in such a familiar manner as because of his bizarre work attire.

'They've been complete assholes all morning,' Elfin Jon Cryer said in a low voice, tugging Jenna along with him with a hand on her lower back, in complete defiance of all the sexual-harassment rules governing the touching of co-workers in the workplace. Jenna stiffened, but he just kept talking and propelling her along in front of him. 'You're the only one who can talk any sense into them. All I want is good television here, it's not like I'm looking to scale the Berlin Wall, for Christ's sake!'

As the last time Jenna had heard someone reference the Berlin Wall in casual conversation was *sometime in high*

30

school, she could only stare at him. She even forgot for a moment that he was still touching her.

'Okay, fine,' he said, as if Jenna had communicated something with that stare. 'I get that they think their video image will be tarnished or something, but come on. Everyone wants to see them play a few songs live. They *can* play live, can't they?' That last part sounded particularly urgent.

'I don't have any idea how to answer that,' Jenna said, very truthfully.

Elfin Jon Cryer sighed heavily and then laughed very suddenly. Apparently, a victim of both mood swings and fashion. Or, possibly, narcotics.

'Well,' he said with another sigh as they approached the doors to the set, 'this is on my head, which means it's on yours. Let's make sure it works out, okay, Jen?'

Jenna opened her mouth to ask him to please not call her *Jen*, as she preferred *Jenna* (which, fortuitously, was also her name), to request that he remove his small elfin hand from her body, and also to ask him who, exactly, he was. But instead, as soon as the doors opened, the voices inside slammed into her like a wave. A very loud and angry wave.

'See?' Elfin Jon Cryer demanded. 'All morning it's been like this!'

He leaned close, put his other hand on Jenna's back – which she felt was an even greater intrusion into her personal space, hello – pushed her none too gently forward, and then let the heavy door slam behind her.

The loud group of people arguing under the lights turned to look at her as she stumbled towards them, making Jenna feel she was the one under a spotlight instead of them.

It was okay, though. Jenna had finally figured out that she was dreaming. Aimee had called her out for her 'Eighties obsession', and so she was dreaming some strange anxiety dream about people with some serious issues in that area, all set at work just to up the ante, and now that Jenna had realized it was a dream she could simply force herself to wake up.

Wake up! she ordered herself.

It did not have the desired effect.

In the meantime, she continued walking towards the group on set.

My subconscious is good, Jenna thought smugly. Because instead of the retro set Eighties TV used every day, *this* set was done up to look like that iconic one from back in the day, when Video TV and MTV had battled it out every night in the ratings and VJs had lived like gods. Jenna had clearly taken note of every detail, from the sunken couches to the wacky videos on the wall, to the faux-trashed look. She had even installed famously sulky VJ Harrison T. in the corner, he of the pouty lips and pouty hair, despite the fact that she had always personally preferred the more preppy and accessible Digby Jones. Her subconscious dream-mind certainly got points for effort and originality!

'Nice of you to show up,' Harrison sulked at Jenna as

32

she approached. 'The band refuses to play acoustic. They say you promised them they could lip-sync.'

Jenna pasted a smile across her face. Perhaps Aimee had a point, if she was remembering the Eighties all the way down to that petulant little pout Harrison T. was wearing, an expression Jenna associated with music from Depeche Mode and the Cure. Jenna restrained herself, barely, from breaking into the chorus of 'Blasphemous Rumours'.

'For fuck's sake,' said a crisp, upper-crust British voice. Jenna saw the speaker uncurl herself from her seat and draw herself up to an impressive height. 'She's some kind of worker bee. What can she possibly add to this travesty?'

'She's the one who takes care of the bookings,' Harrison T. retorted. Which was news to Jenna. Apparently her subconscious had given her a promotion, too. Even more points. 'She can tell you what it says in the band's contract.'

'This is bollocks,' replied the woman.

Who, Jenna realized, shocked, was Eugenia Wentworth.

Jenna had to restrain herself from gaping. Eugenia was skinnier than she looked in photos, and much uglier, not that Jenna was at all biased. Jenna had originally hated Eugenia on principle, of course, because she got to be with Tommy, but there was no denying the fact that the camera found things to love about Eugenia's oddly angled face and ferrety mouth that the naked eye failed to see. Or that *Jenna's* naked eye failed to see.

'Eugenia,' Jenna said in greeting, as if they were acquainted. Because Jenna felt that in a sense they were, after twenty years of watching Eugenia climb to undeserved fame on the back of Tommy's death. She might as well tap dance on his grave, the bitch. 'How nice to see you.'

Eugenia actually curled her lip, like she was some kind of rabid, upper-crust British dog.

But Jenna had already forgotten her, because *he* was stepping around Eugenia, and frowning down into Jenna's upturned face. Jenna stopped breathing. The lights, the voices – everything disappeared. There was only *him*.

Those sea-green eyes, even narrowed in annoyance, made Jenna's heart kick into high gear. His soft, gorgeous hair was dark around his face and curled over the headband he wore.

It said something that he looked so beautiful even dressed in those ridiculous period clothes. That a *headband* failed to detract from the impact of his lean jaw or his delicious mouth.

Tommy Seer was still the best-looking man Jenna had ever seen. She could feel herself melt as she stared at him.

Okay, sure, she had variations on this dream all the time. So what?

But this was the best dream yet. Jenna took a breath and realized that she could smell things – like Eugenia's cloud of suffocating perfume, and the cigarette Harrison T. was smoking, right there on set.

But mostly, she could gaze at Tommy Seer as if he really was standing there, his brow furrowed into that adorable frown. It was a dream, after all, and she didn't need to worry about what Aimee thought while she was dreaming.

She didn't have to wonder if she really was hiding away from real life – she was too busy just dreaming. And in this dream, Tommy Seer seemed to have a kind of electricity that hummed around him, like he was *that much more* than the average guy. He was *that* compelling, even with that frown.

The frown was an interesting touch, Jenna thought with a distant part of her mind, the part that wasn't swooning over Tommy's magnetic closeness. Usually her Tommy dreams concentrated more on the *he took one look at her and realized he loved her* angle. This was new. Not necessarily unpleasant or anything, but new.

'Are you listening?' he demanded.

Funny, for some reason in her dream Jenna had given him an American accent. How weird. Everyone knew that Tommy Seer was British.

'Uh, yes,' Jenna said, playing along, because that meant she could keep *gazing* at him. She felt heat bloom across her cheeks. 'I'm listening.' *And I love you.*

'We don't want to play live,' he said, his frown deepening as he regarded her steadily. 'We never would have agreed to a live show. Not on Video TV. We're just here to do the VJ thing.'

Still an American accent.

'Wow,' Jenna said dreamily, without really meaning to speak. 'It's just so weird that you're talking in an American accent.'

Everyone in the room seemed to let out a collective sort of groan.

'Yeah,' Tommy said, his gaze going icy. 'Weird.'

'I told you to stay in character!' Nick, supposedly the shy one, bellowed at top volume as he vibrated up and to his feet, fists clenched at his sides. 'You arrogant prick!'

Jenna had been so focused on Tommy that she'd neglected to pay attention to the rest of the band. Normally, this sort of dream cut them out altogether and spent delicious time on the *gazing* and Tommy's immediate realization that Jenna and only Jenna could cure his lonely—

'This is getting us nowhere,' too-cool-for-school Sebastian said, except he didn't sound cool at all. He sounded tense. Jittery. His knee was bouncing up and down and he was fingering his bright blond soul patch nervously. 'We have to figure out what we're going to do on the show.'

Richie didn't contribute to the discussion, as he was too busy idly playing with the back of Sebastian's feathered mullet, an act that was quite evidently not in the least platonic. Not that Jenna had ever seen too many examples of any platonic running of fingers through hair, now that she thought about it. In her dream, for some reason, Sebastian and Richie, who'd given long interviews about their many women and their heterosexual whoring ways, were gay. Or, at any rate, together. Jenna didn't know why she was surprised. After George Michael, it was really only to be expected. Men that good-looking never tended to be straight in real life, did they? It was just that she'd never heard a single whisper about Richie or Sebastian's sexuality in all the years she'd been obsessed with the band. Why she'd chosen to out the two of them in her dream, she couldn't say.

It was like they were all strangers, these guys Jenna knew so many details about. They were all acting out of character – especially Tommy, who didn't, as a rule, spend any time looking *annoyed* with her in her own dreams, like he was now. It was a little bit upsetting. This was less a comforting Wild Boys dream – the kind Jenna sank into at the drop of a hat and used to soothe herself – and more an alternate-universe Wild Boys dream where nothing was as it ought to be.

Why on earth would she dream *this*?

4

'What the hell is going on here?' asked a rough voice from the door behind Jenna, taking the words right out of her mouth. Though she might not have chosen such a belligerent tone. 'I take the wife and kids on a much-needed break on a goddamned beach in Jamaica and this is what happens while I'm gone?'

When Jenna turned around, Duncan Paradis was standing there.

The Duncan Paradis, music manager extraordinaire. He was famous for picking one or two acts every decade and managing them right into the stratosphere. At this point, all he had to do was announce a name for the musician to start raking in the fame, fortune, and full coverage in the tabloids. According to *US Weekly*, Jenna's favourite source of celebrity gossip, Britney Spears had begged Duncan to spearhead her comeback following her divorce from K-Fed, and he'd refused because he was all about the new. Obviously. Because the acts that Duncan Paradis managed were always, always, untouchably huge stars who didn't need to rehab their image.

He'd discovered – some said *created* – the Wild Boys, had gone on to manage the grunge queen Lauren Neopolitan herself, had formed the boy band Real almost, it seemed, to prove to himself and the world that he could steal N'Sync's and the Backstreet Boys' thunder if he wanted to, and he was currently raking in the benefits of having discovered the crossover pop, country, and R&B sensation Fuchsia Kelly – his powerhouse answer to all the *American Idol* girls. He was a living legend.

And now he was standing in front of Jenna minus the trademark shock of snow-white hair he'd started sporting in the early Nineties. This version of Duncan Paradis was slimmer, trimmer, and unquestionably younger. This version, in fact, was one Jenna had only seen in those colour-photo centrepieces they always stuck in the Unofficial Biographies.

'Babe,' Eugenia Wentworth purred. 'At last.'

Jenna watched in astonishment as Tommy Seer's fiancée flitted from the stage to Duncan's side. She towered over him, but that only made it seem more lascivious when she leaned down and kissed him. With evident delight, and visible tongue. Ew. Despite the fact she was supposedly engaged to the man standing right in front of her, and Duncan had moments before referenced his wife and kids.

Was it really that hard for engaged people to remember who they were engaged *to*, Jenna wondered – not that she was taking it at all personally.

The most shocking part of the whole thing was that Jenna was the only one who looked the slightest bit surprised by this development. Even Tommy, the nearest wronged party, looked bored.

How someone who could have Tommy Seer would choose . . . anyone else, ever, was a mystery to Jenna. Much less a man who – while admittedly powerful – looked like Karl Lagerfeld's less attractive brother. Jenna wondered if her subconscious had finally gone round the bend, because this dream was starting to creep her out.

'Tommy's being a complete wanker,' Eugenia tattled, obviously enjoying herself. She rubbed herself against Duncan, who didn't look thrilled with the attention – but didn't push her away, either. 'No one seems to be able to talk any sense into him. I told them they have to do the live show, babe, but no one will listen to me.'

'No one will listen to you because you don't know what you're talking about,' Tommy snapped from his place on the stage. He hadn't moved, but Jenna was close enough to him that she could see he'd tensed up almost imperceptibly at the sight of Duncan. Or maybe it was the sight of his fiancée after all, as she practically licked Duncan's face.

'All I know is that we're running out of rehearsal time,' Harrison T. complained. He lit another cigarette and made a lazy smoke circle in the air. 'We've already kicked out the entire crew, who are sitting on their asses somewhere, waiting to hear what happens next, and we have to start

40

the live show in forty-five minutes. This argument has gone on for way too long.'

This was the most Jenna had ever heard Harrison T. speak, given that he had spent the bulk of his on-air time looking pensive and/or troubled and saying things like, 'What can *anyone* say about "Boys Don't Cry" that's not in the title?' He had been emo long before there was a vocabulary word to describe it.

'Why don't you take ten minutes?' Duncan asked him pleasantly. Harrison T. merely shrugged. Jenna wasn't fooled by Duncan's pleasant tone, which was maybe why his eyes turned to her, then flicked to Tommy. 'Who is this?'

'Booking,' Tommy said tersely. 'Apparently.' They both looked at Jenna. Not, she thought, nicely. She could feel it in her stomach, like an ache.

'Yeah,' Harrison T. said, as he drifted to his feet, sounding amused. 'And more to the point, Ken Dollimore's eyes and ears.' He smirked. Or, possibly, that was his smile. Jenna had never seen it before. No one had, as far as she knew. One of the great mysteries of the Eighties, aside from the popularity of the *Breakin'* movie franchise, was whether or not Harrison T. had teeth.

'Jen's his protégée,' Harrison T. continued in that mocking sort of tone, and then headed for the studio doors. 'We consider her Ken in a miniskirt.'

'It's Jenna, actually,' she murmured, but no one was paying any attention to what she was saying. They were all much busier glaring at her as if they would each,

41

individually, like to murder her. Jenna had to lock her knees to remain upright.

'Far be it from me to kick out Ken's eyes and ears, in a goddamned miniskirt,' Duncan said scathingly. His famously heavy-lidded eyes bored a hole into Jenna's forehead from across the room. She ordered herself not to feel for blood. 'Whatever the esteemed vice-president of Video TV wants, he gets. You can feel perfectly comfortable telling him I said so.'

Jenna's head began to spin. Ken Dollimore. The vice-president of Video TV back in the day, credited with the bulk of the creative programming that had made the station a viable contender against the MTV behemoth. Which Jenna knew because she spent a lot of her working hours on Wikipedia, when she wasn't napping behind her desk. Oh, okay, and because she was proud of the fact she worked at Video TV, like her favourite aunt Jen before her. It was practically the family business, she felt, and she knew all the trivia. Like the fact that Ken Dollimore was considered the genius behind Video TV, which was supposedly the root of his bitter feud with Chuck Arendt, the CEO from 1981 to 1989 and Ken's once-upon-a-time mentor—

That was the moment when it occurred to Jenna that Elfin Jon Cryer had looked a lot like those old posters of Ken Dollimore they were forever dragging out of storage and festooning about corporate events.

Huh.

Jenna didn't know what it said about her subconscious

42

that it was this detailed – that it was subtracting over twenty years from everyone's age and waiting for her prowess in Eighties trivia to catch up with the show.

Jenna wasn't sure she wanted to know. Aimee, she was certain, would have a field day with this dream. Adam, for that matter, who had always treated her devotion to the Eighties like a strain of leprosy, would consider it evidence that she'd finally achieved the truly spectacular level of lameness he'd always suspected she would. The jerk.

'Um, I'll be sure to tell Ken he has your support,' she heard herself say to Duncan, who ignored her. But Tommy flicked her a sideways sort of look that Jenna confidently interpreted to mean *faintly amused*, as she was an expert on reading Tommy Seer's numerous facial expressions.

Tommy thought that was funny, a little voice in the back of her head chortled. Jenna tried to hide her smile of pleasure.

'So,' Duncan said when Harrison T. closed the set doors behind him, leaving a cloud of smoke and petulance in his wake. 'I asked what the hell was going on in here.'

'Haven't I just told you?' Eugenia complained. Jenna decided her accent was, actually, physically grating.

Duncan set her away from him, not dignifying her with a response, and marched towards the stage.

'I can't believe what I'm seeing,' he said in a gravelly, low voice that made Jenna nervous, suddenly. And she could see that she was not alone in that. He looked at Sebastian and Richie, who broke physical contact as if scalded. 'You two are all over each other, when I explicitly told you we're selling you both as straight. *Straight.* Save it for your private time. And here's Tommy parading around without even pretending he's English, and who knows who heard him.'

'We're not onstage,' Tommy retorted, in an angry sort of tone Jenna had never heard before. Not from him.

'And you're not likely to be onstage ever again if you don't do what I tell you,' Duncan snarled. He stuck his face close to Tommy's. 'Remember who owns you, you little shit.'

In Jenna's mind, Tommy Seer was like a god, and he didn't take that kind of crap from anyone.

But this *was* Jenna's mind, and instead of smacking Duncan down in some satisfyingly heroic way, Tommy's jaw tightened and he otherwise made no response.

Jenna wanted to punch Duncan in the face on Tommy's behalf. But she caught herself. For some reason, she sensed this was not the sort of dream in which she could suddenly act like Buffy.

'All right then,' Duncan said, a note of triumph in his voice when Tommy continued to do nothing. He turned to look at Eugenia. 'Did I hear you say you want them to perform live?'

'It's high time,' Eugenia said, striding towards the stage, casting an imperious look over the band. 'They've ignored me for years now—'

'Because it's the stupidest thing I've ever heard,' Duncan growled. 'You're supposed to be acting like a besotted, supporting fiancée, Eugenia. Has your job description changed even a little bit since the beginning? No. So tell me, what part of *being Tommy's girlfriend* involves giving the band creative direction?'

Colour flamed bright and high on Eugenia's porcelain British cheeks.

'Everyone's clamouring for a live performance,' she said, her voice notably less strident, 'and this is the perfect opportunity . . .' Her voice trailed away.

'Let's think about your areas of expertise,' Duncan suggested in that quiet, horrible voice. Even Jenna, no fan of Eugenia's, was quite certain she didn't want to hear what he was about to say. Duncan looked Eugenia up and down, his expression cruel.

He didn't have to say another word.

'I'm sorry,' she said, her face even redder.

'Why don't you sit down, shut up, and leave the music to the professionals?' Duncan ordered her.

As Eugenia did so, everyone else seemed to stare off into space, expressionless. Avoiding being the next target, more likely.

'So,' Duncan said when Eugenia was seated, and the moment had become so actively uncomfortable that Jenna had to clench her knees to keep from literally shaking in her boots, while her stomach cramped. 'How much of a disaster is this thing?'

'Video TV wants a live performance,' Sebastian said, jiggling his knee in obvious agitation. 'They've been promised a live performance.'

'And we can't deliver,' Tommy said, in his English accent, which, now that Jenna had heard his American one, sounded odd to her ears. But there was no denying the slightly mocking tone. 'The moment we become a live band on national television, we lose our edge. Look what happened to Duran Duran.'

'Simon is a friend,' Nick retorted, enraged again. Or still. 'Arcadia is a fantastic band and I don't know why everyone's all excited about Powerstation in the first place and besides, they haven't broken up! Why does everyone think they've broken up?'

'*Simon's a friend,*' Sebastian imitated him, with much derision. 'Listen to yourself. You sound like a groupie. The original line-up is gone and I don't know if you've noticed, but Live Aid was over two years ago.'

Everyone started yelling again, while Jenna's Eighties-obsessed brain tried to make sense of what she was hearing. Live Aid, of course, was the brilliant British charity concert to help with famine in Ethiopia. A year or so before the concert, assorted British artists released the fantastic 'Do They Know It's Christmas?' single on an unsuspecting world. Bethie Ridgeway had given Jenna the special ten-inch single for Christmas that year, bless her. The American response was the decidedly sub-par 'We Are the World', which if Jenna never heard it again would be too soon. The very thought of the sickly-sweet chorus, heavily centred on Michael Jackson, made her feel ill.

Which was all a roundabout way of her figuring out

that this bizarre dream of hers was apparently taking place in 1987.

Sometime late in the summer of 1987, if she had to hazard a guess, based on the lack of coats and hats and Tommy's ragged denim vest that he wore in place of a shirt. Which meant Tommy was a mere two months away from careening over the side of that bridge. 1987 was a dark year. Jenna could probably list off the band's every accomplishment during that year – that was the level of her geekiness where the Wild Boys were concerned. She had gone over those accomplishments with a fine-tooth comb many, many times after 1987, and a great deal over the last eight months, believing that there had to be a clue somewhere in those details that would explain what had happened to Tommy. A clue about what was to come in October. So she probably knew the Wild Boys' 1987 schedule better than they did.

Including, now that she thought about it, their revolutionary Video TV appearance in late August of that year.

Jenna's breath caught. Was this supposed to be *that* fateful day?

She looked at each of the band members, unable to contain her sudden joy. This was *the best Wild Boys dream ever*, no matter the weird dream asides regarding accents, faithless fiancées, and Duncan Paradis recast from fatherly supporter to nasty, adulterous bully. All of that was probably her brain's anxiety concerning her usual issues – thirties, Manhattan, betrayed and alone – coming out in strange new ways. But the idea that she might get to take part in that hallmark of Video TV appearances? That was worth whatever weirdness might come!

Jenna could see the whole thing in her mind's eye, as if she was once again twelve years old and sitting two inches away from the television in her parents' study, almost hyperventilating with excitement.

She had only ever seen similar excitement amongst Harry Potter fans. Or those girls screaming over Edward Cullen from *Twilight* in the mall. Or the crazy people in South America or somewhere who nearly capsized the Backstreet Boys' tour bus, that was how much they loved them.

Everyone had expected a live performance. There had been rumours for months in all the teen magazines, on MTV and Video TV. The Wild Boys were in the studio finishing up their next album, the follow-up to their record-breaking international hit *Fancypants Afire*. They were a high-concept band, all about the videos. Their limited live shows were pageant-like events in arenas with enormous video-screen backdrops, during which the Boys paraded around in a variety of costumes and produced huge new videos that became iconic. They put on a slick, visual experience, and, now that Jenna thought about it, probably lip-synced the whole time.

But the rumour was that they'd be playing an acoustic set on Video TV.

Instead, the Wild Boys had made television history by performing their videos.

Not their songs, their *videos*.

As the videos of their hit songs played against the backdrop, the Wild Boys stood in front of the videos and acted them out as they went. Put like that, it didn't sound like anything exciting, but for the twelve-year-old with her face practically *inside* her parents' television, it was breathtaking. Some of Jenna's fellow online fans felt Mystery Science Theater had stolen the idea for their franchise from this groundbreaking appearance.

Tommy's adorable, bashful smile. Sebastian cracking up halfway through 'Lucky Penny'. Richie performing an extended air guitar. Nick dancing the robot during the mournful part of 'Celestially Yours'.

When they'd released the first single from the new album about a month later, the ballad 'Misery Loves Company', it had hit #1 and stayed there for most of that fall. It had just started to slip when Tommy had gone off that bridge, and his death had catapulted the single back to the top spot for the rest of the year.

Jenna got misty just thinking about it.

'Shut up!' Duncan roared then.

Jenna jerked back to attention.

'This is a disaster,' Nick muttered. 'No one asks Boy George for an acoustic set.'

'No one asks Boy George for anything these days,' Sebastian retorted. 'Not even his name, from what I hear.'

'Culture Club broke up in 1986,' Jenna said, not that anyone had asked. And no one paid any attention to her, either, as the squabbling commenced – except for the man standing nearest to her, his toned biceps on display.

'You mean, last year?' Tommy asked, one dark eyebrow raised into a perfect arch.

'Oh, right,' she said, and laughed nervously because his eyes were *so green*, 'because in 1987 you would definitely say *last year* and not *1986*, I get it. That's totally what you would say.'

'Uh, yeah,' Tommy said, raising his eyebrow a little more. And why not? She was acting crazy.

Duncan Paradis turned his steely gaze on her then, which was far worse than any look Tommy might have been giving her.

'Well?' he demanded.

'Well, what?' she asked, nervously.

Jenna realized she was terrified of him. And not in that amorphous dreamy way, where she could sort of sense someone was evil or something and *feel* that they might wish to harm her. This wasn't like that. She actually felt herself break out in a sweat. A nervous, unpleasant sweat.

'The band won't perform anything acoustic, and Ken knows it,' Duncan told her in that awful voice that made her think of Tony Soprano but without the heavy New Jersey accent. 'This is a set-up, and we're two seconds away from walking out of here. I'm betting MTV wouldn't jerk me around like this.'

'There's no need to bring them into it,' Jenna replied, stung out of her fear of him by ten years of loyalty to her employer.

Duncan Paradis smirked.

'So what are you going to do about it?' he asked. He

crossed his arms over his chest and levelled that glare directly at her. 'Tell me how you're going to make me happy, sweetheart, and keep me from taking off. You have thirty seconds.'

Then Jenna remembered that she didn't have to be afraid of Duncan Paradis or his thirty seconds.

She already knew what happened.

'Actually,' she said with a smile that bordered on smug, 'I have a great idea.'

'You're a genius!' Ken Dollimore crowed, not for the first time, and Jenna was so giddy and pleased with herself that she decided to ignore the fact that he had his arm draped across her shoulders. And the fact he was crowing directly into her ear, which meant his elfin lips were tickling her earlobe when he got particularly animated.

There was only so much she could ignore, however, and the next time his lips touched her skin was well over that line, so she edged away from him in her chair.

Ken appeared oblivious, his attention focused on the set in front of him.

The Wild Boys' performance was, of course, phenomenal beyond the telling of it. Not that Jenna had had any doubt, having watched it herself in excess of three million times, thanks to her early VHS tape and later DVDs. The phone lines had lit up seconds into the first video the band performed, with teenaged girls screaming and swooning into their receivers, and Ken had come racing into the studio with the good news that this live broadcast was electrifying the viewing public. Unfortunately, he had also decided to sit with Jenna and watch the rest of the show, which meant there was far too much touching.

But this, Jenna felt, was a small price to pay for being hailed as the visionary behind *the* Wild Boys' video experience of all time.

Best. Dream. Ever.

Harrison T. was thanking the band up on the set, and the closing credit music started to play, and Jenna felt as triumphant as if she'd actually had a hand in making history. It was a very good feeling. Almost as good as the more lurid Tommy Seer fantasies – well, no. Not *that* good. There was no need to get carried away.

Ken Dollimore jumped to his feet then, suddenly. He motioned for Jenna to do the same with an impatient hand.

'Hurry,' he said in an undertone, his eyes on the stage. 'If I know Duncan Paradis, and I'm sad to say I do, he's going to want to talk to me and I'd rather do it in my office. Let's go.'

Ken did not consult Jenna on what she'd like to do, which was, of course, to remain in the studio where she could continue to watch Tommy Seer. Whether he was being silly with his band mates, singing along with the video, or sitting quietly in his chair during the advertisements with that faraway look on his face, she found him equally mesmerizing. Now he was up on the stage, smiling that gloriously crooked smile, and she wasn't sure she could bear to so much as blink and miss even a second—

'Jen,' Ken snapped in a tone that brooked no disobedience, and was completely at odds with his happy-go-lucky, fun-loving appearance. Jenna was on her feet and following him before she knew what she was doing. Like a trained dog, in fact. A comparison which did not exactly thrill her.

Obviously, she thought as she hurried after him, concentrating on his colourful high-tops, he hadn't become a legend by being shy and retiring.

Ken strode to the bank of elevators, Jenna close behind him in spite of herself, and nodded at all the young men in suits who complimented him on the show. All of them, Jenna could see, were blatantly jockeying for his favour, and all of them assumed that the whole thing had been Ken's idea.

'It was totally boss,' one lavender-suited gentleman said, loudly enough to drown out the rest of the chorus of praise. Jenna had to cough to cover an involuntary laugh. *Totally boss*? Really? Who said things like that? Even in the Eighties?

Instead of seeming impressed, or even interested, Ken caught Jenna's eyes for a moment and gave the slightest roll of his own.

Which was maybe why, when Ken wasn't looking at them, the scrum of competing pastel suits glared at Jenna as if they'd like to wrap their hands around her throat. And those were the milder expressions. Others were far more murderous. Jenna gulped, and moved closer to Ken, despite her earlier personal-space concerns.

'Pack of wild animals,' Ken muttered when he'd claimed the next available elevator car – and had denied the other men access to it simply by raising his palm to them and jabbing the CLOSE DOORS button with his other hand. He grinned at Jenna. 'I hate office politics.'

'Everyone hates office politics,' Jenna said, quoting Aimee. 'But that doesn't mean you get to stop playing them.' Aimee said more or less the same thing to Jenna at least six times a week during their usual daily lunches, feeling that Jenna's refusal to pay attention to office politics was the reason Jenna was stuck in a going-nowhere position while she, Aimee, was rocketing towards a VP slot. Jenna thought it actually had more to do with her penchant for naps under her desk, to say nothing of the weeks she did no work at all until midday on Thursday, but she knew better than to share that thought with Aimee, who would only get upset and suggest therapists.

'Play or die, huh?' Ken said, rocking back and forth on his heels. He let out a sort of whoop of triumph. 'This is a good day, Jen. This is a really fucking good day. I can feel it. I think we just kicked MTV's ass.'

Jenna knew that they had. The Wild Boys had received almost as much press as when Letterman went head-to-head with Leno years later.

'I don't know why,' she told Ken with a sort of chuckle, as if she was making it up as she went along, 'but I have a feeling that we skyrocketed past them in the ratings. By an enormous margin.'

'I like that feeling,' Ken said, grinning. 'From your lips to God's ears, babe.'

The elevator doors swished open, and Jenna found herself on the very posh top floor of Video TV. The intense poshness of it was perhaps what kept her from pointing out to Ken that 'babe' was not an appropriate way to address a co-worker. She was far too impressed with all the gleaming wood and the quiet. As this was where the executives spent their days, there were no cubicles, no tiny rabbit warrens of depressing workspaces. The carpet was far more plush, and everything felt hushed and moneyed. The receptionist smiled as if personally delighted that Jenna and Ken had arrived in front of her. It was a far cry from Jenna's own floor, where workers scurried about with their heads down, trying to avoid attracting any attention.

Ken raised a hand in the direction of the receptionist, but didn't slow his pace.

'She's a nice gal,' he told Jenna out of the corner of his mouth, 'but I wish she wouldn't smile like that. It's like one of those puppets in that Genesis video. It creeps me out.'

Not as much as his casual use of the word *gal* creeped Jenna out, but she didn't have time to comment on that or even the reference to the disturbing 'Land of Confusion' video, because Ken was charging down the quiet, very fancy hallway, and only stopped when he arrived at its furthest corner. He threw open the door and stepped into what Jenna quickly realized was an outer office, complete with a couch for visitors, framed movie posters on the walls, and a large, aggressively healthy ficus plant beneath the window. Ken kept moving, and wrenched open the interior door.

'Make him wait,' he said, with a grin over his shoulder, and disappeared inside, closing the door behind him.

Jenna blinked, and made her way across the room to the desk. The brass nameplate read JENNIFER JENKINS, but she didn't have time to absorb the shock of that, because she'd already noticed the pictures. Her stomach dropped all the way to her feet, and she heard herself make a sound that was close to a whimper.

There were photographs everywhere – clipped to the bulletin board behind the desk and displayed proudly in frames. Jenna was in every picture. Her hair was different, sure, and she was wearing clothes she'd never laid eyes on before, but it was Jenna. But a dislocated version of Jenna, because she couldn't identify a single other person in any of the pictures. Not the blonde girl next to her on a roller coaster, screaming in joy with her hands in the air. Not the group of laughing girls in atrocious ballgowns. Not even the adorable mutt she hugged, in front of a Tudor-style house she'd never laid eyes on.

It wasn't just weird. It was full-on spooky. Jenna closed her eyes for a moment, and then took a closer look.

Okay. She blew out a breath. Maybe that wasn't her. It was just someone who looked a whole lot like her. As in, enough like her to pass as her, though Jenna thought that their noses were a bit of a different shape. And she thought her teeth were straighter – as they should have been after years of painful orthodontics. But if she wasn't this mysterious Jennifer Jenkins, who was? And where was she now? Had she woken up to find herself in the Video TV supply closet twenty years from now? Was she even now navigating Jenna's actual life, such as it was?

Of course she wasn't, Jenna told herself sharply, because none of this was happening. It was just a dream. There was no Jennifer Jenkins, and no time travel, for the love of all that was holy. And that was a good thing, because if it was real, she was completely incapable of figuring out the physics of the whole thing, which, if she recalled the movies she'd seen on this subject, was a prerequisite for the inevitable conclusion when she catapulted herself back to the future, pun intended. What she knew about physics was pretty much nil. She'd watched *What the Bleep Do We Know?* with Aimee and Ben one night, if that counted, though she couldn't remember much about it besides the word *quark* and some vague impressions of hippy dancing. She somehow doubted that would prove to be helpful in some kind of time/space/physics emergency.

Jenna sank down behind the desk, and got another shock – she'd never been in this office before, and yet the calendar in front of her was filled with notations in her own unmistakable handwriting. Or handwriting that looked enough like hers to pass for it at a glance, much like the photographs. Everything was *almost* Jenna, but not quite. The *almost* part, she figured, was what was giving her the uncanny sense of familiarity – as if she should have recognized something, but hadn't.

She thought she should have been getting used to the weirdness by this point, but it was all making her feel a little bit dizzy instead.

Rubbing at her temples, Jenna looked around for several more minutes, until she realized that the gigantic machine taking over most of the desktop was a computer. A very old, very out-of-date computer, with an actual floppy-disk drive. There was an intercom box next to a very old-looking phone. There were actual in-and-out wire boxes, stacked. There was a typewriter on the desk's perpendicular return, and Jenna wondered if it was considered cutting-edge in 1987 even though, to her eye, it looked ancient.

She also wondered if Jennifer Jenkins knew how to type, because she certainly did not. She could hunt and peck, and IM and text at the speed of light, but that did not translate into secretarial skills. Somehow, she suspected that Ken Dollimore was not the sort of executive to type out his own various documents, and, clearly, she was his secretary as well as his protégée, which was somewhat less of a promotion than she'd originally thought. Hooray.

The phone rang then, startling Jenna, and her heart jumped into high gear. It was almost as if Tommy Seer had walked into the room – but no, it was only the telephone. Jenna stared at it, until the intercom buzzed.

'Are you planning on answering that?' Ken's disembodied voice demanded through the intercom, sounding even more elfin through a machine, but also authoritative.

'Of course, of course,' Jenna muttered, then had to repeat it in a much more chipper voice into the intercom. She snatched up the phone, thinking, *seriously? I have to work? As a secretary? In my own dream?* Her usually much-maligned job in Accounts was looking better and better by the second.

'Ken Dollimore's office,' she said into the mouthpiece, in an approximation of the way her own boss's assistant answered the phone. It was a far cry from the belligerent way she barked out her own name when her office phone rang, but then, no one ever called her unless there was a problem, or she'd forgotten to remove her old takeout containers from the communal fridge.

Jenna took notes as someone named Gigi got increasingly hysterical on the other end of the phone – about some installation of something Jenna didn't quite catch or care about – and she was replacing the phone into its cradle and wondering how she planned to explain that call to Ken, having not understood it herself, when the door to her office was thrown open.

Duncan Paradis walked inside, his solid barrel body moving low to the ground and his face arranged in a completely fake smile. It made her spine chill along its whole length to look at it.

'There's the hero of the hour,' he said, the smile deepening. Jenna's temperature dropped in direct response. 'That was a great idea. How'd you come up with it?'

'I'm so glad it worked out,' she demurred, suddenly not at all interested in being perceived as a visionary. Or, for that matter, noticed by Duncan Paradis in any way. 'It could have been a disaster.'

Duncan, she thought then, with a sudden flash of insight, had wanted it to be a disaster. She remembered the look on his face when she'd suggested the band act out their videos. He'd started to laugh, but then that considering gleam had taken over his gaze, and he'd stopped himself. Jenna had watched him. And she couldn't help thinking that he'd wanted the band to look ridiculous.

But that didn't make any sense at all.

'Is the big man in?' Duncan asked, through his teeth, with calculation in his cold eyes. 'I have a proposition for him.'

'He's on a call,' Jenna lied, and smiled fakely back at him. She indicated the couch against the wall with one hand. 'If you'll just take a seat . . . ?'

Jenna did not have to be told that Duncan Paradis was not used to being kept waiting. A muscle bunched in his jaw, even as he kept that smile beaming right at her. Once again, she had to restrain herself from checking for lacerations.

She leaned over and announced Duncan into the intercom, and then had to attempt to look busy and untroubled while Duncan Paradis prowled around the room, alternately glaring at the pictures on the wall and the side of her head. This was not easy for her to do, especially when confronted with the dinosaur of a computer in front of her, one that most assuredly was not running the latest Windows operating system. In point of fact, it was not even running in *colour*. Not that Jenna had time to mourn the loss of her workplace Internet access – the widely accessible Internet being off in the future, if she recalled it all correctly – because Duncan Paradis was roaming malevolently in her peripheral vision.

When Ken finally opened the door, what seemed like years later, Jenna was ready to weep with gratitude. Duncan Paradis, for all that he was such an expert talent spotter, scared her on a fundamental, animal level. Plus, he was an entitled asshole.

She sighed in relief when Ken's office door closed behind him.

But she'd barely taken another breath before her office door opened again. And she went right ahead and held that breath, because, this time, it was Tommy Seer who walked inside.

It was like time froze around him. He'd stepped through the door and looked towards Ken's door, but she saw it all in such tiny, spread-out increments. She saw the way the unflattering fluorescent lights cast a shadow across his face, highlighting his high cheekbones and the masculine thrust of his jaw. She saw the fine, long muscles in his arms, and the way his silly vest emphasized the width of his shoulders and the narrow span of his hips, with so much of his smooth golden skin on display.

And she felt him, just the sight of him like a physical

caress, sizzle through her skin, settle into her veins, and heat his way through her body.

'Duncan's in there?' Tommy asked, jerking Jenna out of her daze.

'Yes,' she said. She meant, *yes, love me* and *yes, yes, yes*, but he didn't seem to notice the undercurrents.

'I don't know how long he'll be in there,' Tommy said in a low voice, his American accent back. Along with that frown between his eyes. He stepped closer to the desk. 'But I know what he's going to do.'

'You do?' Jenna asked, far too dreamily. Tommy's eyes narrowed – God, he was beautiful – and she coughed slightly. 'What's he going to do?' she asked, aiming for a businesslike tone.

'He's going to hire you, borrow you, whatever,' Tommy said matter-of-factly. 'He's going to sic you on me, in fact. I have no doubt.'

'I already have a job,' Jenna said. Stupidly. Besottedly.

Tommy smiled a thin sort of smile.

'That won't matter. Duncan always gets what Duncan wants.' His voice was bitter, and his gaze had gone cold.

'I don't mean to argue,' Jenna said, frowning. 'But so does Ken.'

Tommy let out a laugh. A short, bitter sort of laugh.

'Are you kidding? What Ken Dollimore wants is to keep Duncan happy, and away from MTV.' He looked towards Ken's door, and when he looked back at Jenna his mouth had tightened. 'You think he likes you, his little protégée? He likes this company more.'

'Wow,' Jenna said, stung by his tone. And by the way he was looking at her – like she was an insignificant little ant or something, desperate to do Ken's bidding. 'That was a bit aggressive.'

Why, she wondered, did she find this man so attractive, even when he wasn't being nice to her? Was Aimee right that this was all unhealthy? Was it a form of mental illness? Some Adam-related mental breakdown? Surely a sane person would be angry with the man, Eighties idol or no, and wouldn't simultaneously notice that his butt looked particularly tasty in those scandalously tight leather pants, right?

Jenna was beginning to feel she wasn't at all sane. And then she reminded herself that this was her *dream*, and felt that much crazier.

'I want to hire you first,' Tommy said impatiently. Jenna jerked her attention away from his ass.

'Hire me to do what?' she asked, and got caught up in his beautiful eyes once more. They were hypnotic. They were gor—

'I want you to agree to do whatever it is Duncan asks,' Tommy said in that low voice. He looked towards Ken's door, and then back towards Jenna, the line between his brows deepening. 'But before you do anything, talk to me, and we'll figure out how you'll play it. Do you understand?' When Jenna only stared back at him, still mesmerized, he made an impatient noise. His mouth flattened out. 'I'll pay you, obviously. Whatever he offers, I'll double.'

Jenna blinked. This was all getting extremely complicated, and they hadn't even begun kissing. Yet.

'What makes you think Duncan Paradis is going to offer me anything?' she asked, her scepticism showing. 'He looked at me like he'd prefer to choke me, if you want to know the truth. I really don't think he's looking to hire me.'

'Trust me,' Tommy Seer said.

And, sure, he said it in that bleak sort of way, but Jenna's heart had been waiting to hear him say those words for twenty years – or any reasonable variation thereof. It wasn't as if Tommy Seer had to *convince* her to do as he asked. It was a given.

'Okay,' Jenna said with a happy sigh. 'I'll do whatever you want.'

He looked at her for a moment, and his famously perfect mouth shifted to the left in what Jenna could only describe as a smirk.

'Great,' he said, in a tone that completely belied the sentiment.

'Great,' Jenna echoed. Was this when the kissing would start? Was this when he would declare that he could wait no longer, that his feelings could not be denied, that he *wanted her*—

But, no, he was shaking his head. If that was an expression of sexual longing, Jenna had never seen anything like it before.

'I have a feeling I'll see you soon,' Tommy said. Not, Jenna noticed, in a yearning or smoky sort of way that would lead to some kind of cinematic romantic clinch. More in a resigned and dry kind of way that was anything but romantic.

'Um, if you say so,' Jenna said, not bothering to hide her confusion. Why was he looking at her like she was some combination of crazy and pathetic? Because she was familiar with the look in his eyes, having seen it so many times in Adam's. It wasn't any more pleasant coming from him, no matter how green his were.

She expected him to break then, to confess his over-powering feelings for her in ringing tones à la Mr Darcy, or to simply toss the desk aside like King Leonidas might have in *300*, had there been desks in ancient Sparta. She wouldn't mind a satisfyingly over-the-top moment of passion. In fact, she thought one was sadly overdue.

Instead, Tommy Seer, who should have looked ridiculous in his Eighties Pop Star ensemble, turned on his heel and sauntered out of Jenna's office as if he were some kind of great big jungle cat, all rolling gait and confidence. With nary a backward glance her way, to top off the indignity of it all.

Jenna didn't believe he'd really left, for good, until several moments had passed and she was still gazing expectantly at the door.

She shifted in her seat, and tapped her fingers against the blotter on her desk. So far, this dream had involved work, inappropriate touching from Ken Dollimore, bullying from Duncan Paradis, and only the strangest and least-satisfying Tommy Seer interactions imaginable – and this from someone who had imagined just about every Tommy Seer interaction there was, more than once.

And worst of all, there was still no freaking kissing.

6

The only thing worse than an extended dream about Tommy Seer in which a) he found her annoying, b) was kind of mean about it, and c) there was no kissing, was, Jenna discovered, being trapped in the back of a smelly New York taxi with Duncan Paradis.

Jenna wasn't even sure how it had happened.

One moment she'd been sitting at her desk – or Jennifer Jenkins's desk, whoever *she* was, and Jenna didn't quite want to think about that – staring at the place where Tommy Seer had been standing as if the force of her will could make him reappear. The next moment Ken's door had been tossed open, Ken and Duncan Paradis had come strolling out wreathed in fake bonhomie and cigar smoke, and Jenna had found herself summarily dispatched into Duncan Paradis's keeping.

'Just for a few days,' Ken said, waving away Jenna's high-pitched protest with a languid wave of his hand. 'What a great experience for you, to have this kind of exposure to such a big band. Someday, who knows, you can write a book about it, ha ha ha.'

When Duncan turned his back and headed for the door, Ken made a telephone with his right hand and mouthed the words: CALL ME TOMORROW. Then he shooed Jenna out of the office.

Cut to Jenna in the back of a retro chequered taxicab, scrunched in the furthest corner to avoid even a casual brush against Duncan's pant leg, surrounded by the pervasive smell of long-saturated body odour, with a strange woman's purse perched on her knees. It had been second nature to reach down into the desk drawer and pull out the bag sitting there – so much so that Jenna had been halfway down the hall in Duncan's wake before she'd realized that the purse was not hers. Given that it was big, poufy, and neon baby blue, Jenna really ought to have noticed. Instead, she'd been so flustered by the triple punch of Tommy Seer, Duncan Paradis, and Ken Dollimore's willingness to throw her to the lions that she'd run off with another woman's bag. Something women tended not to take lightly, no matter how ugly the bag in question. Just one more thing to blame Duncan Paradis for, she thought sourly.

Not that the mighty Duncan Paradis was paying Jenna the slightest bit of attention. He was far too busy barking orders into a gigantic cellphone that looked as if it required two hands to lift. It was bigger, Jenna thought, than the portable house phone she used in her apartment. It was the size of a book, or one of the small dogs starlets toted about. She was more worried than he seemed to be that it might adhere to his ruthlessly slicked-back hair. Nor could she imagine that the reception was all that great, with the huge antenna sticking out of the top, so long it almost brushed the ceiling of the cab.

Trying to ignore him, Jenna returned her attention to the bright blue bag in front of her. Worrying her lower lip with her teeth, she cracked open the top and peered inside. There was a comb the size of a dinner plate, a selection of mascaras and other cosmetics, a sheaf of papers, the usual pocketbook detritus including a collection of gum wrappers – which made her feel better at once, since *she* did not chew gum and this therefore definitely was not her own life – and, last but not least, a wallet. Gingerly, Jenna fished the wallet out, took a bracing sort of breath, and flipped it open.

She almost screamed.

Almost.

Jenna kept herself from shrieking out her horror by biting down hard on her own lower lip. And between that and the picture on the licence, she was scarred for life. The sudden, shooting pain in her lower lip, though it made her eyes water, did nothing to dispel the horrific sight of a person who looked entirely too much like Jenna, sporting painstakingly sculpted bangs and what amounted to a mullet. *A mullet*, Jenna thought as a dull tide of horror swept through her. A *hairsprayed* mullet with height as well as lustrous frizz on the end. *Hideous, hideous, hideous.* If Jenna had been asked to describe what her worst nightmare bad-hair day would entail, it was the hair she saw on the driver's licence in her hand – hair that might as well have been on her own head, that was how much she and Jennifer Jenkins resembled one another.

She would never get the sight of it out of her mind. Never.

Jenna forced herself to close the wallet, and threw it back into the neon blue depths of the purse. The horrendous mullet danced before her in her mind's eye, however, taunting her. Duncan Paradis's voice grated as he bellowed orders to some poor subordinate – maybe he was talking to his wife, it was hard to tell. Jenna felt shaken. She tried to shrug it all off, along with another lungful of BO that seemed to come from the seat beneath her, and looked out the window to the city streets.

It was like looking into a kaleidoscope.

Outside, the city looked the same – and profoundly different. It was still New York City, but it wasn't the New York City Jenna knew. First of all, it was much, much dirtier. There were too many homeless people on the sidewalks, and garbage in the streets. Times Square, which Jenna thought of as practically a Disney theme park with an amusing red-light-district past, was rife with porn theatres and obvious junkies. Jenna was almost dizzy as she realized that the cab was headed down Sixth Avenue, but instead of the superstores she knew, there were only warehouses. She saw what looked like a Keith Haring mural as the cab roared past a warehouse, but then her attention was drawn to the SILENCE=DEATH posters that covered the dilapidated structures. Her stomach clenched, and her breath went shallow, as if her body was accepting a truth she wasn't ready to face.

As the taxi rounded a corner, Jenna saw a black on yellow street sign instead of the ubiquitous green and white signs she knew, and before she could process that fact and wonder why it bothered her so much, she saw the World Trade Center loom up before her, the towers standing proud and tall to the south. Jenna felt her breath whoosh out of her at the sight of them, and wondered how she'd managed to forget how they'd dominated the sky. She felt a kind of panic rise inside her, clawing at the back of her throat, and knew she was close to tears, or worse. She pushed it all aside, and concentrated on other details – strange-looking advertisements for half-remembered products, like a huge Maidenform ad that featured a leggy blonde who was practically chunky in comparison to the models Jenna was used to feeling badly about. The cars surrounding them on the street were ancient-looking: wide and long. Jenna told herself to breathe, and shut her eyes to keep the strangeness at bay.

Duncan Paradis finished talking on his phone, and turned his attention to Jenna. The fine hairs on the back of her neck stood straight up and her stomach knotted. She opened her eyes and snuck a glance over at him. His expression was not comforting, so she returned her attention to her lap.

'Look at me,' he demanded then, and Jenna did, because she didn't like to think what he might do if she defied him. He swept a rude, dismissive glance over her, from her head to the tips of her ankle boots. She managed not to cringe. 'What's your name?'

'Jenna,' she said. She realized that had come out in what was more or less a whisper, and cleared her throat. 'Jenna Jenkins,' she said in a stronger voice.

'Uh huh.' Duncan's dark eyes were cold and assessing. 'Let me tell you what's going to happen here, *Jenna Jenkins*.' She didn't care for the way he emphasized her name like that. Like someone might say, *Chlamydia*. 'You're quite the little go-getter, aren't you?'

Jenna wasn't sure how to answer that. 'Sure,' she said. It was better than pointing out that everything he was saying was patronizing and bordering on mean, because she sensed he was well aware of that fact.

Luckily, he wasn't really looking for an answer.

'Great,' he said dismissively, as if she hadn't spoken, or maybe he was simply used to instant acquiescence. 'That was a good idea back there. You really made the most of a challenging moment. But what you don't know is that the band is in a bad place right now.'

'The Wild Boys are in the studio, putting the finishing touches on their new album,' Jenna replied automatically, in her role as Little Miss Fan Club Know-It-All. She fervently wished she hadn't spoken when that cold, reptilian glare of his sharpened, like he was putting her directly in his crosshairs.

'Unfortunately, it's not going well in the studio these days,' Duncan told her through another fake smile, this one even more terrifying than the earlier ones. 'There are tensions.'

Jenna happened to know for a fact that this was not true. That, in actuality and according to numerous interviews, the remaining band members marvelled to this day that their final album had gone so smoothly. After twenty years, surely someone would have mentioned it if there'd been *tensions*. It was in fashion these days to have *tensions*. The Police talked about their *tensions* all the time, and still went on sold-out reunion tours.

Not that Jenna was particularly surprised to discover that Duncan Paradis was lying to her. Wasn't this exactly the kind of thing Tommy had predicted? Though he hadn't mentioned how unpleasant it would be to bear the full force of Duncan's attention. Jenna swallowed, and tried to stiffen her spine.

'I want you to be my eyes and ears in there,' Duncan told her, his awful rictus grin widening. Apparently, this was his attempt at charm. Jenna wasn't entirely sure why his attempts fell so flat with her, when the rest of the world talked about his *famous charisma* ad nauseam. Maybe that was code for *scary*. But he was still talking. 'Now that the band has seen how you have their best interests at heart, you can be with them in their more relaxed moments. They'll trust you in no time.'

'They don't trust you?' Jenna asked. Her stomach was in knots, and her voice was too high. 'I mean, why do you need me, when they must already trust you, right?'

Duncan dropped the smile, which was a relief. 'Aren't

you smart?' he said, and not in an encouraging way. Or even a nice way. She shivered, and tried to hide it. 'All you need to worry about is keeping me happy, okay?'

That was a losing proposition if ever she'd heard one.

'By being your eyes and ears,' she echoed, and then tacked on a smile as if the idea thrilled her, because it occurred to her that things would be easier if he thought so.

'Just tell me what they say in there when I'm not around,' Duncan said softly, and then Jenna's blood ran cold because he reached across the back seat and patted her on the knee. It wasn't a gentle pat so much as it was a reminder. That he was stronger and meaner and could crush her.

'Okay,' she squeaked, staring at his hand on her leg. What if he ... She couldn't finish the thought, but she did send up a little prayer of thanks when the taxi careened to the side of the road and discharged her in front of what looked, at a first and traumatized glance, to be a very fancy boutique hotel.

'Especially Tommy,' Duncan told her as she went to close the door, leaning across the seat so she could see how serious he was, up close and personal. 'I especially want to know what Tommy's doing and saying, do you understand me?'

'Of course,' Jenna squeaked, and fled.

7

The hotel was not, it turned out, a boutique hotel. Or any kind of hotel at all. It was instead a four-storey town house on a quiet side street in the West Village, which was impressive enough. It was equipped with a state-of-the-art recording studio, numerous well-appointed guest rooms, a kitchen complete with gourmet cook, a backyard that was more like a garden paradise and included a jacuzzi, and a full service staff including the very imposing butler who had admitted Jenna to the house only after an intensive round of questions better suited to weeding out potential terrorists from airports.

But she soon forgot the indignity of what amounted to an entrance exam, because the butler/bouncer stepped aside and let Jenna in to the marble foyer, where her eye was immediately drawn to a stunning arrangement of lilies in an almost equally beautiful vase, blue and white and nearly taller than she was. Each room of the town house was prettier than the one before – all gilt edges, perfect furnishings, and a riot of art on the walls. Jenna didn't have to know very much about furniture, antiques, or art to recognize the fact that she was looking at extremely good taste supported by excessive wealth. It certainly didn't suck to be a rock star.

Jenna followed the butler's rigid, black-clad back down a set of stairs. He stopped at the bottom of the stairwell, and indicated the door in front of him with a stiff sort of bow, making her wonder for a moment if she was expected to do something like perform a curtsy in return. Luckily, the man backed away before she could commit one way or the other.

Pushing open the door, Jenna stepped into what she'd expected to be the recording studio, but was instead an open-plan living and lounging room that ran the length of the house and opened up to the garden beyond. It took her a moment to get her bearings. The room featured high beams along high ceilings, as if it wasn't in the basement of the building at all, long couches arranged around a fireplace on one end and a movie projector on the other, and was completely empty except for Tommy Seer.

Jenna's heart jumped in her chest at the sight of him, and then started beating wildly. She wanted to massage the thump of it with her hand, because she had the sudden, hysterical notion that its crazy beat was visible beneath her shirt, but kept herself from doing it at the last moment.

Tommy, meanwhile, continued to pick absently at the electric guitar he held across his lap like a lover. The notes he played sounded tinny and distant, since the guitar wasn't plugged into any amp. If he'd looked up when Jenna entered, she hadn't seen it, but somehow she knew he was perfectly well aware that she was there.

Jenna worried her lower lip with her teeth, surprised to feel the nerves dancing through her limbs. She forced herself to walk closer, and sank down on to the couch facing him. It was so soft and comfortable that she was tempted to sink back into it, relax and put her feet up maybe, but some awareness made her sit up straighter instead.

He still didn't look up, much less at her. She felt the dance of nerves turn into more of a jangle and ran her palms along the tops of her legs, trying to stave off that jittery feeling.

'You were right,' she said suddenly, jumping in, because the silence between them stretched out and she couldn't stand it. 'He wants me to spy on you.'

Tommy used a dark brown guitar pick to pluck out a series of notes. He bent over the guitar, and his hair, released now from its headband, fell forward in the sort of careless dark mess that just begged for hands to fix it. Her hands, perhaps. Jenna's fingers, as if alerted, twitched slightly in response, and she quelled the urge to sit on them.

'Did you sleep with him?'

'What?' She jerked her attention away from the luxuriant spill of wavy hair across his forehead. Then what he'd said penetrated. She flushed. He looked up, and his expression was cynical, at odds with the light tone he'd used.

'Of course not,' Jenna hissed, appalled.

'Really.' It wasn't a question. 'Are you sure? Maybe it was just a blow job. Better than a handshake for sealing the deal. That's a direct quote, by the way.'

'I did not touch Duncan Paradis.' She was horrified that he would ask. Then she was more horrified when he smiled slightly, indulgently, as if he didn't believe her. 'I would never touch Duncan Paradis,' she said fiercely. Her skin itched with the force of her mortification.

'If you say so,' he murmured, and returned his attention to his guitar.

Jenna sat there, and grew more and more agitated the longer he continued to play, the pick in his nimble fingers coaxing out a melody that she almost recognized. Her breathing went shallow, and she wondered how she could feel so hot with embarrassment when he seemed to have forgotten she was there at all.

'Where's, uh, the rest of the band?' she asked finally, when she thought she might scream if she didn't speak.

'Out and about.' He didn't look up. 'More out than about, probably.'

'Oh. I thought you were recording.'

'We are. This is called songwriting. It works better without interruptions and idle conversation.'

Pluck. Pluck. Pluck.

As if she did not exist.

Jenna looked down and saw that her hands were balled into fists.

Upon a moment's reflection, complete with that *pluck pluck pluck* sound in the background, she accepted the fact that she wanted to take both of those fists and plant them in Tommy Seer's pretty face.

This was a brand-new, revolutionary feeling. It was also upsetting. She'd never imagined a moment involving Tommy Seer in which she would want to do anything but gaze at him adoringly and love him. Cherish him. Worship him, even. Then again, she'd never previously imagined him to be so irritating.

Not to mention the fact that she was still embarrassed by that cynical look he'd thrown at her, and his assumption that she'd had any kind of sexual contact with the repulsive Duncan Paradis. How dare he? What kind of person did he think she was?

And more to the point, what kind of person was she, that she was still quietly sitting there on that couch, waiting for him to finish being rude to her? At his leisure?

The events of this insane dream whirled around and around in Jenna's mind then, very nearly making her gasp out loud. Why was she so passive and *absurd* that even in her own dreams she allowed herself to be led about, condescended to, ordered around, and talked down to in such a variety of ways, by a variety of people, all of whom seemed to regard her as – at best – little more than a pawn in whatever their latest schemes were? None of it made her feel good, despite the brief moment of joy that she'd had something to do with one of her favourite moments in history. But if being bullied left and right was the price of sharing a moment like that, Jenna wasn't sure it was worth it.

The dream was clearly a metaphor for her entire life, she decided then, comprehension dawning as Tommy's clever fingers poured melodies into the charged air between them. A very pointed metaphor, involving this man she had adored for so long yet never met, and representing some thirty-five years of going with the flow and not making waves and waiting in vain for something to happen, finally, to make all her bending and contorting worth it somehow. It represented hiding away in her new single-woman apartment clutching her old Wild Boys concert T-shirts for comfort for eight long months, while Adam gallivanted about Manhattan with his brand-new, flexible twenty-three-year-old girlfriend and never thought at all about the life he'd thrown away.

It represented far too much, and she was sick of all of it, suddenly and completely – so sick of it she felt her stomach clench in response.

And since it was *her* dream, it was about time she started acting the way she'd be too afraid to act in real life. Otherwise, what was the point? Why dream at all?

'Do you want me to help you or not?' she demanded then, and her tone of voice was aggressive enough to surprise even her. She decided she liked it, and that the sudden thrill she felt shoot across her skin was power. Her chin rose in a show of bravado as she waited for his reply.

Her tone also surprised Tommy, clearly, because he lifted his head, his fingers stilling on the guitar strings and those famous eyes narrowing as he dragged his gaze to hers.

'What did you say?' He knew what she'd said. She could tell from the arrogant tilt of his head, and that deceptively mild tone of voice.

'I have better things to do than sit on this couch while you ignore me,' Jenna announced, in exactly the way she fantasized she should talk to people and yet never actually did. In real life she just . . . faded away. She even got to her feet, and looked down her nose at him, and doing it made her feel like some kind of warrior. 'And if you do want me to help you,' she continued, because why the hell not, 'you shouldn't be so rude. *You* asked for my help. *You* appeared in my office. You have no reason to get all surly now.'

'Surly,' he repeated. The arrogant head tilt came, this time, with an almost-puzzled expression, as if he couldn't quite take it in. '*Surly?*'

'Surly,' she retorted, overenunciating the word. 'It means bad-tempered and unfriendly. Obviously.'

There was a long, tense moment, and then, very carefully, Tommy set the guitar next to him on the couch. Without looking away from Jenna for even a second, he uncurled himself from his sitting position and rose to his feet, with that lethal sort of grace that made him so fascinating to watch in all those music videos.

Except this was not a video, this was three feet across a coffee table, and Jenna's heart stopped beating for a single, startled moment before kicking back into high gear as he loomed above her. Her mouth went dry, and she could feel her eyes widen. Panic. Or lust. She wasn't sure she could tell the difference.

He'd changed out of the outfit he'd worn on set earlier, and was wearing nothing more dramatic than a tight black T-shirt and faded jeans. Both clung to that lean body of his the way she'd often dreamed of doing herself. His feet were bare, long and narrow against the cream-coloured carpet, which struck Jenna as somehow over-poweringly erotic. He was so close that she could see his dark hair, freshly washed, was thick and lustrous and almost shaggy without all its usual product. Suddenly he didn't look like he was stuck in a time warp, he looked like any smoking-hot male animal in any time, and the force of his attention was entirely focused on Jenna.

Like she was a target. Or prey.

She ordered herself to breathe.

'I know the meaning of the word surly,' he told her, his voice low and husky, though she didn't mistake the bite in it. Just as she didn't mistake the way he held himself, all taut and furious and so very full of himself. *Arrogant.*

And yet, what Jenna wanted to do was apologize, for anything at all, just to make him stop looking at her that way. To ease the tension. That was exactly what she'd do in any real-life scenario that got even remotely as intense as this one. She'd all but apologized to Adam as he'd headed out the door, hadn't she? So, of course, she couldn't let herself do anything of the kind. Not here. Not with *this* man. Not any more.

'I'm glad you do,' she told him, and she was ninety per cent sure she hid the tremor in her voice. 'Maybe you can try a little bit harder not to *be* surly, then.' Okay, maybe it was more like eighty per cent, but she had the snooty tone down pat, thanks to practising it so often in her head.

His mouth moved slightly – as if he thought about smiling, and not in a nice way.

'Or what?' he asked, and there was no mistaking the laughter lurking there, in both the fine lines around his eyes and his voice. Laughter directed *at* her. Mocking, arrogant laughter. Not a shared moment of levity, by any stretch of the imagination. It put her teeth on edge.

'I can report to Duncan or I can report to you,' she snapped at him, once again doing the exact opposite of what her instincts screamed for her to do. 'Your choice.'

'My choice,' he repeated. He looked away for a beat, and when he looked back, his face was wild with a sudden fury. '*My choice*,' he said again, spitting out the words. He sounded incredulous. And so, so angry.

'Yes,' Jenna said, or meant to say, because she was caught up in the play of emotion across his face. Emotions she, such a scholar of this subject, had never seen, in any of the hundreds of hours of videos and documentaries and interviews she'd watched. There was that searing fury, something dark, and something else that looked a whole lot like self-loathing, something Jenna had seen on her own face from time to time, but never on his. Never.

'What fucking *choices* do I have?' he hissed at her. Then

84

he abruptly cut his hand through the air, cutting himself off. 'This is bullshit,' he muttered, and turned away, hands on his narrow hips.

Jenna had no idea what had just happened, but she felt the air around them was infused with electricity and any wrong move might send it jolting through her. In response – or preparation – her body thrummed like a live wire. As if she'd had way too much caffeine. Like six or seven venti lattes too many.

And still she wanted more.

When he turned back around, his eyes had gone distant, as if he'd pulled a veil across the emotions Jenna had just seen, but he was smiling a far more familiar smile.

'I'm sorry,' he said. 'I get moody when I'm working on a song.'

'That's okay,' Jenna said at once, and could have kicked herself, because why should she rush to appease him? The familiar, adorably crooked smile deepened.

'I did ask you to work for me,' Tommy continued, his tone apologetic. His smiled widened, and she forgave him. Just like that.

'Duncan told me to pay attention to what you say and do.' She ordered herself not to squirm or otherwise indicate she was moved by his proximity. 'He thinks the band will trust me, now that I proved myself with the Video TV idea.'

'We're a bunch of trusting fools,' Tommy said, though that note of mockery was back in his voice. Whether directed at her or at himself, she couldn't tell. He crossed the room to the bar set in an old cabinet, and made himself a drink with a few economical movements. 'What are you drinking?' he asked, suddenly playing the perfect host.

Jenna opened her mouth to ask for a soda, because she didn't want him to think she was the sort of person who required a drink in the afternoon. Two things occurred to her simultaneously. First, *he* was apparently the sort of person who required a drink in the afternoon, which, sure, made sense as part of the whole rock-star lifestyle, but even so, why worry what he'd think if she did, too? And second, this was supposed to be about going against the instincts that had thus far kept her malleable and passive for her entire thirty-plus years on the planet. Which meant it was high time she stopped worrying so much about what other people thought of her.

'I'll have whatever you're having,' she said with all the bravado she could muster. She walked towards him, trying to feel the way a woman who was about to toss back whisky with abandon and told international rock stars to behave themselves should feel.

Wordlessly, Tommy handed her a heavy-bottomed glass with a generous amount of whisky. But then, who needed words when he had green eyes that reminded Jenna of the sea and storms all at once? She turned her attention to the glass in her hand, and the amber liquid that swirled in it.

'To working together,' Tommy murmured, and reached over to clink the rims of their glasses. He saluted Jenna briefly with that half-smile, and then tossed back the contents of his glass in one easy gulp.

Jenna thought that was a spectacularly bad idea, which meant, of course, that she had no choice but to follow his lead.

The whisky burned down her throat and charged like a wildfire along the length of her oesophagus to warm her belly. It took Herculean strength of will, but Jenna managed to keep herself from making a face or coughing. Though she couldn't do much about the tears that pricked the back of her eyes.

And yet he was still looking at her with that slight tilt of his head, as if she was a specimen beneath a microscope and he the lofty scientist. Arrogant, yes, but also inviting, somehow.

'Yum,' Jenna said, her voice huskier than it should have been, thanks to the fire still raging in the back of her throat. Something in his expression made her think he knew all about that fire, and so she hurried on. 'Working together should be fun,' she said, which wasn't a particularly interesting thing to say, and it was too soon to blame the whisky. 'Assuming you can behave yourself,' she added, frowning at him. Trying so hard to seem tough, to stand up for herself, even though she could hardly remember why she wanted to, with him right there in front of her.

'I can try,' he murmured, and suddenly he was much closer, and Jenna had to tilt her head back to look up at him. His beautiful mouth hovered so near, and she caught her breath against the tide of longing that swept through her. 'How do you want me to behave?' he asked, barely above a whisper, and moved even closer.

Jenna put out a hand, to stop him – but then it was lying there on the hard plane of his chest, and she forgot all about stopping him.

She forgot everything.

She forgot about acting tough. Everything within her melted into that fire already burning in her belly, igniting into something much hotter, much lower, and much more dangerous.

It was all so familiar, so right. He was so close. She could feel the heat of his body through the soft, clinging fabric of the T-shirt he wore, burning into her hand. She could smell the fresh scent of the soap he'd used, mixed with the darker notes that were all him. She could see the perfect lines of that face of his, the face she had loved for so many years, from afar.

She knew the proud thrust of his cheekbones, the dark arches of his brows above those mysterious eyes that were now hooded, his attention focused on her mouth. She knew the hard chin and the sensual lips, so close now to her own that she quivered. She could sense more than see the broadness of his sculpted shoulders, the chiselled length of his torso.

She knew *this* dream like the back of her hand.

She'd had this dream a million delicious times. First he would lower his mouth to hers. Then he would whisper something loving and sexy, sometimes both. Then he would pull her close, and things would get even more amazing. She knew all of his moves, having choreographed them to her satisfaction more times than she could possibly count.

She decided it was high time she stopped being passive in that area, too. Why wait for his moves? It was her dream, she should make her own damn moves.

So she reached over and wrapped her hand around the back of his neck, like she had every right, and pulled his mouth to hers. She felt him stiffen for the briefest moment, and then he was kissing her, hard. Hunger bloomed inside of her, liquid and hot in her core.

This was more like it.

His mouth moved over hers, and his large hands cupped the sides of her face. Jenna lost control of the situation when he slanted his head for a better fit, and she felt it all the way down to the soles of her feet.

He tasted like whisky and something else, something magical.

Jenna was on fire. She moved closer, and made a sound of protest when he pulled his mouth from hers – a protest that quickly turned into a sigh when he turned his attention to her neck. His hands roamed down her sides in long, drugging strokes, then scooping beneath her T-shirt. It was all happening so fast, and her head spun. She shuddered helplessly when he cupped her breasts in each hand and then dragged his thumbs across the rigid peaks.

This was amazing, she thought with what was left of her

mind, *the best dream yet, the most real* – and then she opened her eyes to savour it and saw the look on his face.

Cynical.

Weary. Bored.

If he'd thrown a bucket of cold water in her face, Jenna could not have reacted more violently.

She reared back, pushing away from him. His hands fell from her breasts. She put as much space between them as she could on her shaky legs, which amounted to a few feet. Her breath came in short, horrified bursts, but she couldn't seem to look away from his face. That beautiful, bored face.

'What's the matter?' he asked in that same seductive tone, except this time she knew he was faking. The tone, the whole thing. *Faking.*

If she'd thought she'd felt humiliated before, Jenna now knew that she'd never experienced the emotion in all its glory until this very minute. She was afraid for a long, panicked moment that she might scream, or burst into tears. Anything to release the horror, to get it out. While she had been losing her mind from the pleasure of his kiss, he had been bored. *Bored.*

'Why . . . ?' She didn't want to ask the question, because she was certain she didn't want to know the answer. Real-life Jenna would already have bolted, and would be halfway across the city by now. So she cleared her throat of the tears she knew she would rather die than shed in his presence, and tried again. 'Why would you . . . You're not even interested.'

He flashed that adorable grin of his, but she could see through it now. She could see it was little more than a costume. That it was an act. His act. The act she'd been in love with for years.

'Don't be silly,' he said, with that magazine-ready smile, and she was sure he knew how delectable he looked with his hair spilling across his forehead.

Of course he knows, she thought then. *It's his job to know.*

She saw all of those magazine covers in her head, all of those poses, all the shots in all the seductive positions, and what had she thought? That the photographer had come across Tommy Seer that day and he'd *happened* to be gazing hungrily at the camera, in soaking wet pants and no shirt?

This is part of the job to him.

He'd all but announced it earlier, when he'd asked if she'd been with Duncan Paradis.

'I don't want to *seal the deal*, or whatever you called it,' Jenna gritted out, shocked by the emotion in her voice, by the dark currents that swept through her, over her, threatening to send her tumbling along with them. Her knees felt close to giving out again. He only arched those dark brows of his, and waited. 'That's disgusting! I'm not like that!'

'If you say so,' he said, and while his voice was mild, non-committal, his gaze was so cynical it bordered on bleak.

Jenna backed further away from him, her head spinning, humiliation and shame swirling through her, fighting for prominence.

He thought she was just another groupie.

He thought *she* was a *groupie* – and if that were not heinous enough, she knew she had behaved like one. She had thrown herself at a complete stranger because, what? She thought it was at all likely that an international rock star would have fallen head over heels in love with her the moment he saw her? How often did *that* happen? Even in dreams?

She felt herself flush, and a deep red washed over her.

But she would not let herself run. She gathered whatever dignity she could manage, which mostly consisted of keeping her spine straight and her head high, despite the hectic colour she could feel heating her cheeks and neck. She did not say a word, and he only stood there, gazing back at her, unknowable – a face she knew too well concealing a person she could not, did not, know at all.

So she did the only thing she could. She turned on the sharp heel of her ankle boot and walked away from him, before she burst into tears or collapsed to the floor and made an even bigger fool of herself than she already had.

8

Outside, the afternoon sun was giving way to the long summer evening. Shadows stretched across the street as Jenna stumbled down the front steps of the town house, not that she noticed. She looked around wildly, blindly, and then walked off in the vague direction of the nearest corner – wanting to get that town house and everything that had happened there as far behind her as possible before she stopped and got her bearings.

She wanted to go home, curl up in a ball, and die. Or at the very least, pretend none of this had ever happened. She knew she was good at *that*, at least. Jenna sucked back something that felt like a sob. She couldn't get that awful, bored expression Tommy had worn out of her mind, and she couldn't breathe, either. She was flushed and sweaty and she knew she couldn't blame that on the August humidity, much as she'd like to.

On the corner of Barrow and Bleecker Street, she started to head uptown, her head already way out in front of her.

She could visualize sinking with pleasure into the comfort of her one-bedroom in Hell's Kitchen, where she had great plans to disappear into her sofa cushions and comfort-eat at least six pints of Ben & Jerry's Oatmeal Cookie Chunk and New York Super Fudge Chunk ice cream. Six of each. And then, she vowed, she would eat an entire emergency pizza. She deserved it.

It was not until she'd made it to the V of Eighth Avenue and Hudson that Jenna recollected herself. The ageing hippies and leather boys she'd passed along Bleecker Street hadn't intruded on her brooding, but in retrospect, she should have realized that the fancy hipster mafia was notably absent and the Village was significantly more quaint all around her than she knew it to be. It was not the place she'd loved so much in her college days, either, when she and Aimee had spent endless hours sitting in a café on MacDougal Street planning the ways they'd take over the world. Everything was off. Different. Grimy and wrong.

1987 strikes again, Jenna thought, feeling incredibly sorry for herself. And maybe a little bit scared, too. She kept walking, too weirded out to stop. *None of this is the Manhattan I know.*

There would be no welcoming apartment in Hell's Kitchen, an area Jenna wouldn't dare enter if this was really the late Eighties. Even if she did muster up the courage to go there, in defiance of everything she'd ever heard about the urban blight that had taken over back then, she was pretty sure she would find her apartment building occupied by the crackheads and prostitutes who had helped give the neighbourhood its bad reputation in the first place. There probably wasn't any Ben & Jerry's either, at least not on offer in the corner deli, which struck her as just about as awful as her sudden homelessness. She decided she would go to the office, where she was more than happy to sleep – and then remembered that she no longer had a private office to hide in. No private office, and no convenient four seasons' worth of extra wardrobe inside that private office. How would she explain herself to Ken Dollimore if he was still there?

Not to mention she had no desire to discuss her interaction with Tommy Seer. Not with Ken Dollimore, or anyone else. Not even with herself. Not ever.

Which meant she had nowhere to go.

Jenna removed herself from the flow of pedestrian traffic, put her back to the nearest wall, and took a moment to try to catch her breath. She was perilously close to breaking down into tears, though she cautioned herself sternly that nothing productive was likely to come from sobbing on a street corner. She'd learned that lesson repeatedly back in her NYU days. She blinked back the heat in her eyes that threatened to spill over, and forced herself to look around instead.

The first thing she noticed was the drag queen in full regalia, complaining into the payphone on the corner. A glance up and down the street confirmed that there were payphones everywhere and, stranger by far to her eyes, no cellphones. The people who walked by talked to their companions or not at all, unless they were noticeably and probably certifiably insane. The walk/don't walk signs at the crosswalks were lettered, not flashing electric. The streets were filled with cars as always, but they were all passenger cars, with not a single SUV to be seen. Everyone smoked. Even inside the restaurants, customers waved lit cigarettes in the air to make their points and blew out clouds of smoke directly into their food. Station wagons, some with that awful wood panelling, careened through the intersection. A kid carrying an actual boom box on his shoulder, resplendent in a tracksuit and gold chains, strolled by with Run DMC blaring from his speakers. Phil Collins blasted out of a car window at a stoplight, and Jenna half smiled to hear that it was 'Take Me Home'. How appropriate.

The smile faded, however, as she took in the state of the city around her. It was a much dirtier, more unpleasant New York than the one she knew. There were vials strewn in the grimy corners near the alleyways, and homeless men who looked almost demonic in the summer-evening shadows. Women marched down the street with their purse straps across their bodies and grim looks about the mouth. There were junkies nodding out in boarded-up doorways, and buskers on the corners.

This was the 'edgy' Manhattan everyone bemoaned the loss of. They called it that because time had dulled their memories, and they'd obviously forgotten what it felt like as darkness neared. Just as her terror was hitting a fever pitch, and Jenna was trying to figure out how she was going to survive a night on the original mean streets with predators thick on the ground, she remembered the driver's licence in the purse she clutched in front of her like a shield.

Jennifer Jenkins, she thought as relief rushed through her. She fumbled inside the neon blue depths, her mind racing. What if Jennifer Jenkins, like Jenna, had moved to New York City from somewhere else and never updated her information? What if her licence had an old address from some other state?

But her fears were groundless, because Jennifer Jenkins was clearly the organized type. Organized and living at 457 East 83rd Street. The question was, in a world without a handy Apple store with access to Google Maps, *where* on 83rd Street was that?

A dim memory of her freshman orientation programme at NYU surfaced then, and Jenna scanned the street for the nearest empty phone booth. She couldn't remember the last time she'd used a phone booth, and was slightly afraid that her karma would be such that it wouldn't provide her with what she needed, as payback for belonging to a cellular world. But karma refrained from kicking her while she was down. This time.

Jenna pulled the phone book on its chain up to the little metal shelf, and slapped it over a SILENCE=DEATH sticker someone had plastered there. There, in the front of the phone book, was the Manhattan street-number formula she'd vaguely remembered hearing about. According to this, 457 East 83rd Street was located between

First Avenue and York Avenue. Jenna closed the phone book and let it fall back down, feeling inordinately pleased with herself.

She was practically jubilant as she walked up to 14th Street and headed east, along a street that in her time sported fancy hotels and designer stores. There was none of that tonight. No high-rises. No trendy Meatpacking District restaurants – in fact, she thought she could smell the blood from, presumably, actual meatpacking. Gross. She trudged past the brick building on the corner of Ninth that she knew all too well, because of a spate of bad dates she'd suffered through at an Italian restaurant that had been there. More than once, she'd been forced to shove so-so pizza into her mouth and try to stay awake while her date blathered on about himself. None of the men she'd met there had showed even a smidgen of interest in the fact that the building had also contained Glenn Close's apartment in *Fatal Attraction* – a moot point tonight, Jenna thought with a sigh, since that movie came out in September of 1987 and it was still, as far as she knew, August. Married men could continue to cheat merrily and without fear of boiled bunnies for at least a few more weeks.

Jenna continued along 14th Street all the way to Union Square – a grim-looking Union Square, not the gentrified place with the Farmers' Market she loved, but a disgusting area with a seemingly abandoned warehouse where the Virgin Megastore should be – and went down into the subway in search of the 6 train to the Upper East Side.

The subway station was another shock. Once again, Jenna was aware of a sense of menace all around, perfuming the air along with the ever-present smell of ripe garbage and unwashed humans in the summer heat. She fumbled for her Metrocard, and it was not until her fingers encountered a token in the bottom of the blue purse that she remembered the existence of tokens. She weighed it in her hand, brass with the silver plug in the centre, then inserted it into the appropriate slot and pushed her way through the rickety turnstile.

The subway platform was even dirtier than the sidewalk, and was approximately six hundred degrees hotter than the outside world. Jenna kept her attention focused on the track. She did not look at the potentially dangerous pack of young men to her right, with that undercurrent of meanness in their laughter. She did not want to know what slithered out of sight in the dark down on the track itself, because she had a strong suspicion it was a rat. Possibly in the plural.

The subway car, when it arrived, was not much better. There was graffiti all over the walls, grey plastic benches, and a battered linoleum floor. Jenna missed the new subway cars. She missed air conditioning. Yet when the conductor made his completely incomprehensible announcement, she felt immediately more at home. Happily, some things never changed, and the unintelligible jabber of New York City subway conductors was, apparently, one of them.

Yet other things were completely different, Jenna

thought later, as she made the long trek from the subway towards Jennifer Jenkins's place. No Starbucks. No ATM machines. Just a long walk, practically into the East river. By the time Jenna made it to the address listed on the licence in her bag, which was at least on the block it was supposed to be on, she was dragging. She was exhausted, physically and emotionally, and the truth was, for all the trivia she'd been immersed in all day, she thought she'd finally had enough of 1987 Manhattan.

Jenna was ready to wake up. She was even ready to join the real world Aimee was always going on about. She could admit it – she'd hidden away in a little cocoon after Adam had left her. But she was ready to leave it behind. She would even approach the endless series of blind dates with more enthusiasm, if she had to – just as long as she could escape the Eighties.

First, however, she had to fight her way into Jennifer Jenkins's apartment building through a series of heavy security doors using a selection of keys from the enormous key chain in the inside pocket of the neon blue purse, and then haul herself up five floors to the very top. Jennifer Jenkins's apartment was the highest, furthest apartment possible in the building, Jenna thought sourly as she limped, overheated and panting, to the door of #15. She had to try each key in each of the three locks on the door, but eventually she made it inside, and closed the door with a satisfying *thump* on the city.

For a moment she simply stood there, her back against the door, breathing.

There was a fan blowing from one of the two windows in front of her, in the area that comprised most of the living space in the studio apartment. Jenna hated studio apartments, on principle. She took a few moments to investigate the one she found herself in, which she accomplished by pivoting around on her heels. It was tiny. A bathroom to the left and a kitchen to the right, and one big room to live in. It should have felt like a cell – the way her own studio apartment had felt those three dire years she'd lived in one – but this apartment didn't feel cell-like at all. It took Jenna a moment to figure out why.

It was the pale yellow paint on the walls, she decided, that made the space seem bigger, somehow, and happier. It was also the fact that the place was spotless. Not a speck of dust. Fresh flowers in a vase on the cute mantel above a faux fireplace, and living plants in the kitchen. Between these plants and the ficus in the office, Jenna suspected that Jennifer Jenkins could actually grow things, which she found amazing, having neglected even cacti to death in her day. The futon couch was carefully made up, rather than left open and piled high with clothes and assorted debris, as had been Jenna's way. A quick glance proved that the refrigerator was filled with the kinds of things people who knew how to cook assembled – ingredients rather than takeout containers and pizza boxes. The walls were not plastered with old pin-ups from *Tiger Beat*, but featured pretty prints from the Metropolitan Museum of Art and a few artsy, black and white photographs.

And, of course, more pictures of the woman who looked way too much like Jenna.

Jenna trailed her fingers across the photos in frames on the mantel. A trio of laughing girls, all in their early twenties. Pets. The beach. A mountain somewhere and lush green trees. A college graduation, flanked by beaming parents.

As Jenna stared at the parents, the penny finally dropped.

Because she knew them.

She knew them, just as she knew the girl in the pictures with them – she must have known it at once, though she'd been too disoriented to take it in. How else to explain the resemblance? The name?

Because the parents were Jenna's grandparents.

She was looking at photos of her favourite aunt Jen. Jennifer Jenkins *was* Aunt Jen.

Jenna sank down on the futon, feeling dizzy, and pulled off her ankle boots. She let them clatter to the floor in front of her, then thought better of it and lined them up neatly beneath the futon. No need to unleash Hurricane Jenna all over this pristine little place.

Had her aunt woken up to find herself in the chaos that was Jenna's life in the twenty-first century? The messy office would be a mere precursor to the wreck of her apartment, though at least Jenna had a separate bedroom. Poor Aunt Jen must want to kill herself right about now, sitting nearly twenty-five years in the future in Jenna's dusty, overstuffed home, surrounded by piles of crap and dirty dishes.

Was this why Aunt Jen had always suggested that Jenna learn how to pick up after herself? *Neatness can never be a bad thing*, she'd told Jenna this past Christmas, apropos of nothing. Had she been waiting for this to happen – and hoping to keep Jenna from inflicting her messy ways on her life?

Was this why Aunt Jen had never grown impatient with Jenna's Eighties obsession the way everyone else had?

Get a hold of yourself, Jenna told herself fiercely. *There is no swapping of lives. Tommy Seer has been dead for almost twenty-five years, Aunt Jen is even now living her fancy life in that gorgeous house in Carmel that she bought with her Apple shares, and none of what went on today happened anywhere but in your head.*

So she lay down sideways on the futon, closed her eyes tight, and waited to wake up safe and sound and back in her bed.

9

When Jenna opened her eyes again, the phone was ringing and the walls were bright yellow in the morning sun and she was still, damn it all, on the pristine futon belonging to the ruthlessly organized Jennifer Jenkins. Also known as Aunt Jen.

Which meant she was still in 1987.

Or still dreaming that she was in 1987.

Ignoring the ringing phone, Jenna dragged herself into a sitting position, and scraped her hair back from her face, securing the curly mess in a knot on the back of her head. The phone stopped ringing, and in the blessed quiet she noted absently that there was no answering machine, a concept her brain could not quite absorb.

There was a lot of that going around.

The problem was, she didn't feel like she was dreaming. She'd had epic dreams before, many of them also involving Tommy Seer, in which everything *felt* real – but that was only the kind of thing she'd noticed in retrospect, upon waking. She'd never dreamt in such *detail* before. The weathered faces of the homeless men she'd seen on 14th Street. The depressing and sticky-looking porn shops and theatres in Times Square. The beginnings of blisters on her feet from those damned ankle boots, pink and tender even now. The potent stink of the cab she'd shared with Duncan Paradis. The continuing ache in her butt from hitting the supply-closet floor. The numerous times she'd tossed and turned herself awake during the night, only to lie there, fuming and too hot even next to the fan, until she'd drifted back to a fitful sleep.

The only reason she thought she was dreaming at all was because it was, obviously, impossible to wake up one morning and discover oneself in the distant past, consorting with long-deceased childhood idols. If she hadn't known such a thing was impossible, the idea that she was dreaming would never have occurred to her, since absolutely nothing that had happened felt *dreamy* at all, up to and including her awful interaction with Tommy Seer the night before.

An interaction that was so bad, even in retrospect, that it practically *proved* that none of this could be a dream. In the more than twenty years she'd been dreaming about Tommy Seer, she had never once dreamed him to be cynical and snide. Never. Not one time. Until now.

So if she wasn't dreaming . . . Jenna sighed, and rubbed her face with her hands. *This is crazy*, she thought, and then groaned it aloud.

Which was, of course, the other option. That she was

insane. That she was even more unhealthy than Aimee had suggested she might be – and that she had spent the past eight months preparing for a serious nervous break-down. That she had suffered a catastrophic break from reality and was even now locked away in some mental institution while all of this took place in her head. Like that *Buffy* episode where Buffy thought her entire life (and therefore the entire show) was a paranoid schizophrenic delusion she was having from the safety of a padded cell, complete with a straitjacket and guards.

The phone began to ring again, and Jenna glared across the room at it. It hung from the wall, the receiver attached to the base by a very long, stretchy cord, presumably one that allowed Aunt Jen to wander all over her apartment. Yet still on a leash. Every time it rang, the cord moved a little bit, calling attention to itself and the fact it was not cordless.

Jenna looked around the studio, and let out a long breath.

There was nothing to be done about her situation. Either she had somehow travelled through time, or she was insane. Did it really matter which? She happened to look enough like her aunt to ease right on into the life Aunt Jen had left behind, she'd managed to embroil herself in some high Eighties drama already, and going to sleep had not altered her circumstances even one iota. So whether or not any of this was actually happening, it looked like Jenna was stuck in it.

And that being the case, she'd better stick to the new course she'd set for herself. No more hiding away from life and dreaming of other times. Hadn't that gotten her into this mess in the first place? No more being passive and apologetic, no matter how much the thought of seeing Tommy Seer again made her want to cry. Which it did. And absolutely no more feeling sorry for herself.

She'd spent eight months going nowhere, and now she'd gone too far. It was time to get over herself. She wished she could let Aimee know exactly how right she was.

Jenna blew out a breath, and squared her shoulders. Everyone always claimed they wished they could go back in time and redo things, with all the knowledge they'd gained in the interim. Well, here Jenna was, with 1987 wrapped up in a bow. Thanks to her obsessiveness, and recent quicksand-like descent back into extreme fannishness, she knew pretty much every last newsworthy detail of that year – and many un-newsworthy details, for that matter. Jenna had always worried that her life was boring and lacked adventure, that *she* was boring and lacked a sense of adventure, both while with Adam and after he'd left her. She wouldn't be able to live with herself if, faced with the ultimate adventure, and who cared if it was only in her own mind, she hunkered down like a turtle and disappeared into her shell.

It was time for the new Jenna. The New Jenna Project, in which she would finally be the person she'd always meant to become. The person who stood up for herself, and did not hide somewhere dreaming of a different life but lived the one she had. Even if that involved humiliating interactions with the likes of Tommy Seer.

She could practically hear herself roar.

She surged to her feet and strode across the room, snatching up the phone despite the tangle of the cord and congratulating herself on her confidence. She was *a badass*. At long last.

'Jen, what the hell is going on?' Ken Dollimore, of course, his elfin voice in the higher register. Which she interpreted to mean he was panicking. 'You were supposed to be at the studio an hour ago!'

'Ken,' Jenna said in a confident, New Jenna sort of voice, 'let me stop you right there. I don't know what you're talking about.'

'I am talking about how I look like a schmo in front of Duncan Paradis,' Ken barked at her, which pretty much murdered the confident thing in its infancy. 'Are you *trying* to screw me? Because you screw me, you screw yourself, Jen. I'm not kidding on this. *Watch me.*'

Not an auspicious start to the New Jenna Project, she reflected sometime later, in the back of a cab hurtling downtown at what she feared was literally breakneck speed, but she'd done her best to rally.

She'd assured Ken that there had been no start time mentioned, but that she took full responsibility anyway and would tell Duncan Paradis so the moment she saw him. Only slightly mollified, Ken had told her to get her ass in gear, except he'd been more profane, and he had then hung up with such force it made her ear ring.

Jenna had allowed herself exactly two minutes to feel

sorry for herself, which had then extended through her shower in the bright pink and white bathroom, but no one could tell she was sulking while she was underwater, could they?

Once out of the shower and dry, Jenna had then had the profoundly creepy experience of digging through another woman's wardrobe for something to wear. She'd found out two things very quickly.

One, that Aunt Jen wore an incredibly floral perfume. Anais Anais, if Jenna's nose was right, which Jenna had not worn herself since a junior high school dance but could still identify at a sniff. The vivid memories the scent brought back to her, of standing off to the side of the gym feeling ugly and unloved while Tripp Mason danced to 'Crazy For You' with Kelly St Pierre, took her long moments to dispel – much the way they'd taken most of high school to get over in the first place.

And two, that Aunt Jen actually hung up all her clothes and kept her closet and dresser neat and organized, which was something Jenna had never managed to do no matter how many times she read *Real Simple* and vowed to turn over a new leaf. It made it very easy to pick out an outfit. Feeling as if it was Halloween, Jenna rummaged through a selection of carefully ironed and pressed jeans that were the Eighties version of designer denim: Jordache, Gloria Vanderbilt, Sergio Valenti, and Sasson. All of them with unflattering high waists and straight or tapered legs, in washes that screamed *ancient* and *ugly* to Jenna's eye. Those being among the nicer things that screamed through her brain. The acid-washed pair with ankle zippers almost made her pass out from the visual horror of it all. Jenna didn't recall her aunt looking like such a fashion victim, but then, what had she known about fashion in 1987? She'd been twelve. All she'd wanted from life was a Benetton sweater.

In the end, there was only so much Jenna could do. No matter how organized the closet, it was still filled with Eighties fashions. The Eighties clothing revival of the early 2000s was, she'd discovered, very much *inspired by* the actual Eighties clothes, but not, it turned out, *the same as* Eighties clothes. This was a good thing for the early 2000s, and not so good for Jenna. But that was how she'd talked herself into a pair of stirrup pants (!) with penny loafers (!!) under a formless, gigantic cotton sweater that would have easily fitted three of her. At which point, there was no sense being coy about her hair, was there? She had already been forced to accept the fact that the Eighties did not provide much in the way of appropriate frizz-busting products for curls in the summer heat – or at least, Aunt Jen did not possess any. So she held her head upside down under the hairdryer, used half a bottle of hairspray, threw a bright yellow banana clip into the mess, and that was that. She looked in the mirror and nothing but big hair looked back.

She was about as Eighties as it was possible to get.

And then she couldn't dawdle any longer, because she knew it would result in another apoplectic phone call from Ken, and another call might have her in tears. Very much *not* the New Jenna she was going for.

The cab screeched to a halt in front of the Wild Boys' town house, jerking Jenna back into the moment. She was not at all happy about it – because the moment meant confrontations she would rather put off indefinitely. But wasn't that how she'd ended up in this mess in the first place? She paid the driver what seemed like a laughably small sum and crawled out of the car, the sickly-sweet smell of her head full of Aqua Net hairspray surrounding her for a moment and making her cough.

She really didn't want to go inside. *Really* did not want to go inside, from the bottom of her heart.

The thought of facing Tommy again made that heart pound and her face flush, and not, for a change, with suppressed yearning, but with abject embarrassment. What was she supposed to do? How was she supposed to act? Her instinct was to slink off in shame, or pretend he didn't exist, which was the only way she'd ever handled even remotely comparable situations in the past. She couldn't run away, however, without risking Ken Dollimore's ire – to say nothing of homelessness – and she imagined that it would be difficult, to say the least, to pretend the lead singer of the band she had come to hang out with did not exist.

Grow a pair, Jenna, she ordered herself then, squaring her shoulders and hiking up her chin. *This is not high school. He is an international superstar and will take no more notice of you than any other insignificant groupie – of which he has millions, as you well know. What makes you think the most humiliating moment of your life even* registered *in his?*

Oddly soothed by the realization that Tommy was unlikely to recall the night before, much less deliver knowing or mocking looks or something equally horrifying, Jenna marched up to the front door and submitted to the exact same entrance exam of the day before.

'Name?' the butler asked tonelessly, as if he'd never laid eyes on her. Had she not remembered it so clearly, she might have wondered herself.

'It's Jenna Jenkins,' Jenna said. Her eyebrows arched up. 'Just like it was yesterday. I haven't changed it.'

He did not so much as blink. 'And the nature of your business?'

'I'm supposed to sit in with the band,' Jenna said. 'Again.'

'And are you expected?'

'I certainly hope so. Otherwise, we'll all be awfully embarrassed, won't we?'

Though he did not alter his expression in any discernible way, Jenna was left with the distinct impression that should there be any embarrassment, the butler did not plan to share in it.

'If you'll be so kind as to provide a licence or some other form of identification, such as a passport,' he intoned as if he was auditioning to be an automated system, 'you can wait here in the vestibule while your identity is verified and your appointment is cleared.'

'I think it might be easier to fly carry-on with a full make-up bag than it is to get into this house,' Jenna told him, and not in a complimentary way.

'I beg your pardon?' Delivered in a snide tone, with a

snotty sort of blank look to match, as if Jenna had started speaking in tongues.

'Never mind,' she said, and showed the butler her teeth.

He made her wait extra long as revenge, she was sure, but eventually she was cleared to enter the premises.

Her foot was on the top stair outside the top-floor studio when the door in front of her opened and Duncan Paradis stepped out. Her skin crawled. And then kept on crawling, when Eugenia Wentworth appeared behind him. Her face was in mid-pout, which morphed into a full scowl when she saw Jenna.

'What is *she* doing here?' she demanded, putting her hands on Duncan's shoulders as if she needed assistance to stand, which might very well have been true in the heels she was wearing.

'You're no fucking use to me if you're not where I tell you to be, are you?' Duncan asked Jenna in a relatively mild tone. Jenna wasn't fooled; she could see his expression, flared nostrils and all.

'I had no idea what time I was supposed to be here this morning,' Jenna said crisply. *New Jenna*, she thought. 'I'm so sorry. Ken was appalled.'

'I don't give a shit about Ken Dollimore,' Duncan growled at her. 'And I don't give a shit about you either. Do you have anything to tell me? Were you here last night, or did you fuck that up too?'

Wow, she disliked this man. And the woman hanging all over him, gleeful to watch him light in to someone else. But Jenna ordered herself not to react.

'I was here,' she said as calmly as she could, especially given the images of the night before that paraded through her head. 'Nothing came up. It was mostly songwriting, which didn't allow for much talking.'

Duncan glared at her for a moment, then grunted. Whether to himself, to Jenna, or simply because he was a pig, Jenna didn't know.

'Make sure you're here on time from now on,' he suggested in that soft, evil voice. 'You don't want me on your ass.'

'No,' Jenna agreed. 'I certainly don't.'

When his gaze turned suspicious, she pasted on a polite smile, and stepped to the side with apparent meekness to let them brush past her on their way down the stairs, off to do things Jenna preferred not to imagine.

'Have fun,' Eugenia murmured, wreathed in sarcasm. As if prancing off somewhere with Duncan was any great triumph.

Jenna sighed when they disappeared around the landing, and tried to rub the sudden knots out of her neck with her hand. Then there was nothing else to do but walk into the studio.

Inside, Sebastian was behind the glass, playing a guitar solo. Richie stood off to the side of him, nodding along to the music and waiting for his cue. Nick, angry scowl at the ready, was behind the console with three men Jenna had never seen before. And Tommy was right there in the little lounge area separate from the two closed-off studio areas, sitting directly in her line of vision, his body packed

114

into tight jeans and a white T-shirt, and arrayed across the leather chair with all the bonelessness of a cat.

Awkward.

He did not look as if he had any trouble remembering who Jenna was, or as if she had mercifully faded into the great anonymous sea of his groupies. In fact, his mouth tilted over into that little smirk when he saw her, which was as good as an announcement that he remembered every detail of the night before.

Jenna refused to give him the satisfaction of reacting, so she did nothing. She stood tall. She met his gaze. She somehow kept from turning beet red. She waited.

'Don't be late again,' he told her in a soft voice, without so much as blinking. 'You can't build trust if you're sleeping in while we're working, can you? And then what will you tell Duncan?'

He glanced away for a moment, fighting a smile.

She decided she hated him.

Then he looked back at her, those green eyes wicked and still so clear, and Jenna knew she was a liar.

10

Life – or her paranoid schizophrenic delusion, and Jenna wasn't sure some days which one was the worse possibility – settled into routine. It was amazing what a person could get used to. For one thing, she was immersed in a world she knew a lot about, but which was very different in daily practice from what she'd imagined. Or anyway, her reaction to it was different – perhaps because she was no longer locked in her usual epic Tommy Seer fantasy.

The aftermath of the Iran-Contra hearings, and President Reagan's acknowledgement that 'things had gone astray', fascinated her in a way neither had originally – perhaps because she was old enough this time around to be outraged. She scoured the *New York Times* every day. She followed the Senate hearings on Judge Bork, laughed over John McEnroe's antics at the US Open, skimmed over the visit of Pope John Paul II, marvelled at the way Donald Trump was seen as an actual force to be reckoned with rather than a reality-television hack, and read about Mayor Koch's plan to commit the mentally-ill homeless to Bellevue against their will. The war against terrorism was alive and well in 1987, Jenna discovered – it was not an invention of the 2000s. In fact, it seemed to have a whole lot more to do with the Pan-Am airline hijacking in 1986, the cold war, the Iron Curtain, and Libya.

She took herself to the movies, because it just so happened that the summer and early fall of 1987 were loaded with movies. And not just any movies: the movies that had so thrilled her as a teenager that they'd helped form the foundation of her subsequent thoughts on life and romance, to her shame.

She saw *Dirty Dancing* in the theatre, which her parents had not allowed her to do back when she was a kid, and sighed just as much over Patrick Swayze on the big screen as she had over the VHS tape she'd watched on the sly years before. She saw *The Big Easy* and thrilled anew over the heat between Dennis Quaid and Ellen Barkin. She saw *No Way Out* and managed to restrain herself from shouting out Kevin Costner's true identity in the first scene. She saw *Fatal Attraction* on its opening night, and felt gleeful at the shock and dismay of the males in the audience.

'So much for Glenn Close's career,' she heard one guy tell his friend as they all shuffled out of the theatre, with a punctuating bark of a laugh that clearly meant he was angry. 'She was great in *The Big Chill*, but she's finished. Talk about career suicide.'

'I'm betting you're wrong about that.' Jenna turned

around, looked him in the eye, and announced this, not caring when the two men stared at her in shock. 'I'm betting she'll have a long and glorious career, actually.'

The man shook his head at her, as if she were very dim. 'No man will ever pay more money to see that crazy broad,' he informed Jenna. Condescendingly. He and his friend snickered.

'Just remember you said that,' Jenna suggested, with a smile.

And then there was *The Princess Bride*, which Jenna had never before seen on the big screen. She fell in love with the movie all over again, and saw it more than once, as if she could melt into the movie – *become* it, somehow.

In the bookstores she ran her hands over fresh new copies of her old favourites *Hollywood Husbands* by Jackie Collins and *Through a Glass Darkly* by Karleen Koen. She was thrilled to see Stephen King's *It* and Patrick Suskind's *Perfume* on the bestseller list, both of which had disturbed her when she'd read them sometime in the early Nineties.

But mostly, she worked.

If that was what it could be called.

There was a clever advertisement for Charivari boutiques that she kept seeing everywhere that read: *what is expected of New York is the unexpected*. The same could be said of double-agenting for an international pop star and his devious star-maker manager.

Duncan made a point of lying in wait for Jenna each morning. He pounced somewhere between the butler (who continued his obnoxious entrance exam daily) and the studio door, lurking around the town house doing God only knew what. Jenna wondered if in later years Duncan would perhaps consolidate his power base, and therefore wouldn't find it necessary to skulk around quite so much. At least, she had never read a word about Duncan subjecting his later acts to the sort of scrutiny he demanded and performed on the Wild Boys. She had to wonder if it was a chicken/egg scenario.

Not that she did much wondering while she was experiencing the pleasure of having Duncan vent his considerable spleen all over her.

'I don't believe that pompous little shit isn't talking,' Duncan growled at her today, having cornered her in the kitchen when she foolishly stopped for some caffeine. The lack of Starbucks confounded her, daily.

The good thing was, the New Jenna Project had helped. Not that Jenna was enjoying herself or these little chats, but she wasn't cringing away in fear, either. She called that progress.

'Tommy talks a lot,' Jenna said, pretending she was completely serene as she mixed milk and sugar into her coffee. 'But he generally wants to talk about different tracks on the album, or argue with Nick about whose ego is larger and so who is the bigger danger to the band, like Sting and Stewart Copeland in the Police.'

'This is bullshit,' Duncan growled. 'You've been hanging around with them for a month, and this is the best you can do?'

'I can't *make* them plot against you,' Jenna said, with a little bit of a laugh.

'You think this is funny?' he demanded, stepping closer and trapping her against the counter. He loomed over her – one of those men who was not afraid to use his bigger body to intimidate. He was close enough that she could see the veins bulge in his thick neck, and his Adam's apple bob angrily above his collar.

'No, of course not,' she said, trying to stay calm. 'But I tell you everything they say. I'm not sure what else I can do.'

'We're talking about money,' Duncan hissed at her. 'Not whatever fairy tale you have in your head about rock stars and music videos. This is about *money*. And I have no intention of losing out on my investment.'

'Of course you don't,' Jenna murmured. She aimed for *soothing*, but feared it came out more *strangled*.

'I made that little punk what he is,' Duncan ranted. 'I *made* him! He was *nothing* when I found him!'

Jenna had by now heard a variation on this theme at least once a day. Tommy was ungrateful. Tommy was an upstart. Blah blah blah. She tuned Duncan out, and tried to edge along the counter and away from him.

'Duncan? Where are you?'

Jenna was delighted to hear Eugenia's rancid tones waft into the kitchen, sing-songing in from the next room. *Saved by the bitch*, she thought happily, then schooled her expression to something more neutral when Duncan's head swung back towards her.

'You better hope I don't decide you being here has been a waste of my time,' he hissed, leaning in way too close, so Jenna could feel his breath puff against her cheeks.

'I'll do my best,' Jenna promised, craning her head away from him, and then sagged back against the counter in relief when he stepped back, out of her personal space at last. Note to self: never turn your back to a room, not in this house.

Seconds later, Eugenia stomped into the room, wearing her usual expression of distaste, which only sharpened when she saw Jenna. She opened her mouth.

'I don't have time for your whining today,' Duncan barked, cutting her off before she could start. She clamped it shut with an audible *click*. 'I have meetings,' he continued, running a hand over his tie and his suit jacket, one that made Jenna think of Tony Soprano again. 'Trump,' he said significantly. Eugenia sighed in admiration. Jenna had to force herself not to ask if the two of them were planning to compare bad-hair tips.

Then she had to force herself to look away from the kiss they shared. Duncan held Eugenia's cheek in his palm. It was . . . almost tender. Disturbing on a whole new level.

When he left, barking orders down the hallway in the direction of one of his assistants, Jenna returned her attention to her coffee. She stirred the hot liquid with a teaspoon and quelled her urge to fling some of that liquid into Eugenia's face when the other woman stepped into the personal space that Duncan had so recently vacated. What was with these people?

'You are standing too close to me,' Jenna said, without inflection. 'Do you want coffee?'

'I'm watching you,' Eugenia hissed. 'Don't think I'm not wise to your little games.'

Jenna turned to face her, holding her coffee mug like a shield before her. She would not hesitate to upend the mug on Eugenia's dress, either, despite the fact it was vintage Ungaro.

'I can't have this conversation again,' she told the other woman. 'I keep telling you this, and yet here we are.'

'We'll have this conversation as many times as we have to,' Eugenia snapped. 'We'll have it until you understand that I am not about to sit idly by while you try to muscle in on my patch. Do you have any idea how hard I had to work to get to where I am?'

The worst part of this conversation, which Jenna had been heartily sick of having weeks ago, was having to face the knowledge – again and again – that Eugenia was this jealous and territorial about a sleaze like Duncan Paradis. Jenna was tired of tiptoeing around the real reason she found that so unbelievable – aside from the fact that she had, in fact, *seen* Duncan.

'You were dating Tommy, weren't you?' she asked. Because if she was going to have to have this conversation every day, she might as well ask what she wanted to ask. 'At some point? How did you go from him to Duncan, of all people?' She didn't even get into the fact that Duncan was married. That was practically a moot point here in Eugenia's La La Land.

'You must be kidding,' Eugenia scoffed.

'And yet, I'm not.'

Eugenia blinked, and then shifted her minimal weight on to her other foot, away from Jenna's coffee mug, as if she sensed the danger she was in.

'Tommy and I had fun, at first,' she said, and then shrugged. 'But why date Tommy Seer when you can date the person who *created* Tommy Seer in the first place?'

'I don't see what you see in him, I guess,' Jenna said. Eugenia immediately looked suspicious.

'Like I'll fall for that!' she scoffed. 'Duncan is the most powerful man in music right now. Do you know how many Grammys he's won?'

'If I had to choose, I wouldn't choose Duncan,' Jenna said, and didn't mention that the last time she'd checked, the Wild Boys had won the Grammys. 'That's all I'm saying. And I'm willing to bet right now that if you took an informal poll out on the street, most people would agree with me, because they're not going to care about Grammys.'

Eugenia looked at Jenna for a long moment, as if trying to figure her out, but then shook her head. Her lips pursed slightly.

'Tommy's no prize,' she said finally. 'He can be a right cruel bastard when he puts his mind to it, believe me.'

Jenna knew this to be true. But she also knew that Eugenia had offered the poor man what anyone reasonable would have to consider provocation, in the form of sleeping with Duncan.

'I believe you,' she said.

'Do you think you're going to put me off my guard?' Eugenia asked incredulously. 'Do you think I'm that stupid?'

Jenna gazed at her. Did she think that required an answer?

'Stay away from Duncan!' Eugenia ordered her. 'I'm tired of finding you holed up with him in every corner of this house. It ends now, or you deal with me.'

She was already dealing with Eugenia, but Jenna knew saying so would cause a whole onslaught of outrage that wouldn't be worth the brief pleasure she'd experience in saying it.

'I can't help it if he wants to talk to me,' she pointed out in a reasonable tone. The same way she did every time they had a version of this conversation. She sighed. 'I work for him. He's going to want to talk to me, and I have to talk to him.'

Eugenia made a hissing noise that was simultaneously angry and dismissive, and stalked across the kitchen towards the pantry. As she did not eat, Jenna could not imagine what she was after. But she didn't stick around to find out. She took her opportunity and hustled towards the stairs, as fast as she could go while holding hot coffee.

Up in the studio, she settled into the lounge area with her coffee, pasted a relaxed sort of smile across her face, and tried to come to terms with the worst part of her new work duties over the past few weeks. Tommy Seer.

Today, the rest of the band was absent and he was sitting

behind the glass on a stool, singing different versions of the same song ('Because and Because') again and again into the mike while the producers in the booth played with different effects that Jenna didn't pretend to understand.

She understood other effects. Like the effect Tommy's crooning voice had on the average woman's respiratory system, for example. Or the fact that when they settled on the final effect for the song, it would be so beautiful that a generation would make it their wedding anthem. Or, more to the point, the effect Tommy's proximity had on her.

Jenna knew she should have gotten over it by now. It had been at least a month since that awful scene between them, but the truth was, she was still embarrassed. And the even more upsetting truth was that the humiliation, which she would have sworn should have obliterated every last feeling she had for the man, hadn't done anything of the kind.

Instead, Jenna had spent the last weeks falling for Tommy Seer in a totally different way.

It wasn't about how pretty he was, or what she imagined it would be like to interact with him. It wasn't about Jenna or her fantasies at all – and the more she got to observe the real Tommy Seer, the more embarrassed she became not only for thrusting herself at the man, but for engaging in so many years of hero worship for someone who didn't exist outside his public persona.

It was the way he talked about music, for example, when

it was only the band around. They all had spirited debates about this guitar versus that guitar, this music legend versus that music legend, the importance of a good hook and a kick-ass bridge, and what comprised the perfect pop song. They were all extraordinary musicians, it seemed to Jenna, or at least very good ones, who happened to make pop music, and were therefore dedicated to making sure it was *really good* pop music. She often wished she could let them know that they succeeded – that they'd stood the test of time, and would be remembered and revered long after the end of the band. But, of course, they would think she was a complete lunatic if she did that.

Not that they didn't already think she was, if not a lunatic, something less than terrific anyway.

Something she remembered in a hurry when Nick sauntered through the door, his rangy body in full swagger.

Jenna smiled her hello, and was not surprised when Tommy's angriest band mate failed to return the smile. He didn't quite scowl. He looked at her, then through the glass at Tommy, who had moved around to the console. Then back to her.

'I don't get it,' he said belligerently. The way he said everything, including *pass me that magazine.*

'You don't get what?' She tried to sound bright. Trustworthy.

'If you're not fucking him, or someone, what the hell are you doing here?' He planted his fists on his hips, drawing attention to the parachute pants he wore. To say nothing of the tank top made entirely of mesh.

126

'I'm just, you know . . .' Jenna smiled again, unperturbed by his rudeness. That was mild, for Nick. 'Duncan really wanted me to be here to help out. Since I had such a great idea on the Video TV thing.'

'Interesting,' came a different, smoother voice, and yet this one made Jenna's spine straighten involuntarily. She hadn't noticed that Tommy had left the console booth, and yet here he was, lounging in the door with that mocking gleam in his eyes. 'We're making an album. Do you sing? Play a musical instrument? How can you help out, exactly?'

'I'm strictly here for moral support,' Jenna said, and her smile took on an edge. 'Ken Dollimore's gift to Duncan Paradis, and now you.'

'Politics,' Nick muttered in disgust, and slammed into the booth.

Leaving Jenna alone with Tommy.

'Was that necessary?' she asked him, not quite meeting his gaze. 'You want me here, remember?'

'I want you on my side if you have to be here,' Tommy corrected her. He prowled over to the leather sofa and stretched out on it, propping his head on one arm and his bare feet on the other. 'Not quite the same thing.'

Here were some things Jenna knew about the actual Tommy Seer, as opposed to the one she'd made up in her head. He was, apparently, American, which no one had yet explained. He liked to go barefoot, all the time. He wore T-shirts and jeans and very little else, save the occasional sweatshirt, which was at complete odds with his public persona, who was always decked out in the height of Eighties fashions. It was the same with his hair, which he tended to rake back from his face with his hands throughout the day, but otherwise left alone, thick and with that near-curl to it. He read the paper. He played cards with Richie. He watched PBS documentaries. He swapped paperbacks with Sebastian, and they liked to argue over who was better: King or Koontz. While Nick and Richie battled each other in Zelda on the Nintendo downstairs, Tommy preferred to read. Sometimes he cooked elaborate meals for the band and the producers – and by default, Jenna. One day it would be a massive brunch, with everything from banana pancakes to eggs Benedict. The next week he would announce he was making dinner, and would roast a couple of chickens and grill up some vegetables.

And, of course, he liked to lie on the sofa, stare at the ceiling, and hum to himself, driving his band mates insane when they were in the room. Nick had been known to throw things at his head. Jenna thought they were all missing the key point, which was that the man looked particularly good all stretched out like that.

'You're staring at me,' he said, startling her out of her thoughts. Jenna blinked, and saw that he'd turned his head and was now contemplating her instead of the ceiling.

'I'm sorry,' she said, as if she had not been checking out his abdomen as it peeked from beneath his T-shirt. She no longer engaged in wanton, absurd fantasies about the man, but hello. He was smoking hot. Millions of fan girls agreed. 'My mind wandered.'

'Uh huh.'

She decided she didn't want to hear whatever inevitably devastating thing he would say next.

'Duncan jumped all over me,' she said instead. 'Not literally,' she hurried on when Tommy's brows arched upward. 'But he wants to know what you're plotting. He thinks this is a waste of his time.' She pursed her lips slightly, remembering. 'And he told me it was about money. His money, specifically, and . . .' Her voice trailed away, because Tommy moved then. He swung to a sitting position, suddenly intent.

'He said it was about his money?' His voice was light but his gaze was anything but. 'He said that, exactly?'

'He has no intention of losing his investment.' Jenna searched his face. 'That's what he said.'

'I knew it,' Tommy said. 'I knew he would try to pull something.' He let out a hollow sort of laugh. 'I wouldn't be surprised if he tried to kill me.'

That sat there for a moment, between them.

And Jenna couldn't help but wonder, almost against her will: *what if he had?*

11

The silence in the small lounge stretched out, and Jenna realized she was staring at Tommy in a sort of stricken horror.

He looked away first.

It was absurd. Why would Duncan Paradis kill off his cash cow?

'You haven't told me I'm crazy,' he said quietly. 'That's usually the first thing people say.'

'You've told a lot of people that you think Duncan Paradis is—' His eyes cut towards the booth as she spoke, as if he thought everyone in it might overhear. Jenna broke off, and adjusted her voice to a whisper. 'That you think Duncan Paradis might kill you?'

'Not a lot of people.' He considered her for a moment. 'But you're the only one who hasn't laughed or shrugged it off. Why?'

What could she say? *As it happens, Tommy, you die in October – which starts in a matter of days – and your body will never be recovered, so there's just as much chance that Duncan Paradis killed you as the accepted version, which is that you drove off the side of the Tappan Zee Bridge in a drunken stupor. So that's why I'm not laughing or scoffing – it's my ability to see into the future.*

Somehow, she didn't think that would go over well.

'I don't know,' is what she said, shrugging. She inspected her fingernails. 'Duncan likes to throw his weight around. He likes to intimidate people. He's married and yet he's carrying on with your— with Eugenia. It's not the biggest stretch in the world to imagine him capable of worse things.'

'I don't know whether that makes me feel better or worse,' Tommy said after a moment. 'There's a certain comfort in being laughed at. Better to think you're crazy than that people are really out to get you.'

'But why?' Jenna asked, lifting her head. 'Why would he want to?'

'Money.' Tommy's mouth twisted. 'It's always about money with him.'

'I would think that you continuing to make him money would be a better plan than killing you,' Jenna said, whispering again. Very reasonably, as if what they were discussing was at all reasonable. As if they habitually sat around and had discussions in the first place.

That seemed to occur to Tommy too. The silence between them was filled with the sound of his voice singing as tracks spooled out from the production booth. Jenna was holding her breath. She let it out, surprised to feel that

131

she was a little shaky. Tommy drummed his fingers against his leg for a moment, then stood up abruptly as if he'd made up his mind about something.

'Walk with me,' he said.

'What?' But Jenna was already rising to her feet, as if his voice was connected to some sort of puppeteer's thread and she had no choice. Who was she kidding? If he was the Pied Piper, she'd always come running.

'I don't want Nick to hear any of this,' Tommy confided in an undertone as they walked down the stairs. Jenna followed his lean back as he moved, and tried to banish the usual fantasies. She laced her fingers together.

'He's very angry,' she observed. Tommy shot her a look over his shoulder. 'Nick,' she clarified. 'He's always yelling about something.'

'He's protective,' Tommy said, a smile she couldn't see warming his voice. 'Of the band, but also of me. Nick and I grew up together. If he thought Duncan was even thinking about this kind of thing . . .' He shook his head. 'And the last thing we need is Nick getting in Duncan's face. It wouldn't end well.'

Jenna tried to absorb that description, though it was of a different Nick than the one she'd come to know: blustery, furious Nick. Nick who was always in a rage.

'I'm guessing you didn't grow up in Manchester, England, as advertised,' Jenna said drily.

'No.' This time when he looked at her, laughter crinkled up the corners of his eyes. 'Buffalo, New York. But that's a secret, of course.'

'Of course.'

'If it helps,' he said in the same dry tone, 'I'm pretty sure there's a Tommy Seer who did grow up in Manchester, and I'm also pretty sure Duncan keeps him on the payroll. But I can't say for certain.'

Jenna felt a warm sort of glow spread through her, simply because he was telling her one of his secrets. Even though it was a secret she already sort of knew, given the fact he never bothered with his English accent in the town house. She hadn't known he was from Buffalo, though. He hadn't had to tell her that. He didn't need to talk to her at all. The fact that he was pleased her more than it should have, more than she was willing to admit, even to herself.

Though she couldn't quite figure out why he would want to.

He led her through the quiet house, all the way to the spacious living room where they'd had that awful scene. Jenna generally avoided that room whenever possible. He didn't stop there, thankfully, but continued on out into the garden. Only when he'd gone to the furthest edge of the walled-in space, to the small stone bench fetched up next to the brick wall and protected from the house by trees and the gurgling fountain, did he stop and face her. His expression was serious.

'I told Duncan I'm leaving the band after this album,' he said, with no preamble. 'I'll tour, but then I'm done with the Wild Boys. With him. He went ballistic.'

Jenna's mind cartwheeled around her typical fan girl's

133

reaction to that announcement. It was hard not to show it. But there was a more pressing question.

'Why are you telling me this?' she asked haltingly. She tilted her chin up, braced for his response. 'Why are you even talking to me? It's been nothing but sarcasm since the night we— since that first night after the Video TV show.'

Tommy sighed, and sat down on the stone bench. He stretched his long, denim-covered legs out before him, flexing his bare toes against the warm grass.

'You had the groupie look then,' he said simply. His gaze was challenging. 'You don't have it any more.'

'What—' She stopped, composed herself. She ignored the shaft of pain that lanced through her. She cleared her throat. 'What is the groupie look, exactly?'

He didn't look away. Nor was his expression particularly kind.

'That creepy blank stare.' His voice was quiet. Not quite bitter, more resigned. 'They don't see you, whoever you are. They only see what they think you are. The fantasy. Usually they're dreaming something about you while they're looking at you. You're just the object. You could be anyone. They're like zombies.'

Jenna swallowed. She wanted to deny that she'd ever been like that, a *zombie* for God's sake, but the protest died unspoken on her lips. Because she knew he was right, that she was still fighting it, even in this moment, and it shamed her.

'Um.' She tried again. 'I'm sorry about that.' How woefully inadequate.

'You don't have that look any more,' he said again. What he didn't say was, *that's okay*, or *all is forgiven*.

'You must get that a lot,' she said, aware that her cheeks had reddened. She could feel the heat spread across them, itchy and shaming. She blinked back similar heat behind her lashes before it spilled over and humiliated her further.

'You could say that.' The creases next to his eyes deepened. 'Also,' he said after a moment, 'there's no one else to talk to. Anyone in the band might tell Duncan, if they thought it would help them out. And there's no one outside the band I can trust. That's what happens when you sell out everyone you know to become a big star. Behold my success.'

'So,' she said briskly, not caring to discuss her groupieness any further, or his evident loneliness, because both made her chest ache and there was nothing to be done about it, anyway. 'Duncan going ballistic because you're leaving the band makes sense, given, you know, Duncan's personality. But what makes you think he'd kill you rather than lose you?'

'I don't know that I do think that.' Tommy watched her carefully, his head cocked to one side. 'It's been a weird thought, that's all. But then you didn't laugh it off.'

'You can't be basing it on *that*.' Jenna shook her head. 'You must have other reasons to think it, right?'

'There's Eugenia.' His expression got very distant, as if he was remembering something. 'She's been much friendlier lately. Which is terrifying.' He smirked. 'She's normally vicious.'

'And yet you asked her to marry you,' Jenna couldn't help but point out. His eyes flashed.

'Or Duncan announced our engagement so he could keep his piece of ass available at all times, without his very jealous and very connected wife any the wiser,' Tommy retorted. 'You shouldn't believe everything you read. Or even part of it.'

'You used to date her,' Jenna replied, feeling defensive.

Tommy sighed. He raked his dark hair back from his face with an impatient hand. 'Eugenia Wentworth is a failed model with a very large trust fund, and can tell people at parties that she's one hundred and sixty-seventh in line for the British throne. She's exactly who I *should* have dated when I was twenty-two and in love with myself and our first single hit the top ten.' He tipped his head back against the brick wall, and sighed. 'And then, years later, she was still hanging around. So I dated her again, except this time it was perfectly clear that she wasn't what I was looking for, but it was too late because I finally realized I was trapped and she was banging the guy who put me in the cage.' He let out a small laugh then. 'That's how I ended up engaged to Eugenia Fucking Wentworth.'

He said *engaged* as if it was in quotation marks, and also as if the very word sickened him. Jenna could relate.

'That's a terrible story.' More than that, it made her want to reach out and soothe him, comfort him, but she didn't dare.

'Yes,' Tommy agreed. He shifted on the bench. 'The

136

thing about Eugenia is that she has no filter between her emotions and her mouth. And I know she hates my guts.'

'She told me you can be cruel,' Jenna added helpfully. She did not add that she already knew that from first-hand experience.

'She's right.' Tommy shrugged, as if cruelty was of no matter to him. 'Her being friendly disturbs me. Deeply.'

'Okay, sure,' Jenna said, rocking back on her heels as she considered the situation. She crossed her arms over her chest and frowned. 'But that still doesn't add up to her conspiring to do anything but mess with your head.'

'The only way to get out from under Duncan's thumb is to get out of the band,' Tommy said, looking away again. 'And he isn't the kind of guy to give up his power.'

'But—'

'You want proof,' he said, interrupting her. 'I don't have any. I just have a feeling. It's not like he ever saw me as more than a means to an end, but lately, I don't know, there's something different in the way he looks at me. I can't explain it, but I think he has a big plan.'

'Which isn't the same thing as planning a *murder*,' Jenna argued. Tommy shook his head.

'Duncan Paradis is a thug,' he said matter-of-factly. 'That story he tells about his loving family and his poor child-hood in the Bronx is a lie. There was no loving family. There were foster homes and sealed juvenile records. He lies about everything, he pays people off to help tell the lies, and he really only cares about money. Believe me, I know. I'm his biggest investment. I can't imagine he's going to let that change.'

'I believe you,' Jenna said. 'I think he's a creep. I just think it would make more sense for him to force you to make more albums, and therefore make more money . . .' But even as she said it, she realized that idols who died tragically and at the height of their glory raked in far more money, and for far longer, than bands of once-great heights whose follow-up albums lost listeners. Kurt Cobain versus Simon Le Bon, for example.

'Dead singers make a whole lot more money,' Tommy said softly, as if he could read her mind. 'Indefinitely. To say nothing of the cults that spring up around them. The greatest-hits compilations. The loving tributes and concerts. It's big business.'

Jenna's mind raced. Tommy Seer's body had never been recovered. Theoretically, anyone could have crashed his car through the guard rail and sent it spinning into the Hudson river. She'd seen it done in enough movies, at any rate, to know that it was possible. And if someone had done that deliberately, it made sense that they'd also done away with him. Because everything he'd just said with that bitter twist to his mouth had come to pass. Tommy Seer was a legend. Cut down in his prime, his death had been one of the most shocking events of not just Jenna's young life, but of the lives of her contemporaries. Years later, when Kurt Cobain died, they'd all hugged themselves and wondered why the voices of their generation all seemed to die before their time.

There was no evidence that it had been anything but an unfortunate accident. But there had always been the suspicion – or hope – amongst the fans that it had been an elaborate set-up and Tommy Seer still lived. Kind of like in that wonderful early-Eighties movie, *Eddie and the Cruisers*. The fact that there was no body kept the suspicion stoked no matter what official-sounding statements were made to the contrary.

But it could also mean that someone else had set the whole thing up. And if there was anyone Jenna thought might be not only capable of such an act, but gunning for it, that would be Duncan Paradis.

'It's only a feeling,' Tommy said again.

'I understand where you're coming from,' Jenna said slowly, her mind still spinning through all the reams and reams of news articles she'd read about Tommy's death, the documentaries with the news footage, her own more recent and exhaustive search through everything she could find that vaguely related to Tommy's life in those last months . . . She shook herself slightly, aware that he was still watching her closely. Heaven forbid he see *zombie eyes* when she was just thinking things through. 'So what do we do? Wait to see if he tries to shoot you one day?'

Tommy's mouth pulled to one side, and his eyes warmed.

'That's not the best plan I've ever heard,' he said. 'The trouble is, I can't think of any reason Duncan would share his plans with me. Or anyone else.'

'He thinks I'm an idiot,' Jenna said, pulling on her bottom lip with her fingers as she thought it over. 'If that.'

They looked at each other, in perfect accord. Tommy smirked and Jenna smiled. And at the same time, they said her name.

'Eugenia.'

As it turned out, Jenna did not have to look very far for the other woman, because she was thoughtfully lying in wait when Tommy and Jenna returned to the house. She sneered as they walked in the glass doors from the garden.

'A little early for a nooner, isn't it?' she asked snidely.

Tommy ignored her completely, the way he always did. He walked past her as if the room was empty, as if she was not arrayed across the couch with that spiteful look on her face. Jenna made as if to do the same, and hid her smile when Eugenia barked out her name. Not that she thought Eugenia was likely to spill Duncan's plot at the drop of a hat, but every conversation was an opportunity to get a little bit closer to that possibility.

'What?' she asked. 'I have to be up in the studio.'

'A few minutes in the garden with Tommy and suddenly you think highly of yourself,' Eugenia murmured. 'You shouldn't be so naïve, Jenna.'

'I didn't think I was,' Jenna replied, crossing her arms as she stared down at Eugenia's awful little rat face. 'I thought I was doing my job.'

'Is that what he told you?' Eugenia let out a trill of

laughter. 'He certainly has slipped. Used to be, he didn't have to tell his groupies that it was part of the job – they did it for free.'

Jenna hated that word, *groupies*. She particularly hated it coming from Eugenia's nasty mouth.

'Whatever,' she said. 'Didn't you fall all over yourself in the kitchen earlier to tell me what an asshole you think Tommy is? Why would you care what he does?'

'I don't,' Eugenia retorted. She crossed her legs, and let them slide against each other, as if performing for someone who cared. 'But don't you think you're fooling yourself?' She smiled. It was a brittle thing. 'You're not exactly his type, are you?'

Jenna knew perfectly well that Eugenia was trying to hurt her feelings. She also knew that this conversation was absurd at best, because she knew Tommy had less than no feelings about her. Not to mention she thought there were many other matters she could be talking about with Eugenia.

But, 'What do you mean?' she asked, instead of all the reasonable things she should have said. Eugenia's smile sharpened.

'Well, look at you,' she said, waving a languid hand at Jenna. 'Tommy is one of the most famous men in the world. Sure, he'd sleep with anything, including a garden hose, but it's not like he'd be seen in public with a poor little secretary like you, now would he?'

It was ridiculous to let that hurt her. For one thing, it was true. And for another, it was irrelevant, because he wasn't sleeping with her. So there was absolutely no rational explanation for the stab of pain that bloomed under her breastplate, much less her sudden, violent urge to leap across the coffee table and punch Eugenia Wentworth in the face.

Eugenia uncoiled herself from the sofa like a cobra. She closed the distance between them with one long-legged stride. 'Oh,' she said then, 'I almost forgot. Your boss called. He needs you back at the office.'

'Ken called?' Jenna asked.

'That's what I said.' Eugenia sniffed, and raked Jenna from head to foot with her piercing eyes. 'It must be painful to have such a crush on a man who will never, ever notice you. I almost pity you.'

But her gales of laughter as she sauntered away said different.

Jenna wanted to throw the lamp after her, possibly braining her, but restrained herself. After all, this was the plan. Convince Eugenia that Jenna yearned hopelessly after Tommy, and she would be less territorial over Duncan, which might – *might* – allow for some bonding down the road. Jenna and Tommy had agreed that it was the best – and, really, only – plan they had at the moment.

The downside being, of course, that it was only the fact that Jenna really did yearn after Tommy that made her believe she could tolerate Eugenia long enough to pretend to bond in the first place.

12

Times Square looked sketchy and frightening in the late-morning sun, and Jenna ran from the cab to the door of the office building as if the homeless drug addicts were likely to pursue her if she slowed down. Inside, she ran into the still-snarly Princess-Diana-Haired receptionist in the elevator, and wondered, briefly, why every female she encountered in the Eighties hated her on sight.

She was used to being the kind of woman other women liked. She had primarily female friends, back in her own life. She wasn't one of those alien women who avoided females like the plague and concentrated her emotional energy on men. She had, in fact, long maintained that such women had severe problems of their own, even as she envied them their ease with members of the opposite sex. So what was going on?

As she headed down the lush, opulent hallway on the fancy executive floor, hurrying to do Ken Dollimore's bidding, Jenna suddenly realized that her New Jenna

Project life actually resembled her sad and pathetic Former Jenna life. More than it should. Sure, she was stuck over twenty years in the past, but she still spent all her waking hours consumed with the Wild Boys. She still worked at Video TV, even if she hadn't spent much time in the office lately. She still spent her nights alone in a small Manhattan apartment, with too much Tommy in her head.

You could take the girl out of her time, but you couldn't take the way she spent her time out of the girl. What did that say about her, that she could be catapulted into a different era and still continue doing the exact same things? On the one hand, maybe that spoke of her strength of character, that it stood the test of time, rigorously. On the other hand, maybe she should accept that she was the world's biggest loser, as witnessed across *several* decades.

On that cheery note, she stepped into her office and found Ken Dollimore in a tizzy. He was scowling into the telephone, and didn't glance up as she walked in and stood in front of his desk. Today his outfit once again brought to mind the character of Ducky in *Pretty in Pink*, with the oversized yellow blazer, complete with rolled-up sleeves and FRANKIE SAYS RELAX T-Shirt underneath. He was a bright eyesore.

'Finally!' he cried when he saw her, rising to a half-crouch above his desk, which was piled high with precarious stacks of paper. 'This place is a disaster without you, Jen.'

Jenna murmured something vague and hopefully soothing, but Ken was on a roll.

'I have no idea what I'm doing,' he told her in frenzied tones. 'My calendar is a disaster and I keep missing appointments. I never miss appointments! Gigi Unger called me today and became hysterical – I missed the entire exhibit! How could this happen?' When he saw Jenna's blank stare, he threw his hands in the air, theatrically. 'Gigi Unger? The art broker? She manages three different downtown artists whose work was *finally* getting some respect, and I missed the exhibit.'

The slightest trickle of a memory teased at the edges of Jenna's brain then. She had the vaguest recollection of the name Gigi, and the word installation, and she was almost certain she'd spoken to this person in the three minutes she had been impersonating her far-better-organized aunt before Duncan Paradis had spirited her away. She felt guilty, but not guilty enough to confess.

'Gigi Unger is always hysterical,' Jenna claimed authoritatively, as if she had any idea. She based that assertion entirely on her faint memory, and what Ken had just said. 'And artists generally show their work again, especially if they're up and coming. They have to. I hope you told her to relax.'

'Yes, thank you, I know it's not the end of the world,' Ken said with a groan, and flopped back in his chair. He sighed in a great gust. 'Tell me what you're doing over there in Wild Boy heaven, as Duncan Paradis's little seeing-eye dog.'

Jenna blinked. 'What a delightful description.'

'He's a delightful guy,' Ken said drily. He made a face. 'He's a bully, to put it mildly, and I wish there was some other way, but if I want Video TV to have an exclusive relationship with the Wild Boys . . .' He shrugged. 'There it is. Those bastards at MTV wet themselves when they saw that live show of yours. Brilliant idea.'

'It's going well,' Jenna said. 'I mean, I guess it is. I just sit there. The band doesn't pay any attention to me. Most of the time I read magazines.'

'Money in the bank,' Ken said with a shrug. He ran a hand over his chin, thoughtfully. 'See if you can figure out what they think the first single will be from the new album. If I can get some creative people working on it now, I'm pretty sure I can wow them and get the world premiere. MTV can eat my dust.'

Jenna looked at him for a moment. Once again, loyalty to her employer compelled her to answer.

'"Misery Loves Company",' she said, 'That's the first single. I think they're planning to release it next week.'

'You are a goddess,' Ken breathed. He pointed at her. 'Stay right there. I have to make a few calls.'

Jenna eased down into one of the bright blue and red beanbag chairs that served as visitor seating in Ken's office, and perched there gingerly, her butt making the beans crunch as they compressed.

She couldn't help going over the events of the day in her mind. She'd spent a month doing absolutely nothing – fending off Duncan's rants, exchanging barbs with Eugenia

– and today, suddenly, Tommy had talked to her like she was another person and not just another annoyance.

She knew that it had as much to do with the topic they'd discussed as it had to do with the fact that she'd stopped seeing him as the imaginary creature she'd made up. She didn't know what this new, complicated Tommy might do or say. She didn't know him at all. But she wanted to.

And more than anything, she wanted to keep him from dying in a few short weeks.

How, she wondered, as that thought crashed through her with sudden force, had she managed to put that fact out of her mind? Whether Duncan Paradis murdered him or he got drunk and did it himself, he was still going to die. That was what happened. She knew, because she'd already lived through 1987 once before. So how had she let herself think about anything else?

Oh, she knew that *Tommy Seer, the legendary singer* died on a certain date at a certain time, but in the past month, if she'd thought about it seriously, it had been in the abstract. Only now, sitting on a beanbag listening to Ken light fires under the behinds of numerous creative professionals, did it dawn on Jenna that *this* Tommy was the one who would die. Not the legend she'd made up in her own mind, the one who had been like a teddy bear or a comforter to soothe her as she'd needed over the years. That one would die too, but *this* Tommy was the one with bare feet and a slight smile. *This* Tommy told bad jokes and hummed at the ceiling. *This* Tommy didn't bother to dress in anything but the most casual jeans and T-shirts, and he sometimes went without his morning shower too, turning up in the studio with a day or two of beard growth, and could still look so adorable while he made eggs for everyone. *This* Tommy had to be saved.

He had to be.

And she was the unlikely person to do it, because she was the only one who knew what was coming. He might suspect it, but she could tell he thought he was being paranoid. Jenna *knew*.

'You have a terrifying look on your face,' Ken said, interrupting her reverie. 'I'm proud of you for taking one for the team, kiddo,' he said with a smile. 'But I'm not going to lie and tell you I think it's anything but a crappy job.' He sighed, not unhappily. 'And now I have to go kiss Chuck's ass. What I need you to do is take a break from the Wild Boys and do something with this office, so I can work again. Can you do that?'

'Of course I can do that,' Jenna assured him, with the sort of cool confidence she imagined Aunt Jen, organizer extraordinaire, might exude.

'That is way cool,' Ken said, sounding relieved. He came around the side of the desk. 'Because I can't take the clutter any more. I can't find anything. You're my saviour.' He grinned. 'I've got to book. I'll see you in few hours, when Chuck finishes yelling and screaming.'

Chuck, Jenna knew, was Chuck Arendt, the CEO. Once the best of friends, Chuck and Ken had fallen out by the late Eighties, though no one knew exactly why. People claimed it was because Chuck was jealous that Ken was seen as the creative genius behind Video TV, and felt he was equally responsible. Ken didn't bother to explain, he just scurried out of the room, taking his absurdly bright jacket with him.

Which left Jenna with the unenviable task of having to neaten up and organize his disaster of an office in Aunt Jen style. Not something she was at all sure she could do, actually.

The good news, she discovered quickly, was that he had been unable to completely undo, in a few short weeks, the spectacularly well-organized system Aunt Jen had implemented. Once Jenna sorted through the immediate mess, the architecture behind it was sound. Which meant she could turn her head off and let it return to its new favourite subject: Tommy's approaching demise.

Jenna's mind raced. If he was really Tommy's killer, how had Duncan gotten away with it? Had he really used Eugenia? That seemed unlikely – she might be one hundred and sixty-seven people away from the throne of England, but that didn't mean she was a good choice for a partner in crime. Given how confrontational she was, and how much Duncan seemed to enjoy talking down to her, Jenna couldn't imagine him conspiring with her at all. On the other hand, the two of them were involved in an elaborate charade involving her supposed engagement to Tommy, just to hide their affair. So who knew what was more unlikely for such people?

Having watched every single episode of *The Sopranos*,

Jenna had all kinds of ideas about nearby places where Duncan might have disposed of poor Tommy. She needed to think no further than the New Jersey Meadowlands, a place she saw only when flying into Newark airport, but which her imagination insisted was brimming with mafia-discarded remains. She repressed a shiver.

Was Duncan a shooter? Or did he plan to bash Tommy over the head with something – after all, he was stocky enough to do some damage? Jenna's head whirled with one grisly image after another, until she had to stop before she completely freaked herself out. It was hard enough to walk around the far more dangerous New York she found herself in these days, let alone imagining a murderous Duncan Paradis with a chainsaw, for the love of all that was holy.

She had calmed herself down and was sitting at her desk, going through Ken's mail, when he came rushing back in the door a few hours later.

'Why didn't you tell me that the Wild Boys are going to start shooting the video for the new single next week?' he demanded in lieu of a greeting. 'Dante La Rue pulled me aside after the meeting and told me his secretary had given him the message, but he didn't know how I didn't already know about the shoot.'

'I don't know anything about it either,' Jenna assured him. 'They don't give me a schedule, Ken. They do whatever it is they're doing and allow me to tag along.'

Ken stood there, his skinny arms propped on his skinny hips, his glaring yellow jacket brightening up the whole room, and not in a good way. Jenna was tempted to pull out her sunglasses.

'That needs to change,' he said. 'I can't be kept in the dark. They must have some kind of schedule somewhere. Tell them you need it.'

'I will,' Jenna promised. She indicated his office, behind her. 'I think you'll find everything is back the way you like it.'

Smiling, Ken walked into his office. Jenna followed. Ken beamed as he saw the neat desk, all the piles he'd left for her no more than a memory.

'You are truly a miracle worker,' he told her with a happy sigh.

Which is what she tried to tell herself a little bit later, as she walked from the subway through the Village on her way to the town house again. Maybe she wasn't actually a miracle worker, but she did have the advantage of not only having been through 1987 before, but having been *obsessed* with it ever after. She had so many facts about the last few months of Tommy's life running through her brain that she could probably write an encyclopedia on them.

Maybe it was the fact that she'd just spent hours face to face with organizational genius, but it occurred to her that if she wanted to help Tommy avoid his fate, she should, well, *get organized*.

Thank you, Aunt Jen, she thought, sending that thought spinning out away from her, into whatever mysterious void had brought her here. *I hope you really are in my twenty-*

151

first-century life, because I think you'll enjoy low-waisted jeans. You deserve to look that good, and so much less hippy.

And then she climbed up the front stairs, succumbed to her second entrance exam of the day, and went in search of a pen and paper.

She would start writing down every little fact she could remember about this period. Surely, now that she was actually *in* 1987 instead of thinking back on it from years in the future, she'd be able to discern some pattern. Some answer. *Something.*

She found a notebook and a pen in the library, and settled herself on one of the couches.

Tommy had started to trust her – or, at any rate, had stopped disliking her quite so intensely. This, then, was the very least she could do for the fantasy she'd loved for so long and the real man she'd only just begun to admire. The very least.

It wasn't working a miracle, she thought as she began to write, but it was a start.

Present

Destiny is just another word you use
Don't you wonder what it means?
I'm too afraid to ask the question
Too many shadows in between.

The Wild Boys, 'Careless Lips Kill Relationships'

I only know the stars you claim
Constellations without name
Wherever there is fire, wherever it is bright
Carve our hearts into the night
I am celestially yours.

The Wild Boys, 'Celestially Yours'

13

The secretary was getting to him.

There was nothing about her that should have interested him in the slightest, and *interested* was a strong word to begin with, Tommy thought while sitting through another interminable photo shoot. *Interested* made it sound like he was hot for her, which he wasn't. Because that was impossible.

He could see her through the mirror, while the stylists worked on his hair, plumping it up and out, because the photographer *had a vision* that apparently involved big hair and a serious amount of gel.

She wasn't ugly. She was probably cute, as far as regular people went. Her name was *Jenna*, which struck him as a little silly. She had masses of dark, curly hair, which today she had piled up on the top of her head in a huge, lopsided ponytail. Big brown eyes, too, that he'd seen widen in astonishment and narrow in anger and glaze over with desire, for that matter, though why he'd spent any time thinking about her eyes, he didn't know.

She wasn't beautiful. She wasn't going to grace the covers of any magazines any time soon, which had been Tommy's main criterion for sexual partners ever since the Wild Boys hit it big. He liked models. They always looked good in photographs, and could be depended upon to dress for the camera no matter where they were going. They inspired envy and admiration wherever they went, like luxury sports cars. And they were unlikely to trick him into unburdening himself in the back garden of the town house, as their main topics of conversation were themselves and which other models had finally succumbed to fat.

He couldn't see Jenna's clavicle from across the loft space that was serving as the shoot location, which should have automatically excluded her from his consideration. Not that he was considering her.

On the other hand, he'd been staring at her for whole minutes now, and it wasn't the first time, either. Tommy forced himself to look away. Nick was sitting in the next chair, surrendering to full make-up, and was likely to start noticing if Tommy wasn't careful, given Nick's brooding attention to everything and everyone these days. Tommy couldn't afford to have Nick crawling up his ass about some nonentity of a secretary, not now.

What the hell was the matter with him?

His new policy, developed over the past few years as he'd realized that he was little more than a hamster running endless circles on a wheel inside Duncan Paradis's cage, was to stop lying to himself. He'd gotten so good at it. A consequence, maybe, of selling his soul at the tender age of twenty-two. But that was over now, and it was unflinching honesty for him, even – especially – when it hurt.

So Tommy had to admit the truth as he sat there on the stool, eyeing himself in the mirrors and seeing her behind him. Somehow, for some reason, she was getting under his skin. The worst part was, she wasn't even doing anything. She wasn't prancing around in something alluring, or trying to tempt him. She was sitting across the room with a paperback cracked open in front of her, wearing tight jeans tucked into slouchy boots and one of those off-the-shoulder sweatshirts all the girls were forever tugging back up, drawing attention to the curve of their arms and the slopes of their breasts. Objectively, sure, she was cute, he guessed. But she wasn't anything special. She wasn't a luxury sports car. She was a Chevy. No one else in the room even glanced at her.

And here he was, unable to look away.

It had been one thing when she had been in the grip of the groupie virus. She'd gazed at him with that dazed look in her eyes, no doubt dreaming of her favourite fantasy involving whatever character he was in her head. He'd figured he could use that to his advantage. She'd claimed she hadn't slept with Duncan Paradis – which Tommy had believed since Duncan was definitely more about the blow job when it came to underlings and nonentities – so Tommy saw no reason why he shouldn't use her own rich fantasy life against her. Clearly, she wanted to sleep with Tommy Seer, and who was he to turn her down when it was a means to his own ends?

The first surprising thing about Jenna Jenkins was the fact she'd stopped him. Not only had she stopped him, but she'd been so horrified. Mostly in such scenarios, the groupie in question never noticed that he wasn't into it. But he could still remember with perfect clarity the way her voice had shaken, the way she'd told him she didn't want to *seal the deal* with him. Why that should continue to fascinate him, interrupting his thoughts at strange moments, he couldn't say.

Then she'd been around all the time. Sitting in the lounge every day, smiling. Not prattling on about herself. Not whining for attention. Not intruding, or throwing out unsolicited suggestions or critiques about the music. Not even trying particularly hard to befriend the other members of the band. He'd found himself irrationally annoyed by her very *unobtrusiveness*.

Which, of course, he had dealt with by being as obnoxious as possible.

'You need to leave that poor girl alone,' Sebastian had chided him after a particularly frustrating day, when he'd actually gone out of his way to insult her and though he'd seen the heat rise in her cheeks, she'd only smiled politely in return. He knew she could stand up for herself, so why didn't she?

'She's Duncan's spy,' he'd snapped at Sebastian.

'You're being an asshole,' Sebastian had retorted, and had then proceeded to spend the afternoon chatting with her, to rub it in.

The longer she sat around doing nothing, being unfailingly pleasant and polite no matter the provocation, the more he had the urge to ruffle her feathers. He acted like the sullen teenager he'd been long ago. He was rude. He lounged around in various states of undress, to prompt the groupie reaction. And the longer it went on, she gazed at him with those big glazed calf eyes less and less. Which for some reason outraged him. He, who had maintained a firm no-groupie policy in recent years – it was too much like masturbation, and not in a good way – was *furious* that she was losing that groupie glow.

So, naturally, he'd made it all worse by confiding his paranoid delusions to her.

On the scale of epically bad ideas, that had to rank at the top, right under signing away his life to Duncan Paradis. He didn't know this girl. He didn't want to know this girl. So he was completely unable to figure out how he'd found himself talking to her about things he never, ever talked about.

And now, once again, he was brooding and staring at her. Like a lovesick puppy. It was embarrassing. It had to stop.

So of course she chose that moment to look up from her book, adjust the sleeve that had crept down her arm to expose the tender joint of her arm and shoulder, see him in the mirrors, and smile.

Politely.

Damn her.

Hours later, Tommy's cheeks ached from all the smiling and pouting. He was happy to take a break while they did something with the lights, and wardrobe was consulted about Richie's spandex jumpsuit.

He was sick of having his picture taken, to tell the truth, but had surrendered to vanity like anyone else and had experimented to figure out how to make sure to take a good picture anyway. Sebastian, of course, had been born with such knowledge. Tommy had spent more time than he cared to admit in various poses in front of his mirror. It only took a few unflattering pictures in the tabloids – which band mates were sure to plaster across tour buses forever – to convince a man that he'd be better off discovering his good side.

Even Nick, who had once threatened a photographer with biological improbabilities if he didn't stop taking his picture, had given in. At the moment, he was standing in front of a bank of mirrors, in a wide stance that would have been more appropriate for sports of some kind, *simmering* at himself.

'You look like you have gas,' Tommy offered helpfully.

Nick ignored him, trying the look from different angles.

'I hated those *Vanity Fair* pictures last month,' he

muttered. 'I had a double chin in half of them.'

Tommy sighed by way of an answer. Nick might as well be asking if he looked fat in his pants. Tommy refused to respond for both their sakes.

'That's easy for you to say,' Nick said, glaring at him as if he'd said something. 'You're the pretty-boy lead singer. The world would end if a hair of yours was out of place. The rest of us, who cares?'

'You're pretty too, Nick,' Tommy said drily. Then laughed when his oldest friend scowled and gave him the finger. He turned away from the mirrors and looked around the loft. It buzzed with activity, as it had since they'd arrived that morning. Stylists and PR lackeys and record-company people, all milling around having low-volume conversations. The photographer was deep in conversation with Sebastian, no doubt hearing Sebastian's numerous thoughts on how best to preserve and enhance the Wild Boys' image while still achieving the photographer's vision. Richie was standing near the windows while the spandex controversy raged around him, staring out over Manhattan and smoking a cigarette.

She was still sitting quietly on the same couch. Tommy was irritated. How could she sit still for so long? Why didn't she have to take breaks, go to the bathroom, whatever else? It was unnatural.

So unnatural, in fact, that he crossed the room to tell her so. 'Your ass must be numb,' he heard himself say.

She had watched him approach with that frozen sort of smile he knew she used only on him. And, now that he considered it, on Duncan, which infuriated him. It was obviously automatic, as she waited for the other shoe to drop. The sort of smile she might give a wild animal. Now, her eyebrows crept high on her forehead.

'Excuse me?'

Tommy gestured at the couch, grimly aware that not only did he sound like a lunatic, but the *gloriously deconstructed jacket* that he wore – the stylist's words, not his – had a leather fringe hanging from the sleeves that waved when he moved. He felt like a bullfighter, only more absurd.

'You've been sitting in the same position for hours,' he said.

'Yes.' She thought he was insane. He could see it in her eyes. He felt insane.

'Did Eugenia let anything slip yet?' he asked, as if his leather fringe were not waving in front of her nose. As if that had been the reason he'd come over to speak to her.

Jenna looked startled. She straightened in her seat.

'No,' she said. 'Well. Yesterday she told me the story of how she started in modelling.'

'I'm sure that must have been fascinating.'

'And today she said something about her mother.' Her face lit up with laughter as she looked at him. He felt it everywhere, like a kind of ache. 'I'm going to consider it progress.'

He wanted to sleep with her.

Tommy stared down at her, his mind racing, confused. His body was far more direct. It announced itself in the wholly unwelcome pressure in his groin, a situation not at all helped by the fact he was wearing a pair of white leather trousers that might as well have been painted on.

He couldn't possibly want to sleep with her.

And yet . . . It was something about that unruly mess of curls that today exposed the delicate line of her neck. And that mouth of hers that she abused, like now, as wariness crept back into her expression and she bit down on her full lower lip. He imagined that mouth put to much better use, and then wished he hadn't, when his too-tight pants immediately got tighter. He shifted, uncomfortable.

'Or maybe not,' she was saying. 'I mean, Eugenia's and my current relationship involves me standing there while she rants at me. The only real improvement is that it's been a few days now since she was ranting *about* me.'

He was just barely still man enough to admit to himself that he'd been reacting to her like a teenaged boy – why not just punch her in the arm and get it over with? He was disgusted with himself.

'You are a Chevy,' he informed her. Reminding himself at the same time. So what if it sounded crazy. The whole situation was crazy. *He* was definitely crazy.

'A Chevy,' she repeated, her eyebrows jacking up and her chin lifting. Because there was no way being called a Chevy was a compliment, and she wasn't an idiot.

'A Chevrolet.' In case she was confused as to which Chevy he meant.

'A Chevrolet.' She didn't look confused. She waited. When he didn't speak, she cleared her throat. 'I am an automobile.' Her voice went up at the end there, making it a question. An icy sort of question.

'A Chevy.' He made an impatient gesture. 'Not a De Lorean. Or an Aston Martin.'

'I see.' Her tone was arid. 'Am I a Chevy station wagon? Maybe with wood panelling? Because those were always my favourites. They were so sleek and powerful. Who wouldn't want to be a Chevy Caprice Classic, for example?'

Her sarcastic tone could have peeled paint. He ignored it, and concentrated on her strange use of the past tense. He frowned.

'That doesn't make any sense.'

'But calling me a Chevy does?' She held up a hand before he could answer. 'Silly me, of course it does. It's a secret car code known only to rock stars. I'll just ask Billy Idol the next time I run into him.'

'I drive luxury cars,' he told her. Firmly, as if that settled things. 'Luxury sports cars. Expensive machines that other men would kill to touch.'

'Yes, Tommy,' she replied, soothingly. With that bite underneath. Treating him like a child. An *annoying* child. 'You're a very rich, very famous man.'

'Exactly.' But as he glared at her, and she failed to fall apart before him, he realized that he was in trouble.

And the worst part was, he knew why.

He hadn't always been a very rich, very famous driver of very fancy cars. The Tommy from a trailer park in

Buffalo, who had never been near a De Lorean in even his wildest wet dreams, was the problem. *He* had spent some quality time in the back seats of numerous sturdy, unpretentious American cars, Chevys among them. He liked American cars, and the little slice of heaven Donna Castiglione had showed him in her daddy's Buick. *He* wasn't such a snob that he couldn't appreciate that mouth Jenna was worrying, or the way the tight jeans covered her ass.

The problem wasn't that Jenna Jenkins was a Chevy. The problem was that, deep down, *he* was.

'You're looking at me like you want to kill me.' Jenna's voice yanked him back to the here and now. 'With your bare hands.'

'That's not what I want to do with my hands,' he retorted, before he could think better of it, and there was no getting around it once he'd said it. Her startled gaze flew to his and he felt heat gather where it shouldn't. He pointed at her. 'You're a Chevy,' he spat at her, and then he turned around and escaped back across the room, where all the primping and preening and posing in the world couldn't change the fact that he wanted her.

And he could feel her watching him, making it worse with every second.

14

With the new single out, and the record about to launch, the Wild Boys' schedule got hectic. No more long days of hanging out at the studio – Jenna was instead dispatched along with the band to their never-ending cycle of interviews and press junkets.

Which was annoying for many reasons, chief among them the fact that she was pretty sure she'd figured something out – something that could help Tommy live through 1987 – if she could just work out how to *tell* him about it without sounding like a mental patient. *I've written down everything I can remember about 1987 – because, you see, I am from the future—*

She couldn't seem to get past that point.

She imagined Tommy would be unable to get past that point, too. It was an unpassable point.

'Might as well make yourself useful,' Duncan barked at her the day after the weird photo shoot, the one where Tommy had started ranting incoherently about cars. *Maybe he really does have a substance-abuse problem*, Jenna thought. *Maybe Eugenia wasn't lying all those years later.*

But that was unlikely. Eugenia, the Eighties version, was at that moment lounging in a chair at the kitchen table in the town house, pretending to sip at a cup of black coffee while watching Jenna's interaction with Duncan like a hawk. She would, and did, lie at the drop of a hat. *Maybe Tommy is just insane*, Jenna thought with something like regret. *Paranoid delusions. Chevys versus De Loreans, all out of nowhere and a little too intense—*

'Are you listening to me?' Duncan was outraged, and far too close.

Jenna eased herself away from him, aware of Eugenia's possessive glare, and edged around the breakfast bar in the kitchen. Out of his immediate reach. 'Of course I'm listening to you,' she said smoothly. 'Usefulness, you were saying?'

'People who work for me need to earn their keep,' he growled, fingering the tight shirt collar that was digging into the red folds of his neck.

'They talk about you,' Jenna said, not for the first time. 'They just don't plot against you. I'm sorry.' She felt a sudden boldness. 'They don't like you very much, if that's what you wanted to know.'

'Because this is a popularity contest suddenly?' He stopped messing with his collar and shook his head at her. 'I don't give a rat's ass if they like me.'

'That works out then,' Jenna retorted, with that inter-mittent flash of bravado that she couldn't seem to predict or control. It wouldn't win her any points with Duncan, she knew.

'Welcome to your new role,' he said, ignoring her last remark, though his cold eyes flicked across her face in a manner she definitely didn't like. He handed her a clipboard. 'PR.'

'PR?' Jenna took the clipboard automatically, staring down at it.

'Public relations,' Eugenia chimed in from the table, overenunciating as if Jenna maybe didn't know what PR meant. Jenna restrained herself from flinging the clipboard at Eugenia's head.

'You'll sit in on the interviews,' Duncan said, ignoring Eugenia as always. 'Anything that's on that clipboard doesn't get discussed. Some reporter starts talking about any one of those bullet points? The interview is over. It's your job to make sure the band sits there and behaves, and that the reporters ask what they're supposed to ask and don't get creative. Got it?'

'I guess so,' Jenna said. She frowned at the clipboard. 'You do know I've never done PR before, right?'

Duncan glared at her. The back of her neck started to tingle a warning.

'Does this sound like a difficult job?' he asked, his voice quiet. Jenna hated the quiet voice. Everyone hated the quiet voice. Quiet and so very, very mean. It was as effective as a slap across the face.

'Uh, no, of course not,' she stammered, quaking despite herself.

She was relieved when he left, Eugenia with him – though not without throwing a warning sort of glare over her shoulder at Jenna.

Please, Jenna thought almost scornfully. *Like I'm afraid of you when your boyfriend is so creepy!*

She was getting her breathing back to normal when Sebastian walked into the kitchen, as immaculately turned out as ever. He unapologetically spent hours in the gym, slaving over his appearance. Unlike Tommy, who took a much lazier approach to fitness, meaning that he relied mostly on his metabolism and dissolute lifestyle.

'Good morning,' Sebastian said in his pleasant voice, his English accent by all accounts the real deal.

Jenna smiled her hello at him, and didn't object when he peered over her shoulder at the clipboard she held.

'I'm your PR person today,' she said. She liked Sebastian. He had been the first band member to talk to her like she was a person rather than an appendage of Duncan's, twitching malevolently among them. To be fair, only Tommy had really treated her that way. Richie and Nick had appeared largely indifferent.

'Ah, yes,' Sebastian said with a self-deprecating smile. 'My heterosexuality must be promoted at all costs. You should be prepared for me to make reference to various sleazy orgies involving numerous women. It works best if you jump in and try to cut me off.' His smile thinned. 'Much more believable.'

'Why don't you come out?' Jenna asked, not without sympathy. 'Wouldn't that be easier in the long run?'

Sebastian straightened, and moved over to pour himself a mug of coffee, giving Jenna ample time to kick herself in the noticeably cool silence. What business was it of hers whether Sebastian came out or not? Not to mention this was 1987. George Michael was all over the television singing 'I Want Your Sex' to various women. What did Jenna know about choosing to remain straight in the eyes of the world as a famous person?

It was almost cheering to think that despite everything, things had changed enough since 1987 that Lance Bass's announcement of his homosexuality could cause nary a ripple of backlash. In fact, if Jenna thought about it, it seemed to her that more boy-band members were gay than weren't.

'Have you been talking to Richie?' Sebastian asked after a moment. His voice was still pleasant enough on the surface. He stirred Sweet and Low into his coffee.

'No,' Jenna said. As far as she could tell, Richie didn't talk to anyone outside the band, for any reason. He was the prettiest of the four of them, objectively speaking – the youngest, and the most self-contained.

'So this is simply your unsolicited opinion, knowing nothing about me or my life, then?' His voice was crisp as he turned around to face her again, his dark gaze hard. 'A tidy solution for me, one I've obviously not considered? How thoughtful.'

Jenna cringed. 'I'm sorry,' she said. 'I wasn't trying to be . . .'

'You can't possibly understand,' he started, then stopped,

170

and shook his head. He let out a short laugh. 'It would kill my mum, if you want to know the truth. And even if I decided to do it anyway, I can't. All references to my preferred gender of sexual partner must be cleared through Duncan, according to the contract I signed. So I'm trapped either way.' He smiled, faintly. 'And none of this is any of your business.'

'I know it isn't.' Jenna was appalled at herself. 'I don't know what I was thinking.'

Sebastian raised his coffee mug in a mock salute.

'Why don't you get over Tommy?' he asked in the same polite tone. 'He's adored by millions, dates only super-models, and is actively rude to you. Why not pine for someone else, instead?'

Jenna closed her eyes, and sighed. 'I'm sorry,' she said again. 'Really.'

'I know,' Sebastian said. He sighed. 'I like you, too.'

Later, in the hotel suite, Jenna held on to her clipboard for dear life and wondered how they did it. She felt as if she'd been run through a blender, when all she'd had to do was check journalists in and out, and make sure no one talked about forbidden topics, like sexuality (Sebastian and Richie) or fistfights apropos of nothing (Nick) or tabloid pictures of supposedly engaged Tommy with certain young actresses (staged, Tommy had told her tersely). All she had to do was listen, and interrupt whenever necessary. She tried to channel the awesome CJ Craig from *The West Wing* while she did this. The band, meanwhile, had to somehow sound up and excited and interesting and *themselves* – for hours.

And here Jenna had always believed that being in a famous band must be glamorous.

Glamorous was not the first word that came to her mind as she spent hour after hour listening to the band answer the same questions over and over again. The journalists giggled and laughed and flirted, apparently unaware that their questions were not at all new or interesting. Sebastian and Richie had a running competition to see who could get the most laughs off the same, canned jokes. Nick would spontaneously change his accent in the middle of a sentence, while chain-smoking, to see if anyone would call him on it. Tommy, who began the day in a slouch against the sofa cushions, became more and more prone as the interviews wore on. By afternoon, he was practically reclining, propping his head up with one languid arm and stretching his long legs in front of him, while talking about nothing at length in the British accent that now sounded completely ridiculous to Jenna's ears.

He also spent most of the day staring at Jenna, with that brooding look of his, the one that shorted out her nerve endings and made her feel jittery.

The one that made her feel like prey.

But not, she could admit to herself, in a bad way.

There was no way he suddenly woke up one morning and found her irresistible. She actually laughed out loud at that, and had to cough to cover it when everyone else in the room looked at her.

'Excuse me,' she murmured, and tried to look deeply interested in Nick's sweet story about singing the new single to his grandmother which wasn't even true, and which she had already heard in excess of seven thousand times.

When the journalist was finally finished, and Jenna had escorted her from the suite, she was thrilled to see that according to her list, they were done with interviews for the day. She walked back inside to tell them so. The band reacted to the news predictably – they all raced from the room at top speed, off to stop telling lies and start living their lives, no doubt.

All except Tommy.

He didn't move.

He simply *reclined*. His gaze never left her.

'Don't you have somewhere to go?' Jenna asked, trying to keep her voice light. She wanted to tell him that she had stayed up into the wee hours almost every night since they'd talked, trying to record every single fact she knew about these months, and had reached a startling conclusion, but she couldn't. How would that conversation go? *Here's a list of everything that's happened since late August through next month – I'm very psychic. This is how I know that you will begin to experience a number of what look like accidents but are, I believe, attempts on your life. The first will be tomorrow night, when you are nearly hit by a car. No, no, I won't be the one pushing you, I will be saving you. The insanity isn't really insanity if you consider the fact I'm a time traveller.*

Yeah, right.

'There's some dinner somewhere.' Tommy shrugged. He had dropped the British accent. Jenna liked his real accent better. Warmer, unclipped. She wasn't sure when that had happened.

'You don't want to be late,' she said, but she didn't care if he was late. She felt spellbound by that almost angry look on his face, and the slow way he was getting to his feet then, never looking away.

'I'm expected to make a grand entrance,' Tommy said quietly. The suite seemed particularly, dangerously empty all around them. Jenna gulped down some air. Her feet felt fused to the carpet below them.

'Don't let me keep you,' she said nervously as he stalked across the room towards her. 'I have to call Ken anyway. He likes updates, you know, since he lost his secretary . . .' The babble died out as he stopped in front of her, forcing her to look up at him.

'This is driving me insane,' he said. Definitely with an angry undertone, which was completely unfair. What was she doing except a job she hadn't even wanted in the first place?

'That's pretty much how I've felt since I met you,' she replied, stung. 'And if you mention *Chevrolets* again, I won't be held accountable for my actions.'

'We are way past Chevys,' Tommy said gloomily, a tone that did not match the heat in his gaze.

'I don't have any idea what you're talking about, as usual,' Jenna said loftily.

'I know,' Tommy said. He sighed.

And then he reached over, slipped his warm hand around to cradle the nape of her neck in his palm, and fitted his mouth over hers.

15

God, she was sweet.

Jenna froze beneath him, and then started, opening her mouth as if to gasp.

Tommy took complete and shameless advantage, angling his mouth over hers for a better, deeper fit.

She was like cotton candy. Sweet but with a kick, and she went right to his head. He had only meant to kiss her, once or twice, to remind himself that he'd kissed her before and been bored by it.

Except he wasn't bored now.

Not at all.

She made the softest sound in the back of her throat, and something triumphant raced through him. His hands cradled her face, then traced shapes across her neck, and over the delicious curves of her body. He wanted her naked, and under him. Over him, next to him, he didn't care, he just wanted to be in her.

He thought he might have groaned then.

He put his mouth against her neck, and delighted in her shiver of response. He pulled her hips flush with his, and her eyes opened, dazed. He rocked into her, letting them both feel how hard he was. She was soft against him, and so sweet.

Then he took her mouth again, worrying that lush lower lip the way she'd done all day, then licking into her like she was cream. Like she was his.

She made another incoherent noise, and then she pushed him away, with the flats of her palms against his chest.

'What are you doing?' she asked him. He noted, with satisfaction, that her breathing was uneven and her pupils were dilated. Good.

'I thought it was obvious what I was doing.' He smiled. 'I can try and do it better, if you want.'

'But . . .' She searched his face, and frowned. 'Why?'

He didn't like the question. He reached over and toyed with a dark curl until she batted his hand away.

'You can't just go around kissing people,' she said, her voice stronger, her frown more pronounced. 'I don't know what game you're playing.'

'I am not playing a game,' he said, well on his way to being irritated. She brought it out in him. He was either awash in lust, or annoyed. Usually both.

'Yesterday you're ranting about cars and today . . .' She shook her head, which made her great mass of hair shake too, and slide around and over her shoulders, cascading towards her breasts. He found the sight inexpressibly

177

erotic, and shifted his stance to allow a little more breathing room.

'Yes,' he said. 'Today.'

Tommy had no idea what she was talking about, and he didn't care. She was close enough that he could smell soap and something darker, more mysterious, that he wanted to explore. Preferably with his mouth. So he did, leaning close and kissing his way along her lovely neck, letting her warmth seep into him, and around him, until his groin was throbbing and he thought he might throw her to the ground and bury himself inside her right then and there. God, he wanted to.

But she shoved him away again, and this time danced out of reach, behind the couch.

As if he was too proud to leap over it. He almost did. Her face was flushed, and her chest was heaving, and he knew she wanted him. He knew it.

'You want me,' he pointed out. Unnecessarily. 'Why push me away?'

'I hardly know you,' she retorted.

'That didn't stop you before.' It was all right to throw herself at Tommy Seer, the fantasy, but now that she knew more about him, she had some objection?

If possible, she went even redder.

'That was different,' she snapped. 'What is this? I understand about last time, I guess. You thought I was a groupie. You were trying to prove a point.'

'Last time I was trying to make sure you would do what I wanted you to do,' he said, without a shred of apology.

'Sure, okay, that's mercenary at best but I'm not going to throw stones—'

'This time has nothing to do with that,' he interrupted her. Some of his frustration boiled over. 'I want you. I don't know why, I don't know how, but I do.'

He was immediately aware that that was not the right thing to say. The temperature in the room seemed to plummet about thirty degrees.

'How romantic.' Her cheeks were still rosy, but her spine stiffened, and everything else was icy. *Great.*

'Jenna,' he began, trying to figure out a way to tell her what he meant that would lead to them writhing naked on the couch, which was something he was willing to do almost anything to accomplish, if he could figure out how to get her back to that dazed, wild-eyed state.

'You don't know why and you don't know how,' she continued in that same pissed-off tone. 'Every girl's dream.'

'I'm being honest with you,' he snapped at her.

'This is why you've been scowling at me and acting crazy, isn't it?' He watched the light dawn, and didn't like the way she stared at him. 'Oh, and now I get it. I'm a *Chevy.* That's another way of saying *beneath you.*'

'I wish you were beneath me,' he said, hearing the frustration in his own voice. 'Right now. On that couch. With a lot less talking.'

'How irresistible,' she said in that same voice, sarcasm dripping. 'For the small price of my self-respect, I can sleep with someone who thinks it's beneath him. Who

179

thinks that he deserves luxury cars, while I am a plodding Chevrolet.'

He didn't like any of it, especially the way she looked at him as if he had slapped her.

'Your self-respect,' he repeated. 'Where was that when you threw yourself at a total stranger? At least I know who you are.'

She flinched as if he'd hit her, and he felt about as bad as he imagined he would if he had.

He then proceeded to feel like the biggest asshole in the world when she looked away, and ran her hand across the mouth that he still wanted to ravage. Her lips looked swollen from his kisses, and her eyes were too dark, like she was fighting off tears. He wished he could take back what he'd said. He wished he knew why he cared so much in the first place, when he hadn't cared about much in far too long. He wished for a lot of things, none of which came true in the long, strained moments before she turned back to him.

'I have to meet with Ken,' she said, her voice even. He wondered what that cost her, because he could see the turmoil in her eyes. He still wanted to touch her, but he discovered to his amazement that his hard-on had subsided. He just wanted to hold her.

It was unbelievable.

It bordered on terrifying.

A case of unusual attraction was one thing. But this . . . this was crazy.

'I'll see you tomorrow,' she said, and he let her turn

around and walk away because he didn't know what else to do. Because she'd sucker-punched him and she didn't even know it.

He was still brooding about it later, ensconced in a private booth in the back of Manhattan's hottest club. At least he assumed it was Manhattan's hottest club – all he'd seen were the lines outside before being whisked off to his dinner of schmoozing.

Tommy hated schmoozing.

He also hated record-company executives, but he did not need Duncan's glower from across the table to remind him where his bread was buttered. He knew that he wasn't required to enjoy himself. All he had to do was sit, smile, and look like a rock star.

'I don't feel like a rock star tonight,' he muttered under his breath to Nick, who was slumped back against the banquette next to him. Sebastian and Richie had drawn the short straws, and were seated directly next to the two fat executives with their panting girlfriends. Which meant they were the ones who had to flirt and pretend to care.

'The great part of being a rock star is that it doesn't matter if you feel it or not, you still are,' Nick retorted from somewhere beneath the crooked fedora he wore. He tilted the hat back slightly. 'We're on top of the world, man. Why would you leave it? This is what we dreamed about.'

It wasn't the first time Nick had asked the question,

or one like it. Only Richie had shrugged off Tommy's intention to leave the band after their tour. Sebastian, naturally, had wanted to sit down and plot out how Tommy's departure could be milked for the best coverage, the most emotion, and therefore the most money. Nick had stopped speaking to Tommy for a tense week, maybe two. Then he'd started asking questions like this one.

'We dreamed about music first,' Tommy said. He shrugged, and forced himself to smile and wink at one of the giggling girlfriends. The music was so loud in the club that he knew Duncan couldn't overhear him, which was all that mattered.

'Because suddenly you're a purist,' Nick scoffed. 'Come on, Tommy. Give me a break. You can't tell me you haven't enjoyed what we have going on here.'

'Of course I have.' Tommy shrugged. 'But I want to do other things, too.'

'Phil Collins does solo projects *and* plays with Genesis,' Nick pointed out. 'Why do you have to break up the band?'

'You know why.' Tommy flicked a look across the table towards Duncan, who sat there with his beady gaze trained on Sebastian and Richie, like he was waiting for them to slip up and start making out right there at the table. 'He's had us on a leash since 1980.'

Nick shifted in his seat, agitated.

'But it's a good leash,' he said, his voice low and urgent. 'So what if you have to talk in a stupid accent? So what if he's in control of all the stupid shit? We're rich. Famous. How bad is it, really?'

'Nick—'

'Do you remember where we came from?' Nick demanded. 'That shitty fucking trailer park. We swore we'd do anything to make sure we never went back there.'

'And we did,' Tommy said evenly. 'But I don't want to be rich and famous if it means I can't be myself. Not any more.'

Nick shook his head.

'I don't even know who you are, man,' he said quietly. 'Nothing that you say makes sense.'

Before Tommy could respond, he was climbing to his feet and excusing himself from the table. Tommy watched him go, cutting through the crowd with his fake smile firmly in place. He and Nick weren't the same people they'd been all those years ago, true, but Tommy didn't think he was the one who'd changed. At heart, all he wanted was what he'd always wanted – his guitar and a few words. The Wild Boys were like a fun-show detour, with so much pomp and circumstance disguising the main thing – the only thing. The music.

He smiled again, and pretended to laugh along with some joke a record exec was telling, which he was just as happy he couldn't hear.

He didn't think it was so much to ask. He was tired of the pop-music spectacle, of synthesizers, of the absurd videos that seemed sometimes to overtake the songs. He was tired of band politics, of Sebastian's constant man-oeuvring, Richie's indifference, Nick's anger. He minded Duncan's leash more than he could say, and it surprised him that Nick didn't feel that way. Tommy thought there wasn't enough money in the world to make a cage feel like something besides a cage.

Lately Tommy had had a recurring fantasy, and it was a simple one. A stool, a stage. Just him and his guitar and the easy, quiet songs he'd written recently and had chosen not to share with his band mates. Music that borrowed from folk, and maybe a little bit of country, and fused it all together acoustically. He refused to accept that he couldn't have that, that no one wanted to listen to the kind of music he yearned to play.

He had to believe that there were other people out there as sick of the smoke and mirrors of Eighties music as he was. He was tired of all the histrionics of it – the elaborate costumes, the drama of the keyboards. He craved the simplicity of a voice plus a guitar and nothing else. No embellishments.

And he believed in himself, even if no one else did.

For some reason, Jenna's face swam into his mind then. Tommy smirked. Did his poor libido think that Jenna would support him in his quest for a different musical style? Yeah, sure. She wouldn't even sleep with him when she had the chance. Twice now. It was enough to give an international pop star, named 'irresistible' in any number of magazines, a complex. He wondered if it was deliberate, a strategy – if she knew, somehow, that she was the first woman to turn him down in ages. Maybe ever since he'd become famous, now that he thought about it.

He realized he didn't care. He could still taste her, smell

her. He felt himself harden slightly, and checked a sigh. The last thing he needed was for one of the record executives' girlfriends to think he had the hots for her. Not to mention his reaction was ridiculous. He was a grown man, not a high-school kid. Why couldn't he control this attraction? Why did she get to him when she wasn't even in the room?

'Tommy,' Duncan said then, breaking into his thoughts with that oily voice of his. 'Tell Rod and Jeremy what you were telling me today, about that sweet car of yours.' He grinned at the executives. 'A 1986 Testarossa Spider, gentlemen.'

Tommy thrust the damned woman out of his mind. Or tried to. He smiled like the trained seal he was, and leaned in.

'The Testarossa is a pain in the ass to drive around town,' he told them, his smile widening on cue as they all oohed and aahed, 'but get her free and clear on a highway at about seventy, and she's like a ballerina. Maybe later I'll take her out and show you.'

If he had to be a trained seal, he might as well do the best tricks.

16

Of all the times to seriously question her sanity, lurking on a street corner, waiting for Tommy Seer to happen by and into what Jenna knew would be a near-death experience, was not that time.

The time for questioning had long since come and gone – *that* had been the night before, when she'd sprawled across the futon in the bright yellow apartment, watching *Moonlighting* and *thirtysomething* and wishing that she could bring herself to hate Tommy Seer.

Seriously.

Because if she didn't hate him as she should, then what was she going to do? How could she accept the fact that she wanted someone so desperately, with so little regard for herself, that even after he'd humiliated her and mocked her and made her almost burst into tears, she had still wanted him? She wanted him even now. She'd wanted to be beneath him on that couch, with a desperate ache that had only intensified as they'd stood there, and had not subsided in the slightest, hours later.

She still felt it now, as she lurked in the shadows outside Tommy's personal apartment, far away from the shared accommodation at the town house in the Village. She had a feeling that the term 'apartment' meant something different when one was a pop star of international renown and lived in a fancy building on Central Park West. Tommy Seer, she was sure, did not maintain a bright yellow studio with a pull-out futon at such an august address. She imagined he inhabited one of those absurd New York apartments that were forever appearing on shows like *Law & Order* or *Sex and the City* – all shining wood floors, high ceilings, eat-in kitchens, extra dining rooms, and several bedrooms. Jenna had never, personally, met anyone who could afford to live in or near such places, since they probably started at four or five million dollars. Which was nothing to a rock star, of course.

Jenna had decided to watch over Tommy to see whether or not her theory was true. She'd gone over her notes again and again, and she couldn't believe she'd never noticed it before, but there had been a pattern of incidents leading up to his death. He'd nearly been hit by a car out in front of his apartment building, and after that had had one mishap after another, all of them in the weeks leading up to that night on the Tappan Zee Bridge.

Except, what if they weren't mishaps? What if someone had been trying to kill him that whole time?

What with the kissing and the whole time-travel thing,

Jenna hadn't felt she could advance this theory to Tommy. Especially not when he'd spent the day in what sounded like excruciatingly boring meetings as the band prepared for their first video from the new album. The whole band had looked frazzled and hollow-eyed at the end of the day, and Jenna hadn't had the necessary spine to grab Tommy, inform him they would not be discussing the events of the previous night, and then launch into some explanation about why she thought he might want to be extra careful crossing streets tonight.

Maybe it wasn't that she lacked the spine. Maybe it was the fact that if she'd actually tried to tell him any of the things she suspected, he would no longer look at her with those green eyes so hot and intense. He would look at her like she was a psycho. Maybe the truth was that she couldn't bear the thought of it.

So the obvious solution was to watch out for him herself.

Yes, Jenna was essentially stalking Tommy. Across the country in Indiana, the little girl she'd been (and was? How did this time thing work?) was no doubt weeping over her Wild Boys record collection and wishing she could be sitting outside Tommy's apartment. Jenna remembered those tears, and the force of loving Tommy – it had taken over her whole body, like an extended flu. Jenna remembered believing with all her heart that if she could only place herself in his proximity, she could make him fall in love with her.

But life was much more complicated than she'd understood back then. Sometimes proximity was far more confusing than it should be. Sometimes it made everything worse.

At least Tommy lived on a convenient street. Jenna could sit across from his building on a bench outside the park and stalk to her heart's content without raising the ire or notice of the doorman. After all, this was a public park bench in Manhattan. She was free to sit there as long as she liked, enjoying the September evening. And it might well take hours, since she had no idea what time the supposed accident occurred. She only knew it happened sometime tonight.

It was beautiful out. Clear, warm, yet with that slight snap in the air that promised the coming fall. There was the suggestion of autumn in the gentle breeze that ruffled Jenna's hair every now and again. She was comfortable in the jeans and sweatshirt she'd thrown on after work, complete with slouchy socks and Keds.

The problem was, she had nothing to do while she sat there but think, and the last thing she wanted to do was think. Because there was only one thing to think about, and she was tired of it. Because she couldn't seem to stop herself from fantasizing, from pretending that she hadn't stopped him last night, from wondering what might have happened if she'd stayed silent, if she'd pulled him closer rather than pushed him away . . .

The truth was, Aimee had been right. Jenna understood that now, and didn't want to. She'd used the fantasy of Tommy Seer to keep herself protected, to hide. And the worst part was, she hadn't just done it after Adam had

189

left her. That was understandable. Excusable. But Jenna finally realized that she'd done it long before her engagement had broken up, too. Maybe not consciously. Not deliberately. But no real, live, flesh-and-blood man could live up to the Tommy in her head. Real people were never so understanding, so perfect.

On some level, hadn't she kept Adam at a distance? Always focused on what *he* was doing – was he going to propose? Was he coming home at a reasonable hour? Was he completely emotionally available? But where was *she* in all of that? Hadn't she been hiding then, too? Intimacy was terrifying. Dangerous. Hard. Making their whole relationship about Adam's flaws and needs and failures had, on some level, kept her heart safe. She had never let him penetrate to the secret core of her, the place where she hid the truest part of herself. She'd stayed out of reach, and complained that the man she was supposed to marry didn't understand her, couldn't satisfy her, wasn't enough for her somehow. Who could be?

And understanding all of that, however unpleasant, made her understand Adam in a new way, too. He deserved to be a *necessity* for Marisol, the yoga instructor. Didn't everyone deserve to be a necessity? Shouldn't that be the point, really?

Meeting the real Tommy Seer had sent her into turmoil. She could admit it. First, he wasn't that fantasy in her mind that she'd used as a security blanket all these years. He was real. He wasn't anything close to perfect. In fact, he was mean sometimes. Cruel. Funny, too, and surprisingly witty. She'd never thought about him being *witty*. Because he'd basically been nothing more than her own voice in her own head, for all those years. She had thrown herself at a man, expecting the fantasy, and she was lucky it hadn't gone farther than it had that first night, because then she'd *really* hate herself.

But now . . . She wasn't sure what game he was playing, with his behaviour lately and that scene in the hotel suite that still made her pulse pound when she thought about it. And it wasn't as if she could think of anything else. She felt marked by him, and the craziest part was that something in her thrilled at the idea. She didn't know what he was doing, or why, but what she did know was that she was falling in love with him, and this time it was for the person he actually was. The cranky, pissy, brooding, possibly insane person it turned out Tommy Seer was. She didn't understand where the chemistry had come from, but it had nearly overwhelmed her in the hotel. She'd thought she'd felt the heat of him before, but that had been a pale imitation.

Suddenly, he wanted her back.

And it scared the hell out of her.

Which forced her to face another unpleasant truth – and why not, what better place for unpleasant truths than a park bench in the middle of a stalking expedition – and that was that she was as skittish about the real Tommy Seer as she'd been about the other real men she'd dated. As she'd been about Adam. Which meant, she was pretty sure, that she had severe commitment issues. Emotional problems, as Adam himself had often accused her in their drawn-out fights. Because the fact that she was currently sitting in 1987, having met and touched the real Tommy Seer, was, to put it mildly, an anomaly. The reality was, she'd been using the fantasy Tommy as a shield. It was sad that she was only able to realize it now, while she was trying *not* to use fantasy Tommy as a shield against real Tommy.

Jenna knew with some deep, internal wisdom that if she had sex with this man, this real live living person, with all of his complications and needs and flaws, it would change her on some fundamental level. There would be no waking up the next morning and feeling *normal*. There would be no dismissing it, or minimizing it. She understood that Tommy was different – *more*, somehow. More demanding. More powerful. It had something to do with that raging chemistry that had sprung up between them, that she'd felt flood every cell of her body with the same glorious, terrifying heat.

He had marked her with no more than a few kisses. What would *sex* do? Could she survive it? Did she want to?

She was positive that she was much too afraid to find out.

And equally, recklessly certain that she wanted to do it anyway.

Hours later, Jenna was stiff and cranky and happy she had no access to a cellphone, because the situation begged for some ill-advised texting. WHERE R U, JACKASS? for example.

It was well after eleven when she saw the flashy sports car, black and sinister-looking, pull up to the kerb in front of Tommy's building. Early, really, considering the fact that Tommy was a superstar and not a worker bee. Jenna sat up straight on her bench, ignoring the numbness in her butt and the stiffness of her limbs.

One of the doormen raced to the driver's side, and Tommy climbed out of the low-slung car, unfolding himself with his customary grace, so unexpected and mouth-watering in such a tall man. Jenna knew she should have been able to recognize the brand of car at a glance – it was that kind of car, the sort that screamed its pedigree with every gorgeous line – but all she really saw was Tommy. As usual. He exchanged a few words with the doorman, and smiled. Then, instead of turning towards his building and heading inside, he stopped. His head swivelled around, and he scanned the darkness. Jenna caught her breath, in the shadows. It was almost as if—

He frowned.

Directly at *her*.

Jenna didn't understand how he'd known, but he was clearly looking right at her, standing with his hands on his narrow hips. He looked annoyed. But not surprised.

Cars rushed past him on Central Park West, shooting uptown and downtown in speeding packs, but he was looking across them as if he barely noticed them. And he pinned her into her seat with the force of his glare.

It was like the city faded. The lights changed, and it

was as if the street lamps were only there to shine on his dark head. The horns and the music and the hum of traffic disappeared, and there was only Tommy. Jenna drifted up and on to her feet, then over to the kerb without meaning to move, as if he'd called her somehow.

His frown deepened. He looked as if he intended to take a step, which would have put him directly in the path of oncoming cars.

And then she remembered: he was in danger.

Was this her fault? Would he have walked inside if she wasn't there? Would he have been safe?

But she didn't have time to think about the ramifications of *that*. She put her hands up in the international sign for STOP, and, when there was a break in the flow of traffic, ran across to him.

'You have to get out of the street,' she said, her heart thudding hard in her chest. 'You have to watch out—'

'What are you doing here? Why were you sitting on that bench?' He shook his head, as if shaking off the strange spell they'd been under. He was muttering, and he sounded pissed off about it.

Jenna didn't think there was time for his muttering. She took his arm and tugged. His attention was riveted on her hands, where they touched the bare skin of his wrist. She wished he didn't generate so much heat – it was distracting.

'I'm serious, Tommy.' She was proud of herself for sounding it. She was hardly breathless at all. 'You can interrogate me on the sidewalk.'

'You don't really think you can move me if I don't want

194

to move.' His eyebrows arched up. Heat and annoyance and humour simmered in his gaze. 'You do, don't you?'

'Tommy, please,' Jenna begged, her nerves screaming at her and making the back of her neck tingle.

Tommy laughed, throwing his head back so the strong column of his throat shone in the street lights, and for a moment everything slowed down. But Jenna was looking behind him at the headlights which were accelerating through the stoplight on the corner, and she knew this was it, that the car would hit him and it was her fault after all because if she hadn't been there, would he still be in the street? Would he have paid attention to his surroundings rather than to her?

But then she thought, *who cares why*, and she threw herself against him with everything she had, knocking him backwards and off his feet – knocking them both over and down towards the concrete sidewalk, down as the car roared past her, so close she could feel it just beyond her skin – so close that if she had waited even one second more, it would have smashed into the both of them.

Safe! she thought triumphantly, but that was in the split second before they smacked into the ground with all of the force she'd put into tackling him.

There was a single, silent beat as they hit the ground, tangled in each other. Her knees made contact, scraped. She felt more than heard him grunt as he crashed against the concrete. She thought maybe their heads cracked together, and she landed in an undignified heap on top of him with their torsos on the sidewalk and their legs poking out into the street.

But they were alive.

Which was when the pain started, bursting into flames along her knees and the place on her forehead where she must have cracked into his jaw.

'Jesus Christ,' Tommy said thickly. 'What the hell was that?'

And then the yelling started, and things got *really* crazy.

17

Of course, Tommy insisted on taking her home.

He worried that maybe the bump to his head had been harder than he'd thought, because the moment he'd informed her – not asked her, informed her – that he would be taking her home, he knew it was a bad idea.

The night was already absurd. The press taking pictures, the cops summoned to listen gravely to the story of a near hit-and-run no one would ever be able to solve, an unnecessary trip to the hospital for exactly two stitches on the back of his head and bandages for Jenna's scraped knees and bumped forehead, and there he was at two in the morning announcing he would escort her home like they'd been on a date.

And he really wished they had been on a date. That was the worst part. Everything involving Jenna was the worst part. And here he was, begging for more. He disgusted himself.

'I don't need an escort,' was what she told him. Scowling.

They were in a curtained-off section of the emergency room at St Luke's Roosevelt, and he was awash in irritating protective instincts. His mood had not been improved by Duncan's inevitable arrival – he didn't know who had even called him, he suspected the doormen in his building were on the payroll – or the subsequent medical attention. It worsened as he took in Jenna's body language – arms crossed over her chest, hair scraped into a knot on the back of her head, shoulders hunched over like she was trying to ward him off.

She was trying to keep *him* at a distance.

It made him crazy. It made him want to leap across the small space and show her exactly what he thought of *distance*, and what the hell was his problem that all he could think about was leaping over furniture? What was he, an animal?

'I didn't ask if you needed an escort, I told you I'm doing it,' he snapped at her, unreasonably enraged. At his own response to her, mostly, but he decided that was her fault too. Might as well snap at her.

'Not really interested in the alpha-male thing, thanks,' she threw back at him with extreme snottiness, but she didn't storm off and leave him sitting there on his gurney, she just planted her hands on her hips and glared.

Tommy interpreted this as a victory.

'Why were you sitting in front of my building?' he asked, watching her closely.

She shrugged, and then, suddenly, she looked shifty. Uncomfortable. Had she been waiting for him? If that car hadn't come at them – and Tommy blamed too much alcohol and a bad driver no matter how many times Jenna claimed it had been headed right for them – what would have happened? Would she have come upstairs with him? Was that what she'd been waiting for? An invitation?

Somehow, he didn't think so, despite his body's enthusiastic response to that idea. Which made him that much more surly.

'Are you going to answer the question?' he asked when she didn't speak. He swung his legs slightly as he sat on the high bed, bracing himself with his hands against the edge.

'I don't know,' she said, still not looking at him. The bustle and noise of the hospital swam around them, beeping machines and moans of pain, quiet conversations and occasional announcements, and then the two of them alone in the midst of it.

'You don't know if you're going to answer the question or you don't know why you were there?' he asked, his voice still light. 'Because I'm happy to come up with my own explanations.'

'Really.' She looked at him then. Her dark eyes measured him.

'Of course.' He shrugged. 'I'm Tommy Seer. You certainly aren't the first groupie to sit for hours outside my house, desperate for a glimpse of me. Some girls wait for days.'

A smile tugged at her lips. He wanted her to laugh more than he could remember wanting anything else.

'I'm sure that's true,' she said. 'But I don't think I count as a groupie any more. Do I?'

'I'm not in charge of groupie classifications,' he said, trying not to smile himself. 'I just know them when I see them.' She laughed then, and it made Tommy's chest swell. It was ridiculous, and it wasn't even a big laugh. More of a rueful sort of laugh.

Was he *categorizing* her laughter? What was *wrong* with him?

'Zombie eyes,' she said. Her brows arched. 'Isn't that what you told me? Isn't that the usual way to tell?'

'There are zombie eyes, sure, and then there's sitting outside my house in the dark all night,' Tommy replied. 'It's hard to argue with a good stalking. It pretty much speaks for itself.'

'For all you know I was there for exactly thirty seconds,' Jenna pointed out. 'Hardly stalking.'

'Were you?' He dared her. Because somehow, he knew she'd been there longer. He just knew.

She grinned. 'You'll never know, will you?'

'Why were you there?' He laughed when she sighed. 'Why can't you tell me?'

'I already did.' She shook her head. 'I had some thinking to do, and a park bench seemed like a great place for it. I don't know.'

'I think you do,' he suggested, his voice going lower. 'It's a big city, Jenna. There are thousands of benches. What made you pick that one?'

She met his gaze then, with a challenging sort of expression in her eyes. Her chin tilted up.

'You seem to think you know.' She crossed her arms

over her front again. In defence. 'Why don't you tell me?'

And he would have – in graphic detail – but the curtain was tossed back without ceremony and the doctor hurried in, with Duncan and a tight-mouthed Eugenia in tow.

'Darling!' Eugenia cried in carrying tones, the better to alert the waiting journalists, no doubt. 'I was so worried! I only *just* heard the news!'

She rushed to his side without sparing a glance for Jenna, who, Tommy thought, looked entirely too relieved. *Just wait*, he promised her silently, suffering through one of Eugenia's overwrought embraces because the doctor was watching. *I'm not done with you yet.*

'Practise your smile,' Duncan told him, in a pleasant tone that Tommy assumed was for the doctor's benefit. 'There's a crowd out there.'

'They think it's a publicity stunt,' Eugenia said crisply, the doctor clearly beneath her notice. 'Lead singer in peril, and so on.' She looked from Duncan to Tommy. 'You don't really think that car was *trying* to hit you, do you?'

'Yes,' Jenna said firmly from her corner, even as Tommy shook his head.

'No,' he said, with a quelling look her way. 'I think it was an accident.'

'Doesn't make any difference,' Duncan said, dismissing the entire incident with a wave of his hand. 'You get to look cute, wounded, and brave. The fans will eat it up.'

Tommy forced a smile. That made him sound like a Cabbage Patch Kid, or something else equally toothless and inane. Duncan did wonders for his self-esteem.

201

'Great,' he said, and managed to keep himself from slapping Eugenia's talons off his shoulders.

'And you,' Duncan said, his tone changing as he turned towards Jenna. 'I don't know what you were doing there, but this needs to spin as *Tommy saved by his staff*, not *Tommy with random girl*. Do you get me?'

'Absolutely,' Jenna said, much too quickly for Tommy's taste. 'In fact, I think I'll slip out the back while Tommy faces the press, so there's no confusion.'

'And then it looks like I have something to hide,' Tommy argued smoothly, without meaning to speak. 'They all know I came in with a woman. Why would you slip away if you were only my assistant? It looks as if you're avoiding my fiancée.'

'Touché,' Jenna said grimly. He could feel her glare, but he didn't look at her. He was too busy trying to keep his smirk at bay.

'Good thinking,' Duncan said, rubbing his chin. 'We'll all leave together.'

'Everyone wants to make sure you're alive and in one piece,' Eugenia crooned, still touching him, the very model of the supportive fiancée.

'You're ready to go,' the doctor said then, in a diffident voice, evidently intimidated by Duncan. Or maybe by all of them. Tommy forgot in moments like this that he was supposed to be impressive himself. It was one more benefit of self-loathing, his constant companion.

'Let's do this,' Duncan growled. His gaze swept over Tommy, and hardened.

Tommy stared back at him blandly and buttoned up his shirt.

Jenna, naturally, was staring at the floor, her expression shuttered.

'Try to look pathetic and heroic, Tommy,' Duncan snarled as the doctor threw the curtain back once again. 'Instead of pissed off, if you think you can manage it.'

He not only managed it, he rocked it. Anything to make it end, so he could escape his supposed fiancée and her cloying, faked attentions. And then he'd literally manhandled Jenna into the back of a taxi, jumped in after her, and fled.

'That did not hurt,' he said, again, as she rubbed at her arm and glared daggers at him.

'It's my arm. I get to decide if it hurts or not.' She sniffed in disgust. 'And by the way, I know you're famous and all, but you can't go around physically *forcing* someone—'

'I helped you into the cab,' he interrupted, in a bored tone. When really, he was enjoying himself. 'It's called chivalry. I did not *physically force* anything.'

'You grabbed my arm. It was not chivalrous at all. I think I might have bruises. And then you shoved me into the back of a taxi.' She glared. 'Completely unacceptable.'

'If you were hurt,' he said in a reasonable voice, 'you wouldn't be giving me such a hard time, would you?'

'And now I understand the rise of political correctness,' she snapped. She shook her head. 'What are you, a Neanderthal?'

'I feel like a Neanderthal when I'm around you,' he muttered. He frowned. 'What did you say? Political what?'

'Never mind.' She turned away and faced the front of the cab. 'I could have taken a cab by myself.'

'Jenna.' He waited until she looked at him, reluctantly. 'I think you saved my life. The least I can do is make sure you get home all right.'

That shut her up. Although he was pretty sure he could hear her mind racing as they sat there in tense silence. The cab shot across town in the usual fits and starts, even so late at night. Tommy didn't know why he was so insistent that he see her home. The more she made it clear she didn't want him to do it, the more he took perverse pleasure in doing it anyway.

He'd been kidding about the Neanderthal thing, but now he wondered. Maybe it was true. Maybe he'd gone completely prehistoric.

The cab pulled up on a quiet enough street in the wilds of the distant Upper East Side, and Tommy followed her out into the night and then into one of the buildings. It was a smaller building, no more than five storeys. It wasn't dumpy, exactly, but it bore no resemblance to his own breathlessly fancy building or even the quiet elegance of the town house. It was a place where regular people lived.

They went through two security doors and up flight after flight of stairs. When they reached the top, she was red in the face and short of breath. He was too, to his shame, and he wondered if it was time to take Sebastian's commitment to the gym more seriously. They stared at each other on the landing, and Tommy couldn't help but think of other activities that would lead to the two of them in the same sweaty, breathless condition. Preferably with fewer clothes on.

'Stop staring at my mouth,' she ordered him. Her voice sounded prim, but her expression was not.

'I was staring at your ass all the way up the stairs,' he told her deliberately, enjoying the way her eyes darkened, with temper or desire, he didn't much care. Is that better?'

'This is my door,' she said, waving at the one she stood before. 'You can go now.'

'My mother taught me to always see a lady *inside* her door,' Tommy told her, laughing down at her.

'I don't believe you,' she said, but he saw her swallow. He stepped closer, to see what she'd do, and he wasn't disappointed. She jumped, skittish, and edged away from him.

But not *too* far away from him.

'I'm lying,' he said, almost smiling. 'My mother had no interest in manners. She was more into truckers and construction workers. Why don't you open the door?' That last came out softly, more like a whisper. A plea.

Her eyes widened, and she stepped away again, only to find herself backed into her own front door. Tommy stepped closer, so that if she took a deep breath her breasts would brush the planes of his chest, and settled one arm over her head. That brought them face to face. Lips nearly touching lips.

'I don't want this,' she breathed, but her pupils were

huge and her nipples hardened into little peaks beneath her sweatshirt, and they both knew she was lying.

'Why not?' he asked lazily. He used his free hand to trace a pattern along the exposed skin south of her ear, and felt her pulse skip and hammer against her neck.

'It doesn't matter why,' she told him. She was barely forming the words aloud. He had to lean in to hear her. 'It just matters that I don't want to.'

'So why did you come all the way across the city to sit outside my building?' he asked, in the same soft voice. She shook her head, as if she wanted to escape him but lacked, somehow, the will. 'Why did you wait for me?'

'You're lucky I did,' she told him, her eyes flashing, and she wiggled backward as if she hoped the door might bend behind her and put more space between them. She turned her head away from his touch.

'That's me,' Tommy agreed in a murmur, leaning in to catch the scent and heat of her skin. 'I'm a lucky guy.'

He put his mouth where his fingers had been, hot and wet against the line of her neck, the curve of her jaw. She made a sound that caught in her throat, then became a moan. He threaded his hands into the heavy mass of her hair, like silk around his fingers, and tilted her head back, exposing her full mouth and her lashes that fluttered closed. It would be so easy to prove her a liar, to settle his mouth against hers, to press himself into the inviting cradle of her body. But, instead, he ignored the roar of his own body, and waited.

Her breath was ragged. She opened her eyes. Her pupils

were dilated, and he could feel the shiver that snaked through her.

'Goodnight, Jenna,' he said.

She blinked, confused. He leaned over and kissed her gently, chastely, on the forehead. He heard her suck in a breath, then release it in a rush.

'What are you . . . ?'

He liked the stammer in her voice. The thickness.

When he stepped back, she sagged against the door, and grabbed the frame to hold herself up. She looked dazed. He liked the fact that he'd made her look that way without actually kissing her mouth.

Like hell she didn't want him.

'I'm not going to sleep tonight,' he told her, with very male satisfaction he didn't try to hide. His smile was almost cruel. 'Why should you?'

18

Just as Jenna remembered, and had once upon a time breathlessly assembled into a scrapbook, the papers were abuzz with Tommy's near-death experience. Ken Dollimore was beside himself with joy that he could infuse the station's coverage of 'the event' with real commentary from 'an anonymous source at the scene', and Video TV launched into 'Tommygate' with round-the-clock coverage – above and beyond what the situation merited, in Jenna's opinion.

Jenna was somewhat less delighted, a fact she had time to consider as she made the trek from Ken Dollimore's office towards the warehouse down near Wall Street where the Wild Boys were filming their latest video. Fall had swept in as October began, kicking out the meandering remains of Indian summer and treating the city to the cold winds and rain that heralded the coming winter. More than this, the gloomy weather reminded Jenna that Tommy only had a few weeks left to live.

She knew that the 'accidents' kept happening, until the final one. The trouble was, she wasn't exactly sure *when* they happened. Which meant that she had no option but to trail around after Tommy even more than she already did. Which should have been fine, except her resistance to him waned more and more every day. Or maybe it was that her desire for him expanded, something she would have said once was impossible.

She was forced, in the absence of Aimee, to give herself a talking-to on this subject as the cab lurched down Broadway in the middle of the usual midday Manhattan chaos. The rain drummed against the roof of the taxi, and miserable-looking pedestrians slogged down the grey sidewalks outside the foggy window. Jenna wrapped herself tighter in the wide-shouldered, oversized plaid atrocity that had been the only fall-coat option in Aunt Jen's closet, and settled back against the seat.

Why was she resisting Tommy the first place, Jenna demanded of herself with all the Aimee-esque concern she could muster? Hadn't she loved this man since she was a pre-teen? Hadn't she made her entire adult life a shrine to the fantasy of his perfection? Hadn't she found her own long-term boyfriend and short-term fiancé lacking, in comparison to that fantasy? Hadn't she accepted the fact, just last week if memory served, that she had been hiding from everyone else and the whole world in her fantasy of Tommy Seer and who she wanted him to be?

So why, after he had overcome his initial reluctance

which, no matter how embarrassing to herself, she under-stood, and more to the point after *travelling through time* to meet him, was she now desperately trying to keep him at arm's length like some tragic, dithering virgin? Sure, she had issues with commitment. But it wasn't as if Tommy had proposed marriage. He hadn't proposed anything at all, in point of fact. He didn't need to propose something – all he had to do was touch her and her body went up in flames.

So what was her problem? It didn't make sense to keep saying no.

The fact was, on some level, she didn't believe that he really wanted her. But she couldn't get her head around the way he touched her. She'd experienced the Tommy-faking-it version before, and it had been nothing like this. It had been colder, more distant. It had been nothing so . . . combustible.

And she'd certainly never felt like this before. Not about Adam. Not about anyone. Not even about her own fantasy version of Tommy himself. Even *that* paled in comparison to the reality.

She tried to relax into the seat behind her, but her shoulders refused to come down from around her ears. Or maybe that was the effect of the ubiquitous shoulder pads, which made her feel like she was in a Star Trek uniform.

The thing was, she didn't think she was in 1987 by chance. Unless, of course, she really was locked away in Bellevue and this was a delusion – but that merely meant this was the only reality her poor, broken brain could handle, so it all ended up the same.

Jenna wasn't a particularly religious person. She'd been raised mildly Protestant, and celebrated Christmas, and otherwise didn't spend a great quantity of time thinking about it. Truth be told, she wasn't sure what she believed about God, or fate, or destiny, or the universe, or karma, or whatever else.

But she didn't think that it could be an accident that, of all the people in the world who might have been in that supply closet at the exact moment the lightning hit, it had been her. The one person who knew down to the last nit-picking detail what Tommy Seer had done with his last weeks on earth. The one person who was invested enough in Tommy Seer that she would stay by his side and try to help him, rather than, for example, heading back home to Indiana for a heart-to-heart chat with her former self – a trip that could not only change the course of her own personal history, but could conceivably allow her to mete out a little justice to some of the bullies of her junior high school.

The fact that it had never crossed Jenna's mind to do this – or to buy Microsoft stock, or do any of the other things which would make her own life better or different – had to mean something.

Didn't it?

The truth was, she didn't think the universe – or God, or fate, or whatever had sent her back in time, and she didn't care who or what it was – *cared* if she slept with

Tommy. But by the same token, she couldn't bring herself to believe that the *purpose* of her trip was to finally get it on with the object of her desire. Because that was just ridiculous. The purpose of her trip had to be to save Tommy. To stop that car from going over the bridge. This unexpected mutual attraction was one more obstacle, that was all.

You make everything so much more convoluted than it needs to be, the Aimee voice in her head said softly. *This is not an obstacle, Jenna. You only want it to be.*

Maybe the problem was that Jenna kept waiting for the other shoe to drop. Waiting for reality to reassert itself. Because the reality was that he was *Tommy Seer*. He dated supermodels in line to the British throne. She was nothing more or less than a regular old New Yorker in her midthirties. She wasn't ugly. On good days she thought she was pretty cute. But she wasn't the kind of cute that attracted superstars, and she knew it.

Maybe she was waiting for Tommy to realize that simple truth himself. And maybe she was protecting herself, too, because Jenna didn't know what would become of her if he came to that inevitable realization, say, five seconds after sleeping with her.

Because if she weren't so scared about getting hit in the head with that dreaded other shoe, it would make all the sense in the world to start sleeping with Tommy. What better way to make sure she was with him night and day, alert to the danger he didn't even know was stalking him?

Too bad she was far too alert to the danger *she* was in.

* * *

'This video is particularly asinine,' Tommy said in an amused undertone. 'I think that the video for "Once You Might, Twice Tonight" was by far the most absurd, but this one is coming in a strong second.'

He was sitting in full make-up, complete with drawn-on tattoos all across his face, as the set was being prepared for yet another take of all four Wild Boys, who were expected to crawl across the floor – covered in scarves and sinuous, half-naked models – in full battle regalia that was both futuristic and vaguely reptilian. All this while lip-syncing and attempting to look seductive, naturally.

Up above them, huge steel cages hung from precarious-looking hooks. Jenna knew that the Wild Boys would each spend some quality time in those cages, getting his own moment in the sun for his section of the fan base, but she knew that from her memories of the finished product – it hadn't happened yet in the shoot.

'This video was—*will be* fantastic,' Jenna said confidently, without looking at Tommy. 'One of the best in the Wild Boys catalogue. I have a feeling.'

'I can't help thinking that all of this takes away from the song, somehow,' he said after a moment. He shrugged. 'Don't you think? What's wrong with us *singing* the song, instead of performing kabuki theatre?'

'This is the Eighties.' Jenna smiled. 'And nobody does Eighties kabuki video better than the Wild Boys.'

'I'm not sure that's a compliment,' Tommy said after a moment. He sprawled in his chair, his legs stretched out before him, as if he was some indolent princeling. Jenna, meanwhile, knew perfectly well she was sitting as if she'd chosen to carry a selection of hot pokers with her, lodged in an intimate place. She tired herself out, she thought with an internal sigh, and of course, he thought it was funny that she was sitting there like some prim schoolmarm. She could tell he thought it was funny by that crook in the corner of his mouth, the one that was so much warmer than a smirk.

'You're good at what you do,' she said. 'Of course it's a compliment.' He shifted in his seat.

'What would you think if I changed what I do?' he asked.

'You mean, if you became a car salesman?' Jenna replied drily. 'I don't think that would be the best use of your skills, to be honest.'

'Not exactly what I meant.' He looked at the set. 'What if I wanted to play a different kind of music?'

'Well,' Jenna said, frowning as she thought it over. Did he mean to go all jazzy, the way Sting had after The Police? Not the worst career move in the world. 'The Wild Boys—'

'Not the Wild Boys. Me. I told you, I want to leave the band.' He sighed. 'I want to do something different. Something less—'

He broke off, and indicated his face paint with his fingers.

'Then you should,' she said, staunchly. 'You should do what you want to do. You certainly have the talent for it.'

'But that doesn't mean anyone will want to hear it,' Tommy said. His gaze was intense. 'Maybe I'm only good at pageant and kabuki theatre, after all. Maybe I shouldn't want anything more than that.'

Jenna ached for him in ways she didn't wish to explore. She reached over and put her hand on his, and felt him twitch in surprise. It was the first time in a long while that she'd touched him first, and they both took a breath, then another.

'I think,' she said, and looked him full in the face, so there could be no mistake, 'that you'd be wonderful. No matter what you sing, or how.'

He looked almost taken aback, as if he hadn't expected her to be that direct. His green eyes looked almost dazed. She hoped it was because of her sincerity, and not because he suspected she'd succumbed to the groupie zombie virus once again. She knew she hadn't. She knew she believed in him. The real him.

'Jenna . . .' he said, her name little more than a breath.

'Places!' someone yelled then, and they both jumped.

Tommy flipped his hand over, capturing hers in his much bigger one. He didn't say a word, he only held her hand for a breathless instant, the warmth from his palm sinking into her skin like ink.

Then he got up and walked towards the set without looking back.

Jenna sighed, and looked around the set, trying to concentrate on the various people running here and there, because she knew that all the bodyguard types in the romantic suspense novels she read were always looking around, always watching, always on high alert for any hint of danger. And even though she felt a bit flushed with the pleasure of connecting with Tommy like that, she still had to protect him. That was the reason she'd come back in time. It had to be.

Scowling, she watched the Wild Boys assemble themselves according to the director's orders, with Tommy front and centre and the other three some distance behind, still enmeshed in the models. She let her gaze drift. To the windows, and then back up to those heavy cages.

And that was when she saw it.

She frowned, and squinted – not sure.

The biggest of the cages was rocking back and forth, right up there above the Wild Boys – but not as if there was a wind. Not in a controlled way at all, the way she knew it would rock when the band was in it. It was almost as if—

'WATCH OUT!' Jenna screamed at the top of her voice, leaping to her feet and lunging towards the set. 'It's going to fall! It's going to fall!'

But it was too late, even as she ran. Even as she screamed out the alarm, she could see it happening.

The cage separated from the hook with a screeching noise, not in slow motion at all, and dropped like a stone towards the set below.

Towards Tommy.

19

'I think you have to accept the fact that someone really is trying to kill you, and that was their second attempt,' Jenna said in that bossy voice of hers, which, unaccountably, Tommy found adorable.

She was frowning and generally vibrating with tension in the back of his limo, and Tommy had the sense that if she weren't still afraid to touch him, she would be fretting over him like some kind of mother hen. All hands and worry, like mothers – generally speaking, not his – were supposed to.

He found that cute, too.

'Things happen on sets,' he said nonchalantly. 'And on city streets, too. No one is trying to kill me.'

'You're the one who told me that you thought Duncan was—' she began, her voice cracking with temper. With *concern*, he realized. For *him*.

'I know what I told you.' Tommy sighed. He ran his hands over his face, scrubbed clean of the day's make-up

– too clean, in fact, so that it felt reddened to the touch. 'And I'm not a big fan of leaping out of the way of various heavy steel objects, but I think it's a coincidence. Duncan looked like he wet himself when that cage hit the floor.'

Duncan's response had been the highlight of the experience. It wasn't every day a man got to see his enemy that white of face. Much less reduced to shrieking, like a highly agitated pre-teen girl. He grinned, thinking about it.

Jenna sniffed. 'Maybe he's a good actor.'

'He's a terrible actor,' Tommy retorted, with a laugh. 'I know, because he pretends to like me on a daily basis.'

'I don't agree with you,' she said obstinately. 'I think you're wrong, and it might just get you killed.'

'How refreshing.' He eyed her. 'But it doesn't matter what you think. The fact is, even if Duncan *is* trying to kill me, you can't prove it.' A sudden suspicion flashed through his head then. 'Is that why you were lurking outside my house that night? What was your plan, exactly? To disarm Duncan? He outweighs you by at least three hundred pounds.'

'I thought maybe I'd hang around and see if anything happened to you,' Jenna said drily. 'And aren't you glad I did?'

Tommy didn't answer her. He leaned forward and mixed himself a drink from the limo's bar, and then settled back against the plush seat, ice cubes clanking against the glass. He was tired. It wasn't every afternoon that he was nearly crushed to death, and he was pretending to be far more relaxed about it than he truly was. He didn't have to believe someone was trying to kill him to find narrowly avoiding his own death alarming. He had a healthy attachment to his body as it was, thank you.

He was lucky Jenna was turning paranoid, because if she hadn't screamed bloody murder like that, scaring years off his life, he wouldn't have lunged forward to save her – like some white knight from a fairy tale. He'd leapt to defend her without even thinking, diving towards the sound of her terror, mindless, wanting only to get to her and rescue her from whatever was making her scream – and it had taken him a long moment to hear the huge crash behind him. He'd only been aware of Jenna.

He didn't care to examine that too closely. Or at all.

He shifted against his seat. Jenna sat next to him, her jaw tight and her lips pursed as she stared out the tinted windows while dusk fell across the city. What did he know about this woman, anyway? She was a real person, with a real job, for one thing. Well. A *more* real job than his; he wasn't sure Video TV really qualified as *normal*. In truth, all he knew about her was that she was susceptible to Wild Boys marketing, had lost her head over *Tommy Seer: the Legend*, and was now perhaps too quick to see conspiracies wherever she looked. If he didn't want to sleep with her so desperately, to the point that he was losing sleep and walking around in a distracting state of arousal, he'd be tempted to worry that she was your garden-variety psycho.

It wouldn't be the first time he'd overlooked psychosis

en route to the nearest bed. Some claimed it was an aphrodisiac. Nick always maintained the crazy ones were the best in bed, because all the things that made them terrible human beings – lack of boundaries, intensity, emotional reactions to the slightest little thing – made them fantastic between the sheets. It was the insanity of what happened afterwards that everyone agreed got tedious.

'Tell me about yourself,' he said then, his voice too brusque. Her eyebrows arched up her forehead.

'Did this turn into a job interview?' She smiled. 'I already have a job, but thank you.'

'My life is an open book,' Tommy said with a shrug. 'An open book you, apparently, read several thousand times and committed to memory ...'

'I'm the target demographic,' Jenna snapped at him, evidently stung. 'Wouldn't it be worse if I thought you and your music were bullshit?'

'I think me and my music are bullshit half the time,' he drawled, enjoying the flush that moved across her neck and stained her soft cheeks. 'We could have bonded.'

'And your life is not an open book at all, unless you mean it's a work of fiction,' Jenna continued, colour high and eyes too bright. 'Everything that's supposedly true about you is a lie. Why pretend to be English? Why maintain the fake fiancée?'

'I think Duncan really wanted to play on the Beatles idea, and therefore Nick and I became English, which also keeps people from connecting us to our past upstate,' Tommy said with a shrug. 'I take comfort in the knowledge he has to pay a lot of money to maintain that story. And the good news is that when I leave the band, there goes Eugenia's cover. I'm predicting we break up, destroying the happy fairy tale of our relationship.' He sent her a challenging look. 'See? An open book.'

'Uh huh.' Jenna straightened her back – or he thought she did, beneath the layers she wore and the padded shoulders that winged away from her body. The patterned coat she was wearing was louder than a glam-rock power ballad.

'But you remain a mystery,' Tommy pointed out. 'Where are you from? Why did you want to work for Video TV? How do you feel about being plucked from your ordinary life and forced to hang around us, doing nothing, for weeks on end? Do you have a boyfriend? These are only sample questions,' he said smoothly as her brows clapped together. 'Feel free to answer any of them, in any order you please.'

'I grew up in Indiana,' she said after a moment. He watched her closely, sensing that she was concealing something. It was the way she paused after she said it, as if her home state was a delicate subject.

'Are you afraid the New Yorkers will rise up and eject you because you're a corn-fed Midwesterner?' he asked.

'I wasn't until you said that.' Her nose wrinkled as if she was fighting off laughter.

'I don't think they do that any more.' He made a languid sort of gesture with his tumbler. 'Not openly. Only when the smell of corn overwhelms them and they're forced to act.'

He had no idea what the hell he was talking about. From the odd look she shot his way, neither did she.

'I grew up in Indiana, and I always wanted to move to New York City,' she continued. He suspected she was speaking to save them both from whatever nonsense he kept spouting. She shrugged. 'My favourite aunt lived here when I was a kid and it always seemed like the best city in the world to me. "If you can make it there, you'll make it anywhere," you know? My parents would have preferred I felt that way about Chicago, probably, but only New York would do. I came to attend NYU and I never left.'

He waited, but she didn't seem inclined to continue. He sighed.

'And? That's it? Who you are can be summed up in your choice of university?' He shook his head. 'Your entire personality is an alumni magazine?'

Jenna shrugged, but he knew she was lying. He didn't know why she felt she had to lie, or what she could be lying about. He entertained the notion that this normal, everyday girl could have a whole secret life he knew nothing about. Much as the idea intrigued him, he rejected it. He'd seen where she lived. He saw *her* every day, with her puppy-dog eyes and curly hair and secretarial outfits. He knew who she was, no matter what she thought she was concealing.

'I don't know what you want me to say,' she said, her voice defensive. 'I'm a normal person. I live a normal life. I have pictures of beach vacations and hiking trips on my mantel. I live in a studio apartment and I'm good at my job.' She glared at him, but he could see the emotion there, rolling underneath. And despite the fact he'd thought much the same thing about her normality moments before, when she said it herself, it put him on guard. It was like the people who self-identified as *nice*. Untrustworthy and notably not *nice*, every one of them.

'I'm sorry,' she said in that snippy tone when he didn't answer, 'but I didn't put out hit singles or get on any magazine covers in my twenties. I just worked.'

'Do you have thoughts? Dreams?' he asked, his attention on her expression, and the distance there. As if he could see her lies written on her skin. 'First you tell me you're all about NYU, now you're defined by Video TV . . .'

'I'm sorry to disappoint you, Tommy,' she said in a voice that was in no way apologetic. 'But I'm not complicated. I dream about whether or not to get a cat. The pros? Cats are awesome. The cons? I don't like cat litter. See? Exciting stuff.'

'And that's it,' he said. Mocking her. 'To cat or not to cat, that's the central question of your existence. That's your internal life.' He shook his head. 'If I believed you, I'd be sad.'

'I used to be a big fan of this one band,' Jenna said tartly. 'But no more, unfortunately. I think the front man is a jackass.'

'No, you do not.' Tommy grinned, despite himself and his suspicions. 'You sound very boring to me. I hope you

223

don't take this the wrong way, but I think you need to get a life.'

'I have a very rich, very fulfilling—' She broke off, and rolled her eyes. 'Whatever. Listen, who cares about my life? My life is great and I don't care what you think about it. I'm more concerned about yours. No one's tried to mow me down on the street lately. Or thrown a seventeen-ton steel cage at my head. It's a miracle you're not in the hospital right now. Or worse.'

'This may come as a shock to you,' Tommy replied, 'but I don't particularly want to talk about near-death experiences. I would rather get to know you, which seems to terrify you, for some reason. Did you really *announce* that you have vacation pictures on your mantel? What does that even mean? Why does that need announcing?' He shook his head, and swirled his drink around in its tumbler, staring at it instead of her for a moment. 'I think the so-called near-death experiences are a coincidence, anyway.'

'How many near-death experiences do you have to have before you think they're more than a coincidence?' she asked, her mouth twisting. 'When does it become a pattern?'

'Two events are not a pattern.'

'Not yet.' She rubbed at the back of her neck with one hand, as if it ached. 'Are three?'

'And it doesn't count if you throw me off a balcony, Jenna,' he teased her. Her lips twitched.

'Don't tempt me.'

'I think it's cute that you're so convinced I'm in danger,' he told her.

'Great, and in addition to ignoring me, he's now patronizing me,' she said, as if she was narrating to a third party. Tommy found himself laughing without even meaning to start.

'Genuine concern,' he told her. 'That's what I meant. It's nice to see it.'

Jenna shook her head, and then leaned forward to peer out the window.

'We're at your building,' she said. 'I think I'm going to walk across the park and go—'

'No,' he said. Having not meant to say anything, having planned to leave her and go about his business, he was as surprised as she looked. He blinked. 'I have a party I have to go to, and I don't want to go alone.'

'You should call Eugenia,' Jenna suggested without missing a beat. Or looking at him. 'Your fairy-tale princess.'

'I want you,' he said, and then had to clear his throat, because that came out far too husky. She pretended not to notice, but he saw her swallow, and she was staring out at the sidewalk as if it fascinated her beyond measure. 'If you come, I can claim it's a work thing and I have to leave sooner.' He eyed her. 'Why? Do you have plans?'

She didn't answer him. Maybe because he'd asked it in that snide way, insinuating that she couldn't possibly have plans to rival his. Which might be obnoxious, but was also probably true, assuming she cared about *the*

225

high life and all it contained. Finally, she turned back and nodded.

'I'll go with you,' she said. 'If you won't look out for yourself, I will.'

'Excellent,' Tommy murmured. He smiled. 'A babysitter.'

Of course, he failed to mention that it was a sit-down dinner party, a fact that Jenna obviously found infuriating. She hissed something about *couture* that he didn't catch, and looked mortified, sitting amid a collection of Manhattan stars and their assorted sycophants in a Greenwich Village town house.

He wanted to tell her that she stood out from the glittering crowd, but not in the way she probably thought. *They* were all flash and surface, and she, by contrast, was real. Not quite normal, whatever that was, but real enough to still blush with shame or embarrassment. Real enough to look more than bored when surrounded by various famous people. Real enough to feel out of place, instead of grasping her way towards some higher social level.

He found her endlessly refreshing.

'Did you bring your secretary?' the woman next to him, some pop singer he knew he ought to recognize, trilled in scandalized tones.

'My assistant travels everywhere with me,' he replied in a bored, affected tone that was calculated to make everyone around him think he was unable to wipe his own ass without assistance. Something he suspected was true of half the people there.

From across the table, Jenna glared at him as if she'd like to strangle him.

Which had the usual effect of cheering him right up.

'You had no business putting me through that,' she snapped at him when they finally made their escape – long before the main course arrived. Tommy didn't know why anyone bothered serving food at these things. None of the guests ate. As policy. 'Not to mention it was rude to the hostess.'

'The hostess will comfort herself with the large amounts of cocaine she and the rest of the party will be consuming,' Tommy said drily, ushering Jenna out of the building and on to the bustle of the street. 'They probably won't remember you were there.'

'I felt like an idiot,' Jenna bit out. 'Is that what you wanted? Was that the plan?'

He had no plan. He only wanted to be near her. He accepted that, suddenly, as he looked down at her scowl and the blush on her cheeks. He knew it didn't make any sense, that she should hold as much interest for him as a lamp-post, but he had never been able to ignore her or relegate her elsewhere. The less beautiful he told himself she was, the more beautiful he found her to be. The more out of her reach he thought he should keep himself, the more he insisted on being close to her.

He was infatuated, she was looking at him as if she thought he was a lunatic, and he felt absurdly and unreasonably pleased with the entire, ridiculous situation.

He reached over and traced a pattern across her rich

mouth with his thumb, then took her hand in his when she shuddered.

'Come on,' he said. 'It's a Friday night and we're in Manhattan. Let's go dancing.'

20

When Tommy Seer talked about *dancing*, Jenna learned, he was not referring to the sorts of experiences she had had in her time: paying some insulting cover charge to listen to mediocre music spun by so-so DJs before drinking too much and rocking out on the dance floor, surrounded by Bridge and Tunnel clubbers. Oh, no.

Tommy Seer did not wait in lines, or pay cover charges. *Tommy Seer* sauntered up to doors guarded by very large bouncers and smiled slightly as they leapt to whisk the velvet ropes out of his way. *Tommy Seer* was converged upon by club kids and promoters – one of whom looked a great deal like Dr Cuddy from *House* – and then whisked away to a private room where the likes of Linda Evangelista, Andrew McCarthy, Tama Janowitz and Keith Haring lounged about being wildly famous in the Eighties.

Tommy Seer (and whoever happened to be with him) was plied with free drinks while astoundingly pretty girls shook their barely clad butts at him. Jenna sat next to him in her tacky overcoat and couldn't find it in her to be anything but delighted.

This, after all, was the club scene everyone talked about in reverent tones more than twenty years later. Artists and club kids and supermodels and actors all mixed together while a very short man Jenna suspected was Steve Rubell, founder of Studio 54, held court. Out in the main part of the club, DJs played Bananarama, some hip-hop, Madonna, Duran Duran, the Cure, the Smiths, the Bangles, the very beginnings of what would turn into house music some day soon. And the Wild Boys, of course.

It was fun and glorious, but it wasn't *dancing*. It was the Palladium in 1987, long before it became the cheesy club Jenna recalled from her college days. It was an experience.

And it was no surprise that Jenna found herself a little bit tipsy, especially when she'd been forced to contend with some German princess of taxis – well, no, that didn't make sense, but that's what Jenna thought she'd said – and had nearly collided with Ally Sheedy on her way to the bathroom. To say nothing of Molly Ringwald herself, looking at her famous pout in the bathroom mirror. How was someone who had originally been a starry-eyed adolescent in 1987 supposed to deal with so much Brat Pack goodness?

It was all a little too much, and then, of course, so was Tommy.

He watched her, his green eyes alert, his mouth in that faint smile, and Jenna might not have known why, exactly, he had brought her here, to this once-famous and now (in the 2000s) demolished club, but she knew it had something to do with that expression he wore. As if he was waiting for some sign that only she could give, though she couldn't imagine what that sign might be.

So she did the only thing she could do. She danced. She sang, *I'll be alone, dancing, you know it baby* to herself. She danced for what seemed like hours, at the best Eighties night imaginable, until he came and took her arms in his warm hands and looked down at her, and she knew it was time to go.

'What was that about?' she asked as they burst outside into the cold night. Her skin was hot and her hair was wet with sweat on the back of her neck. 'You didn't dance at all.'

'I watched you,' he said simply, as if that was an explanation. 'Did you have fun?'

'Sure,' Jenna said, but she was confused. It must have shown on her face, because his smile twisted and he reached over to thread his fingers in her curls.

'You looked like you were in heaven,' he said. 'You really do like the music.' His hand was hot against the top of her head, his fingers making even her skull sensitive. He moved his hand over her temple, then along the line of her jaw.

'I really do,' she said, and then she whispered, 'What are you doing?'

As if she didn't know, but she didn't really know him then, with that odd, tender look and the soft touch against her skin. This wasn't the dizzying fire she had come to expect when he touched her, nor the calculating distance even while kissing her that she knew he was capable of – this, she knew on some deep level, was much, much worse. This was quiet and awful and sweet. This could hurt her in ways she didn't dare consider. This was everything she was afraid of, right there in front of her.

He didn't speak. His mouth settled into a grim line and he searched her face for something in the passing lights of the busy Manhattan street, something she was afraid he wouldn't find – or worse, that he would. Something tightened in her gut, something sharp and barbed and made of heat and fear and more.

'Let's go,' he said in a quiet voice, and he took her hand. Jenna felt his fingers close over hers, and felt the calluses on his fingers from his guitar playing, hard and rough and perfect, somehow, against her skin.

He hesitated, and Jenna thought, *I have to tell him, right now, that whatever he's thinking can't happen—*

But she didn't open her mouth at all. His hand tightened on hers when she failed to speak, and a very male sort of expression flashed across his face. Jenna felt a flash of answering heat deep in her belly.

And then he was moving, and she felt unable to do anything at all but follow him. She told herself she was tipsy, that she had no control over what she was feeling, but she knew she was lying to herself. The last of her tipsiness had vanished the moment the night air hit her, and everything she'd felt since then, she knew, was Tommy. Pure and simple.

The truth was, she was surrendering. She knew it.

She wanted it.

She couldn't remember, any longer, why she'd fought him in the first place. She didn't care if he was faking, or if he had an agenda. She could feel every nerve ending in her body standing at attention, thirsty for him, and she didn't know how to deny that any more. She didn't want to.

They didn't speak on the taxi ride. Jenna felt his heat and his pulse through their linked hands, and watched the city slide by outside the windows, red tail lights and street lights gleaming, brightly lit bodegas on the corners and clumps of pedestrians walking along the cold sidewalks.

It was as if an electric current hummed inside of her. Desire pooled in her belly and spilled outward. She felt the urge to throw herself at him even in the back of the taxi, with the need to taste him, touch him, explore him. It was making her so dizzy she thought that if she let go of his hand, she might spin off into the darkness.

Then, finally, they were outside her apartment building. On some level that surprised Jenna, but she let him lead her inside and up the stairs, until they were standing in the little yellow studio and there was no more pretending this was a dream. This was happening, right now.

Her breath was coming in short bursts. She could feel the rapid thump of her heart against her chest, like it was fighting to get out.

'Why here?' she asked, her voice sounding to her as if it came from far away. 'Why not one of the many rooms in your apartment?'

Tommy smiled, and looked around the yellow room, which Jenna thought was closing in on them. He seemed bigger somehow. Or maybe it was just that she had never experienced the studio with another body in it before. There was hardly enough room for one.

'Why not here?' he asked. 'I like this place. It's cute.'

'Uh huh.' She felt anger sear through her then. 'The international superstar thinks my little studio is *cute*. That's why you live in a palace on Central Park West.'

His head tilted slightly as he regarded her for a long, cool, moment, with her sarcasm hanging between them like a blanket. *Thumpthumpthump* went her heart, picking up its pace.

'It's okay,' he said finally. 'I get it.'

'You get what?' she demanded, and then sucked in a breath because he closed the distance between them, and she felt edgy and terrified and desperate, and were those *tears* pricking the backs of her eyelids?

'We don't have to fight or banter to mask it, you know,' he murmured, too close now. 'It's intense, isn't it? But it's going to be okay.' His grin was crooked, and his eyes were far too knowing. 'I promise.'

'I don't know what you're talking about,' she said, but her voice was nothing more than a croak, and it was a lie anyway.

'Yes, you do,' he said, so softly, and then he settled

234

his mouth over hers, his hands wrapping around her upper arms and anchoring her there, holding her still while the kiss went on and on and Jenna slowly lost her mind.

Tommy kissed the way he sang, she thought, with all of that heat and yearning and sweet, hot sex. Somehow they ended up sprawled across the futon, and it no longer mattered if the studio was big enough, because they were finally, finally touching each other with all the frustration of the weeks – years, in Jenna's case – they hadn't touched. His hands were everywhere – learning the shape of her curves, tracing them, and tasting them, too. He yanked off his shirt and Jenna kissed her way across the hard planes of his finely moulded chest, then gasped when he pulled her up and kissed her, hard. He stripped her clothes from her body, and laughed when their hands tangled trying to get his pants off. He grabbed a small package from the back pocket of his pants, sheathed himself in one quick movement, and then they were both naked and it was really, truly happening.

'Relax,' he said then. He reached over and smoothed away the frown between her eyes. 'You look very serious all of a sudden.'

Because this is not a dream. Because this is happening. Right now.

'I'm totally relaxed,' she lied, which made him smile.

He swung over her, rolling her beneath him, and she could feel him all along the length of her body, head to toe. The crisp hair on his legs against her smooth ones, the breadth and strength of his shoulders above her, and between them, his erection pressed hard against her belly. She shivered, and he smiled.

She loved all of it, and it was too much at the same time. So much heat and contrast. So much skin. She tasted him. *Salt and sweet.*

She wondered if it would change her. Shouldn't sleeping with such a huge crush change her somehow? What if, after all of this, it was terrible? What then? Was it possible for chemistry to just . . . *fizzle out?*

'I can hear your mind going,' he murmured then, amusement lurking in his voice. 'What are you thinking about? So loudly?'

'Oh . . . uh . . . nothing,' she said, embarrassed. 'I'm not thinking anything.'

'You're not mindless and begging, either,' he said in that silky tone that made her shiver. 'I don't know where you went, Jenna.'

'I'm right here—'

But her protest died when he claimed her mouth with his own. This time his kiss was hard, possessing. This time, he used his hands. They cupped her breasts, holding them while he moved down and took first one peak, then the other into his hot, demanding mouth.

Jenna tried to catch her breath but he kept moving, tasting her belly, licking his way down between her thighs, where he settled his mouth on the molten core of her. Jenna gasped, but he only held her hips in his strong arms, held her down, and ravished her with his mouth

236

until she was sobbing out his name, begging him to stop
– or finish – or something, she didn't care what.

But he didn't stop. He teased her and toyed with her,
bringing her closer and closer, and then, just as she shim-
mered on the edge, he released her, and kissed his way
back up her body.

'What are you . . . ?' She was out of her mind. Red-faced,
panting, and she wanted to kill him, too. 'Why would
you . . . ?'

'Much better,' he murmured, and then he twisted his
hips and drove into her.

Jenna shattered into a million pieces.

When she came back to herself, he was motionless above
her, braced on his arms and watching her, determination
and satisfaction written all over his face. She reached over
and touched that wicked mouth of his with her finger,
astonished to see she was still shaking.

'You better hold on, Jenna,' Tommy told her, his voice
rasping in the quiet room, and she could see how much
his effort at patience was costing him. His eyes gleamed.
'We're just getting started.'

He was as good as his word.

Dawn was greying the dark outside the windows and
just starting to light the room. Jenna disentangled herself
from Tommy's limbs and got to her feet. Her thighs felt
like jelly beneath her. She pulled a shirt from the pile on
the floor and tugged it on over her head. His, she realized belatedly. She guessed that her hair had redefined

the word *bedhead*, and she had a feeling she would not want to see what that looked like.

In the soft light, Tommy lay sprawled across the futon that they'd finally pulled out to make into a full bed at some point. He looked like some kind of god lying there, his big body taking up most of the space. Fast asleep, that clever mouth relaxed and the too-knowing eyes hidden, he looked different. Softer.

Every muscle and bone in her body hurt. Her skin hummed with leftover electricity, and she desperately needed water. Her eyes burned from so little sleep and she was sore. Oh, so deliciously sore. Something in her thrilled at it, but there was no denying the twinges every time she shifted position.

Tommy, it turned out, was a creative and inventive man. That should not have surprised her as much as it did. On some level, she'd been expecting him to be selfish and inconsiderate, like the famous rock stars were always accused of being in memoirs. But not Tommy. He'd been the opposite of selfish. So unselfish, in fact, that she didn't think there was a single spot on her body he hadn't made his own. She wondered if that came from the legion of women he'd undoubtedly slept with, a subject she thought she should probably care about. But she couldn't rustle up any outrage or insecurity. How could she?

He'd made her limbs do things she didn't think they could do. He'd laughed and teased and practically made her go blind from the sheer, overwhelming pleasure of it all. And then he'd done it again, and again. And again.

She'd lost track of how many times he'd reached for her, or she'd reached for him. One touch blended into another, and swirled in her head like some extended montage scene of sex and sighs and *more*.

And even grainy-eyed and exhausted, she wanted him. Even sore, and unsure how or if she could walk, she still wanted him. She had the disconcerting thought that if she could figure out how, she would burrow into his skin and lie there with him. Was that insane?

No, just incredibly creepy, she retorted silently, disgusted with herself. She would not be sharing that decidedly freaky thought with Tommy, that was for sure.

She turned away, and moved across the floor towards the tiny kitchen, aware of her body and all the new and various aches. It was a sin tax on dying from pleasure, she thought, feeling a little bit smug. She hadn't had many nights like the one she'd just had with Tommy. In fact, if she was honest with herself, she'd never had anything that came close.

She poured herself a glass of water and gulped it down, imagining that she could feel it racing to soothe her poor, ravaged body. She put the glass down on the counter with a click, and when she turned back to the door, Tommy was lounging there, sleepy-eyed.

And also naked. Jenna's gaze fell across that famously beautiful torso, then down towards his narrow hips. Then she remembered that she was sore, and jerked her attention back up to his face.

His dark hair stuck up at odd angles and his beard had

grown in during the night, leaving him with rough stubble she'd felt along the smooth skin of her thighs long before she'd noticed it with her eyes. He rubbed a hand over his face and then blinked at her, looking drowsy.

It was hard to look at him. It was harder still to look away. Everything, Jenna knew with a bone-deep conviction, was different now. Especially her.

'Water?' she asked, even as she was handing him a glass.

He took it without comment and drained it, then put it on the counter.

'Why are you out of bed?' he asked, his voice rough with sleep. He reached over and pulled on one of her dark curls, tugging it straight and then winding it around his finger.

'I needed a drink,' she said, fascinated to hear the huskiness of her own voice.

'You look good in my shirt.' He slid his free hand around her waist, then let it drift down to squeeze her butt. 'Very good, in fact.'

'You can't possibly . . .' She trailed off when he kissed her. The sweetness and electricity of it hit her again. She thought she might never be able to get enough of his taste. Of him. He pulled back, and laughed at her expression.

'God, no, woman,' he said. 'What am I, a machine?'

'I have some concerns about that, to be honest.'

'Get back in bed,' he growled at her. 'It's too early to be awake.'

Jenna let him lead her back to the futon, and felt her

240

heart clench when he wrapped her in his arms and settled back against the pillows, burying his face in her hair. She could hear the steady beat of his heart beneath her ear, and smell the salty-sweet scent that was uniquely his.

She had loved him long before she met him, and then even more once she'd grown to know him, and she had known full well that sleeping with him – what a ridiculous euphemism, after such a sleepless night – would change her. And maybe she was exhausted; maybe that was why she was trembly and on the verge of tears, but that didn't alter the way she felt.

Tommy – alive and well – was a necessity. She got that now, in every possible way.

She would save him. She had to. No matter what saving him entailed.

21

Tommy didn't think anyone was trying to kill him, because unlike Jenna, apparently, he knew that shit happened. People drove like idiots on New York City streets. Steel cages that weren't supposed to hang from ceilings in the first place sometimes fell. And sometimes, people were required to jump out of the way of these things. That didn't make an accident a plot.

Along those lines, there were accidents in set dressing rooms all the time. Fires, even. People were always forgetting cigarettes, or whatever else they happened to be smoking, and racing off to film something. Sometimes cigarettes – or whatever, Tommy wasn't into the harder stuff these days but he didn't cast stones – burned out in ashtrays, and other times, they caused larger problems.

Had Tommy been napping the way he'd claimed he was, rather than trying to convince the delectable Jenna to while away the time with him between boring video takes in a far more interesting fashion, the fire in his dressing room might have caused some serious damage. But he hadn't been napping, and he'd smelled the smoke long before it could do much more than singe the wall, and there was no harm done.

'No harm done?' Jenna hissed, when the crowd had dispersed, Richie had sauntered away with the fire extinguisher still dangling from his hand, and it was only the two of them in Tommy's dressing room once more. 'You could have been killed! *Again!*'

'But I wasn't.' He closed the distance between them, ran his hands over her hair and nibbled his way along her neck. He loved the scent of her skin, something citrus and vanilla all at once, sharp and smooth. He loved how quickly her body melted against his, as if she couldn't help herself. 'Weren't we doing something much more interesting?' he asked. He slid a hand down and slipped it beneath the jacket she wore, seeking and finding the tight peak of her breast. 'Like this?'

'Be serious.' She batted his hand away, and stepped back, that frown of hers clamped down between her eyes. He'd never had a woman frown so much around him. The models were afraid to change expressions too often because they might get lines – and, if he was fair, because they didn't have the sort of thoughts that required a change of expression. Jenna, on the other hand, seemed hell-bent on lining her lovely face sooner rather than later.

'I've never been more serious in my life,' he assured her, and the crazy thing was that he wasn't kidding. He was focused on the sweet curve of her breast like he was a teenage boy and he thought it might be the only breast he'd ever see. Jenna Jenkins, it was turning out, was addictive.

'I would ask you if you had to go to the hospital before you would take this seriously,' she continued, ignoring where his attention was focused and moving away from him to lean against the arm of the couch. 'But you've already been to the hospital, and you don't seem to care.'

'Of course I care.' He didn't, actually. He would, however, pretend to care if it would make her happy. And he could tell she knew that. The furrow between her brows deepened.

'If you took the energy you put into sex and put it into self-preservation—' she began.

'And where would that leave you?' he interrupted her, unable to keep the smile from his lips. He stalked her across the room, grabbing her hand and tumbling them both lengthwise on the couch. 'You act like you're not enjoying yourself.'

'And that can't possibly be true.' Her voice was heavy with sarcasm, but her eyes were shining. 'Not with your immense skill.'

'And yet,' he pointed out, his mouth moving over her neck as he positioned himself in the cradle of her thighs, 'I can't help noticing that your heart is beating very, very fast. And you're holding your breath.'

'I can put my attraction to you aside to focus on other things,' Jenna said primly.

He took her mouth with his, and moved suggestively against her, making them both sigh.

He thought he might die if he couldn't get inside her. Again.

'Sure you can,' he agreed, his voice rough with need. 'But why would you want to?'

'I thought you were anti-groupie,' Nick threw across the conference table in Duncan's office with no warning whatsoever.

There were any number of places Nick could have broached the topic of Jenna, and none of them would have been as inappropriate as an official band meeting. They were supposed to be talking about the new album and their press tour and upcoming concert dates. Not Tommy's personal business. Granted, *he* had been amusing himself by wishing Jenna into the room rather than off at Video TV appeasing her boss, but that was his prerogative.

'What?' He made his voice as menacing a voice as possible, hoping Nick would take the hint.

Meanwhile, everyone else stopped staring off into space – the usual reaction to one of Duncan's annoying speeches about band unity or whatever else he was obsessed about that week – and stared at Tommy instead.

Nick, the bastard, ignored Tommy's tone. He even leaned in closer, putting his arms on the smooth table in front of him.

'The secretary,' he said, as if maybe Tommy was confused

as to his meaning. 'Since when did you start banging your groupies? You used to be against it.'

'You're banging the secretary?' Duncan's pig eyes went all cunning, and he smoothed a hand over his shiny, gelled hair. 'Interesting.'

'The next person who uses the word "banging" in connection to Jenna is getting my foot up their ass,' Tommy said conversationally, though the glare he sent around the table could have cut through steel. Richie raised his eyebrows and looked down, hiding a smirk. As he did not use the word 'banging', Tommy ignored it.

'Jenna is a nice girl,' Sebastian said, in evident disapproval. He drummed his fingers against the table, scowling. 'Are you sure she can handle the full Tommy Seer experience?'

'I'm not a carnival ride, Sebastian,' Tommy snapped. Sebastian's elegant brows rose.

'She's not your usual type, is she?' he asked mildly. 'I think she might have a thought or two in her head.' He shook his head, managing to convey his disappointment in Tommy and support of Jenna. Tommy was unreasonably furious that Sebastian thought Jenna *needed* his support.

'This is my business,' Tommy gritted out, aware that Duncan was watching his every move like some fat predator. 'Not band business.'

'You don't have a private life, asshole,' Duncan threw in then, malice in his voice. 'Unless I tell you otherwise.'

'Which is one more reason I'm leaving,' Tommy threw

back. He sensed more than saw his band mates shift in their seats, and ruthlessly thrust away the stab of guilt he felt. He didn't understand why he was the only one to feel the desperation, the horror, that the idea of staying in the band raised. But he was tired of fighting about it.

'Not quite yet, you're not,' Sebastian said, breaking the silence, his crisp accent calibrated to soothe. 'And we all have a lot of work to do before then.'

Tommy could feel Duncan's eyes on him from one side, but he turned to Nick instead.

'What do you care anyway?' he asked his oldest friend, hating the hard set to Nick's jaw. Hating that he'd put it there.

'What do I care that you're breaking up our band?' Nick asked, incredulously. 'Are you insane?'

'No.' Tommy refused to talk about breaking up the band any more. 'About Jenna.'

'I don't give a shit about Jenna, brother,' Nick said with a short, angry laugh. 'But I am fascinated that you've become such a fucking hypocrite all of a sudden.'

Tommy felt himself smirk. 'I don't think it's *all of a sudden*,' he drawled. 'I'm pretty sure I've been astoundingly hypocritical for years now.'

Richie let out a guffaw at that, and Sebastian's lips twitched into a smile. Nick only glared for a moment, before shaking his head.

'I guess you got me there,' he muttered. Not quite smiling.

It didn't really solve anything, but it smoothed the

moment over well enough. Duncan continued braying on about appearances and tour dates, and eventually the meeting was over.

Tommy caught up with Nick at the elevators.

'What the hell was that?' he demanded. 'Why are you riding me?'

'I don't know what you're talking about,' Nick grunted, barely sparing Tommy a glance.

'Like hell you don't.' Tommy ordered himself to modify the aggressive tone. Nick was a brawler. He heard aggression and responded with more of his own. 'The last time you gave a shit about my personal life we were sixteen years old.'

'Yeah, and the reason I cared was because you stole Ursula Freitag from me,' Nick retorted, turning on him with anger written across his face. 'Kind of like now, when you're destroying my livelihood and all you care about is fucking some secretary.'

'That's not all I care about,' Tommy said stiffly, and opted not to punch his best friend in the face for discussing Jenna like that.

'Then what do you care about, Tommy?' Nick asked in a hiss. He stepped closer. 'You never even asked what *we* want in all of this.'

'I have to get out,' Tommy said, with a helpless shrug. *Or die,* he thought, but did not say. They were men. There was only so much drama allowed.

'I get that.' Nick shook his head. His mouth twisted. 'And whatever you want, we'll all fall over ourselves to

248

make sure it happens. Because you're Tommy Seer. You're the fucking legend.'

Tommy hated the bleakness in Nick's expression, but he didn't know what to do to change it. Because he couldn't fix it and also save himself. He had to choose.

Still.

'Nick—'

'Hey! Assholes!' Richie's voice – which he hardly used, much less raised – made both of them turn back towards Duncan's office. Richie was running down the corridor, his face bright. 'Duncan just got the call – "Misery Loves Company" is the top of the charts! We hit number one the first week out!'

Nick didn't look at Tommy, he just brushed past him and headed for the conference room – as if Tommy was already gone. It made Tommy feel worse than anything that had been said. He followed Nick more slowly, clapping Richie on the back.

Inside the conference room, Duncan was popping champagne and oozing that fake bonhomie that usually made Tommy's skin crawl.

'Congratulations,' Duncan said when he drew close, handing Tommy a glass of champagne even while he aimed another of his nasty glares his way. 'The world goes to hell in a hand basket, but you know how to go out on top, don't you?'

It was not until he was out on the street that Tommy let himself breathe easy again. How was he going to make it through an entire world tour if things were already this bad and they had yet to play a single gig? Not for the first time, it occurred to him that he could have made all this easier on himself if he'd kept his plans secret. Gone on the tour, kept everyone happy, and then just up and quit when it was done.

But no, he'd tried to be a stand-up guy for once. He'd tried to do the right thing and let everyone prepare themselves. He wasn't sure he'd be inspired to try such a radical notion again, that was for sure. Screw the right thing.

The October night was dark and cold, and Tommy pulled the collar of his bomber jacket up to protect his neck from the chill. He loved New York. Pull a hat over his hair and keep his head down, and he could be anyone. Just another guy on the street, minding his own business. Of absolutely no interest to the millions of others doing the same.

The anonymity thrilled him.

He was aware of the shift – the irony of it. He'd have given anything at eighteen to be *known*. That was all he'd wanted. The music, sure, but he'd wanted adoration. He'd wanted people to know his name. He'd been so sure that he was better than the place he came from, and he'd wanted to prove it. He'd have given anything and everything – and he had. The worst part was, he hadn't even cared what he was leaving behind. His mother, his kid sisters, his extended family. He'd shaken the chains of his childhood off without a backward glance, and that was that. Little Tommy Searcy of the shittiest part of Buffalo

250

disappeared, and a few years later, Tommy Seer rose to take his place.

He didn't know why he regretted it so much now that it was far too late. When Nick didn't regret a thing. He didn't know why his lack of freedom bothered him so acutely – because who was free? He was walking down a street in midtown Manhattan, surrounded by suits. Men and women who were chained to jobs, careers, families, and would no doubt change places with him in a heart-beat. Who wouldn't want to be a rock star if they could?

He thought of Jenna then, of the ever-present frown between her pretty brown eyes and the way she pressed those full lips of hers together. He felt something he hoped was as simple as longing spread through him. He didn't know why she'd gotten to him the way she had, but he did know that he felt freer with her than he had in years. Maybe it was because she was so determined to solve the mystery he thought was mostly in her head, but how could he resist someone who thought he was at risk and wanted to save him? When was the last time that had happened? Had it ever happened? And he didn't care what Nick or Sebastian thought about it – he couldn't let go of that, of her concern, if he tried. He didn't want to try.

The lights on Madison Avenue clicked over, and Tommy slowed his pace, looking over his shoulder as he approached the corner and trying to avoid being knocked in the head by a woman's unnecessary umbrella. It was cold, but not wet, he thought. *Crazy New Yorkers*.

He felt only the slightest pressure near his ankle, and

looked down in surprise. Even as he registered that something – a foot? – was hooking around his leg, there was a terrific shove from behind and Tommy found himself lurching forward, pitching into the street – and directly into the path of an oncoming bus.

There was no time. Tommy heard screams, and the shrill shriek of brakes.

He knew he was dead.

After all this—

He knew it, but he threw out his arms and wrenched his shoulders back as far as he could. He crashed down against the concrete, sliding face down into the gutter.

Pain exploded through him, but he couldn't deal with that, he had to move—

The bus skidded. Tommy rolled.

His life did not flash before his eyes. There was only cold pavement, pain, and his fury that it had all come to this.

But somehow, the bus missed him.

By about a centimetre.

Tommy knew the precise measurement because his head was right there, too close, too *fucking close*, and he was too scared to close his eyes or even wet himself – both completely reasonable urges, he thought, as he realized over the sound of his racing heart that he would, in fact, live.

I'm still alive.

The crowd surged forward. Two suits pulled Tommy to his feet, while a woman continued to scream. Only now that his head was not a pancake could Tommy make sense of the words.

'Pushed!' she hollered. 'I saw it! He was pushed!'

Tommy brushed himself off, dazed. He was man enough to admit that he was shaking ever so slightly, adrenalin and terror combining in his gut and making him feel sick.

'Hey,' one of the suits said, peering at him in surprise. 'Aren't you—?'

Tommy jerked his arm out of the other man's hold. Not much of a thank you, but what was he supposed to do? Notify the press that once again, Tommy Seer had met with an accident on the streets of New York? He just . . . couldn't do it.

'No,' he told the man briskly. 'I'm not.'

Then he turned and dove into the crowd, letting his legs move him as far away from the scene as he could go. He didn't quite break into a run, though he wanted to.

But he had the feeling that running wouldn't help.

Because he hadn't needed the screaming woman to tell him he'd been pushed – he'd felt the shove. He'd been *thrown in front of a bus.*

Someone was trying to kill him.

Future

You say your ice age hasn't started to unwind
Your tricky cold war, cruel designs
Lucky penny, lucky penny
How can I make you mine?

The Wild Boys, 'Lucky Penny'

Half a mind to quit this desperate dance
Am I defined by what I want or what I do?
Imprisoned in my choice and circumstance
But I still want to follow you.

Tommy Seer, unpublished song lyric

22

Jenna tried to hide her impatience as she did her best to organize Ken's office yet again. You would think that if someone knew that he was sharing his secretary with a rock star, and that she would therefore be unable to do her job every day, he might take it upon himself to be that little bit neater in her absence.

Not Ken.

It took her hours to reorganize his files and get his calendar into shape, hours that she could have spent doing far more interesting things, like figuring out how to save the man she loved from his fast-approaching certain death, had Ken taken a few moments here and there to keep up with his own clutter.

It didn't take much. A few minutes of straightening every day, that was all, and *voilà!* – a clean and neat office.

Funny, that was a whole lot like what Aunt Jen used to tell her. Had she turned into Aunt Jen? Or was it that Aunt Jen had completely taken over Jenna's life at this point – and vice versa? Not that she'd thought about it in any great depth, but Jenna had initially felt that the very least she could do was leave the life she was using the way she'd found it. It seemed only polite. The plants still thrived, amazingly enough. And now she couldn't bear messiness. *There's a place for everything, and everything in its place*, she could hear her aunt sing-songing in her mind, as she'd done so many times throughout Jenna's childhood.

Her new interest in tidiness probably also had a lot to do with the pages of detailed information she'd written out, all of it neatly organized into dates and times, facts and rumours – as much as she could remember of the last two months of Tommy's life. She'd had to write it out again and again, until it was as neat and clear as it could be, so that she could reference it all with ease. Having forced herself to be so organized in that part of her life, how could she slack off everywhere else?

Jenna looked out her office window at the evening falling over the city, already so early. Too early. Summer was truly gone. Tommy had about a week left to live. Thinking about it made her feel panicky – and being trapped back at Video TV while he was out there unknowingly risking himself only made it worse.

'You look annoyed,' Ken said, bounding into the office, resplendent in parachute pants, a jaunty fedora, and a sparkling midnight-blue ascot. Jenna started in her chair, as much at the outfit as at his unexpected arrival.

'Hi,' she said brightly, as a secretary should.

'And now you look guilty.' Ken eyed her. 'Is it that rock star of yours? Duncan mentioned in our phone call yesterday that you and he seemed close.' His eyebrows rose suggestively. 'If you know what I mean by *close*.'

Jenna blinked. 'You and Duncan talk about whether or not I'm *close* with Tommy?' she asked, incredulous. What she did not ask was, *is this junior high school?* Though it was the logical next question.

'Oh, dear.' Ken searched her face. 'I thought he was kidding. Or that it was wishful thinking on his part, since he thinks everyone in the entire world is as slimy as he is.'

'I don't think Duncan knows anything about—' Jenna began stiffly.

'Jen. This is no good.' Ken sank into the visitors' couch, crossed his legs at the ankles, and sighed. 'These stars, they're not like regular people. You can't trust the things they say when they want to get lucky. I thought you knew this by now.'

'Why are we having this conversation?' Jenna could feel her cheeks redden. No doubt her neck and ears, too. She was practically a beacon of shame and embarrassment.

'This is my fault,' Ken said in a musing voice. 'I never should have let Duncan pull you into his stupid games. I knew better, but I really wanted to kick a little MTV butt, is that so wrong?'

'Ken.' She waited until he looked at her. 'I don't know what you think is happening, but I assure you, it's not.'

259

Her boss's elfin face twisted, so that he looked almost rueful. And very nearly wise.

'You're not sleeping with Tommy Seer?' he asked. The answer must have written itself across her face, because he laughed to himself. 'That's what I thought.'

'I don't think . . .' Jenna's mind reeled around, trying to figure out what to say. 'It won't affect my job, if that's what you're worried about,' she managed eventually.

'I don't care about the *job*,' Ken said with a dismissive wave of his hand. 'Please. I can put up with Duncan's crap for a little while longer, and then you'll be back here and he owes me a serious favour no matter what you did or didn't do for him.' He shrugged. 'It's you I'm worried about, Jen. You're not exactly the rock-star girlfriend *type*.'

What every girl dreamed of hearing. Truly.

Especially when she knew it was true.

Jenna felt her teeth were on edge, and ordered herself to stop it.

'Of course I'm not,' she said, although it cost her. 'Don't you think I know that better than anyone?'

Ken sighed, and his expression changed. He looked sad. Jenna wished herself a thousand miles and as many years away from this conversation.

'Some people love power more than they'll ever be able to love anything else,' Ken said. 'They might not even mean to be that way, but they can't help it.'

Jenna nodded sagely, though she didn't think *power* was the reason she and Tommy would never last. It was probably a lot more to do with, to pull a couple of reasons out at random, his fame and beauty versus her lack of same. The fact that she was only supposed to be twelve years old here in 1987, not old enough for Tommy at all.

Oh, yes, and his imminent death.

But Ken wasn't paying attention to Jenna any more. He was looking at her, but he was focused on something far away.

'You have to accept that they can't help it,' he said in that same urgent but low voice. 'It's that or go crazy.'

'Ken,' Jenna said, very softly, so as not to kill the mood, because she wanted to know what made him look so wistful. 'Are you telling me you . . . ?' She couldn't complete the sentence. Not because she was suddenly so delicate, but because he was, no matter his confessional mood at the moment, her boss. 'You and a rock star?'

'A different kind of rock star,' Ken said with a weary sort of sigh. 'A more corporate version.' His mouth curved. 'I know you know already. I'm talking about Chuck, of course.'

'Chuck,' Jenna repeated, confused but trying not to show it. And then she understood, and suddenly everything fell into place. Ken Dollimore and Chuck Arendt's famous partnership and even more famous falling-out made a lot more sense if it was romantic. A romance explained the ferocious fights the two of them were known for. The bitterness of it all. 'But doesn't he . . . ?'

'Have a wife and kids in Greenwich?' Ken asked with some bite. 'Of course he does.' He shook his head, his lips pressed into a thin line. 'And that's part of the problem.'

He pulled his fedora from his head with one hand, and ran his other hand through his hair. 'It's the fucking 1980s, not the 1950s, but Chuck can't handle it.' Ken made a noise in the back of his throat. 'I've been out since I was sixteen years old, and sure, sometimes that sucked, but I did it. But now it's 1987 and half of my friends are dying or dead, and the other half are HIV-positive or soon to be HIV-positive, and I'm trying to have a relationship with some closeted, married guy?' He rolled his eyes. 'I couldn't do it any more. He can't admit who he really is – not because he's afraid, mind you, but because he thinks admitting it would be giving up his power. And Chuck will never love anyone as much as he loves his power.'

'If that's true, I'm sorry for him,' Jenna said. She shook her head. 'It doesn't sound like any way to live.'

'I'm not telling you this to make you feel sorry for Chuck,' Ken said. 'Or, hell, even me. But you've always been here for me. You were totally cool about the sexual harassment thing—'

'The *what*?' Jenna practically yelped.

'It's not every secretary who would let her boss pretend to sexually harass her, just to confuse co-workers about his sexual preferences,' Ken said with a laugh. 'That was the best idea you've ever had. I'm pretty sure half the people who thought they knew what happened between Chuck and me now doubt the whole thing. It's rad.'

'That's me,' Jenna agreed with a weak sort of smile. 'I'm rad.' But at least she now knew why her gay boss spent so much time in her personal space. And the truth was, she suddenly – retroactively – forgave him for all the inappropriateness. Jenna had always drawn a line between gay space and straight space. Gay men could cross boundaries that she would slug straight men for looking at funny. *Go Aunt Jen*, she thought, admiringly.

'That's only one of the reasons I don't want to see you heartbroken over this guy,' Ken said, far too kindly. 'And heartbroken is where you're heading. Believe me, I know.'

'Ken . . .' But Jenna didn't know what to say. She looked down, and noticed to her surprise that her hands were clenched into fists on her lap. She uncurled her fingers, let them spread wide. 'My eyes are open,' she said simply.

'How could they be?' Ken asked, in that same, kind tone that made Jenna want to cry. 'He's Tommy Seer. He's already a myth. Who prepares for a myth?'

'Sure,' Jenna said. 'But I know who I am, too. I do.'

Ken smiled at her, then slapped his hands against his knees. 'I hope so,' he said in his usual brisk voice. He got to his feet, and Jenna knew the moment between them was over. She straightened. 'Don't you have a rock star to shadow?' Ken asked, walking towards his office. 'That bottom-feeder Duncan Paradis apparently feels that you are not providing him with enough information, just so you know. He claimed he was on the warpath.'

'He's mad because I can't give him details on a conspiracy that exists only in his head,' Jenna said with some heat. 'What am I supposed to do? Make something up?'

'Be careful,' Ken advised her, pausing at the door to his

office. It wasn't clear whether he meant with Duncan, or with Tommy. Or both. He gave Jenna a wry sort of smile. 'I warn because I care.'

There was, Tommy thought as he walked through Central Park, heading north-west towards his apartment building, a huge difference between knowing that you were going to die *some day* and having a near-death experience *today* – especially one that had clearly been engineered by someone looking to hasten *some day* along.

How had Jenna known? He bent his head against the bite of the wind, and scowled at the ground. He knew that he'd set her on the path, with his half-formed suspicions about Duncan, but she was so certain. She had been waiting for him outside his apartment the night the car had nearly hit him – almost as if, he thought now, she had been anticipating the car. And she'd been the only one to see that steel cage start to fall . . .

But that was impossible. Even if he believed that she'd been somehow involved in both, the fire in the dressing room exonerated her.

Because Tommy had been the one to stop what they'd been doing, and Tommy had been the one to sniff the air and announce that there was smoke and *maybe* they should do something about it. Jenna had been lost in need, making those killer little moans of hers and writhing beneath him. He'd had to *demand* she get up, and she hadn't wanted to. He remembered how much she hadn't wanted to. She'd very reluctantly opened her eyes, and only then had she smelled the smoke herself. He'd watched the panic flood through her, and he didn't think she was a good enough actress to fake the wild, raw fear. Tommy couldn't imagine anyone with an assassination agenda putting *herself* in harm's way like that.

Then again, he wouldn't be the first guy in the world to get played by a woman.

Tommy hissed out a breath, and shoved his hands in his pockets. His body ached, he thought he was bleeding from hitting the road and skidding into the gutter, and thinking about Jenna betraying him was definitely not making any of it any better.

The trouble was, he had no idea who it could be otherwise. Tripping him into the path of a bus did not seem like a Duncan Paradis move. Duncan was about flash and show. Tommy could see Duncan orchestrating the steelcage incident – that seemed far more up his alley. It had flourish and a certain irony. And while Eugenia would certainly not be above shoving Tommy off a busy sidewalk, she didn't drive, which meant she couldn't have been the driver of the car that had almost hit him. And one of the only things Tommy remembered about that car was the fact there was only one person in it.

It had to be someone close to him, he reasoned, because they'd had access to the set and his dressing room. While Tommy supposed that could make it any one of the numerous crew members, make-up artists, or various support personnel, he had the feeling that whoever wanted him dead had a very personal reason for it. Wasn't that what the mystery novels he devoured on tour always told him? That murder was personal? And personal in his case meant the band.

Except Tommy's mind baulked at the idea. His band mates were his brothers. The only family he had left – the only family he would claim, anyway. They'd been through so much shit – how could one of them be capable of *killing* and Tommy hadn't known it, all this time? How could he have that kind of history with someone who now wanted to kill him?

None of it made sense.

Except, in an awful way, it did. He hated himself for how easily his mind turned – how quickly he went from not being able to imagine one of his band mates wanting to kill him to understanding how one of them could.

Even though he felt the faintest trickle of fear in the recesses of his mind at what wanting to hold her at a moment like this might mean, all Tommy wanted was Jenna.

For no reason that made any sense, or that he would allow himself to consider, he knew that if he could see her, he would feel better.

So he turned on his heel, and headed east, away from his apartment. And towards hers.

23

When Jenna had left the Video TV building, she'd pushed Ken's dire warnings out of her mind, and she'd headed to West 57th Street instead of further uptown and east towards her apartment. She'd found Eugenia where she'd expected to find her – where, in fact, she'd heard her claim to one of her vapid model friends that she *always* went in the evenings – the Russian Tea Room.

Jenna had entered the famous restaurant exactly once before – at the insistence of her mother and grandmother, who thought the place was the height of elegance. Though Jenna had spent about two weeks at NYU before concluding that it was, in fact, the height of tacky, there was no telling her Indiana relatives that all those years later. It had been early 2000, if she remembered correctly, and a lot had changed in New York by then.

Tonight, however, it was 1987. She thought she remembered reading somewhere that earlier in the Eighties, or maybe the late Seventies, Madonna had worked as a coat-check girl at the Russian Tea Room, and Jenna figured there couldn't be a better arbiter of cool than Madonna in the Eighties. Too bad that would change so drastically as time went on.

Jenna had wrapped her scarf over her hair, slunk inside trying to exude *don't look at me* from every pore, then made her way to the bar. It had taken a moment for her eyes to adjust to the dim, golden light in the famously opulent restaurant, and then a few moments more to locate Eugenia sitting in one of the plush red booths facing the bar. Eugenia was nursing a Martini and, as far as Jenna could tell, was practising her version of come-hither looks on a tableful of businessmen nearby.

'I don't know why you recognize me,' Eugenia had cooed, loud enough to be heard clear across the room. Jenna had expected to hear the clatter of her batting eyelashes next, but Eugenia had settled for flipping her hair over one bony shoulder, then the other. 'Have we met somewhere, do you think?' she trilled, clearly mugging for an imaginary camera, and just as clearly waiting for one of the men to get the hint.

As the last magazine she had graced in furtherance of her own career – rather than as Tommy Seer's significant other – had disappeared from news-stands shortly before Reagan won a second term in office in the November 1984 elections, Jenna did not anticipate that anyone would take that hint.

Jenna had ordered her own Martini, and settled in for a long night.

That had been nearly two hours ago.

Stalking someone had to be the most boring thing Jenna had ever done. Waiting for Tommy hadn't been so bad, but Eugenia kept trying desperately to make herself the centre of other diners' attention, even though they were attempting to eat and/or enjoy their own parties, and that tried the nerves. She had even left her table several times to parade through the restaurant, ostensibly to hit the bathroom, though Jenna suspected it was actually to pretend she was on some kind of catwalk. Needless to say, Eugenia did not receive the kind of attention she was looking for – except from the staff, who all but salaamed at her feet.

'No doubt why she comes here every damn night,' Jenna muttered, not realizing she'd spoken aloud until the bartender smiled at her.

'That one?' he asked, pointing his chin at Eugenia's latest stroll-by. 'Every single night without fail. Sometimes with her boyfriend or some girlfriends. But mostly by herself.'

'How sad,' Jenna murmured, insincerely.

'Women like that,' the bartender told her, 'make a man's life a misery. Too beautiful to be kind. Not pretty enough to be worth it.'

Translated: even the bartender thought Eugenia was high-maintenance and annoying. Jenna was getting cranky, though she was wise enough not to be getting drunk at the same time. She'd switched to soda after the first Martini, and any buzz she might have had had long since dissipated. She thought of all the detective novels she'd read over the years, and how they always seemed to gloss over the extreme boredom that accompanied surveillance. Or maybe Jenna had skipped over those parts when she'd read them. Either way, watching a spectacularly boring person spend an evening alone was, unsurprisingly, also spectacularly boring.

Jenna wasn't sure what she'd expected. Eugenia to hold up a sign, perhaps, announcing her murderous intentions? Duncan to appear in a black cloak, twirling a sudden handlebar moustache? Even if Eugenia wanted to kill Tommy, it was unlikely that she'd proclaim that plan to the Russian Tea Room in the middle of a dinner service.

Jenna kept her back to Eugenia, though she was banking on the other woman's self-involvement to keep her from being seen. *If you don't want to call attention to yourself*, she told herself acidly, *you should stop drinking all this soda, since it's making you fidget like a hyperactive five-year-old*.

She heard a commotion behind her, and the next time she dared to look, Eugenia was wreathed in smiles and practically humming with pleasure. That was something different. Seconds later, she saw what had Eugenia all excited as Duncan Paradis slid into the booth with her.

Jenna didn't worry about them seeing her – they never broke eye contact. Not even for the merest second, as if they were drinking each other in and couldn't bear to glance away. She had the sense that the Russian Tea Room could explode and the two of them would hardly notice. Duncan picked up Eugenia's hand, and stroked it between his palms. She coloured with delight. He actually looked ... tender.

Jenna bit back her urge to descend into hysterical laughter at the thought of Duncan Paradis exhibiting tenderness of any kind. She reminded herself that she had also seen quite a bit of Duncan snapping Eugenia's head off – hardly tender at all. She waited for the real Duncan to pop up and do his damage.

But as the illicit lovers smiled at each other and snuggled close in the lush red booth, giggling and touching and doing God knew what beneath the table, Jenna was forced to entertain the possibility that Duncan and Eugenia really did care about each other.

It boggled the mind.

She'd been so certain they were only using each other. Because that was what made sense. That was who they were – a thug with pimp-like ambitions and a woman willing to play fiancée in order to stay close to her married lover. But this was something else entirely.

On some level, maybe it made sense, Jenna thought then, trying to rationalize. Maybe they were a cosmic sort of balance for each other. They gazed at each other as if no one else existed, and she couldn't shake the notion that if that was true, then they were hardly likely to spend their stolen time together stalking around Manhattan setting up accidents for Tommy to stumble into.

That wasn't *proof*, exactly. But her gut feelings hadn't steered her wrong yet. She turned back to the bar, and stared at her drink. She *wanted* it to be Duncan and Eugenia.

They were both so loathsome. Duncan was the bottom-feeder Ken thought he was, if not something worse, and Eugenia was a nasty piece of work from her clothes-hanger frame to her *hey-look-at-me* designer shoes. But *wanting* didn't make it so. Maybe their very hideousness made them the perfect match for each other. They looked at each other like they were the stars of a romantic movie – like there ought to be swelling music and not a dry eye in the house.

Feeling chastened, somehow, Jenna paid her bill, and then headed back out into the night. She felt unsettled. She wanted to blame the large quantities of soda she'd consumed on an empty stomach, but she knew better. She thought about Duncan and Eugenia, what they would gain from Tommy's death and what they would lose. And realized that the problem with her conclusions about the pair of them was that if she was right, that meant she had no idea who was trying to kill Tommy. She bent into the October wind and trudged across 57th Street towards the 6 train. Meanwhile, she'd wasted all this time thinking it was Duncan and Eugenia while the real culprit was off somewhere plotting. She was furious with herself.

On the subway, she brooded over how to tell Tommy what she knew. Or suspected, anyway. The minute she told him her suspicions, he'd use it as reason to blow off the whole thing. It wasn't as if he'd accepted the fact that someone was trying to hurt him. He still thought it had all been a series of coincidental accidents.

Another problem was that Jenna hated the fact she wasn't being honest with him. How could she be in love with him and hide things from him? Hadn't that, on some level, been the entire problem with her relationship with Adam? She'd thought Adam was *almost* the right one. He'd *almost* married her. She'd *almost* loved him the way she should have. But what if they'd been honest with each other from the start? Didn't she owe Tommy the truth – no matter what it cost her to tell him, and no matter what he did as a result?

She was a coward. The way she'd always been a coward. Too afraid to break up with Adam when she should have, years ago, long before he'd met any aspiring yogis. Too scared to admit that she was keeping herself at arm's length from her entire life for years, and too chicken to figure out why. She climbed the stairs out of the subway and started the long walk east towards her apartment, trying to face the ugly truth about herself as she moved. She had hidden away with her fantasies of Tommy Seer for years, and now that she had something good with the real Tommy, she was taking the easy way out once again. It wasn't as simple as her fear that he wouldn't believe her – of course he wouldn't believe her. Who would believe such an insane story? That wasn't why she didn't want to tell him.

She didn't want to tell him because he would leave her. Of course he would. He would think she was the lunatic groupie he'd originally believed her to be. He would hear only insanity, and he would wash his hands of her. Who could blame him? And she was so selfish, so desperately in love with him, and she didn't think she could bear it.

But he was going to die. She knew he was going to die, unless they stopped it somehow, and Jenna knew that if she was any kind of person at all – any kind of human being – she would find a way to tell him. Even if she lost him in the process.

Better to bear losing him personally, she told herself, than to lose him altogether.

Tommy saw her coming from far down the street. She had her head down, bent against the cutting wind, and a bright scarf wrapped around her neck, but he would know her anywhere. He straightened in her building's doorway, and enjoyed watching her without her knowledge.

As she came closer, he saw the frown wedged between her brows, as usual. She worried her lower lip between her teeth, and looked as if she was debating nuclear disarmament with herself. How had he managed to fall so hard for such a serious woman? It was a mystery. But he felt absurdly light-hearted as he watched her worry and frown and march with such force down the city street. She might be serious and strange, but she was his.

He saw the moment she spied him there, waiting for her. Her face went blank with surprise, and then she beamed. Tommy felt the power of that smile all the way to his toes. He smiled back as she picked up her pace and hurried towards him.

'How long have you been here?' she asked, closing the distance between them and climbing the stoop. 'You look like you're freezing to death.'

'I'm fine,' he said, and then helped himself to her mouth. It was like a punch to the gut, heady and sweet. He couldn't seem to get enough of her, so he kissed her again, and then again. He couldn't explain it to himself, and maybe he didn't want to explain it. He wanted to sink into her and forget anything else existed.

When he pulled back, her eyes had gone starry and she smiled up at him, dazed. He watched her take a breath, then collect herself.

'Wow,' she murmured. She reached for him, and frowned when he yanked his hand out of her grasp with a hiss of pain. 'What happened?' she demanded.

'It's a long story,' he said, as she carefully took his hands in hers and looked at the scrapes, her frown deepening.

Jenna made a clucking noise, and then hurried him inside the building. Tommy's hands stung, and he was cold, but there was no denying the warmth that spread through him as he surrendered himself to her. It felt strange and good to have someone fuss over him. To have someone who took his pain personally.

Inside her tiny studio, which Tommy loved despite himself, because it was so normal and so bright – so *happy* – Jenna, tore off her coat and threw it and her bag in the direction of the futon. The bag slid off the couch, tipped over, and spilled its contents everywhere. Tommy stood in the archway between the kitchen and the living room and watched as the usual female things slid out across the hardwood floor.

'Someone pushed me into traffic,' he said, looking away from the bag. Jenna stepped out of the bathroom to stare at him, her eyes wide. 'Obviously, I'm fine,' he said. 'But my head was *this close* to a bus.'

When he showed her the space between his two fingers, he suspected he was as pale as she looked. He tried to shake it off.

'Thank God you're okay,' she said, her voice low. She disappeared into the bathroom again, then reappeared with an armful of first-aid items and a determined set to her jaw.

Tommy let her lead him to the futon, and sank down on it. She kicked her spilled purse out of the way with complete disregard for her own belongings, and knelt in front of him, making more adorable clucking noises as she looked at his palms. He was tempted to hurt himself more often.

'Are you hurt anywhere else?' she asked.

'I don't think so.' Tommy took a quick inventory. 'My knee aches a little bit, but I took the brunt of it on my hands.'

'Did you see who did it?' she asked. Her gaze was serious.

'Just their foot,' Tommy said. He frowned. 'Definitely a male shoe. I'm pretty sure.'

She leaned back, sitting on her haunches with her hands on her thighs. 'What time did this happen?'

'Maybe two hours ago?' He didn't have any sense of time. He'd only known he had to get to her. 'A little more?'

Jenna blew out a breath. 'I had already decided that it couldn't be Duncan and Eugenia,' she told him. 'But I didn't have any proof.' She told him what she'd been up to that evening, and what she'd reluctantly concluded. 'Eugenia, at least, was there for hours. It definitely wasn't her.'

'I don't think it was Duncan, either,' Tommy said. He shook his head, and then winced when she touched one of his raw palms, probing the scrape for bits of the New York street. 'Duncan would never be satisfied with simply pushing someone into traffic. He's too much of an egomaniac. He'd want me to *know* he was the one doing this.'

Jenna nodded as she poured something foul and stinging across Tommy's hands. He hissed his reaction, and she slanted an amused look his way.

'There, there,' she murmured, as if he was a baby. 'It only hurts for a second.'

'Easy for you to say, isn't it?'

She smiled. 'I've had scrapes before, I promise.'

'I think it's Nick,' Tommy said. His voice cracked slightly as he said it, which he hated. It was the first time he'd said it out loud. It made him want to weep, or hit the walls.

'Nick?' Jenna repeated. She looked stunned. She sat back again. 'But you and he have been friends forever.'

'It's about money,' Tommy said bitterly. 'Right? Isn't it always? Or fame. It's the band. It's always about the band.' *Never the music. Always the fucking band.*

'Do you really think so?' Jenna whispered. 'I know he's mad at you—'

277

'More than mad.' He tilted his head back. 'I don't want to believe it, but he's been the angriest. Consistently. The most vocal about me leaving. He was furious about it earlier tonight at our band meeting.'

'You're the one who knows him,' Jenna said carefully. She looked down at her own hands. 'Do you think he's capable of something like this?'

'I don't know how to answer that.' Tommy's voice was hoarse. 'I want to tell you there's no way. But Nick and I aren't who we were back then. He's not the guy I knew.' He blew out a breath. 'So I think he could be capable of anything.'

'He's certainly angry enough,' Jenna said, making a face. He didn't know which temper tantrum of Nick's she was thinking of, but wasn't that the point? That there were so many to choose from? Going all the way back to when Nick would mouth off in high school and get himself thrown out of classes, over and over again.

'He's always had that temper,' Tommy agreed. 'Fight first, talk later, that was always Nick.'

'Okay, so, now we know to watch him.' Jenna's frown was back. Tommy reached over and smoothed it out with his thumb. She smiled, but it didn't reach her eyes. 'That's good. It's like a heads up.'

'Sure,' Tommy said. He was professionally trapped and his oldest friend wanted him dead, but in that moment he felt better than he should have. It was the way she wore her concern for him like a cloak around her, and how seriously she listened when he spoke. It was the way she'd patched him up.

He knew what it was. Maybe it had been inevitable, ever since that first kiss when she'd pulled away and in so doing, confused the hell out of him. *I'm not like that*, she'd told him, horrified. And she'd been telling him the truth. She wasn't like that at all. He wasn't sure how he'd confused the issue.

He watched the sway of her hips as she rose to her feet, and took her bandages and iodine away. He wanted her naked, under him, over him, he didn't care. Just as long as they were skin to skin. Just as long as he could feel her with his hands. Just as long as he could keep believing in her.

He sat forward, and picked up her empty purse. It was giant and very, very blue, and was exactly the kind of thing that made him think women were a different species. He shovelled her things back into it – lipstick, stockings, for some bizarre reason, a wallet. But his attention was caught by the notebook that had fallen open in front of him, the pages cramped with writing. Was Jenna a writer? He wondered why she'd never mentioned that to him. Then again, they'd really only known each other a very short time. There were all kinds of things she probably hadn't mentioned. All kinds of secrets and passions he had yet to discover. He couldn't wait.

Tommy picked up the notebook, meaning to close it properly, and saw his name.

He looked closer, thinking that maybe he'd found Jenna's diary, or something equally private. He was delighted – and definitely not too mature to put it away.

October 3 – Tommy almost hit by car, rushed to hospital –
FIRST ATTEMPT?

That did not read like the girlie diary entry he'd been expecting. So he read on.

And wished he hadn't.

Because it got worse, and then much worse.

TOMMY DIES, of course, was the worst part. It had a page to itself, and a date that was under a week away. She had it circled in red and written in block capitals.

Tommy felt frozen through to his core.

Jenna walked back into the room, her hair around her like a cloud, and stopped when he looked up at her. He watched her notice what he held in front of him, and he watched her swallow.

'What is this?' he asked, and he sounded so calm, so quiet, when all he could hear inside his own head was the screaming.

'I can explain,' she said, her voice quivering. 'Really.'

'"Tommy dies",' he read. His eyebrows shot up. 'I can think of only one reason for this, Jenna. Only one, and it makes you a fucking psycho, among other things. So by all means, explain it to me. Please.'

24

God, the way he was *looking* at her.

It made her stomach muscles clench and her knees go weak. Jenna remembered his weary cynicism that first night, when she'd realized to her horror that he wasn't emotionally or even physically involved, not at all. That he was going along with it because he wanted something from her, but not because he wanted her.

This was much, much worse than that.

He sat there on the futon, the same futon where he'd put his mouth and his hands on every inch of her skin, where she'd cried out his name and made him growl with desire, except now he was looking at her with that arrested expression, like he'd never seen her before. It was horrible. The green in his eyes had gone glacial. Frigid. He was holding himself so still. So rigid.

She knew on some deep level of intuition that it didn't matter what she said. He'd already convicted her of whatever crimes he believed she'd committed. Judge, jury, executioner. She could feel it in her bones, see it in the way he looked at her, like she was a stranger. Worse than a stranger. A monster.

There was nothing to be done about it except tell him the truth. She'd known it would have to come to this, eventually. She'd simply been too cowardly to bring the topic up of her own volition. Too afraid of . . . exactly this.

Jenna took a deep breath, held her hands together in front of her like she was giving a speech, and dove in.

'I'm going to tell you something,' she said, through her suddenly parched mouth, 'and you're going to think it sounds absolutely crazy. Believe me, I know how crazy it sounds. I know how crazy it *is*.' She paused, and discovered that she'd started sweating. Terrific. 'And I probably should have told you a long time ago, but I didn't know how. I still don't know how.'

Tommy said nothing. He didn't move. He didn't seem to breathe. It was as if he'd turned to stone.

I couldn't get so lucky.

'The thing is,' she said, plunging on, 'I've known since before I met you that you're going to die in a few days. I've always known. And the reason I've always known . . .' She wasn't sure she could do it. She *had* to do it. '. . . is because this is not the first time I've lived through 1987.'

Tommy didn't so much as blink.

'I came back in time,' Jenna said. She sounded so bright and cheery. So matter-of-fact. It was ridiculous. She felt ridiculous. She moistened her lips with her tongue. 'And I can hear what I sound like when I say that. But if you

282

can just trust me on the part that sounds crazy . . . I know it might be hard, but if you can, I don't know, suspend disbelief for a few days? The key thing to remember is that someone is trying to kill you. And I know that they were successful once before.' She wanted to faint. She could hear herself, and she sounded like a crazy person. An unhinged lunatic.

'You came back in time,' Tommy said after an endless moment of him merely watching her like she was an exhibit in a zoo. He stretched his legs out in front of him, and suddenly he almost looked relaxed. If Jenna didn't look too closely at the harsh glitter in his eyes, or the hard cast to his jaw.

'Yes,' she said simply, because what else was there to say?

'From where?' He smirked. 'Excuse me. I guess I mean, from *when*?'

She ignored the smirk, and told him the year.

'The twenty-first century,' Tommy said. He nodded. 'Not so far off. Things must be pretty much the same.'

Jenna thought of the Internet. Facebook and IM. Email. Cellphones and Blu-ray. Starbucks and iTunes. Voice-activated cars. Smart houses. Her beloved TiVo.

'Some things,' she said.

'So much for the theory that the world will blow up in the year 2000,' he said in that same conversational tone, as if they were discussing one of the PBS shows he liked to watch. She knew better than to believe it. 'Look at you. Living proof that we survive the millennium.'

He thought she was a maniac. She could feel the edge in his voice as it cut into her. But she didn't know what else to do, what might ease the pounding of her heart or that sick feeling in her gut, so she kept talking.

'The millennium was really no big deal,' she shared with him. He cocked his head slightly to the side, as if fascinated. She knew that she was digging her own grave, as far as he was concerned. But she couldn't seem to stop. 'The world didn't end, the computers didn't explode, and the Four Horsemen didn't appear. It was kind of a let-down.'

'I'll keep that in mind.' His hands tensed over the note-book, then he set it down beside him on the futon. Like it was alive, and had teeth. 'And what's it like in . . . how do you say it? Aught two? Aught ten?'

'You say two thousand,' Jenna said. Teacher to student. As if this was a normal conversation. 'Two thousand eleven. Or twenty. Twenty twelve. Like that.'

It was almost as if he was interested in these details, but Jenna knew he wasn't. She could feel the tension in him, emanating out in waves. Slicing into her like the wind through the concrete canyons.

'I can't tell you how fascinating this is,' he said after a moment, and when he looked at her, Jenna saw a complete stranger.

'Tommy, please,' she said desperately. 'I know this is impossible to hear. I know you don't want to believe me – that you can't. But you have to know that I would never tell you something like this if it wasn't true. Why would I?'

'Why would you?' he echoed softly, and pulled himself to his feet. She saw a hint of despair cross his face, but then his mask came down and it was as if he was made of steel. Blank. Unyielding. 'I can think of a few reasons,' he said shortly. 'But first and foremost, you're obviously out of your fucking mind.'

'I understand—'

'It's all in that book, isn't it?' he demanded, cutting her off. 'Your whole plan of attack. I have to hand it to you, I really do. It's certainly the most creative approach I've ever seen.'

'I don't know what you're talking—'

'Bullshit.' His voice cracked like a whip, and Jenna flinched. 'You know exactly what I'm talking about. Make me think I'm being stalked, then save me from the stalker. What a hero you are. How could I do anything but fall in love with you?'

'You think I—' Jenna held up her hands, palms out. 'That doesn't make sense. How could I drive the car that almost hit you – and me?'

'How did you know it was going to hit me?' he fired back.

'Because I knew,' she said fiercely. 'Because it already happened. And why would I endanger myself – with the car, the fire – if the plan was to lure you in somehow?'

'I don't know why,' he snapped. 'But we're talking about someone who thinks she was *sent back in time*, so I'm not exactly looking for rational explanations at this point. You're lucky I don't call the cops.'

'The cops.' She couldn't believe it was *this* bad. Her heart was hammering against her ribs. 'Why on earth would you call the cops?'

'Because that's what you do when you find out you have a crazy stalker with absolutely no grip on reality,' Tommy threw at her. He jabbed a finger in the direction of her notebook. 'Especially one with a detailed plan leading up to your death.'

Jenna put her trembling fingers to her temples.

'Tommy,' she said, fighting to stay calm, 'you can think I'm crazy. You can think I'm a stalker. I don't blame you. But you have to believe me – *someone is trying to kill you.*'

'Yeah,' he said. His gaze bored into her. 'I'm looking at her.'

'It's not me!' she yelled. 'For God's sake!'

'Stay away from me, Jenna.' His voice came out in a hiss, and his eyes narrowed to slits. He looked dangerous. She felt fear skate down the back of her neck.

'You have to be careful—' she tried again.

'Stay the fuck away from me, or I really will have your ass thrown in jail,' he told her in that low, ominous voice. 'Unless, of course, you can go back to the future like Michael J. fucking Fox.'

He brushed past her, not even trying to avoid it, and that slight bit of contact rocked her.

'Tommy . . .' But she only whispered it, and anyway, the door slammed hard behind him.

He was gone.

*   *   *

286

Tommy spent a long time walking the streets before he calmed down enough to notice where he was. Even when he recognized that he was near the Midtown Tunnel, which was nowhere near anywhere he'd want to go, he didn't care.

She's fucking crazy, he told himself over and over. It was like a song in his head. *She's a fucking crazy lunatic.*

His heart had broken. He'd actually felt it happen. Every word she'd said cracked it into pieces, smaller and smaller. Until there was nothing left but rage and despair, because he'd thought he'd found someone. Finally. He'd thought he wasn't alone.

Wake up, Tommy, he told himself harshly. Bitterly. *You're always alone.*

He couldn't even begin to unravel the levels of insanity involved. He couldn't allow himself to think about what she'd said, but at the same time, he couldn't think of anything else. How could he have spent so much time with her and seen no sign of it until now? She had to throw *time travel* at him before he noticed the fact she was a stark, raving psycho? Where was the yellow light, for God's sake?

Time travel. Of all fucking things. The twenty-first century. She'd even mentioned the millennium. Of course she had. *Time travel*. All the while looking at him with her huge brown eyes, *wounded* that he somehow couldn't swallow the nonsense coming out of her mouth.

How the hell had he failed to see this before?

287

Tommy heard himself take a ragged breath, and decided that it had to stop. Enough. The person he'd thought he was falling in love with didn't exist. He'd been played. It wasn't the first time and it probably wouldn't be the last, not with his luck. It was one of the prices of fame. Yet another cost no one warned you about, but it happened to everyone. It was unavoidable, really. So what if his heart had shattered? He shouldn't have let his heart get involved in the first place.

He knew better. And he'd pegged her from the get-go. How had he let her worm her way under his skin? *He knew better.* He hated himself for his weakness. His loneliness. Because that's what it was. He'd been so desperate to be listened to. Heard. What a fucking chump.

But no more. He was done.

Once he made up his mind, he moved fast. His long strides ate up the distance, and soon enough he was back at Duncan's office building. After all this time, he knew his scumbag of a manager too well. No way, on the night his band made a new number one, did Duncan Paradis stay out celebrating with Eugenia. Hell, no. That was what lesser moguls might do, but Duncan had much sturdier ambitions.

He didn't look surprised to see Tommy standing in his doorway.

'What the fuck do you want?' he grunted, barely sparing Tommy a glance before returning his attention to his desk. 'Missed me?'

'Jenna Jenkins,' Tommy said in a clipped voice. It hurt

to say her name. He planned never to say it again after this conversation. 'Fire her.'

'A few hours ago you were up Nick's ass about this girl, jumping to her defence like some demented white knight, and now you want to fire her?' But Duncan seemed amused. He shifted in his chair and smirked. 'Trouble in paradise?'

'There's no conspiracy,' Tommy said, folding his arms across his chest. 'No one's whispering anything behind your back. You never needed her in the first place.'

'She was either going to report on you, or do you,' Duncan replied, meeting Tommy's gaze with a bland one of his own. He shrugged. 'I didn't care which.'

'I appreciate you pimping for me,' Tommy said drily. 'I'm a lucky guy. You picked me a fiancée, too.'

'I'd wipe your ass if I had to,' Duncan said, leaning back in his chair. 'But I'd take it out of your royalties, believe me.'

Tommy hated him. But he also knew him. Duncan could not surprise him, or shock him. Not any more. Duncan was a known quantity. After tonight, he decided that was comforting.

'Someone's trying to kill me,' Tommy said, watching his manager's face just in case. Duncan's eyes narrowed, but he didn't otherwise change expression. 'All these accidents lately. I think Jenna might be involved.'

'She's gone,' Duncan said immediately. He tapped his fingers against the desk. 'The car thing happened right around the time she came on board. You think she's going to escalate?'

Tommy saw the last page in that notebook. *TOMMY DIES.* The date. He blew out a breath, and ignored the stab of pain in the region of his chest. His heart was ashes anyway. It was a phantom pain.

'Yeah,' he said. 'She might.'

'Any proof? Something we can hand the cops?'

'Nothing like that.' Because he couldn't bring himself to touch that notebook again, he'd left it behind. He felt dirty even knowing it existed.

'I understand the urge to kill you,' Duncan said, his shark's smile on full display. 'I share it. But I can't allow it. There's too much money involved, and I don't accept your resignation from the band anyway. There's way more cash to make out of your sorry ass.'

Tommy rolled his eyes. There was no point responding in any more detail.

'I'll hire a couple bodyguards in case she goes to DEFCON 1,' Duncan said. 'Is that what you want? Is that enough?'

'Make sure I don't see her,' Tommy said. He looked away. 'That's what I want.'

'Done,' Duncan replied.

'You know, you didn't need a spy.' Tommy was surprised to hear how bitter his voice was. 'You could have asked me what you wanted to know. I hate you enough to tell you the truth.'

'Where's the fun in that?' Duncan asked, his voice hard. 'And don't worry, asshole. I hate you too.'

290

Tommy let out a short laugh, and then headed for the elevators. He didn't bother saying goodbye. He felt hollowed out.

And even so, that exchange with Duncan had been the most honest and real of the night.

25

Jenna woke up in a sudden, inexplicable panic, her mouth dry as Death Valley and her eyes gritty and swollen. It took her long, stupid moments to realize that the phone was ringing.

The most immediate source of panic identified, she launched herself up and across the floor – knowing even as she lurched towards the shrieking phone that it was not going to be Tommy.

It hurt even to think his name – she felt a sob roll through her chest and she ruthlessly clamped down on it. No more sobbing. She was sobbed out.

And she knew he wouldn't be the one calling her. There was no coming back from *time travel*.

But her heart still pounded like she was running a marathon.

Jenna snatched up the receiver and muttered something into it, hoping it approximated a greeting.

'Oh, Jen.' It was Ken Dollimore, which was not in itself

surprising. But the fact that he sounded almost ... nurturing?

That anomaly woke Jenna up like a triple espresso. She rubbed at her abused eyes with her free hand. God, she missed espresso.

'Ken?' She wanted to ask if he'd been body-snatched or had suffered a head injury of some kind, but restrained herself.

'I warned you,' he said in that same, almost-sweet voice, the one that surely belonged to someone else. Because Ken was many things – including, yesterday, unexpectedly confiding – but caring in a vaguely paternal way? Never.

And yet, he made a distinct *clucking* sort of noise over the phone, like some kind of mother hen.

'I don't have any idea what you're talking about,' Jenna told him truthfully.

'I just hung up with Duncan Paradis,' Ken said, making a strange sort of wheezing noise that Jenna knew meant he was propping his feet up on the desk she'd so diligently cleared the day before. 'The long and short of it is, your services are no longer required.'

Jenna let out a sigh. 'I figured,' she said. Then she caught on to the strange tone. 'Why are you being so ... *careful* with me?'

She felt certain, somehow, that whatever Tommy had reported to Duncan or even to Ken, *time travel* had not come into it. It was, happily, entirely too crazy for casual conversation. She had that to hold on to.

293

'I feel for you,' Ken said in that same *careful* tone, 'I do. And don't worry, I don't believe whatever bullshit they're saying about *mental-health issues*. It's so transparent. These famous types will say anything to avoid having to deal with real-life issues like real-life people—'

'Mental-health issues,' Jenna repeated dully. It was only to be expected, of course. It was acceptable code for *she started talking about coming back in time*. Yet it still stung.

'Look,' Ken said matter-of-factly, a veritable font of advice all of a sudden. 'You have to be practical about these things. It was never going to work out. He's who he is, and you and me, we're normal people. This is how it goes. You have to figure out a way to be happy about the time you had. Like it was a gift.'

'A gift,' Jenna repeated. She realized she sounded moronic. Part of that was the cotton-mouthed, woolly-headed thing she had going on, thanks to a long night of heartbreak, but another part was her inability to process the fact that her supercharged, elfin boss was *consoling* her.

And, moreover, that he thought he was one of the normal ones.

'I want you to take a week off and rest,' Ken continued. 'And I'm not being nice here, Jen, believe me – I've had secretaries who got dumped before, and I can't cope with the weeping and the phone calls and the downer of it all.'

'You,' Jenna said drily, 'are truly an amazing man.'

'Sleep, eat chocolate, watch videos of *Romancing the Stone*

294

and *Streets of Fire* – whatever you have to do,' Ken said magnanimously. 'I'll see you next Wednesday. Okay?'

'Um, sure.' Jenna replaced the receiver in a daze. Only Ken Dollimore could give a vacation on one hand, and be so profoundly shallow on the other. Complete with a Michael Paré reference. She supposed it didn't much matter – in the end, she had a week to herself.

A week to save Tommy, who would die in five days.

It would be harder now, but it wasn't as if she could stop trying to save him simply because he thought she was a psycho. *Spoken like a true stalker*, she told herself sourly.

Jenna sucked in a ragged breath, then let it out in a rush. *Breathe*, she ordered herself sternly. In. Out. In. Out. She felt a little dizzy, and certainly not calm. Maybe she just wasn't going to feel calm until this was over.

She could not let him die.

She could not.

Jenna scraped her hair back into a knot at the nape of her neck, and told herself, sternly, that she didn't have time to indulge her broken heart, her hurt feelings, or her desire to curl up in the foetal position for several months.

It was time to follow Nick.

Tommy thought that if filming of the stupid video didn't stop soon, he might spontaneously burst into flames. Or pieces.

He stood on his mark and pouted at the camera, as

directed. He lip-synced the lyrics on cue, which sounded more and more inane to him every time he did another take – and he'd written them in the first place. He was irritated well above and beyond the level he normally was at this stage in the proceedings.

It wasn't that the filming had gotten any more strenuous, or even any more stupid than usual. It was that Jenna wasn't there to amuse him, and he hated himself for how much he missed her.

It was a ridiculous way to feel. He'd been making videos for years now, and had done so happily enough without her presence. Why should her absence now seem so unbearable?

Surely, he raged at himself while he was supposed to be transmitting sultriness towards the camera, his feelings for a woman should disappear in a puff of smoke when she exposed herself as a lunatic psychopath. Surely he should not feel this bad. As if several of the goddamned steel cages were perched on top of him, crushing him. Robbing him of breath.

Damn her. And damn him for once again playing the gullible fool, the one he'd thought he'd banished years before, right around the time he'd realized what it meant to sign his whole life away.

'Uh . . . Tommy?' The director sounded apprehensive. Tommy blinked, and wondered how many times the man had called his name. 'Lovely expressions, really lovely. Totally raw and hot. But I'm wondering if we can do it one more time with a little *more* sex and a little *less* mayhem?'

'You look like a bloody serial killer, mate,' Sebastian chimed in from his chair behind the cameras. There was a burst of laughter from the rest of the band. *Ha ha*, Tommy thought sourly. *If only you knew.*

'Of course,' he said out loud, in as even a tone as he could manage. He even smiled, because he was a goddamned professional.

The music swelled around him, and he resumed his place. He waited for the verse to start over again.

He couldn't get that creepy book of hers out of his head, no matter how hard he tried to focus on some-thing – anything – else. All the tiny writing and the nota-tions – like an encyclopedia of a psychotic breakdown. Careful flow charts of how and when 'accidents' had befallen him – or would befall him. How had she done it? How had she managed to arrange all of it so well? She'd had no reason to suppose he would ever see her as more than a secretary and a spy for Duncan.

He tried to shift and think sexy thoughts as he mouthed the words to the song, and the shitty thing was how hard it *wasn't*. He had only to think of Jenna, laid out in front of him, her soft skin with a sheen of sweat and her hair tousled all around her – and something roared through him, hot and loud. *Mine*, he thought, against all reason and sense. When he didn't even want her any more.

When he refused to want her any more.

'Cut!' the director yelled again. He rubbed at his temples and then smiled – in a noticeably strained way – at Tommy.

'Why don't we take a break? Regroup, think happy thoughts, that kind of thing?'

Another burst of laughter from the peanut gallery, as punctuation.

Tommy didn't trust himself to respond. He walked across the set towards make-up, and sat there while they fussed around him, moving the same strands of his hair this way and that and powdering his skin.

'Who pissed on you today?' Nick asked, coming up from behind Tommy to lean against the counter. He looked like he wanted to find whoever the pisser was, and congratulate him. He smirked when Tommy glared at him. 'I'm sorry I asked. But you look like you could spit nails.'

Tommy watched his oldest friend walk off, and hated himself even more for the way he'd turned against him. Thank God no one knew. He would carry the shame of it to his grave. Nick and he might not have been as close as they'd once been, but how the hell did you throw decades of friendship down the toilet so easily? How could he have suspected Nick? In that moment, Tommy loathed himself.

What the hell had he become?

It came to him then, out of nowhere. He hadn't been to Buffalo since he'd left it behind in Nick's rear-view mirror. They'd driven his piece-of-shit Chevy as far as it would go down the New York State Thruway, and left it in a smoking heap by the side of the road when it broke down. They'd hitch-hiked the rest of the way into New York City. And Tommy had always viewed that journey as a kind of rebirth. Fuck Buffalo. Fuck the generations of his relatives who lacked the imagination to leave the trailer park, much less the city. He'd vowed he'd never return.

But he wasn't the same guy any longer. And it occurred to him that maybe Buffalo was exactly what he needed. If he saw where he came from, maybe he'd get a grip on where he'd ended up. Maybe he'd figure out how to move forward.

Maybe he'd even get over her.

'What do you think you're doing?'

Jenna did not mistake Nick's quiet tone for calm. She could see the look on his face, as he towered over her in the dark, swanky bar, and what she saw there made her squirm on her barstool.

'Oh,' she said, stalling. She smiled brightly. 'Hi!'

Nick glared at her. He did not say hello and he did not change that grim expression even one iota.

'Why are you following me?' he asked instead. Not nicely. His hovering had already attracted attention. The other patrons in the bar were looking over, especially the three coltish-looking eighteen-year-old girls Nick had abandoned in order to speak to Jenna.

'Following you?' Jenna repeated, and tried to look confused. 'I don't know what you mean.'

'I mean, you've been following me all night,' Nick said, his voice getting lower and tenser with each word. 'Every time I look up, there you are. Does this have anything to do with whatever's going on with Tommy?'

Tommy. Jenna could not allow herself to think about

him. She thrust the sharp surge of pain away, and ordered herself not to burst into tears. Somehow.

'I don't know what's going on with him,' she said in a steely tone, forcing herself to be tough. This was not entirely untrue. It had been almost two days since Tommy had stormed out of her apartment. He could have any number of things going on with him by now.

'So this is for my benefit?' Nick smirked at her. 'No thanks. I don't go for dumpy secretaries.' The look he swept over her, raking her from head to toe, was beyond insulting. Jenna was fairly certain it would leave scars behind in its wake.

'I'll keep that in mind,' she snapped, her temper getting the better of her. Who was he to look at another person that way? And she was not *dumpy*, she simply wasn't an eighteen-year-old *skank*. She made a face. 'Why are you and he even friends?'

Nick shook his head at her, like she was pathetic beyond comprehension.

'He's not my *friend*,' he spat out. He didn't say, *you stupid little bitch*, but it was strongly implied. 'We're family. You couldn't understand.'

Because Jenna could see how much he meant that, she didn't understand how he could want to hurt someone he cared for so much.

'Maybe not,' she murmured, stalling again while she puzzled over it.

'What did you do to him?' Nick demanded, still with that horribly insulting glare. 'I've never seen him this bad.

300

He was even talking about going back to Buffalo, of all places. Is that because of you?'

'I . . .' Jenna didn't know how to answer that. 'Buffalo?'

'The pit of hell,' Nick said darkly. His lips tightened. 'I think he might be about to do something colossally stupid.'

'I don't get it,' Jenna said then, the words bursting out of her. 'Why do you care? And if you do really care, why are you trying to hurt him?'

Nick stared at her in shock, and fell back a step.

'What are you talking about?' he demanded. He looked pale around the eyes. 'What the *fuck* do you mean by that?'

'Someone is trying to kill Tommy,' Jenna said matter-of-factly. Not that she wasn't afraid he might hurt her, but at this point she was in for a penny, in for a pound. If she was dead, she was already dead. Plus, sleep deprivation apparently made her brave. She shrugged and met Nick's stare with her own. 'He thinks it might be you.'

Nick's mouth actually fell open. For a moment, he did nothing but look at her in confusion.

'What?' he asked again. It was more of a gasp. He shook his head slightly, as if he was dizzy. 'I want to kill the guy, sure, but not *really*— I would never—' He cut himself off. When he looked at Jenna again, his expression was bewildered more than anything else. 'Does he really think I would do that?' he asked.

Jenna shrugged, because, of course, Tommy now thought *she* was the person trying to kill him. Since she

301

knew he was wrong, she didn't feel compelled to share that titbit with Nick.

'That stupid bastard,' Nick muttered, but Jenna could see he was off balance. He threw her a look of intense dislike, and opened his mouth as if to say something. But he stopped himself. 'I guess I'm glad you told me that,' he gritted out. 'Now I can go kick his ass.'

Jenna failed to come up with an appropriate response for that, so they looked at each other in awkward silence for a moment, and then Nick turned and stalked away. Not back to the eighteen-year-olds (and Jenna was being bitchy – maybe they were twenty), but directly to the door and out into the night.

Jenna let out the breath she'd been holding, and smiled sweetly at the pissed-off eighteen-year-olds when the three of them glared daggers at her.

Yes, girls, she thought but did not say, *I can repel any famous musician with the power of my dumpy, secretarial words.*

It was great for Tommy that his oldest friend wasn't the killer, assuming she believed Nick, which, for some reason, she did. He'd looked too shocked by the accusation, too appalled that Tommy would think that kind of thing about him. Of course, he could be an excellent actor who had fooled her. It wasn't as if she knew the first thing about reading people to determine if they were lying to her about their murderous intentions. She wasn't Sherlock Holmes. Hell, she wasn't even Maddie Hayes from *Moonlighting*.

But she didn't think he was lying.

Which meant, with four days to go until Tommy went over that bridge, she still had no idea who the killer was.

Jenna tossed back the rest of her drink, and got to her feet.

Back to square one.

26

Buffalo was some seven hours and whole worlds away from Manhattan, and light years away from *Tommy Seer*, the lead singer of one of the decade's biggest bands. The culture shock, he thought at one point during his impromptu tour of his home town, might just kill him.

But it didn't. He drove around the city, and through the trailer park where he and Nick had grown up. The place looked exactly the same. If he squinted he could almost see the two of them, feverish with their longing to escape, making up songs and telling lies about their futures on the front steps of one of the double-wides. He drove out of the trailer park and this time, he didn't look in the rear-view mirror. He just drove. He had no idea where he was headed, but he wasn't surprised when he found himself outside his old high school.

It was a battered brick building that sat on the crest of a hill, squaring off against the encroaching city and looking the worse for the battle. The place exuded neglect.

Chipped paint and faded graffiti marked the walls. Around the back, temporary classroom trailers abutted the main building – the very same ones that had sat in that exact spot when he'd been a student there. The football field out in front was mowed and tended, but the track surrounding it looked cracked and unsafe. He remembered how completely he'd hated this place when he was a kid, and it was strange to feel so disconnected from it now. Not that the school had become smaller, but the surrounding world so much bigger. Maybe it was Tommy's own ability to put this shitty, forgotten urban high school into its proper, minimized context.

He dropped his head forward in defeat, because he still had all that rage inside him. He still felt trapped, and doomed. Not because of Jenna and her fucking book, but because of the choices he'd made. All that time and all that space, and he'd been doing nothing but running in circles.

He'd left here years ago, determined to outrun his demons, and yet here they all were, together again. It was like a goddamned reunion.

Tommy stood for a moment and stared up at the school, empty in the late-afternoon shadows, and then he walked up to the benches out in front, surrounding a desolate-looking flagpole. As he had more times than he could possibly count, he sat down there, and waited. For his heart to stop aching. For the night to fall. For all of it to make sense, somehow – his past and his present and his murky future. For some kind of sign.

He waited.

He lost track of time. The sun went down, and the temperature dropped. He hadn't thought of Buffalo's famously cold winters, the ones that started in early fall and often brought snow, and he wished he'd brought something warmer to wear than his leather bomber jacket.

Stars came out, so many of them, and Tommy watched them for a long time. He had the sense of the city spread out around him – the Rust Belt city of his youth in the middle of its rapid decline. He still felt Buffalo as a great darkness pressing in on him, crushing him into his predestined life, the one his family had expected of him before he was born – a life he'd always hated. City of Light, his ass. This had always been a city of pain – of lost opportunities, closing factories, and diminished hopes.

Tommy wondered, not for the first time, what kind of man he would have been if his father had lived. Would he have escaped Buffalo? Would he have worked steel like his father, or defected to the police force like so many of his uncles? Would he have accepted those as his only choices? Would he be sitting here now?

He would not be Tommy Seer, he thought. He would not have had this bright, shining life, however fake it might feel to him now. He would never have met Jenna if he'd lived that other life, that lost, dark life he'd never wanted. He would never have trusted her, or lost himself in her body so fully. Sitting there, it almost seemed worth the trade. Surely a life of misery on the line couldn't be worse than the way he felt now.

He thought it was nearing dawn when another car pulled into the otherwise abandoned school parking lot, riding low and tight to the ground. Tommy jerked to attention, and wondered if he'd fallen asleep after all. He felt only a detached sort of interest as a figure climbed out of the car, stood for a moment beside it, then trudged up the hill towards the flagpole.

As it drew closer, Tommy saw that the figure was Nick.

His first thought was that he'd been right all along – Nick was the killer. Was Jenna working with him? Would he die in this horrible place, surrounded by the remnants of the life he'd been so desperate to escape? There would be a certain sick poetry in it – even he could see that.

Don't be ridiculous, he snapped at himself. Jenna was a psycho. She wasn't working with anyone. He shook her off.

'You're an asshole,' Nick said, lowering himself to the bench next to Tommy.

'Nice night for a drive,' Tommy said, in the same conversational tone.

They didn't look at each other. They kept their eyes trained on the football field, and the city beyond. Tommy didn't know what Nick saw, but he saw only their past, stretched out before them and dancing in the dark, like ghosts in a Springsteen song.

'It's colder than balls,' Nick muttered.

Nick blew on his hands and rubbed them together, and Tommy had the strangest sense that it could have been any year at all – that he and Nick could have easily been fifteen years old again. Same conversation, same actions. Déjà vu in reverse.

'Buffalo,' Nick said in disgust. 'This fucking place. You make me chase your pansy ass all the way to *this* shit hole.'

'No one invited you,' Tommy said calmly. 'You didn't have to come.'

'Like hell I didn't.' Nick let out a little snort. 'No good can come of being back here, man. No good at all.' He shifted against his seat. 'Please don't tell me you went back to Lakeshore Park. *Eyesore* Park. What a nightmare.'

'You don't have to be here.' Tommy kept his voice low.

'Why do you?' Nick turned to look at him then. 'What is going on with you, Tommy? You're acting crazy.'

'I'm not acting crazy.' Tommy laughed, without humour. 'You don't even know the meaning of crazy, believe me.' *Time travel*, he thought bitterly. *Fucking* Back to the Future *bullshit*.

Nick shook his head, his knee bouncing up and down – telegraphing his impatience. His agitation.

'I'm not trying to kill you, you stupid motherfucker,' he said in a low, angry voice. 'If I was trying to kill you, first of all, you'd be dead. And second, you'd fucking know who did it.'

Tommy was absurdly touched by this declaration.

'I'll keep that in mind,' he said after a few moments. He knew better than to smile. 'You'll come from the front.'

'You better believe it.' Nick hunched his shoulders into his jacket. 'You're my brother. Family. You know that.'

'I know it.' Tommy's voice was as quiet as Nick's.

Up above, the sky was beginning to show hints of navy. Soon it would grow bluer. Dawn was coming.

Because they were very old friends, and men, they did not talk about the wedge that had grown between them over the years. Too much money, too much fame. Nick did not apologize for his anger. Tommy did not explain, once again, his reasons for wanting out. But as they sat there together, where they'd sat so many times before, the anger and the distance faded away. And soon enough they were simply Tommy and Nick again, troublemakers and dreamers, destined for far better things than the lives they'd been handed.

'It's supposed to snow on this godforsaken city today,' Nick said eventually. 'I checked, so I could be pissed off about it. How long are you planning to sit here in the dark? Are we going to read poetry and hold hands or something?'

'Not much longer,' Tommy said, fighting another smile. 'Prick.'

'Because this time I think we should race down the Thruway,' Nick said, ignoring the insult, though his mouth kicked up in the corner. 'And let me tell you something – that sweet De Lorean you see parked next to your overrated Ferrari is not about to break down like that crappy Chevy back in the day.'

'That Ferrari is a work of art,' Tommy protested. 'Bite your tongue.'

'Let's go,' Nick said. He stood up, and his gaze swept

over the school, the field, the whole of their home town. Then he looked back at Tommy, and his expression was compassionate. As if, finally, he understood. 'I think we're done here.'

Forty-eight hours later, and Jenna was dry-eyed, exhausted, and so caffeinated her skin seemed to hum.

She hadn't slept. She'd gone directly home after speaking to Nick in that bar, she'd spread out all the pages of her notebook in front of her, and she'd studied. She'd remembered. She'd talked her way through the two months leading up to Tommy's death again and again, looking for something – anything – new. She'd racked her brain for any detail it could give her, desperate to find the piece that she was missing. But there was nothing.

She was getting a fresh cup of coffee in the kitchen, ready to start the process all over again, when she noticed that the sun had come up outside.

'Two days . . .' she murmured to herself. She thought about how quickly the last forty-eight hours had passed, and shuddered.

Two days was no time at all.

Jenna sagged against the counter, despair swamping her, sapping the strength from her limbs. What was she going to do? For all that she touted herself as a walking encyclopedia of Eighties trivia, the truth was, she would give anything for access to the Internet. A good Google search. She was running out of time, and she'd long since run out of ideas.

'What is the point of this?' she demanded, feeling hysterical and addressing the air around her – the unseen force, whatever it was, that had brought her here. 'Why would you put me through this?'

She sank down then, all the way to the linoleum, and sat there with her back against the cabinet. From this angle, she could see the small stove and the tiny refrigerator. If she turned her head to the right, she could look out the window at a brick wall. If she turned the other way, she could only see images of Tommy, naked, lounging there.

Jenna buried her face in her arms, and tried to breathe.

Her mind baulked at the images, but they came anyway.

The grainy news footage of the broken guard rail on the Tappan Zee. Reporters huddled against the rain, speaking in those serious, yet still excited, tones. The search of the Hudson river as the rain continued, as if the skies were mourning him. The battered car, pulled out by a crane, swinging like a crumpled black metronome against the grey river.

Then, later, the funeral. They'd packed St Patrick's Cathedral. Fans had jammed themselves behind the barricades on Fifth Avenue despite the bad weather, while every last famous musician anyone had heard of had filed solemnly inside. MTV and Video TV had shown live coverage of the funeral, and then played nothing but Wild Boys videos for the next six hours.

Jenna had cried through all of it.

This time around, she didn't know what she would do.

She was sure she couldn't watch that funeral again. Now that she knew Tommy, all those words and songs seemed egregiously inadequate. All she would do was grieve for him – and try to see if she could spot his killer amongst the glittering, star-studded crowd.

Which was when something occurred to her.

Every muscle in her body tensed, and her head shot up, though she wasn't seeing the kitchen. She ran through her memories of the funeral again, and then again to be sure, but there was no doubt.

Jenna couldn't believe it hadn't occurred to her sooner. She'd been so caught up in what happened *leading up* to Tommy's funeral that she'd forgotten the funeral itself. And it had been spectacular. Sting, Elton John, Prince. Madonna, Cyndi Lauper. All the kings and queens of the glittering Eighties music scene, gathered together to pay their respects.

All except one.

Richie.

At twelve, Jenna had fully understood Richie's absence that day. He'd released a statement announcing that he was too distraught, and Jenna had found that convincing – after all, *she* had been too distraught to do much besides flail on the floor and scare her parents into hiring a child psychologist.

But Jenna wasn't sure she found 'distraught' acceptable any longer. Not now that she knew that someone was making that funeral happen, that it wasn't a suicide or an accident. Maybe Richie hadn't been distraught at all – maybe he'd simply felt it would be too much to pretend to grieve at the funeral of the man he'd killed.

Jenna knew it had to be someone close to Tommy. But she'd never considered Richie. Why would she? He hardly opened his mouth. Yet, somehow, upon consideration, she had no problem imagining him capable of killing Tommy. In fact, she'd had no trouble imagining any number of people killing Tommy.

She climbed to her feet, and took a deep drag of the coffee she'd left on the counter. Two days wasn't long, true, but it was better than nothing. And with adrenalin coursing through her veins, she felt almost normal.

She would clean up, try to look like she'd slept recently and was not, in point of fact, a lunatic. Then she would track Tommy down, and tell him her suspicions.

Her heart leapt at the idea, even as her brain knew better. Seeing him would be awful. There was no doubt about it. He would be nasty, in all likelihood – and that was if she got anywhere near him in the first place. She somewhat doubted she would still have her all-access pass to the Wild Boys.

But it didn't matter, because she wasn't afraid of his reaction any longer. How could she be? She'd already lived through it. She had much bigger things to be afraid of than his reaction.

Jenna blew out a breath, and squared her shoulders.

She had two days.

She would have to make them count.

27

The gallery opening was glittering. Literally.

Everywhere Jenna looked there was more sparkle, more shine. Disco balls hung from the ceiling. Diamonds and other assorted precious gems flashed at earlobes, throats, wrists. The art on the walls seemed to take a distant second place to the über-fabulous types who were supposedly looking at it. Jenna had been in the gallery for about twenty-five minutes so far, and she hadn't so much as glanced at a painting. Not that such things mattered.

'Fabulous pieces, visionary, *genius*,' one stout society grande dame pronounced to her entourage, though Jenna had been standing next to her for most of the past twenty minutes and knew the woman had no more looked over at one of the paintings than Jenna had. 'Marty and I plan to invest,' the woman drawled, setting off an excited murmuring from her friends.

It was nearing one in the morning, and Jenna's exhaustion was making her loopy. She almost turned to the grande dame and demanded to know when, exactly, the woman had had time to notice the art on the walls while gossiping so strenuously. She restrained herself – barely.

It had been a very long night.

Jenna had been forced to track Tommy down through a variety of sources, none of them her own. Rumour and supposition – plus a pleading phone call to one of Duncan Paradis's fleet of underlings, pretending to enquire on Ken Dollimore's behalf – had finally led her to an art gallery on the border of SoHo where, apparently, the Wild Boys *might* show up. The underling in question had been deliberately vague on this point.

'I can't promise you a rose garden or whatever,' she'd informed Jenna in ponderous tones, which had led Jenna to conclude that this creature was yet another early-twenty-something Manhattanite overimpressed with her own literacy. A citywide scourge, even in Jenna's day. 'But if I were you I would tell your boss that he should be there around eleven thirty, and that is all I can say.'

'Ken thanks you from the bottom of his heart,' Jenna had lied, conscience perfectly clear, and then she'd hung up without further ass-kissing because it had already been getting late.

The Wild Boys had played an 'impromptu' set at the stroke of midnight. Everyone was still talking about it, and Jenna could see the raised white stage in the centre of the gallery's main room with the instruments still on it and video screens scattered here and there, still playing the videos that would have enhanced the performance.

She had not experienced the set herself, however, because she had instead spent that time standing outside, trying to look cute enough for one of the bouncers to let her in. When that had failed, as she did not possess hips the approximate width of a Twizzler, she'd snuck around the back and had climbed in the nearest window – which had, unfortunately, led directly into the men's bathroom.

The less said about *that* psychologically scarring experience, the better, she thought now with a shudder – and resisted the urge to run off and scour her hands once again.

Expecting Tommy to be less than happy to see her, Jenna had taken the precaution of looking like someone else. She'd picked up a blonde wig on her way downtown, and shoved all her dark curls beneath it as best she could. She'd knocked the wig askew on her way in through the window, and had wasted precious minutes readjusting it. Now, her scalp itched and she was rapidly overheating, but she hoped she could use the disguise to get close enough to Tommy to warn him about Richie.

And beg him to trust me— But that was not tonight's objective, no matter how much she wished otherwise. *Not to mention, he would say no*, her caustic side felt the need to point out.

Shut up, caustic side, Jenna thought.

She manoeuvred her way through the crowd. Models and artists and the glitterati, as far as the eye could see. But no hint of Tommy. Jenna saw Sebastian chatting with Basquiat in the corner, and there was Nick making time with Linda Evangelista. But neither Richie nor Tommy seemed to be around – which, of course, terrified Jenna to her core. What if she was too late?

But no, Tommy's car had to go over that bridge ... Except, what if her being here had changed things? What if Richie decided to go ahead with his plan earlier than scheduled? Jenna wasn't exactly conversant on the geekier aspects of time-travel philosophy – it was Aimee's husband Ben who read all the science-fiction novels and could expound on the ramifications of disrupting the space/time continuum – but even she could grasp the concept that the very fact of her being in the wrong time could disrupt the sequence of events in that time.

Which meant that Richie could act whenever he chose. As long as he killed Tommy, did it really matter how or when? Tommy would still be dead.

Scared now, and more determined, Jenna pushed her way into the series of smaller rooms, skirting the edges of pretentious conversations – *I adore* the insouciance of the artist's pastels, don't you? – and incomprehensible ones – *I told her max it out to the ultra max, you dig?* And then, finally, she saw him.

Relief swept through her. *He was still alive.*

But he certainly did not look happy. Jenna tried to pretend that she didn't feel a surge of triumph upon seeing that, but she couldn't maintain the lie. He looked tired and, around the eyes, shattered. *Just like me*, Jenna thought, and there was a small and petty part of her that was glad. She tried to shove it aside because it was terrible to take pleasure in something like that, *even if he should have trusted her no matter how crazy she sounded*, and because the important part was that he was still breathing.

Tommy stood with his back against a pillar, nursing a cocktail and – if his expression was any indication – not paying the slightest attention to the conversation going on around him. Two society types and a short, round sort of man in a suit of many neon colours – possibly, upon reflection, Elton John – were bickering over something, their gestures and laughter so animated and over the top that Jenna suspected the use of narcotics.

She eased closer. She was wearing the blonde wig, so it wasn't as if anyone was going to pick her out of such a densely packed crowd without a good look at her face. She figured she could saunter on over, drop the necessary information in Tommy's ear, and then retreat before he picked up where he left off and insulted her further. She was not going to drink him in, or manufacture a reason to touch him. She didn't even need to touch him to have the almost tactile sense of what his skin felt like beneath her hands.

Jenna moved around the pillar, and kept Tommy in her sights. She would not let him see the yearning she felt raging through her. She would not defend herself any further than she already had.

She was only steps away from him when he looked directly at her, the suddenness of it stunning her – pinning her with those shocking green eyes. Something washed over his face – a spark of hope, followed quickly by the dark fury she recognized all too well.

'Nice try,' he said, in a kind of nasty-edged drawl that she was sadly close enough to hear.

'I have to tell you one thing,' she said calmly, even though nothing felt calm, especially not inside her. She was all tilt and spin, and it was because he was near. 'One thing and then I'll go, I promise.'

But then Jenna froze as two beefy-looking men in suits appeared as if from thin air and marched with grim purpose towards her.

She only vaguely understood what was happening as they grabbed her arms. But she understood what she saw on Tommy's face. The betrayal and the hopelessness. The anger.

And then she was being hurried through the crowd. Dragged, in fact – or that was what it would turn into if she stopped walking along with them. The pretty people broke off their conversations and stared at her, and Jenna could do nothing but hang between two men who each individually outweighed her by a hundred pounds at least, keep her feet moving or risk being hauled out like a sack of potatoes, and let them gape at her over their cocktails.

Her stomach ached and the blood rushed to her face, and she realized with despair that he really, truly, thought she was a psycho. A complete lunatic, and not in any sort of casual way. In a serious, hired-bodyguards-to-keep-her-away-from-him way. He had *hired* these men to *intercept* her.

Jenna thought she might throw up. Or, worse, burst into tears.

The bodyguards wrestled her out of the gallery through a side door, and Jenna found herself in one of Manhattan's less attractive alleys, complete with upended garbage cans and the upsetting sound of scurrying in the furthest, darkest corners. The men holding her released her in a deliberate way that was more like a push with the momentum, so she staggered to keep her balance and found herself grabbing on to the slimy wall to keep herself upright.

She was the trash. Tommy had ordered them to remove her like she was no more than *trash*.

I will not cry I will not cry I will not cry—

'Stay away from Tommy Seer,' one of the bodyguards growled in a full Jersey accent. 'Next time, we won't be so gentle.'

'You hear that?' the other one demanded.

'I hear it,' Jenna said dully, and turned herself around to face them. There was only the dim bulb over the gallery door to light the alley, and it cast the two men in shadow. They looked bigger, more menacing. She swallowed.

And then behind them, the door opened, and Tommy walked out.

Jenna's heart leapt in her chest, though she knew better. But he was there, and he was walking towards her despite the objections of the two giants – he even told them to go back inside – and it was almost like a dream.

It was only the two of them in the alley once the door thudded closed. He was wearing some kind of cloak-like thing that flowed around him and made him look like

320

Heathcliff. It was almost romantic, really. If she squinted, she could pretend that wasn't fury on his face but passion, and he wasn't coming towards her for any reason but that.

'What the hell is this?' he demanded in that cold, awful tone, and Jenna had to release the fantasy and stop squinting. He looked so tired, with near-purple crescents beneath each eye. She wanted to reach out to him.

But she couldn't. She was the reason he looked that way. He thought she was a stalker. A mental-health risk. There would be no reaching out.

'Richie,' she said, her voice thick. She coughed to conceal it. 'I think it's Richie.'

'Oh, really?' Tommy did not sound impressed. He stopped in front of her, and for a moment it looked like he might reach across the distance between them. His hands moved – and then he remembered himself. He shifted his weight and planted his hands on his narrow hips. 'What a surprise. Richie. You're just going down the list, aren't you?'

'There were reasons to suspect every one of them,' she said, stung into defending herself. 'But I really do think it's Richie.'

'Of course you do.' His lips flattened, and it hurt that he was looking at her with such contempt. It was much worse than when she'd first met him. So much worse, because now she knew what it felt like to be looked at as if she was the only woman in the world. 'Do you have any reason to suspect Richie, Jenna?' he asked, angrily. 'Any reason at all?'

321

'Of course,' she said, her temper kicking in. Because it was better than bawling. 'He's the only one who—'

'Let me rephrase that,' he interrupted her, his tone vicious. 'Do you have any reason to suspect him that involves *actual evidence*, and does not involve supernatural claims of any kind?'

Jenna could only stare at him, mute.

'That's what I thought,' Tommy muttered. He took a step closer, and then seemed to think better of it, though he didn't move away. His voice lowered, and every word pounded into Jenna as if he was using his fists. 'Explain to me why you're doing this. Look at yourself. You're wearing a disguise and creeping around an art opening. You just got bodily removed, and you still keep going. Why? Give it up, Jenna.'

'If I give it up, you die,' she gritted out, reeling from his tone as much as his proximity. She could almost taste him. If she just reached out— but she was afraid of what he would do. 'It doesn't matter if you believe me. *I* know, and I have to do something about it.'

'It might interest you to hear that there have been no "accidents" since I last saw you,' Tommy growled at her, his gaze piercing. 'What a coincidence.'

'It's not a coincidence, Tommy,' Jenna said, willing him to believe her, to hear her, but knowing he wouldn't. 'There are only a few days left and he's waiting for the big finish.'

'You have an answer for everything,' he said. 'And every one of them crazy.'

'I know it sounds crazy,' Jenna assured him. She held

up her hands, palms out – so close to grazing the planes of his chest. 'Come on, Tommy. I *know* how crazy it sounds. Did you ever think I was crazy before? Even a little?'

'No,' he said, and his mouth twisted. His gaze darkened. 'Which doesn't help your case. It makes me a gullible idiot.'

'Or maybe it's not crazy,' Jenna whispered. 'Maybe it's true. How else would I have known—'

'Because you planned it!' he burst out. 'You planned all of it!'

'Of course I didn't plan it,' she hissed at him. 'Before anything happened between us the one thing you knew about me was how much I worshipped you. Groupie zombie worship, right? I would never hurt you. Somewhere inside you have to know that.'

'There is no *somewhere inside*,' he gritted out. 'There's only the reality. You're nothing but another unhinged fan. I can't believe I was stupid enough to overlook that.'

'Tommy—'

'Don't do this again, Jenna,' Tommy warned her, stepping back and condemning her with a sweeping look, one that took in the blonde wig and made her cheeks heat. 'Next time I'm calling the cops.'

'Tommy, *please*.' She was begging. She should have felt humiliated, but maybe that would come later. At the moment she was only desperate that he hear her. 'Please, whatever you do, think about the *possibility* that I'm not completely off my rocker. What if Richie really is planning to kill you? What if I'm not making all of this—'

323

'What if I get you committed to Bellevue?' Tommy interrupted, his tone lethal. 'What if you spend the rest of your life in a straitjacket? These are much better questions, and ones I think you should consider. Who knows? Maybe John Hinckley is getting lonely in his psychiatric wing.'

Hinckley, who had attempted to assassinate President Reagan in 1981 for the love of Jodie Foster. What a lovely comparison. Jenna sucked in a breath.

'Just keep an eye on Richie,' she managed to say, hearing the tremor in her voice. 'Please.'

Tommy stared at her for a moment, and she could see his temper and his disgust. He swayed closer, whether to touch her or berate her, she couldn't tell. Something flashed between them, and Jenna held her breath. Tommy's mouth twisted in anger and then he wrenched himself away from her. He turned abruptly and stalked back across the alley, throwing open the door and disappearing inside. His two security guards glared through the doorway at Jenna, who was relieved when the door slammed shut once again.

She stood there in the dank, dirty alley and told herself to breathe. To calm down. To let it go.

She felt something like a sob, or a scream, roll up from deep in her gut, and she let it wash through her, gathering steam until she tore the blonde wig from her head and hurled it with all her might at that door he'd let slam in her face. It hardly made a noise at all – it just fell to the ground and lay there, blonde hair bristling in the cold night air.

324

Jenna drew in one breath, then another.

Well. This was one hundred per cent commitment, nothing held back, everything on the line, wasn't it? Everything she'd always been too afraid to do. And now she knew why.

I will not cry I will not cry I will not cry—

And then there was nothing else to do but go home.

Tommy stalked through the gallery, furious.

That ridiculous blonde wig. What had she been thinking? Did she believe for one second that he couldn't pick her out of a crowd? That he hadn't seen her the moment she walked in? It was the way she held herself. The way her hips moved. The way she held one wrist so tightly with the other hand, like a little girl. He would know her anywhere, and more than that, he would know her even if he was blind. It was like she was superimposed over him and he had to fight through her to see anything else at all.

But his real fury was reserved for his own pathetic, sorry self. He called her crazy – what about him? What was the point of having bodyguards to protect him when, at the first sight of the reason he needed them in the first place, he raced to her side? And then, instead of letting them do their job, he'd run after her like a panting dog, desperate to have one more interaction with her. He couldn't lie to himself – he'd *wanted* to talk to her. He'd *wanted* to be that close, to be able to smell her perfume and watch the emotions cross her face. What was he *doing*?

Maybe Jenna couldn't help her delusions. Maybe she had some mental disease. He, on the other hand, was supposedly sane and in possession of all his faculties. So why had it made his chest ache to see her look at him like that – like he was hurting her? Why did he want to turn around right now, run outside, and beg her to pretend she'd been kidding around so he could be with her again?

'This party is boring,' Richie said from Tommy's side, making him start with surprise. He immediately stepped away from Richie under the guise of snagging a drink from a passing waiter, but that wasn't the real reason. The real reason was that she'd warned him about Richie – and apparently, he listened to the ravings of madwomen.

'Of course it's boring,' he replied calmly, as if his crazed stalker hadn't accused Richie of plotting his death, and as if that accusation hadn't taken root somewhere inside of him. He raised his drink towards the mass of people around them. 'Look who's here.'

Richie sighed, and looked around. Tommy looked at Richie. The real issue was not that Jenna had planted suspicions of Richie into Tommy's head. The issue was that no small part of Tommy *wanted* Richie to do something, he was forced to admit to himself. Bash him over the head with his wine glass, knock him out, *anything* that proved Jenna right. Tommy couldn't accept the time-travel thing, of course, but he'd overlook it if the murder thing panned out.

He realized what he'd just thought to himself, and was appalled.

326

'What's going on?' Richie asked then, frowning slightly. 'You look annoyed.'

'Tired,' Tommy said.

'I think I'm going to leave,' Richie said. 'Play some cards, if anyone asks.'

'Fine.' Tommy knew that by *anyone*, Richie meant Duncan. Sebastian never seemed to want to know Richie's whereabouts – which Tommy had always assumed meant he either knew them already, or preferred not to know, an issue that Tommy had no interest whatsoever in learning more about.

After his band mate walked away, Tommy sucked down the rest of his drink and felt sorry for himself.

His life was completely empty. That was not exactly news, of course, but it hadn't hurt as much before Jenna had made him dream about something different. Something more. But that wasn't his life – this was. He was standing in a room packed full of people, all of whom would claim him as a friend, none of whom knew him at all.

He felt like a ghost.

Later, Tommy sat in his expensive apartment and stared out at his expensive view. He cared about neither.

He'd bowed out of the party not long after Richie had left, and had made his way back uptown alone despite the offers of several enterprising ladies. Now he sat in the dark and brooded. About being a ghost. About the choices that had led him here. He thought about Jenna, of course

– he couldn't seem to avoid it. Specifically, he thought about what she'd almost said out in that alley, before he'd interrupted her.

What if I'm not making all of this up?

It wasn't that Tommy suddenly believed her. He didn't. Of course he didn't – she was a nut.

But if his life had taught him anything, it was that everything could turn on a dime – and given the opportunity, probably would. A wise man was not likely to take the advice of an unhinged woman who was obviously a deranged fan, with Hinckley aspirations. A wise man would do exactly as Tommy had done, and distance himself from that train wreck as far as he could.

But a wise man, because he had seen a few things in his day, might take a few precautions.

Just in case.

When he woke up the next morning, he called his lawyer.

28

It had been easy to track Nick around the city, Jenna reflected sourly while clutching her third cup of deli coffee between her palms. She'd ordered each cup extra light and extra sweet, because after the night she'd had, she needed a boost – and she was about fifteen years away from a Starbucks on every corner, complete with a shiny espresso machine and luscious frappuccinos.

But she digressed.

Nick was a creature of habit. He liked the same bar, which he went to every single evening he could, because the bartenders knew him and he could be as famous or as anonymous as his mood dictated. All of which Jenna knew because of the weeks she'd spent hanging out with the band, learning their idiosyncrasies while supposedly spying on them for Duncan.

Richie, on the other hand, was not Nick. He did not have the temper or the predictable bar routine. In fact, the only thing Jenna knew for sure that Richie liked was

Sebastian. She had therefore installed herself at the bodega across from Sebastian's preferred residential hotel, and waited.

And waited.

The coffee kept her warm, and jittery. The half-and-half was entirely too delicious, and she couldn't help but love the sugar. Who didn't love sugar? It was an extra light, extra sweet treat – practically dessert.

And Jenna definitely felt like she deserved extra desserts.

Not that she was brooding over last night's hideous interaction with Tommy, because she wasn't. She refused to give in to brooding. She refused to give him the satisfaction – as if, from across the city, he would sense her brooding somehow.

And, anyway, she was slightly concerned that she might have sprained her tear ducts. Or cried them raw. She'd wept herself into the exhausted sleep she'd desperately needed when she'd finally gotten home last night, but had still managed to drag herself out of bed and across town by noon today. If that wasn't dedication to one presently horrible man, she didn't know what was. She hoped Tommy was sleeping soundly, surrounded by feather pillows and his bedrock belief that she was a crazy person.

Sebastian, she knew, jerking her thoughts away from Tommy, liked to get up early and spend a few hours at the gym every day. Richie, on the other hand, preferred to be known as a more old-school rock-star type, and had often complained about the early hours at the recording studio. He was, he'd claimed, the kind of guy who liked to roll in around dawn, and rarely got up before the afternoon. Which meant he'd staggered in bleary-eyed and muttered, *this fucking sucks* or *why the hell does this have to happen at dawn* to whoever happened to be sitting there, that being whole treatises of discussion where Richie was concerned.

Jenna was therefore pretty sure that noon was far too early for Richie to have roused himself. It certainly felt far too early for her, and she did not have any rock-star street cred to worry about. So she planted herself near a display of fruit, bought a satisfyingly pre-Tina Brown *New Yorker* to read, and waited.

Waiting was even more boring when there was no possibility of a Tommy sighting, she concluded glumly some time later, when she was getting herself yet another delicious cup of coffee, the better to avoid succumbing to the cold. She was considering a second hot dog from the guy on the corner – her protesting stomach be damned – when she saw Richie barrel through the doors of the hotel and head off down the street on foot.

Startled, Jenna tossed her coffee into the trashcan on the corner. She pulled her turtleneck sweater high up on her chin – it was one of those awful *Facts of Life*-ish sweaters, all ribbing and big arms and an unfortunate blazing red colour – and her baseball cap lower over her forehead. (Aunt Jen, apparently, was a Red Sox fan in a Yankees town, a fact which at least two gentlemen had already taken exception to. Loudly and profanely.) She'd braided her hair and tucked it into the back of her sweater, hiding

331

it and hopefully disguising herself without use of another wig. Jenna had not dared look in the mirror on her way out of the house, but she felt reasonably certain that if Richie glanced in her direction he wouldn't recognize her immediately.

She set off after him, keeping the back of his head in sight as she walked south. On some level, following various Wild Boys around New York was probably an exercise in futility. Sure, she might learn something new about Richie today – like she'd learned about Eugenia and Duncan and their unlikely feelings for each other, for example. Anything was possible. But the reality was that most people lived boring lives. Even superstars. And even if they were killers plotting away merrily, they wouldn't necessarily put up signs to that effect while walking into Hell's Kitchen.

The fact that they were in Hell's Kitchen – the scary Eighties version rather than Jenna's beloved twenty-first-century neighbourhood – was her first clue that Richie was perhaps the exception to the rule. She watched him go in and out of about three different places along the increasingly crappy street – never for more than a moment or two – before he disappeared into a dry-cleaner's. After he'd been gone about ten minutes, Jenna ventured closer and peered in the window. The interior looked pretty much the way a dry-cleaner's was supposed to look. And Richie wasn't standing at the counter.

Jenna felt herself biting down on her lower lip, and stopped herself. There was no point dithering about it. She couldn't think like Jenna Jenkins, Eighties Encyclopedia – she had to think like her idol Veronica Mars, Kickass Private Detective. Which meant she had no choice but to go in. She opened the door and eased herself inside, looking around carefully – half expecting Richie to leap at her from one of the plastic-covered garments hanging on a hook beside the counter.

'There was a man . . .' she said to the impassive woman behind the counter – the one who was looking at her as if she'd just discovered Jenna on the bottom of her shoe. The woman's eyebrows, already plucked perilously thin, arched high.

'There's always some man, honey,' the woman replied, snapping her gum and rolling her eyes simultaneously. She snorted with laughter. *Hilarious.*

'He came in a few moments ago?' Jenna wished her voice had not gone up at the end like that. How wimpy. Veronica Mars would never be so fearful or cowed by someone standing bored and annoyed at a register. Veronica Mars would grind such a person beneath her sassy little shoe, or decimate her with a few sharp words.

The woman stared at Jenna for a moment, then sighed, and jerked her thumb behind her.

'Go to the back,' she ordered. 'Can't miss him.'

Interesting, Jenna thought, because there was a certain inflection there that she didn't understand. She smiled her thanks – and was, unsurprisingly, ignored. Carefully, slowly, she picked her way down the crowded aisle of the store, hemmed in by carousel machines and plastic-covered clothing on both sides. She reached the back of the store and was confronted with three doors. She was starting to feel a little bit like Alice in Wonderland.

She went to the closest one and inched it open, mindful of the fact that she didn't exactly want to hurl herself into some room containing Richie, because how could she explain herself? She peeked through the crack she'd made and saw a dark supply closet. She moved to the second door, put her hand on the knob, and then asked herself what the hell she was doing.

Possibly this was a long overdue question.

What if Richie was sitting there, right on the other side of the door? Seriously, what was her plan? *Oh, hi, I happened to be wandering around the streets of Hell's Kitchen, as you do, and I saw that you came in here and didn't come out, and I was worried about your* health, *so that's why I have appeared here, at the back of a dry-cleaner's* . . .

Jenna took her hand off the doorknob.

Because if Richie wasn't the killer, it would still be an unpleasant scene. He would rightly accuse her of stalking him. He might call the police. He might call Tommy, which would be even worse than the police, since at this point Jenna would rather spend a night in Riker's Island than have to see that look of contempt on Tommy's face again.

Okay, maybe not.

But it was a close call.

And then, of course, if Richie *was* the killer, everything was even worse. Seriously, upsettingly worse. Maybe he'd kill her himself, then and there. For all Jenna knew, this was one of his criminal hideouts. Or a place where he practised murdering his friends and colleagues. And aside from how very much Jenna did not want to die personally – how very, *very* much she would prefer to stay alive – she also didn't want to die because that would mean no one would be around to save Tommy. And Jenna really couldn't see the point of this whole exercise if Tommy wasn't saved.

She rubbed at her temples in an attempt to force herself into a decision – and then froze as she heard heavy footsteps coming towards her from behind that second door.

Looking around wildly, Jenna leapt for the supply closet and closed herself inside, leaving only the tiniest crack open, so she could see out. Why had her life become reduced to critical moments in supply closets, anyway? Was that a metaphor? But she didn't have time to ponder that, because her heart pounded frantically and then went into triple time when the door she'd been standing in front of slammed open and Richie walked out.

She felt almost faint with relief – that she'd moved, that she'd hidden, that she hadn't opened that door – and had to hold her breath to hear what Richie was saying over his shoulder. She couldn't, not over the churning clatter of the dry-cleaning machines all around them. But then another man came out, and it was impossible not to hear him.

'Don't give me that shit,' he advised Richie, in one of those braying voices that had never known less than a dull roar. Jenna did not need to see his face to understand that he was a scary individual with thug tendencies to match his overly-broad shoulders and that *I'll mess you up* strut. 'You show up here, with all the money you owe? What the fuck am I? A charity?'

'After everything we've been through together,' Richie said bitterly, facing Jenna's hiding place so she could hear him this time, and not seeming as cowed by the thug as she felt he ought to be. 'You won't even throw me a bone?'

'A bone you can have,' the thug said, with a snort. 'But a ten-grand buy-in? Like I owe you some Christmas present? Forget it. You're a bad bet, Richie. A bad fucking bet.'

'All I need is one good game—' Richie began, almost wheedling. Almost desperate.

'You're running out of time.' The thug's voice was quieter then, but no less lethal. 'You should think about that, and stop worrying about *one good game*, 'cause it ain't gonna happen.'

'Fuck you, then,' Richie raged at him. 'Don't you know who I am? I can make ten grand in ten minutes!'

'Then you don't need me to help you, do you?' the thug threw back at him, obviously unimpressed. 'And that's big talk – last I heard, you were in a five-million-dollar hole.'

'Go to hell,' Richie snarled, and turned on his heel.

The thug watched him go for a moment, then turned around himself and disappeared behind the door again.

In her supply closet, Jenna tried to process what she'd overheard.

Richie in five million dollars' worth of debt made him an excellent candidate for Tommy's murderer.

In the dark, Jenna squeezed her eyes shut, and braced herself. She knew she had to take this new information to Tommy, as little as she wanted to see him. Which was itself a lie – because there was a sick part of her that didn't care that he would be mean, that he hated her, that he would look at her in that awful way again. The sick part wanted to be near him no matter what he did, or said. She had become masochistic where he was concerned, and that appalled her.

But it didn't appal her *enough*.

So, after waiting a while to make sure Richie was gone, she fought her way out of the shop, back into the cold and sketchy neighbourhood, and headed back uptown towards Tommy's place.

The good news was, she had spent that whole night watching Tommy's building not so long before, so it wasn't very difficult to sneak inside and make her way up to his apartment eventually, having long since figured out the schedules and habits of the doormen. She figured she'd camp out at his door, and try to reason with him when he appeared. The element of surprise would be her presence at his door – she assumed she'd avoid the bodyguards that way.

The bad news was, when she rang Tommy's doorbell, he answered.

They stared at each other.

He did not look particularly worse for wear. Perhaps he

hadn't spent the night weeping, or the afternoon creeping around in a ridiculous red sweater, subject to extremes of temperature and unwise hot-dog selections on street corners. Whatever *he'd* been doing with himself, it had led to tousled dark hair, moody green eyes, and those lips of his twisted to one side in a sardonic manner that should have been more insulting than sexy.

Oh, and he was wearing nothing but a pair of battered jeans with the top button undone.

It was enough to give Jenna heart failure. She wanted to press her face into the valley between his defined pecs, and kiss the hollow there. She wanted to feel the heat of his skin, and smell him all around her. She *wanted*.

'This is like a bad dream that never ends,' Tommy snapped, breaking the spell. He glared down at her. Jenna tried to stop thinking about *want*.

But then he walked away from the door, leaving it open behind him. Since he hadn't slammed it in her face or notified his security detail, Jenna decided this comprised an invitation. She followed him in warily, shutting the door behind her.

Inside, Tommy stood over by the window with his back to her, looking out at his amazing two-storey view of Central Park. Jenna let herself drink in the expensive, if somewhat personality-less furnishings. The tasteful art on the walls, the spiral staircase to the next floor.

'I told you I'd call the cops,' Tommy said without turning around. Jenna wondered if he could see her reflection in the window, or only his own. 'I wasn't kidding.'

'So call the cops,' Jenna said, with unfeigned weariness. 'I don't care. But listen to me first.'

'Listen to you.' He let out a hollow sound, not quite a laugh. 'All I do is listen to you, Jenna, and what happens? You get more and more insane.' He turned, but his face was thrown into shadow from the afternoon light outside. 'So why should I listen to some more of the same?'

'I know it's hard to get your head around—'

'Your argument is based on you travelling back in time to save me from my tragic death, about which only you know,' he interrupted, his voice arid. 'Yeah. That's a little *hard to get my head around.*'

Jenna sighed. She pulled the braid out from the back of her turtleneck where it was making her skin itch, and tilted her baseball cap back on her forehead. She felt sweaty and frumpy, and it irritated her to feel that way when he just lounged about in unfastened jeans and looked like some effortless god. It was so unfair.

'Fine. Don't get your head around anything. Just listen.' She shrugged, and decided there was no point in sugar-coating anything. Not at this stage in the game. 'I followed Richie today.'

'Terrific'

But Jenna ignored that acidic tone, and told him. What she'd seen, what Richie had said, what the thug had said. When Tommy only stared at her, and the silence stretched out between them, she reminded him that dead legends sold a ton of records – much more than living stars who faded into obscurity. As Tommy himself had pointed out, in that town-house garden, what felt like ages ago. And Richie had every reason to cash in. Five million reasons, apparently.

When she was finished, she could tell it didn't matter. He hadn't moved, and she couldn't see his expression, but she knew. She could feel his disgust.

'You have to stop stalking the band,' he said, much too quietly, when he finally spoke. 'I really will call the cops the next time I see you.'

Jenna sighed, and looked down. Her hands were clenched into fists at her sides, though she had no memory of doing that. She ran her tongue around her teeth and fought for calm – but it wasn't that she felt angry. Anger would be easy. This, she feared, was defeat, and the panic that went along with it.

'I know you don't believe me,' she said into the shadows where he hid his face. Because she had to say something – anything – or accept the despair that threatened to suck her under. 'I know you can't. I even understand why. But I know that you're going to die tomorrow if I don't do something to stop it.' She heard her voice crack. Tommy moved forward, out of the shadows, so she could see that he was frowning.

'Jenna—'

'I have loved you my whole life,' she said, stopping him with a raised hand. 'Since I was a little girl. I remember sitting in my bedroom when I was eleven, listening to "Lucky Penny" and *just knowing* that you understood me. I loved you so much that I wrote my diary entries to you, like letters. After you died, I hid in memories of you my entire adult life. Every time something went bad for me, I had you to make me feel better.' She sucked in a shaky breath. 'I mourned you, and I didn't even know you. All I knew were interviews, posters, videos. Your public face. But I loved what I knew. I listened to that song that Bono sang at your funeral for decades, and it always made me cry.' She laughed slightly, her eyes filling. 'I mean, Bono and Sting? Singing an acoustic version of "The Unforgettable Fire"? It gives me chills just thinking about it.'

Tommy made a noise then, and Jenna assumed it was something cynical or derisive. She wiped at her eyes with impatient jabs of her hands, curled into defensive fists again.

'The thing is,' she said quickly, afraid he would interrupt her again, and knowing that she had to get it out before it was too late, 'I know that everything I felt was infatuation. I knew it once I met you, here. Once I got to know you. And I'm so glad I did, Tommy, because . . .' Jenna's voice cracked again, and she couldn't bear to look at him. 'Because you're really so, so much more than I ever imagined you could be.'

'Jenna.' His voice was harsh, but no more than a whisper.

'It doesn't matter if you believe me,' she continued, ignoring the command in his voice. She realized tears were streaming down her cheeks, but she ignored them, too. 'It doesn't matter if you think I'm crazy. I love you so much, I love you enough for the both of us.' She thought she ought to be afraid to say that so baldly, with so little hope of a reply in the same vein, but she was past that, anyway, so she kept going. 'Someday I hope I get to hear you play your guitar and sing, all alone on the stage, with no costumes or mascara. I believe I will, if we can just make it through tomorrow. And it doesn't matter what happens between us, because I'll still love you. I just want you to live.'

Her voice seemed to echo for a moment, but then was gone. Jenna heard a ragged sound, and realized it was her own breathing. She looked at him, but quickly looked away, because everything felt too intense. Too raw.

He stood there, so close but still so unreachable. He was silent.

That was it then. She'd extended herself as far as she could go. What more could she do? Say?

She turned, because there was nothing else. She was empty. Her head felt light, and her skin felt almost feverish. Her feet were unsteady beneath her, but she headed for the door.

She didn't hear him move, but suddenly he was turning her around, and his face was tormented. She saw only the glitter of his green eyes, hard and almost angry.

'Tommy—'

But she never knew what she might have said, because his lips came down on hers, and he kissed her like a desperate man. Like he was drowning.

Like he felt the way she did, and hated it.

Tommy didn't let her speak.

He didn't speak himself.

It was only flesh. Only mouths connecting, the scrape of lips and teeth against skin. The sigh and murmur of two bodies coming together, again and again.

He made love to her fiercely, desperately. As if he might die the next day, as predicted. As if she might disappear.

How can I let her go? How can I ever let her go?

The afternoon turned into night, and eventually the dawn followed, and still it wasn't enough. Still, he couldn't hold her close enough or love her deeply enough to satisfy himself.

To keep either one of them safe.

When he finally fell into an exhausted sleep, the sky was far too light, and Jenna looked haunted. He refused to think about why.

And when he woke up, she was gone.

29

Tommy waited for her outside her apartment that afternoon, which was less fun than it might have been thanks to the cold October rain, and was pleased to watch her jump when she saw him. The heavy outside door to her apartment building slammed shut behind her, but she was frozen there on the stoop.

She was dressed in another bizarre outfit, although this one was better than the horrible sweater she'd had on yesterday. Today she had the great mass of her hair pinned up on the back of her head, and it looked like a tornado wouldn't move it so much as an inch. She was also wearing jeans tucked into what looked like Doc Martens – which he was surprised she owned – and a dark sweatshirt. What made that combo bizarre was the grim way she moved, like she was a guardian angel on the prowl. He liked the way her eyes went huge as she looked at him.

'You're soaking wet,' she said.

'I would have come up.' He straightened from the car he'd been leaning against. His car, as a matter of fact – because he might have a date with destiny, but the parking gods were still looking out for him. 'I couldn't decide whether I wanted to yell at you for taking off, or pick up where we left off.'

'I know you're supposed to go to that party thing at that hotel,' Jenna said, as if he hadn't spoken. As if he couldn't feel the electricity sizzle between them. 'You and Eugenia have a big fight there, that much I know. So I was going to go and be there, to, you know, keep an eye—' She broke off, and walked down the steps until she was on the bottom one, putting her at his eye level. 'What are you doing here?' She smiled slightly.' You can't call the cops if *you* stalk *me*, right?'

Tommy closed the distance between them. He liked the way her lips parted in surprise, and he liked the way she tipped her head back to take him in. He didn't touch her, he only stood close enough so they could both feel the sizzle.

'Number one,' he said. 'That song, "The Unforgettable Fire".'

Jenna nodded. She looked wary. 'Bono sang it at your funeral. Sting sang the harmony. It was beautiful.' She smiled as if she was trying to keep from welling up. 'It was haunting.'

Tommy searched her face, looking for something – anything – that would prove her guilt. Her insanity. But there was only Jenna looking back. Jenna, who wanted so

345

badly to save him from a destiny only she could see. Jenna, who worried that he was out in the rain. Jenna, who knew a secret he'd never told another living soul – that he had forgotten about.

'I ran into Bono earlier this year at the Brit Awards,' Tommy said. Behind him, he heard the swish of cars down the wet street, but he could see nothing except Jenna. 'It was only the two of us. We were standing backstage, and no one was near us. I told him that someday I wanted him to sing "The Unforgettable Fire" at my funeral, and he agreed. Said something about hoping it didn't happen anytime soon, and that was that. I never told anyone. To be honest, I hadn't thought much about my funeral before meeting you.'

Jenna swallowed. Tommy saw her throat move, and eased away, watching her chin drop as she followed him with her eyes.

'So either Bono has spent the past few months racing around telling everyone about a completely throwaway conversation he'd have no reason to think about while enjoying the insane success of *The Joshua Tree*,' Tommy continued. 'Or . . .'

'Or . . . ?' Jenna prompted him, her voice barely above a whisper.

'Which brings me to number two,' Tommy said. He reached over and traced the shape of her cheekbone. 'I'm in love with you.' It felt good to say it. Right. 'Even though I don't think I should be, and even though I tried not to be.'

'How romantic,' she said with a wry smile, and he felt his heart thump in response, because that was so Jenna – so completely who she was, and he was a goner. Had he known that, even back at the start, when she'd made googly eyes at him and he'd been so much more cruel than he'd had to be?

'And my major problem here is that I can't come up with a rational explanation for it,' he said softly.

'Love?' She smiled again, and looked away for a moment. 'I don't think it's rational. I think it's chemical. And then emotional.'

'Not love.' He sighed. 'The truth is, I can't figure out how you could possibly know about that song. I mean, what are the odds that you would guess it? I'm not even a particularly big U2 fan.' He considered. 'Although I do like the new single.'

'"Where The Streets Have No Name",' Jenna said, and surprised Tommy with a laugh. 'I don't think I've been able to listen to that song all the way through since the mid-Nineties. That's how overplayed it is.'

'That's crazy,' Tommy said, but without any accusation in his voice. She frowned. 'What you just said is completely, unarguably crazy.'

She opened her mouth to say something, and he put his finger over her lips. She trembled. Heat coiled inside of him, and he knew she could see it on his face.

'I can't wrap my head around it,' he said quietly, seriously. 'But you're the most sane person I know. So I believe you. I don't know how any of what you're saying can be

347

true, but I believe you. It can't be any crazier than a born loser from a trailer park outside of Buffalo becoming a rock star, right? And I don't think I care, as long as we're together.'

Jenna's eyes shone. She reached over and took his face between her hands.

'I love you,' she managed to choke out. 'I'm not crazy. I promise.'

'I love you too,' he said, and couldn't help smiling. So what if it was raining and nothing made sense? So what if she thought he would die before the dawn? He felt like bursting into song. 'So . . . what do we do now?'

It was an excellent question. Jenna blinked. In all the scenarios she'd run through her head, none of them had involved Tommy showing up at her door and spontaneously *believing* her. So much for her plans for great martyrdom and sacrifice.

'We get the hell out of New York City,' she said, pulling back from him. 'I know that you go to this party, and then afterwards you die. So let's avoid the whole thing. Let's go to . . . I don't know, Maine. We'll stay in a bed and breakfast near Penobscot Bay and come back a week from now, safe as houses.'

'Penobscot Bay?' He shook his head at her.

'I've always wanted to go there.' Jenna shrugged. 'Granted, I always wanted to go in the summer, but beggars can't be choosers.'

'Why will I be safe a week from now?' Tommy asked, sounding far too reasonable. 'Why won't Richie just wait?'

348

Jenna frowned. 'I don't know. Everything I know leads up to this night.'

Tommy shook his head. 'That doesn't make sense.'

'What makes sense? We're talking about time travel!'

'No, we're talking about my untimely death.' He tapped her on the nose with a long finger.

'Well,' Jenna said, 'thank you for that condescending gesture, but—'

'We have to figure out why,' Tommy said, cutting her off. She wanted to push his wet curls back from his forehead, but restrained herself. 'Otherwise, what's to keep him from trying and trying until he gets it right?'

'I told you why.' Jenna willed him to finally listen to her. 'Money, Tommy. Lots and lots of money.'

'He could ask for a loan,' Tommy pointed out. 'That's what normal people do, isn't it? You don't jump right over *loan* and go to *murder* without a good reason.'

'Obviously, he hates you,' Jenna said matter-of-factly, earning a dark glare. Jenna thought that most people, upon finally exchanging *I love yous*, probably did not stand about in the rain discussing time travel, death, and murder. She and Tommy certainly were unique little snowflakes, weren't they?

'You're talking about someone I've known for over a decade,' Tommy said, choosing his words carefully. 'I need a little more than that. I think we should go to the party and see if we can figure out why he chooses tonight to kill me.'

'This is the part in every movie ever made where the

audience starts screaming at the screen,' Jenna informed him. 'You are walking into your own deathtrap. It doesn't make any sense.'

'We've fingered three other people for this already,' Tommy pointed out. 'Duncan, Eugenia, Nick.' He grinned. 'Four, if I count you. Who's to say it won't turn out to be Sebastian in a surprise twist?'

'I really think—'

'I want to go to this party,' Tommy said, his gaze serious. 'I want to look each and every one of them in the eye. I want to know why. Will you do that with me, Jenna? Please?'

And what exactly was she supposed to say to that?

'Yes,' she said. She sighed. 'Okay. But we have to be careful.'

Except there was no need to be careful, Jenna discovered a few hours later, as she clung to her champagne glass. The party was boring, setting aside the many stares she was getting thanks to her decidedly uncool outfit, or maybe it was the presence of her supposedly stalkery self with no security team around Tommy, and more to the point, Richie wasn't even there.

'Oh, you know Richie,' Sebastian murmured, smiling blandly.

'Not really,' Jenna replied. Tommy was across the room, fending off a cross-examination from both Duncan and Eugenia – and Jenna knew the topic under discussion was her. Something about Duncan's murderous glare, directed right at her head, clued her in. She turned her attention back to Sebastian, who appeared to be drinking his way through the bar's entire selection of Scotch.

'Duncan's furious because he thinks he wasted money on security when it was only a bit of romance gone awry,' Sebastian said, rolling his eyes. 'He'll get over it.' He clinked his glass to hers. 'Congratulations, by the way. I've never seen Tommy care at all, about any woman. You're a first. And I would have said you're not at all his type.'

Jenna couldn't deny the thrill that raced through her at the first part of that statement, but she could try to hide it, especially with the unnecessary second part.

'His type is what, exactly?' she asked. She nodded across the room. 'Eugenia? That's worked out well.'

'Touché,' Sebastian murmured. 'I suppose I'm surprised he's finally chosen someone who isn't an intellectual void.' He looked arch. 'Tommy is not the dummy he sometimes pretends to be.'

'You don't seem like a dummy yourself,' Jenna said. She eyed him. He looked drunk, and he had struck up this conversation, not her. 'But I can't get a handle on Richie. Is he fascinating in private?'

Sebastian laughed, and took a drink from his glass.

'Why are you so interested in Richie?' he asked, his gaze assessing despite the laughter. 'Believe me, you don't want to be one of his extra-curricular activities. And I can guarantee you that Tommy won't accept it.'

'You think I want to . . . ?' Jenna couldn't finish the sentence. Sebastian only gazed at her. She felt her face redden. 'I thought Richie was gay.'

'I'm gay,' Sebastian said. He waved a hand in the air. 'On good days I think Richie can go either way. On bad days, I suspect the way he goes has more to do with opportunity than desire.' He laughed again, but it didn't reach his eyes. 'I must have drunk more Scotch than I should have.'

'Then why are you with him?' Jenna asked softly. 'You could be with anyone.'

'Fear,' Sebastian said, with a wry smile. 'Loneliness. And don't forget love. That's the kicker. That's the one that always tears your guts out, isn't it?' He sighed when he saw Jenna's expression. 'Don't worry,' he said. 'I'm always maudlin after a fight. It hasn't broken us up yet.'

He excused himself shortly thereafter.

Jenna was stilling mulling it all over when Tommy walked up to her, and settled himself next to her on the couch. After Sebastian had abandoned her, she'd stationed herself in prime position, where she could scan the whole room – the better to enjoy the way they scowled at her dowdiness and complete inappropriateness for a superstar like Tommy Seer.

The truth was, Jenna kind of liked the fact that she was dressed for a grunt mission, and all these sparkling beauties had to stand around and wonder what she had that they didn't. In fact, she kind of loved it.

'No fight with Eugenia,' Tommy announced. 'If anything, she thought Duncan was being too harsh. And still no sign of Richie.'

'Sebastian and he had a fight,' Jenna said, tearing her

attention away from a leggy redhead who was scowling at her.

'And Sebastian got all bitter and a little bit nasty,' Tommy said, sounding bored. 'Blah blah blah. It's like clockwork.'

'That's kind of what he said.' Jenna shrugged. 'And also that Richie is bi. Did you know that?'

'Sure.' Tommy shrugged. 'If it's hot, Richie wants to nail it.' He looked amused. 'You know they have an open relationship, right? Are you interested? Is that why you're asking?'

Jenna made a face. 'Let's survive 1987,' she suggested. 'Then we can discuss the parameters of our relationship.'

'That's not a no, I notice,' Tommy said, grinning. 'Maybe women from the future are more open-minded than the ones in the Eighties. Hope springs eternal.'

Jenna only shook her head at him.

An hour later they were both fed up. There was no sign of Richie, and no reason for them to be suffering through a boring party. Even though nothing had happened – or seemed likely to happen – Jenna felt antsy.

'You wanted to come, so we came,' she said finally. 'Can we go now? Can we disappear for a while? Penobscot Bay, Tommy. Little islands. Pine trees.'

'We can leave this stupid party, anyway,' Tommy said, smiling his rock-star smile for the benefit of the public. 'Liz Smith is giving us the evil eye.'

Jenna felt relief surge through her as they walked through the lobby of the hotel. She didn't know why, exactly, and it quickly subsided. Nothing seemed to be

353

going the way she'd expected it to. Eugenia had barely spoken to Tommy, and certainly hadn't fought with him. And yet Jenna still had that itchy feeling, as if it was all about to go bad.

'I suppose Eugenia could have told everyone you had a fight later,' she mused aloud. 'That would make her seem more central to your death, after all, when maybe it had nothing to do with her. And maybe if she didn't manufacture a fight, someone might remember that she was way more interested in Duncan Paradis than her doomed fiancé that night.'

Tommy shot her a look as they stepped outside.

'What an imagination you have,' he murmured after he handed his ticket to the practically genuflecting valet. 'Are you sure you don't work in PR?'

'Very funny,' Jenna said with a laugh. She curled her hand around Tommy's arm, and was about to say something else when she saw the figure walking towards them.

Richie.

Jenna froze.

Tommy looked up, and Jenna felt him tense, though his expression didn't alter.

'Richie,' he said, by way of greeting.

'Already leaving?' Richie asked, with an edge to his voice. He looked at Jenna much like she was a worm. Then back at Tommy. 'You're back with Loony Tunes?'

So when Richie decided to start talking in her vicinity it was all about name-calling. Nice. Jenna fixed a polite expression on her face, and tried to rise above the Loony Tunes comment.

'The party's pretty boring,' Tommy said calmly. 'No surprise. You okay? You look tense.'

'I'm terrific,' Richie muttered. But he looked tweaked, and twitchy, and Jenna didn't think that was her imagination working overtime.

The valet roared up in Tommy's sleek, ferocious car. Jenna happily climbed inside. Tommy gave Richie a slap on the shoulder, then walked around to the driver's side.

'Drive safe,' Richie said in a snide kind of tone – and it gave Jenna chills. But then she remembered that she was the only one who knew what had happened – would happen – tonight. Wasn't she?

Was Richie threatening Tommy? Or was he just saying something for the sake of saying something, and sounding dark and strange because – hell – he was dark and strange?

Tommy put the car in gear, and Jenna tried to convince herself that it was a coincidence.

Which was hard to do when she turned around, and saw Richie standing there with an angry look on his face, staring after them as they drove away.

'Tell me more about the crash,' Tommy said as he manoeuvred the car through the rain-slick Manhattan streets. His mind was racing. He'd had the most amazing thought. 'The car – this car – goes over the bridge, but how?'

'No one knows exactly,' Jenna said. She frowned, as if she was picturing it, which Tommy found creepy. Maybe it would be strange *not* to find a discussion of the particulars of your own death creepy.

'And my body was never found. Only the empty car.'

'The empty, crushed car,' Jenna said. She shifted in her seat, and he could feel her eyes on him. 'It wasn't pretty, let me assure you.'

'Of course it wasn't pretty,' Tommy said absently. 'This car is a work of art. It's not just a *vehicle*. Crashing it is a sin.'

'I was more concerned with the part where you died,' Jenna said drily. 'But we can mourn the car, too, if you want.'

He heard her, and wanted to laugh or throw the appropriate comeback her way, but the idea in his head was picking up speed and consuming everything else in its path.

'What's the matter?' she asked. 'You have the weirdest look on your face.'

'Jenna,' Tommy said slowly, jerking the car to the side of the road and stamping on the brake so he could turn to face her. She threw out a hand to brace herself. 'What if this isn't about my death? What if this is about *escaping*?'

'What are you talking about?' She was still bracing herself against the door.

'Think about it. No body was ever found. Maybe that's because there wasn't one to find.'

'I liked *Eddie and the Cruisers* too,' Jenna said slowly, shaking her head. 'But it was a *movie*, Tommy.'

'I'm not talking about a movie,' Tommy said impatiently. 'I'm talking about my life. I could just . . . walk away.'

Jenna was quiet for a long moment. Tommy was already envisioning it. A small cabin somewhere, up on a mountain. Just the two of them, and his guitar. It sounded like perfection.

'I think you're too famous to disappear,' Jenna said, shattering the image of a mountainside. 'Where can you go where people won't recognize you?' She put a hand on his leg when he turned to her. 'I understand the fantasy, Tommy, but I don't think you understand how—'

'Look at the facts,' Tommy said, interrupting her. He knew he sounded desperate. Hell, he was desperate. 'You only *think* I died. You have no *proof*. Not everything happens the way you think it will – look at the fight with Eugenia.'

'That's true.' Jenna rubbed a hand over her face, and for a moment she looked so tired that he wanted to cradle her in his arms, and take her away the way she wanted him to. But he didn't think that would be enough. As long as people knew to look for him, how could he ever escape?

'I would know if there had been any sightings over the years, and there haven't been,' Jenna said slowly, as if she was thinking it through. 'I assumed that meant you were dead. But I guess I don't really know for sure.'

'All we know is that the car goes over the bridge,' Tommy said triumphantly. 'So all we have to do is send the car over the bridge. And then we're free, Jenna. *Free.*'

He saw the way she looked at him, and he knew that if he suggested they climb up the side of the Twin Towers, she would do it.

Even if she thought he was as crazy as he'd accused her of being.

Was that love? Or were they both nuts?

Tommy didn't much care.

'Okay,' Jenna said. She looked resigned. But she was smiling. 'I'll do it. But how do we crash this car *without* you in it?'

30

Jenna had seen the Tappan Zee Bridge so many times before, exactly as it was tonight. She'd seen *tonight* over and over again, as a matter of fact – or at any rate, the cold pre-dawn hours after tonight, when the news reports had begun to trickle in. She'd pored over the footage, looking for clues in the wet pavement, the skid marks, the gaping hole in the guard rail. She'd cursed the rain that fell from the low clouds above, and she cursed it again as she followed Tommy back out to the scene of what she'd always assumed was his death.

She was driving one of his other cars – yes, he'd used the plural – and she did not have enough car knowledge (or, to be honest, interest) to know what kind of car she was driving. She suspected it was a very nice one indeed, the kind of car that her father would occasionally sigh over when watching Bond movies. Should she be reverent? Alarmed? Terrified of chipping the paint or something? She didn't know – which was just as well, given the limited visibility in the rain. The storm had moved in over the New York area, and was pounding the hell out of it. Jenna's wipers flew back and forth across the windshield, doing what almost looked like a dance.

They had packed up a few of Tommy's things – very, very few of Tommy's things. After all, they'd reasoned, Tommy couldn't very well pack up his home and all of his belongings and take them with him. He had to walk away. When he was finished, he had only a messenger bag's worth of his life, and that bright, excited look in his eyes that made Jenna's heart swell for him.

She would do anything to keep that hopeful look on his face, she'd promised herself then and there, and she repeated it to herself now.

Anything.

'There isn't much I want to take,' he'd said, standing at the bottom of his spiral staircase, and looking around, though Jenna had doubted he was seeing his apartment. He'd let his hands fall against his sides. 'If that doesn't say all there is to say about this life of mine, I don't know what can.'

'Come on,' she'd said, on her feet and at his side, wanting to soothe him any way she could. 'Let's go get you a new one.'

And soon enough, they were pulled over on the side of the Tappan Zee Bridge, which was remarkably empty for ten o'clock at night. The two of them were the only ones foolish enough to be out in this weather. Jenna tried to block the rain and wind with the hood of her sweatshirt, but it only soaked in the wetness, and clung to her frozen skin. She walked up from where she'd parked a short distance behind Tommy's car.

'Are you ready?' she asked, pitching her voice to be louder than the pounding rain.

'I have to make sure there's enough speed to break through the rail,' Tommy called back. 'I'll rev her up, let her go, and then jump, okay?'

This was what they'd discussed. This was the plan. Jenna didn't know why her stomach clenched in reaction, as if she was hearing it for the first time.

'You'll have to jump out the window,' she said nervously. 'They'll be able to tell if the door was open. You can't use the door.'

She'd spent the drive over thinking through all that footage, all the police reports, the *Vanity Fair* and *Rolling Stone* investigations that came out later and sifted through every last detail. The door had to be closed, definitely. She wasn't sure about the state of CSI departments or forensic evidence in 1987, but why risk it?

'I might get banged up a little bit,' he said, but his green eyes were bright with amusement. 'Can you handle that?'

He thinks this is fun, Jenna realized. Of course he did. How . . . male.

'Why don't you try to land on your face?' She suggested. 'That way you can blend in later on, no problem.'

'You're funny,' he said, as if he didn't think she was, though she could see that he did. She was acutely aware

361

of all that rain and wet between them. He didn't say goodbye, or touch her. She didn't either. Her nerves couldn't take it.

'Be careful,' she said, or maybe she only thought it. He nodded once, definitively, and then climbed inside the car.

Jenna could feel the rain, pounding against her. She was wet everywhere – her wet jeans were heavy and scraped against her thighs, her wet socks scrunched in her boots. Her hair dripped against her neck, a sodden mass. The Ferrari's engine raced like the growl of some gigantic jungle cat. She heard the screech of rubber against pavement, the roar of the powerful engine. Then the car took off. It burst into life, and speed.

Jenna wasn't breathing. She couldn't breathe.

She didn't want to look – but she couldn't look away.

Tommy drove for a few yards, building up speed. Then he aimed the nose of the car for the side of the bridge. It was all so fast. Just as Jenna started to scream, because he had to be trapped, she saw the blur of his body as he hurled himself through the window. He hit the ground, and rolled. The Ferrari kept going – ploughing through the guard rail and disappearing over the side.

So smoothly.

So completely.

And then, improbably, everything was quiet, and once again Jenna could hear nothing but the rain.

But Tommy didn't move.

She was running before she knew she was moving. She

couldn't think – she could only see Tommy's motionless figure on the ground. What if they had played right into it? What if—

No no no no—

She reached his side, skidding on to her knees, her hands reaching for him and turning him over—

'Ouch,' he said, his voice a little bit shaky, and then he opened his eyes, and Jenna felt a rush of relief so powerful that she almost collapsed from it. 'Your bedside manner sucks.'

Jenna touched his face, his throat, his torso. She felt for broken bones, and just to feel him, solid and real, beneath her hands. She took a breath that felt like a sob.

'I think I'm okay,' he muttered, climbing to his feet.

'You better be,' Jenna muttered right back.

It was as if they couldn't speak in regular voices, as if they were hushed by the enormity of what they'd done. Jenna eased over to the gaping, torn hole in the bridge's guard rail and felt a shimmer of cold wash through her. She had the faintest sense of vertigo as the wind buffeted her. She was afraid to get too close. Down below, the Hudson river was dark, with only a flat patch and ripples spreading outwards, soon to be swallowed up entirely.

As if nothing had happened.

'Let's get out of here,' Tommy said, his hands strong on her shoulders.

They didn't speak much on the way back into the city. Jenna stole looks at him, and wiped the water from her face. Tears, rain – it made no difference at this point.

He was alive.

Tommy was alive.

The car was in the river, and he was not.

She should feel jubilant. Triumphant. Safe.

But instead, adrenalin was still coursing through her body, and her lungs still felt tight. She was still on edge. Jittery.

Maybe when the night is over, she thought. *Maybe when everyone thinks he's dead. Maybe when we're far away from here.*

Once in the city, they parked Tommy's car in his private garage, where there were no cameras and no one to report their movements. Then, because they were already soaking wet and they had nothing but time, they walked across the park to Jenna's place.

It was a long, cold, improbably magical walk.

Central Park was dark and should have been scary. It was 1987 and not safe at night, but it was almost as if the two of them were sealed away in some bubble where nothing outside it could touch them. Jenna didn't care about the various physical discomforts she felt – the faint tenderness between her legs from the night before, the spot even now being rubbed raw by her wet sock against her cold foot. All that mattered was Tommy's arm slung across her shoulders, and the way they walked in tandem. As if their bodies recognized each other, and were effortlessly in tune. No words necessary.

By now the hole in the bridge would be noticed. The teams would be called to drag the river, and Tommy's car would be discovered. It was already happening even as

364

they walked along the streets of the Upper East Side, hoods pulled up against the rain, totally anonymous.

Tommy Seer was about to be declared dead. Meanwhile, Tommy was holding on to Jenna's hand like it was a lifeline, and no one else knew where he was. He was free. And she was with him.

The night spun around them, alive with all the possibilities.

'I think we really did it,' she whispered in wonder as they approached her stoop.

Tommy looked down at her, grinning.

'I think we did,' he agreed.

But Richie detached himself from shadows around Jenna's front door, and stepped into the light.

It wasn't the flat, angry look on his face that scared Jenna the most, or the sneer on his lips that she'd never seen before. It wasn't even the incontrovertible evidence – right there on his face – that he really, really hated Tommy. That was surprising, but that wasn't the terrifying part.

The terrifying part was the gun Richie held.

The one he aimed right at Tommy.

'What the hell?' Tommy demanded, but all he could think was *Jenna – have to protect Jenna.* He shoved her behind him. For once, she didn't fight him. 'What are you doing here?'

He didn't mention the gun Richie was pointing at him, because really, as if anyone was likely to overlook it. Mentioning it was redundant, wasn't it?

'I knew you'd be back here with your stalker bitch,' Richie said. He looked at Jenna, and his eyes were cold. Mean. He was a complete stranger to Tommy. 'You're not the only person who likes to follow people around, Jenna,' he said with a disturbing little laugh. 'Did you think I didn't see you following me yesterday? Are you that stupid?'

Jenna muttered something that sounded like *Monica Stars*. Tommy ignored her, keeping all of his attention focused on Richie.

'You're pointing a gun at me,' Tommy said conversationally. Or as conversationally as he could after faking his own death, running around in the pouring rain for hours, and discovering his band mate waving a gun in his face. 'Is that really necessary?'

'You have to die,' Richie said. Somewhat more calmly than Tommy thought was appropriate. 'I've thought about it, and it's the only way.'

'The only way for what?' Tommy asked. He scanned the dark, quiet street, but there was no one around. So much for the city that never slept. There were only dark windows and distant sounds of traffic tonight. He could shout for help, but what would that do? People were likely to turn over, hide their heads beneath the pillows, and praise whatever they prayed to that it wasn't them. That was life in the big bad city.

'I've always been the expendable one,' Richie said. 'You and Sebastian and Nick can get other gigs, no problem, but what about me? There are a million keyboard players.

The Wild Boys is my one shot, and you want to walk away from it, no thought for anyone else at all. Well, you can't walk away from this, can you?' He moved the muzzle of the gun, pointing it at Tommy's head rather than his heart. Not a vast improvement.

'The Wild Boys,' Tommy said, derision flaring in his voice. 'It's just a band, Richie. You can play in another band.'

'It's not *just a band*,' Richie gritted out. The gun in his hand wavered. 'What the hell is wrong with you, man? Why can't you see what a good thing you have going? We're in the hottest band of the decade and you can't even see it!'

'I see it,' Tommy said, trying to sound placating. 'But the decade's almost over. It's time to do other things.'

'That's nice for you,' Richie sneered. 'But what about me? What am I supposed to do? I owe people money, Tommy. Lots of money.'

'We make lots of money,' Tommy snapped. He could feel Jenna behind him, her hands digging into his back. Was she holding on or holding herself back? He wasn't sure he wanted to know.

'And we can make a lot more,' Richie tossed back at him. He raised the gun again. 'Keith Moon. Sid Vicious. Ronnie Van Zant. John Lennon.'

'They're all dead, yes,' Tommy said. 'That doesn't mean you have to go crazy here—'

'Don't call *me* crazy!' Richie snapped at him. 'You're the one throwing it all away. For what? Some bullshit solo career? *What about me?*'

'Make your own solo career—' Tommy began, but it was a mistake.

'You're worth more to me dead,' Richie said angrily, and this time when he took aim, Tommy knew with perfect clarity that he was going to die. Jenna had been right all along.

'What's your plan here?' Jenna demanded suddenly, startling both Tommy and Richie. Tommy wasn't sure who was more surprised when she stepped out from behind him.

'Please don't do whatever you're doing,' Tommy hissed at her, but she ignored him.

'Seriously,' Jenna said, her gaze trained on Richie. 'Did you think this through?'

'Tommy dies, the Wild Boys become legendary, I collect,' Richie said matter-of-factly. 'Even a lunatic should be able to grasp that.'

'Yeah, well, this lunatic is wondering what you're going to do with his body,' Jenna said, sounding as if she was discussing some random pleasantry. Like the weather, or her groceries, rather than his murdered corpse.

'That's a nice image,' Tommy said. 'I think I'd like to be cremated and thrown in the faces of my enemies, now that we're discussing it.'

Jenna continued to ignore him. Richie, on the other hand, was staring at her.

'What are you talking about?' he asked.

'You can't plan to leave it in the street, can you?' Jenna continued in that same brisk voice. As she talked, she eased the strap of the messenger bag from Tommy's shoulder, and let it drop to the ground in front of them. Maybe she was getting ready to run? 'And you'll have to shoot me too, of course, which means you can't claim it was his crazed stalker who did it. They'll ask, you know. I mean, you can try to say it was me who shot him, but it will be your word against mine and I won't be the one with gunpowder residue on my hands and five million dollars in debt. I'm just saying.'

Richie gaped at Jenna, then at Tommy.

'I don't know,' Tommy said, and shrugged. 'She's always thinking. It's her fatal flaw.'

'I'll figure it out later,' Richie said, his voice grating. 'Crazy bitch.'

'Watch the way you talk to her,' Tommy suggested. Without much heat – after all, the man was pointing a gun at him. Still, it was the thought that counted.

'You're about to be dead, Tommy,' Richie sneered at him. 'So you might want to give up on the hero crap.'

Richie raised the gun again, but as he did, Jenna exploded from her frozen position. She let out a noise Tommy had never heard, like a banshee howl, and she swung his bag with all her might at Richie's head.

There was a loud BANG.

Tommy dove to the side, even as he heard a crash and the shattering of glass from the car behind him. He heard Richie shout something, and as he rolled over, he saw Jenna winding up with the bag again while Richie was sprawled over the hood of a nearby car, shaking his head in a daze – but with his attention fixed on Jenna.

It was time to take control of the situation.

Tommy lunged to his feet, and let Little Tommy Searcy out – the scrappy no-account trailer-park rat who had used his fists before he could walk. It had been a long time, but Tommy still knew what to do. Some things never left you.

He hauled Richie up by his collar and smacked the gun out of his hand. Then he socked him a good one, right in the face. Another punch in the gut, and a knee for good measure, and then he dropped Richie to the ground.

'Let's go,' he said, holding out a hand to Jenna, who was crouched next to her stoop and panting, his bag clutched in her hands. Along the street and up above them, windows were lighting up. They had to move if they wanted to avoid being seen, and they had to move *now*.

Richie was already coming round.

Jenna grabbed Tommy's hand, and let him propel her to her feet. She looked pale, but determined. A surge of feeling for her rolled through him, making him more emotional than he would ever admit.

He dropped a hard, fast kiss on her mouth, and then tugged her with him as he began to move.

Away from Richie. Away from that gunshot. Away – though he didn't know where he was going.

'I think he's going to chase us,' Tommy said as they rounded the corner. He cursed himself – he should have taken the gun, at the very least.

Up above, the sky split open. Lightning zigzagged across the night, and moments later, thunder boomed. Jenna stopped moving. Thinking the storm had frightened her, Tommy turned back to her – but she had her head tilted back and was staring up at the sky, and she didn't look in the least afraid.

'It's okay,' Jenna said, rain running down her face. She made no attempt to avoid it. 'I have an idea.'

'An idea?' Tommy had a lot of ideas, and most of them involved getting as far away from Richie and New York City as possible. And fast. 'Please tell me it's something more substantial than *Penobscot Bay*.'

Jenna made a face. Up above, lightning crashed and illuminated her triumphant smile – though why she should feel triumphant at the moment, Tommy couldn't begin to guess. It seemed to him that a bad situation had just gotten significantly and inarguably worse.

But then again, he was not a woman who supposedly leapt about through time, saving random singers along her way.

'It's okay,' she said again, as if she knew what he was thinking and found him silly. She held out her hand. 'I know exactly where we're going.'

31

Everything made sense.

Finally.

Jenna didn't know why it hadn't occurred to her sooner, but she supposed that fleeing for her life down First Avenue was as good a time as any to realize that everything was wrapped in a bow. It was the pattern she'd been searching for this whole time, but she'd never thought to look for it in quite this way.

She and Tommy were keeping up a gruelling pace, running as fast as they could, trying to put distance between them and Richie. And they were running out of time.

'I think I see him back there,' Tommy grunted, looking over his shoulder. 'Don't stop!'

'We have to get to my office,' Jenna panted. Thunder rumbled up above. 'Before midnight!'

Time travel. Tommy's missing body. Her unnecessary overload of knowledge about what had happened on the night Tommy died. All of these things taken together added up to exactly one possible answer.

She had to get Tommy out of here.

Out of danger, and out of 1987. Lightning flashed across the sky, punctuating the thought.

Thunder crashed – as loud and as terrifying as a gunshot.

'Watch out!' Tommy yelled. 'He's gaining on us!'

Meaning . . . it had actually been a gunshot.

Jenna ducked around a hapless pedestrian, and pumped her arms for greater speed. Richie could not shoot them on the street, could he? Surely *someone* would notice that those sounds weren't thunder – wouldn't they?

A store window shattered beside them, and Jenna had to gulp back her scream of terror.

'Run!' Tommy shouted.

Like she needed encouragement – there was flying glass!

And besides, she'd finally figured it all out. They couldn't die now.

She had to take Tommy back to Video TV, to that damned supply closet. They had to be there as the clock struck twelve, just like Cinderella, because that was when lightning struck the building. She remembered thinking about it the night she'd come back in time, and then, somehow, never again.

Lightning. It has to be the lightning. It knocked out the power and sent me here. It can send us both back. Why didn't I think of this earlier?

She might not have thought of it at all if it hadn't been for Tommy's theory that the car was supposed to be empty.

373

She ignored her screaming lungs and aching legs and kept moving. If Tommy hadn't died, he'd either kept himself hidden away for twenty years, or something else had happened, and Jenna was the best something else she could think of.

It had to be the lightning.

'Don't lag behind!' Tommy cried, and Jenna pumped her arms and legs harder, desperately tired and winded but afraid to stop. Afraid to look back.

Another loud crack. Richie? Or the storm?

Jenna kept hauling ass.

It was a matter of life and death and naturally there were no cabs anywhere. It was easier to travel through time than it was to find a taxi in a torrential downpour in New York City.

Some things never changed, no matter what year it was or how bad the storm might be.

'Keep going, keep going,' Tommy called, almost as if he was chanting.

Jenna tucked her chin down, ignored the stitch in her side and the lack of oxygen in her burning lungs, and kept running.

They made it to Video TV's iconic building as the clock in Times Square announced that it was 11:55.

'Do we have enough time?' Tommy panted at her.

'We have to move fast,' Jenna managed to say, trying to force air into her lungs. She smiled at the security guard – desperately trying to look calm despite the fact she was both sopping wet and sweating from exertion – and headed for the bank of elevators.

Inside, they both slumped against the walls, pulling in gulps of air, but neither one of them spoke. Hell, they'd just run across Manhattan, dodging bullets all the way. Jenna, for one, was exhausted.

'What's the plan?' Tommy asked softly. He raked his fingers through his wet hair, shoving it back from his face.

'Time travel,' Jenna said, and grinned a little bit at his expression. 'Destiny.'

'Uh huh.'

'Just trust me.'

'You got it,' Tommy said, and shook his head. 'I am all about trust. Obviously.'

'Let's face it,' Jenna said. 'At this point, that's pretty much all you've got.'

Tommy's eyebrows arched up. 'You said that,' he pointed out. 'Not me.'

Jenna was still grinning as they got off the elevator. She walked past the desk where Princess Diana Hair had sat and hated her, for reasons she had never discerned and had forgotten to wonder about. It was one more thing she intended to ask Aunt Jen about – one more thing on a long list. Then it was down the hall past her office – or, in 1987, Peter Hale's office.

'I still don't know who Peter Hale is,' she said, scowling.

'I don't care who Peter Hale is,' Tommy retorted, shifting his weight from foot to foot and looking over his shoulder every few seconds.

He held his bag, which contained the only worldly possessions he'd planned to take with him. Jenna looked at him for a moment as she stood in front of her old office. He was the man she had always loved, and he was the man she'd fallen in love with – two different men in the same delectable package. He was wearing jeans and sneakers tonight, both of which would have to be discarded on the other side, so that he wasn't mistaken for Ralph Macchio circa *Karate Kid* on the street. And that hair would have to be modernized, certainly. But that was cosmetic. The reality was, the man was beautiful. Outside, certainly, but inside, too.

And he was hers.

And she was really going to save him, the way she'd promised herself – and him – that she would.

Take that, fairy tales, she thought proudly. *He's the damsel in distress, not me!*

The office was silent all around them. Maybe that was why they could both hear the elevator bell *ding*, announcing the arrival of a new car. Jenna felt her eyes widen, and forgot all about reassigning gender roles.

'How could he know where we are?' she hissed, panicked.

'He probably watched the elevator go up and noticed where it stopped. It's easy enough to do,' Tommy said, his voice tense. 'It's time for your plan, Jenna. Like right now.'

Jenna lunged down the hall for the supply-closet door, which was, of course, locked tight.

'Hurry,' Tommy warned as she fumbled with her keys.

There was a shout from the end of the hallway. Richie.

'He's coming!' Tommy cried out – unnecessarily, as Jenna

could hear the thud of his feet against the royal blue carpeting.

Jenna pushed the door open with her hip, and tossed herself inside. Tommy crowded in behind her, making the space seem much smaller than she remembered. He slammed the door behind him.

'I'm filled with trust,' he said in that same low, tense voice, 'but I can't help noticing that this feels like a trap.'

'Hush,' Jenna commanded him. She remembered the scrape on her palm, the shattered glass. She pointed towards the ceiling. 'Lift me up.'

Tommy complied, wrapping his arms around her waist and hoisting her into the air as a heavy fist connected with the door from the outside. Jenna winced, as if it was her body Richie was pummelling instead of an industrial office door that would, she fervently hoped, withstand it.

And then she took a deep breath, looked down, and kissed Tommy.

He kissed her back, and for a moment it was almost as if Richie's hammering at the door was her heart, kicking up its usual fuss at the very thought of Tommy. She pulled away and leaned her forehead against his.

'I'm about to change your life,' she whispered. 'And I don't think you can ever change it back.'

'I love you,' Tommy whispered back, his green eyes clear. No misgivings. No doubts. 'No matter what happens.'

'I love you too,' Jenna said, and then she reached up and smashed the light bulb with her hand.

*   *   *

Tommy almost dropped her, as shards of glass rained down on him, though the light remained on – only broken.

'What the hell?' Jenna yelped. 'Why didn't anything happen?' Then, after a moment, 'That *hurt!*'

Tommy was forced to divide his attention between Jenna and the door, which appeared to be buckling beneath Richie's assault.

'You broke the light bulb?' he demanded, setting her on her feet – dropping her, really – and jumping to hold the door. It took all of his strength, and he could hear Richie ranting from the other side. 'That's your plan?'

'Of course that's not my plan,' Jenna said, sounding like her teeth were clenched. She started climbing the metal shelves, hoisting herself up towards the remains of the light bulb with one foot braced against the opposite wall. She muttered something beneath her breath that sounded a whole lot like *where's the fucking lightning?*

Which, of course, was completely insane. But that was par for the course.

'You think you can hide?' Richie shouted. 'You think you can get away from me? This is your destiny, Tommy! This has to happen!'

'Someone else might be tempted to point out that this kind of proves that you're crazy,' Tommy grunted at her as Richie's attack intensified – the door was bending around the force of his blows, and Tommy doubted the hinges would hold much longer.

'I am not crazy!' Jenna yelled at him.

'Then get something to hit him with, because this door won't hold much longer!' Tommy shouted back.

But she didn't listen.

Like that was anything new.

And then it was too late, because the door bowed open and Richie shoved himself into the gap, his face red and furious.

'Gotcha, asshole,' he snarled at Tommy.

'If you're going to do something, do it now,' Tommy threw at Jenna. But he was ready to fight. He'd been born ready to fight, and the fact he hadn't done it in a long time before tonight didn't bother him at all.

But he hadn't counted on Jenna.

She was up above him, hanging off the metal shelf, and he heard her move before he saw her – before her clunky Doc Marten landed square in Richie's face. Richie made a grunting sound, and then collapsed, hitting the floor on the other side of the door with a sickening sort of thud.

'That was for Aunt Jen,' Jenna said proudly. 'So she doesn't have to wake up with him in her face.'

'What does your aunt have to do with anything?' Tommy demanded.

But she ignored him. She was crouched above him like some kind of goddess – frowning, of course. Ferociously.

She grabbed him around the neck with one hand and he saw her punch out with the other one – out towards the light again – and he knew she was going to fall.

'You're falling!' he yelled – or thought he yelled, but

then everything got mixed up and he thought maybe *he* was falling—

Something buzzed in his ears like a wasps' nest and something sizzled through him and he thought, *is this a heart attack?*

There was a loud noise, like a POP—

And he was falling again, through something long and dark, and he couldn't see anything or feel anything.

Jenna, he thought, panicked—

And then everything went black.

32

Once again, Jenna woke up to find herself on the floor of the supply closet.

Once again, her butt hurt.

But as she rubbed at her eyes and pushed herself into an awkward sitting position, she could feel another body tangled up with her own, and she knew there was at least one major difference this time around.

'Tommy,' she said, and shook his shoulder. She watched as his wonderful eyes opened, and then sharpened. He sat up slowly, and blinked a few times. He rubbed the back of his head with one hand.

'Well,' he said after a moment. 'I'm not dead. So there's that.'

'Does your butt hurt?' Jenna asked. She shrugged when he gazed at her. 'I thought maybe it was a time-travel thing. Aching butt. No? That's just me?'

'Time travel might be real,' Tommy said. 'And I say *might*

because all I've seen is this closet – not a single flying car—'

'There are no flying cars.' Jenna tried to look sympathetic. 'The Jetsons lied. Sorry.'

'—but that doesn't mean you're not crazy,' Tommy continued. His eyes creased in the corners, the green in them gleaming.

'Amusingly eccentric, you mean,' Jenna said, wrinkling her nose at him. 'I can live with that.'

But she didn't move.

'Did we really do it?' Tommy asked quietly. 'Can you tell?'

'I don't know.' It crossed her mind that the supply closet could have thrown them anywhere – what made her think it would be the right year? For all she knew they'd just started their own personal *Quantum Leap*.

'Only one way to find out,' Tommy said.

He got to his feet, and helped Jenna get up. They both brushed shards of glass from their clothes – the shattered light bulb, presumably. Though once again, Jenna's palm was only faintly scarred – not cut. Tommy slung his bag over his shoulder. Jenna squared her shoulders, and opened the door.

Outside, the carpet was grey with age. An excellent sign. Jenna's pulse began to tap out a rapid beat. She walked the short distance down the hall towards her office, looked at the nameplate, and smiled.

'Look,' she said when she felt Tommy come up behind her. He ran his finger over the little plate that read JENNA

382

JENKINS. He looked at her, almost shyly, and smoothed a hand down her back.

'I guess you're real,' he said.

Jenna let out a breath she hadn't known she was holding, and opened the door to her office. Everything was exactly the way she'd left it, just over a month and more than twenty-odd years ago.

Except for the fact the place was immaculate.

The posters of Tommy still pouted from the walls. Duran Duran and Wham! still held their iconic poses, too. But it was an adult's office with vintage posters, not an overgrown adolescent's den. Jenna could see the difference. She could even appreciate the new ficus plant that stood near the window, looking strong and healthy.

Thank you, Aunt Jen, she thought. *I get it now.*

Then she watched Tommy, who was taking in all the posters of himself with an arrested sort of look on his face.

'What?' Jenna asked, with only a hint of defensiveness. Okay, maybe a strong hint. 'You're a good-looking man.'

Tommy didn't respond. He walked over to the window, and looked out at a very different Times Square from the one they'd just raced through the night before. She heard him make a soft noise. She remembered what that felt like, that first long look – how disorienting it was.

'I'm going to go get us some coffee,' Jenna said, unzipping her soggy sweatshirt and hanging it on the the coat rack, where there was no sign of an alternative wardrobe. At least the T-shirt she had on underneath was a dark colour, or she'd be putting on quite a show.

'Coffee would be good,' Tommy murmured, sounding taken aback. He moved away from the window and collapsed into Jenna's desk chair. He looked at the computer, and she could see him swallow. He reached out and touched the screen. Then he looked at the desk calendar in front of him, and Jenna heard his breath come out in a rush.

'It's weird, I know,' she said.

'It was one thing to *accept* that you believed what you were saying,' Tommy said, still sounding dazed. 'But this . . .'

'I know,' Jenna said.

She slipped out of the office and headed down the hall to the little kitchenette and break area. She couldn't believe it had worked. She couldn't believe she'd brought Tommy with her. And she had so many things to discuss with her aunt. Jenna fixed two cups of coffee, and turned to head back to her office—

But instead, she came face to face with Aimee.

Aimee's perfectly made-up face went from a happy smile to a concerned frown in seconds. It was so good to see her that Jenna overlooked the frown.

'Hi,' she said, unable to contain her grin. 'How are *you*?'

'Are you okay?' Aimee asked, her eyes wide as they travelled over the length of Jenna's waterlogged body. 'Why do you look so . . . *bedraggled*?'

'I'm fine,' Jenna said. And she was, finally. But what could she possibly say? *I was running through the pouring rain in 1987* . . . Sure. Aimee would have her committed on the spot. Or, worse: burst into tears.

Jenna stepped around her and started back down the hall towards her office, with Aimee following close behind.

'You look like you were rained on,' Aimee said gently. 'Not that there's anything wrong with that, but it rained last night.' It was so nice to hear Aimee's actual voice, instead of the one in her head, that Jenna didn't even mind the too-careful tone her friend was using. 'Not this morning.'

'I really am fine,' she said. 'Haven't I been more than fine the last month and a half?'

She glanced over her shoulder, and saw Aimee blink.

'Well, sure,' she said. 'You got that promotion, you dress much more professionally . . .' She looked at the all-black, still-damp clothes Jenna was wearing, but rallied. 'Most of the time. You even spring-cleaned that office of yours.'

Jenna only smiled. That answered one question. Yes, apparently, Aunt Jen really had taken her place in Jenna's life. Jenna wondered who *she* had saved. And then realized that it had been Jenna's career, at the very least.

'See?' she asked. 'I've let go of all that crap, Aimee. Adam. The past. Whatever. I've moved on. Just like you wanted me to.'

At Jenna's office door, Aimee sailed right on in behind her.

'And doesn't it feel *good*?' Aimee was asking, her voice filled with obvious excitement for this whole new Jenna, but then she looked at the man sitting behind the desk and stopped dead in her tracks. Her mouth actually dropped open.

Jenna exchanged a glance with Tommy, who was lounging there like the international superstar he was, and set his coffee down in front of him.

'I loved you before,' he said fervently, grabbing the cup and lifting it to take a gulp. He shoved his hair off his forehead with his other hand. 'But this takes it to a whole different level.'

'He really likes coffee,' Jenna told Aimee, biting back the smile she couldn't seem to control.

Happily, Aimee wasn't paying her any attention – she was too busy staring at Tommy.

Jenna wondered how she was supposed to handle this introduction. He couldn't go around calling himself *Tommy Seer*, could he? But what was he going to call himself?

Not, of course, that his *name* was the real issue here.

Aimee looked at the wall of posters behind Tommy, all of them showing his face from different angles. She looked at Tommy. Then back at the posters.

Then, finally, she looked at Jenna, her eyes wide and, yes, *concerned.*

'A Tommy Seer impersonator?' she asked, in a small, horrified voice.

Jenna saw the wicked amusement bloom across Tommy's face, and could do nothing but shrug.

'You know, he's got a great talent,' she said, managing somehow to keep from laughing. She had to press her lips together.

'It's true,' Tommy agreed. 'I'm the best Tommy Seer

impersonator around. People think I *am* Tommy Seer, that's how good I am.'

'Oh, Jenna,' Aimee said, her voice just as sad as the last time Jenna had heard it. '*Really?*'

But this time, Jenna just laughed, and gave her best friend a quick, fierce hug.

'Trust me, Aimee,' she said quietly. 'I finally know what I'm doing.'

One month later
Tommy liked the future.

He liked Pixar movies, and the Internet, though he still had trouble with his cellular phone. Which he never remembered to call his *iPhone*. He liked his hair shorter and his jeans baggier. He liked coffee on every corner, the cleaned-up version of Times Square, and the stunning variety of available channels on the television. He was obsessed with catching up on everything he'd missed – television shows, DVDs, the grunge era, Barack Obama.

Most of all, he liked being anonymous. He liked being *TJ Searcy*, which was, when all was said and done, his name. *Thomas John Searcy.*

And he loved Jenna.

He loved how embarrassed she was by her creepy apartment, the shrine to her obsession with him which she'd made clear was actually the result of a bad break-up, and not an ongoing life choice. But how creepy could he really think it was, when her obsessiveness had saved his life? The woman liked her research. It had saved them both.

'Richie was suspected but never charged in your murder,' she'd told him the morning after they'd arrived in her time.

Tommy had been lying in her bed while she explained the Internet and Wikipedia and it had all gone over his head. He'd just liked to hear her speak. And he'd definitely liked his first glimpse of HDTV, despite the fact she claimed she couldn't see the difference.

'After he was found almost beaten to death in an alleyway, Sebastian not only told the world that he had all that gambling debt, but broke up with him and came out. All in the same week.' She'd tapped at her keyboard, her curvy little body practically vibrating with excitement. 'Everyone thought you were having an affair with my Aunt Jen, but she, Eugenia, and Duncan all denied it and the rumour eventually died. And then she cleaned up on the stock market. That's how she got so rich. Oh, and Ken Dollimore is alive and well. He moved out to Los Angeles and opened his own—'

He'd silenced her the only way he could.

He loved her because she hadn't been excited when he'd told her he'd had his lawyer transfer his considerable fortune to a numbered Swiss bank account – she'd been worried that someone could trace him and discover his secret. He loved her because she thought he should buy one of those ugly hybrid cars, but pretended to understand why he insisted on buying another Spider. And a wicked Corvette. He loved her because she refused to even consider giving up her new VP job. He loved her because she'd flatly refused to live in an apartment like his old one – because, she claimed, it had been soulless – so they'd found a sweet pre-war building with a floor-through apartment in the newly fancy West Village, with enough room for Tommy to think about making his own studio some day. He loved her because she'd packed away all those posters and 45s and teen magazines that featured him, but she'd refused to throw them away.

He loved her because she didn't seem to mind that he morbidly watched all the documentaries about himself and wondered what he should do with himself, now that he was dead.

He loved her because he'd told her that someday he might try to find a way to reach out to Nick, the only person he missed, and she'd only nodded as if that was a given.

He loved her because when he'd pointed out that he was really in his fifties, not his thirties, and he was therefore robbing the cradle, she'd laughed and told him she'd always wanted to be a Geezer Pleaser.

But most of all, he loved her because he'd given her about an hour's notice and one cryptic phone call, and she'd come anyway.

He could see her over the heads of the few people in the crowd – who had come for the beer, not the open-mike night. He played a few chords, and started to sing.

Jenna walked towards the stage, her smile bright with

love, and joy, and promises Tommy had every intention of keeping.

He wasn't a ghost.

He was real, and so was she.

And he knew that finally, all his dreams had come true: just a stool, a guitar, and the love of his life.